Starlight

<u>You</u> are like starlight itself.

Keep shining.

Lauren Jade ✦

Starlight

THE STARLIGHT TRILOGY
BOOK ONE

LAUREN JADE CASE

ISBN eBook: 978-1-9168887-0-8
ISBN Paperback: 978-1-9168887-1-5

Front cover image and design by Gabrielle Ragusi
Book design/interior by Evenstar Books

First printing, 2021

This is for you, Dad.
Thank you for sharing your love of stories.
I know you're proud.

Content Warning

My intent with this book and this story is never to harm and I don't want to risk someone's health by not disclosing that which may cause such things. While some triggers may appear in one chapter, in one line, in large or small quantities, I never want or mean to hurt another person. And while warnings aren't required, I don't want to compromise anyone with anything. Below is a list of what the following book does contain and so now please be aware that these things are present in the story of STARLIGHT to some degree.

This book contains the following content warnings:
Adult language
Injuries/ injury detail
Blood/ Gore
Torture
Violence
Pregnancy
Anxiety
Scenes of a sexual nature
Death
Imprisonment

Pronunciation Guide

I've always loved seeing little pronunciation guides in books I've read, especially if there are difficult names or places to learn throughout them. This is my version. Obviously, as these books go on, you will come across more and more Monster types, so the list will keep expanding, but for now:

Welcome to **STARLIGHT MONSTER PRONUNCIATIONS 101.**

Scorpio – Scor-Pee-Oh
Calefaction – Kale-fack-shun
Jij – Jih-j
Kifflegger – K-iff-leg-er
Poena – P-oh-nah
Mitter – Mih-ter
Shadow – Shah-doh
Siltapolia — Sil-tah-poh-lee-ah

Prologue

THERE ONCE WAS A BEING, a Being of nothingness; no light or dark, no matter or time, no life or death. It was a lonely existence.

So they created.

Out of their hands came life and light, death and dark. Time began and matter spawned.

And six Gods, with a seventh to follow, were breathed into being.

But with their existence, something else followed too. As if the world needed an equal, a balance.

So with the Gods came Monsters. *Things* with no souls that wanted nothing more than to destroy what the Gods attempted to build. But they were separated by Veils - walls in existence itself keeping Earth and Heavens away from other lands and the Hells. It's said, at the very beginning of time, those walls began to break and crack, allowing some Monsters to squeeze through from their side to another. And with time, those cracks grew, and so more came.

No one knew why, but the Gods couldn't rid the world of Monsters. Some say it was because they were equal. All they knew was that they came.

The Gods searched for answers until they found one. They could merge with Humans and create their own kind of species. Those special enough became Creatures and *they* could ruin the Monsters with their newfound powers and ability.

It would be an endless fight, *a war*, the Gods and the Being knew, but it needed fighting for all souls were worthy of life. And so the Creatures would pass down these gifts through the generations, trying to rid the world of Monsters and give life to those who deserved it until one side emerged victorious.

This destiny wasn't chosen by them. It was chosen *for* them.

And so, from the Being's loneliness, there came Creatures and Monsters and a great balance that may one day shift all worlds forever.

1
A Birthday Surprise

"HAPPY BIRTHDAY DEAR, NATALIA. Happy birthday to you."

Natalia blew out the candles on the cake her dad held. As she smiled at him, the lights cut out. She blinked into the darkness.

"I'll meet you downstairs," she said.

She heard her dad shuffle out of her room and moved once he was gone. She searched for some clothes on the floor and hoped they were the right way round when she found some. February mornings were still dark – truthfully, most of the day was – so hardly any light came through the window to see with as a guide.

She dressed anyway and hurried downstairs.

Rain and wind howled beyond the front door. Natalia braced herself and stepped into the deluge to reach the little electrical cupboard attached to the side of the outside of the house.

Yellow light flashed when she pulled the cord. She shivered when a spider ran across a wire in front of her and sighed when it disappeared into the brickwork.

It was an old house so lights going out or electrics tripping wasn't unusual. But as she searched the board, she was stumped.

Nothing has tripped.

For good measure, she flicked some switches before turning off the light and retreating, leaving the spiders and their silky webs behind – two things she didn't care for.

Instantly, the wind slapped thick droplets across her cheeks. Shielding her face with an arm, Natalia turned to the front door.

As she did, movement shot by in the reflection of the glass and she froze.

Spinning with little grace belonging to a former dancer, her gaze spotted a wolf.

What?

How could there be a wolf? No wolves existed on this island – there were no woods for them to live and no zoos for them to have escaped from. It *must've* been a dog. Nevertheless, Natalia stepped into the rain, eyes searching for answers to whatever she'd seen.

Blinking, she spotted a brown shape running away.

Definitely a dog. It probably escaped from someone's house or garden, she thought as thunder rolled across the sky. Only it didn't sound *right*. Normal thunder had a resonating crack. This sounded like a snappy firework.

"Get back inside!"

Natalia wiped her eyes in time to see three people blast past her. They sprinted in the same direction as the dog. Were they warning her that the animal was dangerous?

Whoever had shouted and whatever their meaning, the warning of *something* was clear.

Another chest-rattling noise burst through the air. This time, Natalia was entirely convinced it wasn't thunder. She turned toward the sound, heart pulsing with ominous dread.

Distinguished billows of black smoke rose into the unclear sky.

The smoke wafted closer and closer as a shape emerged from the far end of the street. One that was unmistakable. A scorpion. But this wasn't one that could be crushed under a foot. This insect was *at least* double the height of a person. Natalia choked on her own saliva, her body shuddering. She tried to back up yet her legs wouldn't cooperate, paralysed with hopeless fear.

Out of nowhere, the brown 'dog' returned, barrelling past Natalia, directly for that giant *thing*.

The dog leaped suddenly and Natalia looked for why.

Blood had pooled in the street, leaking towards a drain. Blood from a body that was cleanly snapped in half.

The lower abdomen was down the road a few paces, legs dangling from the path. The top half was closer to Natalia, just in front of her dad's crappy car, but close enough that she could see the wide, lifeless eyes.

Natalia's legs unfroze and she darted toward the front door.

Whatever was happening, it *had* to be in her head. She was dreaming, her brain not yet awake to comprehend reality and had instead offered a nightmare.

She reached the door, her back pressed against it as the rain continued its assault. Still she couldn't turn away or wake.

Three figures sprinted back down the road, paces behind the wolf-dog – Natalia was convinced they were the same ones. If they looked at her, she hadn't noticed; she was too focused on the giant bug as it snapped its massive pincer.

That was the noise!

A lump formed in her throat. Fear either gave the ability to fight or to run. Natalia was unable to do either – a heart solid with fear and wonder was a potent mix apparently.

Natalia's field of vision grew wider the closer the figures got to the giant scorpion. One of them broke away, brown hair whipping about their faces, while the others disappeared into a pillar of smoke.

Their stare was direct as they lifted their arms and Natalia cowered in panic.

When she lifted her gaze once more, all was gone. No one was running about. There wasn't a giant scorpion snapping somewhere at the distant end of the street. There wasn't even a dog. All that remained was the storm.

The dream had ended. She was awake. She *had* to be.

Unease settled into her stomach as she stepped inside, and she blinked in confusion, unable to shake the feeling she was walking away from something important.

The smell of strawberries wafted up her nose, chasing away most of her thoughts. She followed it to the kitchen where her father was bent over the small table, cutting her birthday cake into near equal sized sections, just as he always would.

Natalia sat at her usual spot, tucked into the corner of the small room. She put her hands shaking hand on the table for only a moment before squirrelling them onto her lap. Her dad didn't seem to notice as he passed her a china bowl, took one for himself, and sat opposite with a toothy smile.

"Happy birthday," he chimed, green eyes blazing. The lights above him were on, yellow and soft, like they'd never been out for even a second.

Natalia tried to smile. "Thanks, Dad."

Is the wolf-dog still out there? The body? The scorpion?

The intrusive thoughts made her choke on her first bite, earning a raised eyebrow, but she played it off as a cough.

Of course they're not out there. There never *was a wolf. There wasn't a scorpion. And there wasn't a body.*

Yet the thoughts didn't leave, no matter how hard she tried replacing them with cake.

In another attempt at distraction, she watched her father.

They shared a lot of features. The same tree-bark brown hair which they wore unstyled; Natalia's fell to her elbows with a side parting, while her father's was much shorter, greying at the roots already. The pale complexion, oblong face, small nose, and the dark eyebrows and eyelashes.

Natalia's eyes were the same almond shape as her father's, but hers were a dull brown and his a calm green. She'd never worn braces for her straight teeth while he had wonky teeth he was unbothered by.

Between her shoulder blades began to itch as she thought about the oddest difference. Sometimes, when she became flustered or blushed, a subtle sparkle rose on her cheeks. It didn't happen *every* time, and Natalia didn't think others noticed it when it did. If they did, nobody had mentioned it. She herself had assumed it was residue glitter from something – probably from all the cake decorating she did regularly.

"Did Katherine make this?" She stabbed the last piece of her icing and saw the design on it: intricately small flowers made of tiny dots.

He winked. "Of course she did."

Katherine Santos was their overly cheerful neighbour who owned her own café and cake shop along Main Street. Natalia now worked there too, cooking and baking and cleaning.

She sighed, her gaze drawn to the window and the storm outside.

She caught a hint of her father's voice as it trailed off. She blinked and looked back at him. "What?"

He smiled. "Something's caught your attention."

Wolf. Giant Scorpion. A trio. Dead body.

"It's nothing. Just think about a dream I had." She paused, her stomach twisting. "What were you saying?"

"I was saying," he pushed his bowl away, "that your birthday comes round quicker every year."

"It's the same time every year, Dad. It's just that we're always so busy it seems to come round faster."

"Can't you stop growing up for one year?"

At that, she relaxed and smiled. "I don't think that's how it works."

"Then I *suppose*," he emphasised the word dramatically, "I better give you these."

From under the table, he drew out two presents wrapped in

silver paper. Natalia became an impatient child, no longer distracted, wanting to grab her gifts. She did just that and her father chuckled.

Ignoring how her hands still shook, she tore into the smaller present first.

Inside a black box sat a sight of wonders. Two silver stars, hanging off short hooks, glistened with a hint of something that resembled the essence of starlight itself. Her mouth opened in awe. For *months* she'd asked for these earrings. She'd been drawn to them from the very first moment she'd seen them. How had her dad afforded them?

Her fingers glided over them and then picked them out. Carefully, she pushed the first into one ear and then the second on the other side. The stars hung just below her lobe. They caused little rainbows to dance on the walls as the lights caressed them.

"Dad..." She trailed off, unable to finish. She touched the earrings. They were *hers*.

His smile was a proud one. "You have another present," he reminded, pointing at it.

With a thumping heart, Natalia wondered if she could handle a second present. These earrings were more than enough. They were everything. Knowing her father would only push until she relented though, she grabbed the second gift.

"They're from Katherine too," he said. "She wanted to get you something and remembered me saying about your headphones."

"Dad." She touched the box of her new green headphones. "This is too much."

He climbed from his chair to kiss Natalia's head. "*Nothing* is too much for my Natalia."

"How—"

"I've been saving. It's why you didn't get much at Christmas."

Natalia kissed his soft, shaven cheek. "Thank you," she whispered. But no amount of thanks, whether said or showed, would ever come close to expressing how truly grateful she was.

The doorbell rang and her dad left to get it, knees cracking as he moved. Natalia stayed. She didn't dare blink in case her incredible gifts puffed out of existence. Were they taunts, things in front of her, in reach now, but things she would never really possess? They were too incredible and yet she'd been given them.

"Guess who?" Teased an overly familiar voice, drawing her back.

Noah entered, flashing a wide smile to show off his coloured braces. His neatly-cropped black hair showed off his ears – one ear was missing a chunk at the top thanks to an infected piercing from a couple of years ago. The kitchen lights gave his umber skin a golden sheen.

Natalia stood and Noah enveloped her in a secure hug. She caught her father's eye over Noah's back. He winked – his way of offering encouragement – and walked off.

"I heard it was someone's eighteenth birthday." Breaking apart, Noah thrusted a brown papered package at Natalia. "The birthday Fairies might have left something for you at my place."

"There's no such thing," she argued as something niggled at her stomach.

"Today *is* your birthday, right?"

"It's February nineteenth, right?"

Noah snorted as he laughed. "Then there must be such things. Come on, Princess. You've turned eighteen, not one hundred. There's still enough life in you to joke around."

"But what if they're bad?"

He fake gasped. "I'm offended. I'm cancelling our friendship."

She grinned. "That's the fourth time this week."

"Only the fourth?" Noah laughed at himself as Natalia unwrapped her present.

Long ago, Natalia had grown out of believing stories about Fairies and Witches and the rest; they belonged to the worlds inside her books, the ones now collecting dust in the loft. The idea of them was nice but silly now, and childish. They were a children's wish, not an adult's reality. Maybe that was why her brain had conjured what it had earlier, to hold onto what innocence it could. But Natalia was eighteen now and had to put those things away for good. Though she wasn't old, she was old enough.

A brown box was hidden inside the brown paper package. She tore off the tape and beamed.

On the top was a giant box of Malteasers - her favourite. Putting them on the table as Noah slid into a chair, she found the second gift. She laid down the box to unfurl the piece of clothing, laughing as she held it up.

It was black with writing made from sequins that, when shook, flipped to a rainbow pattern. No matter the way the sequins hung, the writing remained the same: *I'm a Fairy, bitch.*

She looked to her best friend. "Is *this* why you were going on about Fairies?"

He shrugged nonchalantly. "It might've had something to do with it."

"Thank you." She shuffled over and kissed his cheek.

"Though," he paused, "it *might* have something to do with the gossip about a wolf roaming the streets last night." Natalia's breathing hitched but Noah didn't notice. As her heart pulsed loudly, Noah took her hand and kissed the back of it. "Princess," he said - his nickname for her because "Nat" wasn't good enough and he needed a perfectly cheesy name for all the time they'd been best friends.

She blinked. "What?"

"I was just saying I'm glad you like the gifts."

"Old age is kicking in," her father commented as he returned. "She zoned earlier too."

"A mind of jelly at eighteen. It's a sad affair." Noah shook his head, grinning, more so when Natalia's father handed him some cake. "Thank you, sir," he said.

Natalia's father turned to her, looked the t-shirt up and down, and said, "Suits you." He smiled and she smiled back. "Do you two have plans today?"

"Have you got work?" Natalia asked back.

"No matter how much I want this house to run itself, it won't."

Her father, Tony Whitebell, worked hard for what little he had and was proud of that. He gave whatever he could to Natalia despite her constant, incessant protests. But she was everything to him and she knew it, he made sure she did. Usually by doing small things - picking flowers from the garden so she could look at them while washing up; buying a postcard from the market by a local aspiring artist that would brighten her bedroom; trying out new recipes to change her moods. Whatever he could do, however he could do it, he did anything and everything to make her happy.

"Eleven hours today," her father answered, leaning against the sink.

Venderly Island wasn't big. It was close to Nantucket Island but still awfully far - oddly the U.K. had claim over Venderly despite it being geographically closer to mainland America. There was one large general store. Nearly all produce was shipped from mainland America. Two deliveries a week, sometimes three, and then the shelves needed filling. That was what Natalia's father did, often pulling long shifts. But a job was a job.

"I applied there last week," announced Noah.

Natalia's head whipped toward him. "Since when?"

"Since I got rejected for every other job I applied for." Noah rolled his eyes heavily. "Apparently I'm too young and don't have enough experience for anything. But how am I supposed to get experience if no one is willing to offer a chance for me to earn it?"

"Unfortunately, that's how the world works." Natalia's father sighed. "You'll get there, kid."

Even though Venderly was reclusive, the only way on or off being by boat, plenty of people lived here. The entire Island was one town of sorts. There were shops, a market, the grocery store, as well as houses, two hotels, three different schools, a dance studio, a swimming pool and gym combo, and a combined shipping and transport yard and dock – both on the West side, which was how you got from the mainland to here. But jobs were rare and hard to obtain when one did rise.

"I'm going to water the sea and declare that as my job," Noah joked.

Tony laughed. "Let me know how that goes. If it pays well, and the hours are good, I might join you."

"I'll stick with the job I have," Natalia threw out. "I'm guaranteed my birthday, Christmas day, Boxing day, *and* New Year's Eve and day off every year. Plus, the boss is rather nice."

"She is indeed," her father agreed, not meeting her gaze as he spoke. He pushed off the counter with his hands and folded his arms, crumpling the t-shirt he wore. "And that brings us back to the fact that you have today off."

Natalia turned to her best friend. "I was thinking we could visit the new rooftop bar?"

"No more exams?" Noah asked. Natalia shook her head. "Then it just so happens, I have midday reservations for that place."

She looked at her father. "You're ok with that?"

His smile was toothy. "You're eighteen. Technically, I don't have to be ok with anything anymore for you to do it. But of course I'm ok with it!" He unfolded his arms. "It's your birthday and you've finished your exams. Celebrate. *Please*."

Natalia threw herself at her father, wrapping her arms around his neck tightly. "It's impossible not to love you," she whispered.

"My job is to make sure that doesn't change." He kissed her head so gently it felt like bird's wings fluttering against her skin. "And I love you too."

He promptly pushed Natalia into the hallway where she shuffled into shoes and a February appropriate jacket.

"I'll grab something on the way home for tea," she promised.

"I won't be home until after nine!" Her father called from the kitchen.

She smiled to herself. "I'll wait."

She could picture him shaking his head as he said, "I know."

Noah shoved past Natalia. "To the roof party!" He unlocked the door and ran out.

Natalia followed cautiously, searching for a body first and laughed nervously when there wasn't one. There wasn't even a drop of blood in sight. The ground was sodden and the winds had picked up, yet there were no signs of anything mysterious - why would there be? Natalia cuddled herself as she struggled to keep up with Noah's long strides.

Venderly Hotel soon came into view down Main Street - the road that ran directly through the centre of the Island, from one end to the other. The lavish grey brickwork showed style and how it was newer that its surroundings. Gold double doors flashed to those passing, pointing out this was the entrance. An old fashioned chalk board sat out front with "*Rooftop garden now open. Come and get your drinks*" scrawled across it in cursive writing.

Natalia's heart lept as Noah pushed the doors.

They were guided to the lifts by a worker once they'd expressed why they were here. The friends hopped inside the box of gold, along with five others, and were taken up to the fifteenth floor without any music playing above them.

When the doors slid apart, Natalia grabbed Noah's coat sleeve, unable to comprehend how there was somehow more to see.

Here, the whole Island - despite being vast and needing a near quarter day to calmly walk from one end and back - was visible. As was part of the sea beyond; the sound of the waves lapped the shore. Seagulls flew and dived overhead, making a horrible din, but they didn't swoop too low. Car horns tooted, bus doors shushed, and the tram bell dinged below in the streets.

This rooftop was delicate and vast too. Little circular wooden tables were spread out with chairs tucked beneath. Candles sat at their centre, most unlit. Lavender bushes lined the edge of the space and their smell was currently subtle. Other potted plants were placed around, adding greenery to hide the concrete structure it was the best it could. The balance of natural and industrial was incredible. Especially the little path that was lined by plants that led to a wooden shack at the furthest end of the rooftop. The wooden shack being the bar.

To Natalia, it was everything she'd been expecting from the new construction.

No waiter or server came to escort them, so Noah and Natalia took themselves to a table. It wasn't at the edge yet close enough they could see across some of the water the Island was captured by.

Being up this high, able to see so much, was like flying without having wings or the fear of falling. The salt air mixed with the lavender as Natalia tried to take it all in - if only she could package this combination into a jar.

"My treat, birthday girl," Noah said as he handed over a menu from the table behind.

She perused it. Half of the list was compiled of things she'd never heard of. Eventually her eyes found something familiar. "A glass of—"

"Red wine," he finished before she could.

She folded her menu. "It's like you know me."

"You know what? I think I might." He walked off to the bar and returned minutes later with drinks, his ID stuck between his glass and hand, and a puzzled expression. He handed Natalia her wine and sat opposite her, face unchanging. "Those women," he nodded to two tables over, "were at the bar too. They were saying there's a new family moving into Opal."

Natalia was glad she'd not taken a sip or she would've choked. "Opal House? Someone's moving in?"

"Apparently they have a large dog too."

"I heard it was a wolf," said a man in passing, clearly ear-wigging. He moved on quickly.

Natalia's hands shook as she raised her glass. "A wolf." The rich wine did nothing to drown the bitterness she could taste lingering on the tip of her tongue.

"It ran past my window!" Shrieked someone from another table. Clearly they were having a similar conversation. Natalia peered over and spotted the man that had commented to her and Noah moments ago now chatting lively to the women who had been gossiping about Opal House. "A wolf ran across my grass in the night. It unearthed half of it! I'm angrier about my lawn than I was scared. Bloody beast."

Noah raised an eyebrow at Natalia and whispered, "Did you see anything?"

"I don't think it was a wolf," Natalia replied, her stomach twisting an inch.

She realised then that while people had mentioned Opal House and the wolf – *dog,* her mind corrected – no one had said anything about a body. If that had been real, surely everyone would've been talking about it. But there wasn't even a whisper. That alone convinced Natalia, in that moment, that it hadn't been real. Maybe the other bits had been; the storm, the smoke, even the figures and the wolf. But not the body and *certainly* not the beast.

Noah huffed. "I'm pissed I didn't see anything! I heard about it, obviously, but..." He sipped his drink.

Natalia laughed nervously. "There might be a next time."

"Bloody better be. I seem to miss out on all the good stuff."

Natalia drank, hoping there wouldn't be a "next time". Noah drank too. And that was how they spent the next few hours. They talked, mostly about his failed job applications or of Natalia's preparations to start her nurses' course – she'd graduated from High School a term early, hence the recent exams as they were end of term ones and her college entrance exams.

"Come on, Princess," Noah said as he stood, wobbling. "I think it's time to go."

The sky above was sinking, not because the day was done, but because another storm was brewing on the horizon – Island's had benefits and problems.

Natalia gathered her bag as an idea popped into her head. "What about pizza? Home-made?" Despite what she'd drunk, she felt no affects as she stood.

"Like we used to?"

They stepped back into the lift and rode it down, the bell dinging once they reached the ground floor. The doors opened with a swish and they stepped out together.

"You're the birthday princess," Noah continued. "If that's what you want to do, we will."

Umbrellas were thrown up to protect those passing. The older generations kept their heads down while the younger ones looked to the sky. All seemed unsure of when the storm would break, only hoping they could beat it to their destinations. Natalia lifted the hood on her jacket and Noah copied with his coat.

They tried to outrun the heavens too. They made it to the front doors of the general store before water touched them.

Noah grabbed a basket and they walked along the aisles where a few other shoppers were browsing. Natalia picked up some essentials but found herself growing increasingly more distracted.

Her eyes kept wandering to the windows and the shadows as if something was lurking there, watching. Even though nothing jumped out, her heart refused to settle. The events of the morning were plaguing her, her mind unable to decipher what was real to what wasn't.

Once they'd checked out, they chose to venture back up Main Street as it provided the best shelter from the storm. Trams were slower in the rain and walking would give them the best chance to investigate the rumours surrounding Opal House. It took one passing look to decide what to do.

As they turned up Opal Street, Noah pointed to the parked yellow moving vans.

"Them old ladies were right," Noah whispered as they stopped under a tree.

Opal Street had no outlet, though Waverly Road intersected it from halfway down - the way back to Natalia's house. But the dead end gave way to the Island's biggest level-topped hill. Stone steps placed into the earth led up to one of the oldest residencies on the Island.

Opal House had remained mostly empty for as long as Natalia could remember; few had bought the house but no one lasted more than a few months. Every kid on Venderly used to play by the House at some point in their lives; they chased around it in summer and slid down the hill in winter.

"How long do you think they'll last?" Noah asked.

"Someone's finally bought it," Natalia said at the same time. It felt like the end of an era; these yellow vans seemed like serious business.

Noah wiped the rain from his face. "Who?"

It had to be someone off Island buying it. That would make the most sense since no one here had ever claimed it. Natalia adjusted herself and spotted a builders van parked closer to the House. Why would anyone choose to move here though? Not many people in recent years had moved to the Island in general, let alone claiming a rather large house. Maybe it was to be a holiday home?

The wind gusted and rain blew through their little tree cover, coating Natalia and Noah, spraying into their unsuspecting faces. All talk of the House died as they rushed on again.

Luckily the rest of the sprint home was no longer than ten minutes. Natalia handed her things to Noah so she could unlock the chipped, green front door. She shoved him inside and followed, her face immediately flushing.

After putting their coats on the radiator, Natalia led the way into the kitchen. There wasn't much shopping to unpack but Noah insisted on helping. So Natalia flicked on the light and radio, and everything was fine.

Then, for the second time that day, everything shut off.

When the lights didn't miraculously turn on again, Natalia sighed. Throwing open the front door, she hurried into the electrical cupboard. When she was done she paused, eyeing the road.

There was no sign of anything suspicious, but her heart-rate peaked as if expecting there to be. She squinted and a scorpion flickered into hazy existence and then out in a blink. She took a sharp, shallow breath.

It's not there. There's no scorpion now and there wasn't one before.

Touching the handle, she caught a glimpse of a shape in the glass of the door. Her head whipped round. A roll of thunder echoed and she pictured a snapping pincer. Was her mind playing tricks again? It had to be. There were no such things as giant scorpions.

Another rap of thunder crashed and there came no image this time.

Definitely in my head, she thought.

She went back inside, closing the door slowly behind her as if waiting for something to happen at the last second. When nothing arose, she pressed her head against the cold door, steadying herself before going back to the kitchen, picking a jumper up from the stairs in passing.

"I've already started." Noah side-stepped to show a floured countertop. "Hope you don't mind." He must've seen something written on her face because he asked, "Everything cool?"

"Just the electrics."

Noah grinned. "No wolf?"

She swallowed the lump in her throat, refusing to portray her unease on her face. "Not this time."

"Then how about these pizzas?"

Natalia forced a laugh and bumped him aside to join. Eventually she did settle into singing and dancing and cooking with Noah like when they were kids, but something deep in her stomach wouldn't allow her mind to rest – like an idea blooming in her subconscious, slowly coming together.

As they continued, lightning flashed and Natalia gasped. Noah bumped her hip again and she smiled at him. Though it wasn't the lightning that had alarmed her. She could've sworn the flash had illuminated the shape of a wolf in the garden, its eyes staring directly at her.

But as time passed, so did the worst of the storm, and the wolf never returned.

2
Remnants of Storms Last

THE CREAM WALLPAPER IN THE LIVING ROOM WAS PEELING. It had been for years, so it didn't surprise Natalia when a piece fell away as she touched it, the centre having a little orange kite - the overall decorative design of the paper.

She flicked the paper away. The whole house was dilapidated in one way or another. If the wallpaper wasn't peeling, paint was chipped. If a cabinet wasn't missing a handle, it was hanging on by a single hinge. If a sink didn't block, a tap would spray out icy water.

Natalia wouldn't change it for the world.

Her parents had bought this house as their forever home. Natalia had literally been born in this house; they'd never made it to the on Island mini hospital, so she came to breathe in the middle of the kitchen floor.

The best bit to her was the usable, *unbroken*, balcony attached to her room. She could oversee the garden and the ocean beyond it. The entire house resided close to the Northern edge of the Island. The garden and the little public footpath beyond it were separated by a fence. But there weren't too many onlookers here who used that path as it ran by a steep yet small cliff edge.

This house didn't need to be pristine or perfect. It was home. And homes that kept people safe and secure were hard to come by. But here, her heart could be free and her mind could wander unhindered.

Natalia looked at the hanging wooden clock before walking into the dim, pear green hallway. She locked the door behind her as she stepped out.

The previous day's storms were gone, as was the headache Natalia had been cursed with for most of the night. She'd barely slept. Images of wolves and dogs, giant scorpions, and three figures had run through her mind. She'd whispered into the dark that those things weren't real, no more so than her other dreams. But that didn't help her drift off for longer than three hours.

She marched down her road but stopped on Opal Street. The looming House stared down at her. Unease settled into her stomach as she peered at what she could make of the wooden porch.

Like one thousand spiders tapped along her skin at once, she shivered. The hairs over her body stood to attention.

The rest of the walk to work was brisk.

Standing halfway down Main Street, attracting lots of attention for simply being in the right place, was "Katherine's Koffee & Kakes", announced with a neon orange sign. The shop served all sorts of treats and beverages – healthy or not – for all occasions, or nothing special.

Natalia by-passed the queue of customers, keeping her head down. She slipped round the main counter and into the kitchen, and dropped her bag and coat onto the free stool in the corner. She nabbed a waist apron from one of the few wooden pegs.

The oven pinged and Katherine appeared out of nowhere as if summoned. She didn't smudge her pink lipstick as she flashed a white toothed smile. Like always, she wore pink eye-shadow and dangling golden earrings to match. Her little gold nose ring shone under the yellow light of the narrow kitchen, her shoulder length black hair tucked behind her ears.

"I've got this," Natalia told her boss, springing into action.

Katherine stepped closer from the store side of the building. "I didn't see you come in."

"With all those customers, I'm not surprised." Natalia bent to the oven and pulled out the fresh, fruity smelling tray of muffins.

"It's been one hell of a morning."

Natalia laid the tray to rest in front of the open window. "You've been open for an hour."

"Seems to me everyone's hunting for a treat after the storms. Like normal." Katherine's laugh was hearty. "I can't complain."

"Speaking of treats," she smiled, "thank you for my birthday cake."

Katherine's face lit up further. "You liked it?"

"How could I *not*? And how did you find the time to make it?"

"There's always time for you."

Katherine tucked Natalia into her. Her hugs were always warm and motherly – she didn't have children of her own, but it felt like Natalia was a daughter of sorts. Katherine was so easy to love and want around. She was like her creations – absolutely sweet without being overwhelming.

Pulling back, Katherine asked, "Did you have a good day?"

Natalia went in for another hug. "For the headphones!" Guiltily, she'd forgotten until then.

Katherine laughed. "I'm glad you like them."

"They're exactly what I wanted without knowing it." She pulled away first. "I haven't tested them out though."

"What about after work?"

"If the weather holds, I will."

The little bell out front tinged, indicating someone had entered the store. "Excuse me," Katherine said, rushing into the main café. She served whoever was there while Natalia started prepping more muffins in the next tray, and then returned. "What else did you get then?"

Natalia smiled and rattled off the list. As she presented her new earrings, having saved the very best for last, Katherine's eyebrows rose.

"What?" Natalia asked.

"They're gorgeous." Katherine's smile returned, measuredly. "Your family has always liked stars is all. Your mother especially."

Natalia blinked. "My mother?" Had she heard correctly?

"They were her favourite thing to watch, like she was connected to them somehow."

"Dad never told me that."

"Maybe he forgot?"

Natalia scowled, her stomach pinching. Why and *how* would he forget something like that? "Maybe," she agreed, half-heartedly.

Katherine licked her lips, as she did whenever she was nervous about something. "What I meant was that I didn't realise he could afford them."

Natalia touched her earrings. "Apparently he saved."

"Oh, I've no doubt. He loves you and wants to give you the best."

Natalia nodded and settled in to serve the next wave of customers as the bell was activated again.

When the rush was over, Natalia swapped with Katherine who wanted to clean the counters and tables so she could start filling the cooled muffins she'd retrieved from the oven about an hour ago. No amount of liquid chocolate however could distract her. If anything, when it came to patterning stars on top as a decorative centre point, it reminded her more that her father had neglected to mention how her mother had enjoyed them, especially since he'd told her plenty about her mother over the years.

Once complete, Katherine took the muffins. She displayed them in the case out front and peered back in the kitchen doorway. Natalia kept mixing the new cake batter, pretending she wasn't aware of her boss' presence.

Katherine's voice was soft when she said, "Nat, he probably forgot."

Natalia let go of the bowl with a little more force than she'd intended, clanging it on the worktop. She turned to Katherine.

"How could he forget? He never forgot what she looked like, that her favourite fruit was apricots, that her favourite smell was vanilla, that she loved watching the waves of the sea despite being afraid of water. But somehow he *forgot* she liked the stars, the one thing that would appear most in her life."

Katherine folded her arms - a difficult feet for a woman with curves. "Have you considered," her voice was still calm but a fire burned in her eyes now, "that he *forgot* on purpose?"

Natalia listened to one beat of her heart. "What?"

"Having his daughter enjoy the stars as much as his wife might just hurt him more than it makes him happy. That's not me saying you're causing him pain, but maybe he didn't share the memory because he connects the stars with her being gone? So *maybe* he kept quiet to let you enjoy the things you love without tainting them for you."

Natalia cheeks flushed. She hadn't thought of that. Maybe her father *had* locked the memory away, "forgetting", so she could have them as her own. If Natalia's mother did love them, like she now did, then he'd want to keep that separate if all he saw was how she'd been lost and didn't want the same fate for Natalia - like a curse he was forever reminded of in the sky. He hadn't hidden anything to be selfish. In fact, he'd hidden it to be selfless, giving her more love than she'd ever known.

"I didn't—" She started.

"I know," Katherine jumped in, unfolding her arms. "I know you didn't."

Natalia's face heated further and she dropped her face to hide. "But you remembered," she said quietly. "*Please.* Tell me more."

Katherine's face twisted into something close to a wince. "There isn't much to tell," she murmured. "I didn't know her well. Whatever else there is, it's not for me to say or know." She turned abruptly, calling over her shoulder, "We have work to do."

Natalia nodded. She served the new customers and said goodbye to those that left, not saying more than she needed.

During a slower period, Natalia started wiping tables and chairs, pushing them back to their original places before sweeping the black and white tiled floors with the tired old broom.

As she went, she wondered how long she'd be here. Not just today, but in the future. Her nursing entrance course exams were over and now all she needed were the results. Yet she couldn't help but wonder, not for the first time, if she should be doing something else. There always was a knot in her stomach when she thought it, like she was missing an opportunity somewhere.

Sweeping harder, the stars in her earrings wiggled, and her thoughts wandered yet again. They were overtaken by curiosity about her mother's love of stars. Why exactly *had* her father buried something so explainable? It couldn't just be about paint because surely everything about her mother would've been painful, to some degree, to talk about.

How complicated could it be? It was one *story.*

The storms had finally passed and without much incident. There *was* a casualty, a local resident who had been in the wrong place at the wrong time - but their death had been quick, thankfully.

It had worked though. The hunt and execution of the Monster last night had been near perfect. There had been another moment, one single moment, where Jasper hadn't been convinced that it would. The bloody thing was huge. Yet they'd been blessed with the cover of a storm - which happened to confuse the insect too.

He stomped down the stairs, the wood creaking as he jumped the last two steps, and landed in the front hall. The stained glass windows of the double oaks doors formed a complete picture: the right side a sun rising over a hill while the left had a moon setting behind a snow-capped mountain.

"You coming?" Archie's voice echoed from the stairs behind him.

Jasper twisted his head awkwardly to face his brother and his brother's girlfriend, Peri, who walked beside him.

"For what?" Jasper asked back.

"Breakfast."

"No. I thought I'd stand in the hallway all day, unable to enter a new room until someone invited me in like the Vampire I'm not." Jasper smirked when Peri shot him an encouraging grin she half-hid from Archie. "Are you cooking?"

"Why should *I* cook?"

They walked through to the newly remodelled kitchen and dining area. Jasper slid onto the nearest rose gold bar stool. "Because I set fire to the kitchen last time," he reminded them. He could see the little blaze he'd put *into* the frying pan, of course by accident.

"Expect burnt toast."

"As long as it's done by accident. Otherwise, I'll complain."

"Like the baby you are?"

"I *am* the baby. I'm the youngest."

Archie tied himself into the nearest apron, glancing at what he'd chosen. Jasper blinked as the words on the apron shimmered in the light. *"The best ok cook"* they read. Archie frowned but Jasper smiled innocently.

"How about," Peri moved around the island and untied the apron from Archie, slipping it over her own head, "neither of you cook? The only reason you," she pointed accusingly at Jasper, "set fire to the kitchen was because you were trying too hard to prove a point and you," she moved her finger to Archie, "let him take it too far. To save this house *and* us, I'll cook."

"Are you going to burn my toast?" Jasper whined despite preferring it burnt.

Peri waved her right arm, showing off the stump in place of where a hand should be. "I still have one working hand." Proving her point, she wiggled and waved the fingers on her left hand. "*If* I feel like living on the edge, I'll call on you."

Jasper settled into a chair as Archie moved through the kitchen, helping Peri when she asked.. They'd always worked well together, supporting each other's weaknesses and boosting their strengths. Jasper would never admit it, but he'd always liked Peri and seeing her and his brother together made him happy.

Minutes later, a plate of sadly unburnt toast and peppered eggs was placed before him, followed by orange juice and coffee. Jasper dug in. Archie and Peri shifted into the other bar stools beside him.

No one spoke as they ate, until a light voice came from the doorway.

"How did you sleep?"

Jasper lifted his head and saw his mother enter, dressed in a white suit and red heels.

"Like a log," Archie answered. He kissed his mother's cheek.

"That's how you always look. Asleep or awake," Jasper commented.

"Like a thick piece of nature?"

"Close. I was thinking more like a lifeless plank."

Their mother pinched the back of Jasper's neck, leaving a red mark on the pale skin. "Enough," she warned. She walked round the island to face them all. "Peri, dear?"

"Well enough," Peri answered.

Jasper looked at his mother. "Where's dad?"

"Talking to the Council." Her tone was serious, as was the look on her face. Her blue eyes were focused yet distant all at once. "He's giving the details."

"About last night?" Peri stood, walking her empty plate and cups to the sink, then turned to lean beside the boy's mother. "They sent us in there."

"Who sent who in where?" Alex strolled into the kitchen, her usual brown curls a tangled mess on top of her head.

Jasper snorted. "Did someone drag you through a bush last night?"

"Did a bird come to nest?" Archie asked cheekily.

Alex threw up her middle finger at both of them and kept it there as she walked, only stopping when she kissed their mother's cheek. "Morning ma," she said, her Seattle accent still present despite not having lived there in years.

"I was just explaining how dad's on the phone with the Council," their mother said. "They wanted an update and a conclusion on how the situation was handled."

"That's *why* they sent us here," Archie scoffed. "To handle the situations."

Jasper pushed his plate away, no longer hungry. Not because of what had transpired yesterday, but because his brother was right.

Before coming to Venderly, they'd all been peacefully living in Home City. Apparently *too* peacefully. The Council had decided that more areas of the world needed guarding and protecting as breaks in the Veils were widening and the Veils themselves were weakening – they were searching for a way to slow the process but there were no positive signs.

The Darby's had been on the short list to be moved. That didn't mean they could never be relocated again or were refused re-entry into Home City, it just meant, for now, they were on an Island without much company besides themselves.

Jasper didn't mind so much. He hadn't had many roots back in the City. He'd only been interested in training, which he could do just as easily here. Moving did have its perks. Here, he could acquire real life experience, something the City couldn't provide as it was a safe haven, a bomb-shelter of sorts, from the outside world and its troubles. Now, he could kick start his life's Purpose, the thing he'd been training *for*.

Jasper's father, strode purposefully into the kitchen. His shoes were as pristine as his suit and pin-straight tie. His dark hair was combed and slicked back. His green eyes were bright on their own, not needing the fake kitchen light to make them gleam.

Archie and Jasper were near perfect combinations of their parents. Jasper had their father's dark hair, though his was wavy like their mother's, and it hung at a medium length – mother was constantly complaining about it needing a cut – and Archie had their mother's light brown hair that was short all over and shorter still at the sides. Both had their father's upturned green eyes and both had their mother's freckles; Archie's only presented after long exposure to the sun but Jasper's were spread across his cheekbones and nose all year round. They stood at six feet tall, inches off their father, inches taller than their mother. Archie physically carried more muscle, with wide shoulders and thicker arms, though Jasper had enough of his own, his being slimmer and smaller but toned all the same. From time to time, like their mother, Archie got red cheeks too.

Alex, though indeed their sister, was adopted. Her wild shoulder length brown curls, with a fringe she'd cut in herself over winter, and her light brown monolid eyes, often lined with dark black, were her own. She was nine months younger than Archie, almost to the day. She was toned and had muscles she proudly displayed. Her skin was a tawny brown and her eyebrows were dark, with a stud piercing through the left one, matching the stud on the left side of her nose – both of which her mother told her repeatedly to remove, which she ignored.

"What did they say?" asked Peri, breaking the silence. She ran her hand through her black cropped bob, displacing the longer front bits.

"Nothing much," Jasper's father admitted sourly.

"I feel so disconnected," Jasper's mother groaned. "It's not that I don't like it here, James. It's beautiful! But we were in the City for *so* long. I grew up there!" She attempted to smile, blue eyes resting on her husband. "What did the Council want?"

"To know how last night went."

"And what did you tell them?"

"I told them the truth, Sarah, that all was fine. They just noted down what happened for their records. They did some checks, and apparently the Human who died had no family so the Council said they'd see to it."

"And?" Archie pressed.

"And that was that."

"So," Alex dragged the word out. "It was pointless."

"Talking to the Council always is," Jasper mused.

"Boring too," added Archie.

"*You* haven't had that many conversations with them," Alex said.

"I've spoken to them a handful of times," Archie admitted. "That was enough."

Jasper gave him that. All it took was one conversation with the Council to decide talking to them was the biggest mistake ever. Jasper didn't want to know why they insisted on updates every time something happened, major or not. Yet they kept requesting and everyone complied.

Jasper stood up. "I'm going for some fresh air."

Alex perked up, "Want company?"

Peri stood taller. "I'm up for a walk."

"Sure." Archie got up. "Why not. Me too."

Walking backwards from the chairs, Jasper rolled his eyes sarcastically. "Why don't we all take a nice stroll around the Island? We can hold hands and get ice-cream? Maybe feed it to each other? Skip over the cliffside head first?"

Alex rushed into the hall. "That won't scare me!" she called.

Jasper groaned. "The God's can't blame me for trying."

Natalia shuttered the blinds and flipped the door sign to "CLOSED." She stacked the final chairs and mopped the floor properly before switching off the lights.

"You in tomorrow?" Katherine asked, facing the calendar by the back door. "Damn," she clicked her fingers, "you're off."

Natalia didn't have plans but sometimes days without them were the best. They offered endless possibilities and time.

Katherine let them out the back door and locked it. As they moved around the building, coming around to the front, bright car-lights illuminated them. Natalia grinned.

"Want a lift?" Natalia's father called out of the car window.

Katherine twisted her keys around their chain. "If it's not too much trouble?"

"You live down the same street," Natalia told her, beginning to drag her boss by her sleeve.

They climbed into the rusting blue Ford Escort. Her dad never minded offering a lift to Katherine.

The car took off, a little jittery at first. Natalia caught a fleeting glance at Opal House as they passed. A few lights seemed to be on inside. But too soon it was gone and they were stopping down their road.

Once her dad had turned off the engine, she climbed out, the adults following. Katherine turned to Natalia's father, clutching her keys. "Thank you, Tony," she said, not looking directly at him.

"You know it's never a problem," he said lightly.

"Yes, well, I don't expect it."

"I'm always willing to offer."

The streetlights highlighted the smile Katherine gave. They awkwardly nodded together and then Katherine dashed off across the road, scurrying inside her house. Natalia spotted the pink tint to her father's cheeks as she looked at him but remained quiet.

She'd wondered before if her father would ever find someone else. Even without having known her mother, she knew she'd want it for him. Who wouldn't want the one they loved to be happy if they themselves could no longer occupy those spaces?

There had always been tension between her father and Katherine, a lingering pressure that built every time they were close. But neither of them made a move or even acknowledged that there was anything. Was Natalia the only one who sensed it? Or were they too scared to admit it was there?

Natalia unlocked the front door and stepped inside, her father close behind. The hallway was cold. So much so that Natalia shook off her coat and shoes, and raced up the stairs at the end of the hall to get her blood pumping. She dashed into her bedroom and threw on the biggest jumper she could find. The longer the day had gone on for, the icier the air had become; winter was lingering.

Ready to shut her blinds for the night, she turned to her window. The sky ignited.

Natalia swayed. Her heart pounded inside her head, bad enough that she had to put her hands to her chest to quieten it.

She stepped forwards, lifted the latch on the window, hoisted it up, and climbed out. The breeze immediately hit her cheeks. She climbed out and onto the balcony, touching the wooden railing. Her breathing grew short and her legs shook. Jitters ran along her spine, tiny sparks jolting the space between her shoulder blades.

What's happening?

She searched for an answer.

Out of nowhere giant white paw swung towards her and black nails savagely clawed her right leg. Natalia screamed as the nails tore her skin. Gasping for breath, she reached towards the two deep bleeding gashes in her right calf. The throbbing pain sent an unsettling heavy pulse up her body to her temple, blurring her vision.

The paw swung for her for the second time and she was swiped sideways into the railings like a cannonball. The wooden railings snapped and she tumbled.

Her body smacked against the sodden ground. Red hot pain seared through her. She tried to roll away but couldn't. A scream lodged in her throat, her chest telling her to stop as pain bled along her lungs.

Lying motionless on the ground, her attacker came into focus.

Whatever it *really* was, Natalia didn't know, but it resembled a massive polar bear. Though this was evidently deadlier. It had giant paws with claws the length of knives, one perilously closer to Natalia's fallen body.

The beast rolled its head back and roared. Natalia's stomach recoiled. Her body ran cold, halting her more than the pain had. Then it roared again, but at the end of its display, fire spewed from inside its mouth. Though the beast towered above her, the heat warmed her skin all the same.

I need to get away, she thought. *This can't be real, can it? A giant polar bear?*

If anyone had said those things to her face, trying to convince her of their existence, she would've called them crazy. But she remembered the storm and the mark it had left inside her head. First, a giant scorpion in the street. Now, she was beside a beast the size of a house with pain shooting through her leg as a result of meeting it.

"Stay down," whispered an unfamiliar voice.

Natalia was in too much distress and pain to argue. So she bit her lip to subdue the building scream.

"Close your eyes," whispered the same voice, this time deeper.

I will not, she thought. She wanted her eyes on the beast at all times. While it didn't seem to notice she was there, that could change at any moment.

"You might want too," the voice said, making Natalia realise she'd spoke aloud.

A face suddenly appeared above Natalia, peering down at her. Then another. One had dark wavy hair and green eyes. The other had brown eyes and short black hair.

The two people moved, coming into focus. Natalia realised the one with brown eyes, as they came to rest on her left, was female. The one with green eyes moved to Natalia's right. They appeared to be male and Natalia realised he'd been the one that'd spoken to her first.

The girl took Natalia's hand. "This might sting," she said, keeping her voice low.

"I— I— I—" Natalia took a breath. "I—I hurt already."

"Even a little more pain will affect you."

"You'd be surprised," the boy added as if Natalia was about to argue.

Natalia glanced at the girl. She squeezed Natalia's hand, making her suck in air sharply and wince as a stabbing pain zapped along her ribs. "*Mi dispiace, amore*," the girl said. "Feel free to squeeze my hand if anything hurts."

The boy shuffled closer to Natalia's throbbing leg. How bad was the damage? How deep were the cuts? How much blood was she losing?

Natalia could almost forget she was beneath the *thing*. Until it reared up on its hind legs.

Fire oozed from its mouth. Natalia gaped as her body shook. Yesterday, she'd wanted to know if what she'd seen had been real or her imagination. Today, she wanted no such answers. Today, she wanted everything to stop.

Agony ripped through her leg and she whimpered, squeezing the girl's given hand as hard as she could, nails digging in like claws.

The next thing Natalia was aware of, something tight was being secured around her leg and the throbbing returned. It could've only taken mere minutes between the start of the incident and now, but Natalia was exhausted as if it'd been an entire day. Mentally and physically she was in two different places at two different times.

The boy leant back and Natalia saw him open his mouth to talk. But the beast caging them in reared up again. Then its head flopped down. Pure black eyes stared straight into Natalia's soul.

Jolts of adrenaline soared through her body.

Her arms struggled but they started to carry her backwards, making her look like a faulty crab. The beast's mouth gaped at her desperate movements. But her heart completely sank when her shoulders hit something solid; the familiar wobbling noise said she'd hit the garden fence. There was nowhere for her to go now.

The *thing* stomped its feet and the ground shook, toppling the nearby stone bird-bath. Natalia thought of her father as the beast continued to flatten the earth. How had he not noticed this happening in their back garden? How had *no one* on the Island seen this beast?

Natalia's heart pounded heavily as her eyes searched for something to defend herself with but there was nothing.

The beast's mouth opened again, this time at Natalia. An overwhelming calm washed over her, like this was the end and she was at peace with knowing she was about to be cremated alive. Still, she managed to lift her arms, to shield her eyes. Not that it mattered. Soon she'd be a puddle of bones, flesh, and blood – if anything at all.

She focused on the distant sounds of seagulls. A single tear rolled out of her eye.

Mother? She called out. *I'll be with you soon.*

She willed her mother to respond, to say that she was waiting for her daughter. Not even a roar came from the beast. Was this what the end became? She wondered if the world had been silenced and her heart had stopped, her soul now well on its way, without ever feeling a tinge of pain.

Then she smelt the salt of the sea.

Natalia took a ragged breath, the salty sea air flooding her senses. She dared for move her arms from her face, confused.

She wasn't dead.

Paralysed with pain and fear, she still couldn't move, but she was alive. There was to be no afterlife, no wanderings after death. She still belonged to the side of the living.

Realisation hit her and she looked around for an explanation.

The two who had patched her leg were throwing things at the polar bear that was now further away in the garden and partly into next door's. The beast kept trying to burn them, the fire edging closer to licking their skin but they continued to dodge.

Another pair of bodies had joined them at some point. They all danced together, in a way, around the beast while stabbing at it. One of the four – it was unclear exactly *who* as they were all moving so fast – landed a solid hit on the beast's front leg.

All four attackers stopped.

One crouched, letting out a noise like a howl. Two others moved around the beast as a distraction. The last one, the boy with wavy hair, was stood still and waving his hands. He said nothing, or at least Natalia couldn't hear him if he did.

The beast didn't roar as it thrashed its head from side to side.

Out of nowhere, a riptide of wind tore at Natalia. Her eyes watered but she kept her gaze focused on the waving boy.

Pink sparks ignited from his hands.

The beast roared, though sounded strangled. Smoke rose from its nostrils and, with another roar, it crashed onto its back. It didn't seem to be using its fire anymore and Natalia saw that it also couldn't reach anyone to even bite. It was as if something was stopping it from the inside.

When it tried to snap its jaws, it choked more; smoke leaked through its bared teeth and flared nostrils.

"Natalia?"

Her head lolled to the side to see her father in the kitchen doorway. He'd finally seen.

More than ever, she wanted him. She wanted him at her side, singing a childhood lullaby, keeping her tight.

At once, a tearing pain split through her body.

She slumped to the side, desperately grabbing for her leg where the pain was most intense. Her eyes blurred but she could still make out the blood soaked bandages.

I'm dying after all.

Her body was heaved into warm arms and she hung limply in them. Her father's face appeared, his eyes scanning her pale face. The burning tore through her. Sweat broke across her forehead and down her back. Invisible fire was ripping her apart, her body encapsulated by it.

"Don't you dare," her father ordered, his voice audible but distant. "We'll get you help."

Natalia tried to speak but her body went lax; her head sank, her eyes stuck half-open and unseeing as she faded into the black pool that awaited.

3
Upside - Down

THERE WAS FIRE AND BURNING.

There was Heaven and Hell.

There was death.

There was life.

Unbelievably Natalia's eyes opened. They were crusty and sore but blinking and awake. Blood rushed to her face and her heart thudded consistently, beating like a drum on her ribs as she took steady breaths.

She tried to shift, but the effort sent sharp needle-like stabs along her sides. She flopped back, her head hitting the pillow.

What happened?

Something wasn't right. She tried to move her eyes without twisting her neck or rolling her head, and failed. Besides the white ceiling, there wasn't much else she could discern.

Holding her breath, her heart whispered not to try. She ignored it. Her neck cracked as she turned it. Thankfully, no other pain came. *Success,* she thought, and believed it when she noticed the lit candle on the wooden cabinet beside her.

A cabinet and candle that weren't hers.

Where am I?

Then her mind fractured, offering the memories it had suppressed. Images flashed like fireworks in her subconscious. The sky ignited in orange and she stepped towards it. Suddenly she was on the ground, a gigantic polar bear looming over her. Her forehead broke out in a sweat as she remembered her damaged leg and the burning. She could picture two faces working around her, but then they were gone as Natalia died.

"Look who's awake."

Natalia half managed to swallow the thick lump in her throat and rolled her head to the other side. The girl from the garden was there, her black hair cut neatly to frame her round face, showing off her blue painted lips.

The girl edged closer, stopping next to the bed. "How'd you feel?" She asked keeping her voice minimal.

"What happen—" Natalia couldn't finish, it was like she'd swallowed sand.

"Things will be explained, *amore*."

"My dad?" Natalia croaked.

The girl offered a smile. "He's here. D'you want him?"

What did she want? She wanted to know what had happened, how she'd lived, and where she was now. She wanted to know what was going on around her.

Though she could no longer feel the fire's kiss, she had the memory of it scorching her veins which was bad enough. She didn't know whether to throw up or to stay very still. Like her body knew the best thing for her, it moved; her hands flipped back the duvet as she strained to sit.

She *did* feel better for it, like some pressure had been released.

And then her eyes wandered.

Her right leg, from ankle to knee, was hidden beneath white bandaging with white gauze underneath it. There was something against her skin too, something slick like cream. The wound must've been bad or she wouldn't be as patched as she was. Were there stitches? What muscles had been exposed or torn? Did things run deeper than that? Her bones? Was she going to lose her leg?

Her breathing became ragged and sharp. Panic was all she had.

"You won't lose it," the girl assured.

Natalia bit her lip, realising she'd spoken aloud. The girl kept smiling the way nurses did when they were trying to be comforting. Natalia didn't feel the pressure inside her chest release, but nor did she feel it grow.

"I'd know a thing or two about lost limbs," the girl continued. She waved her right arm, showing a missing hand, the arm ending at a stump where her wrist would be. "Yours will be fine."

Natalia gulped anyway. "How bad is it now?"

"My hand or your foot?" she teased lightly. Natalia gave her a weak look. "Bad enough. It might take days or up to a week to completely heal. Possibly longer? But it *will* heal. Though, for a while after, you could have a limp."

Natalia could see the open skin and blood in her mind. Quickly, she averted her gaze. "Where am I? What happened?" She looked back to the girl. "Who are you?"

"I'm Peri. Peri De Costanzi."

"And the rest of my questions?"

Peri's expression turned uneasy. "That depends."

"On?"

Natalia didn't fancy waiting any longer than she already had. She was hanging over a pit, looking into bottomless darkness. Too many things rattled inside her head. She *needed* to know what was happening. No matter how crazy it seemed, she'd seen too much to attempt convincing herself that it was all unreal and just her imagination any longer.

"It depends on how you feel," Peri answered. "Do you think you can walk down some stairs?"

"If I say yes, will things be explained?" Natalia knew she sounded rude, and she would apologise later, but there was no place for niceties now.

Peri nodded, tucking her hair behind her ear. "They will."

Natalia eyed her leg. "I might need some help."

"That's why I'm here."

Peri stepped to Natalia's side. Natalia swung her arm over Peri's shoulder and a tearing pain spread from her ribcage to hip. Natalia winced, but Peri didn't draw attention to it.

Slowly, Natalia twisted her hips and touched her toes to the floor. Her leg came alive with heat and searing pain as her weight pressed it to the ground.

Natalia whimpered, but Peri didn't stop. They hobbled across the room and then down the wooden steps. She bit her lip the entire time. Peri didn't free her once, nor did she seem to struggle under the strain of Natalia causing resistance. For an ex-ballet dancer, Natalia had become rather graceless.

The guilt finally bubbled over. "I'm sorry I snapped," Natalia mumbled.

"No need." Peri made them rest on the bottom step. The girls stood nearly two inches apart, Natalia being taller at five eight. "I understand you're frustrated."

An ache burrowed into Natalia's chest. She pushed it away and turned her head, spotting a long mirror.

Dirt smeared her face. Her jumper was frayed and her trousers had been torn or cut up to her thigh. Blood had crusted in patches around the main bandage on her leg and there was more dried blood on what was left of her trousers.

Upon closer inspection, she also noted blood on her right palm from where she'd grabbed for her wound. Her stomach rolled. She tried scratching her palms on her hips; the blood drew lines on her clothes but some remained on her skin.

"Once this is done, I promise you can have a bath," whispered Peri. Peri tucked some hair behind Natalia's ear. Her fingers lingered on the star earrings Natalia thankfully hadn't lost. "These are pretty."

"Birthday," Natalia mumbled, staring at the beautiful pieces in the mirror.

"You were attacked yesterday, on your birthday?" Shock laced Peri's voice.

Attacked, her mind echoed. "My birthday was the day before."

Peri sighed, relieved. "Whoever got them did well."

"My dad."

"Padre. He's a good soul and we shouldn't keep him waiting. He's been pacing non-stop since we brought you here. Think you can manage a few more steps?"

For her father, Natalia could manage a marathon. So she nodded and bit her lip to gather strength.

They walked round the stairs and headed down a wooden hallway. The next time Natalia raised herself was when Peri was forcing her onto a bar stool that didn't do much for her aching back.

Before she could complain, arms encompassed her. Despite the pain, she wrapped her arms around her father and sobbed into him. He kissed her head many times over. He was warm and smelt of vanilla.

They still had one another. The Whitebell's were still together.

Her father receded, but not far, holding Natalia's face, wiping her tears. "You scared me."

"I scared myself," she said. "I don't know what happened."

His forehead wrinkled in the centre. "We're going to fix that." He moved away, leaving Natalia cold despite being one barstool apart.

She sniffed and wiped her eyes. There were others in the room. She forced her attention to them. She wouldn't give them the satisfaction of thinking she was weak; she may have been crying and confused, but she wouldn't let them hold it over her. Her strength was in recognising her own weaknesses and once she spotted them, only she held the power then to make herself feel weak or strong.

Do I want to know? She thought suddenly, fear clawing up her spine.

A man, dressed in a suit, presented himself. He had familiar dark hair but nothing else of him registered. "What do you know of Creatures and Monsters, Natalia?"

She blanched and looked to her father. "I don't understand."

The man nodded. "Before we go further, I'm James."

A woman came to his side, her light brain hair glistening in the light. "I'm Sarah." She laughed when James rested his chin on her head. "James' wife." She shuffled away to point. "You've met Peri, she's my eldest son's girlfriend," she pointed to a wide-shouldered, light brown haired boy who stood beside Peri, holding her, "Archie."

"I'm Alex," claimed another girl. She forced her way round James and Sarah, smiling in a way that reminded Natalia of Noah. Alex had curly brown hair and a sloped, choppy fringe. "I'm the adopted one."

"You're a Darby," Sarah argued. Alex flashed Natalia a bigger smile and sank back, rolling onto the beanbag in the room. Sarah seemed unfazed. "My other son," she continued, "Jasper, is currently on a run or something hopefully as undangerous."

"Your last name, Natalia," James said, taking over again, "is rather interesting."

"It was my mother's," Natalia admitted. "When my parents married, they kept her name."

"Do you know where it's from? Or what it means?"

Natalia spied her father out the corner of her eyes shifting in his seat. "No."

"I'll ask my first question again. What do you know of Creatures and Monsters?"

"Other than the storybooks ones?"

"Yes, dear," Sarah answered kindly.

"They're from *stories*," Natalia stressed. Her shoulders sank. This was getting nowhere and reminded her of the conversation with Noah on her birthday. "I'm sorry," she said. "But what has this got to do with last night?"

"Unfortunately, dear, *everything.*"

Natalia halted.

She glanced about the room, trying to find the courage to ask what they meant. Whether she asked or not, somehow she knew the answers would come. So while there was a minute of peace, she selfishly stole it.

The room was expansive. The floor was comprised of large grey stone tiles. Natalia shifted against a white marble counter that was sturdily placed in the middle of a white marble kitchen. Cupboards lined the deep, red-tiled walls, silver appliances dotted around the counters. At the back of the room, pressed against the wall, was a long stone table with seats facing the wall and a bench against it. At Natalia's right, closer to her father, was an entire glass wall with rails at the top and bottom which she assumed helped it slide open. A fenced-in luscious green garden lay beyond followed by a clear drop-off near the edge of the Island, one that led to the sea.

For a house that Natalia had always assumed was decrepit and decaying on the outside, it didn't match up. This part, at least, was modern. Maybe the Darby's, as they'd called themselves, had updated it? Had Natalia just never noticed builder's vans?

Natalia turned back to those who were waiting patiently. The air weighed heavily in her chest, thick in her nostrils and lungs, like tar. Even the smells were bland. A tiny whistling sung into her ears.

Out the corner of her eyes, she saw her father wink. She took a shaky breath and her leg trembled; she bit her lip to stop from yelping.

"I know nothing," she admitted once the pain had subsided. "Unless they're from stories." James was studying her. She wanted to shy away from the stare but refused. "Why are Creatures and Monsters important? Why do I need to know about them?"

"Because they don't just exist in stories," James stated plainly. "Creatures and Monsters are made of life and breath, as much as Humans."

"No..."

"There are seven recognisable types of Creature."

"No!" She screeched louder. She *couldn't* be hearing this.

James continued as if she'd never spoken. "Werewolves. Vampires. Fairies. Mermaids or Mermen. Witches. Angels. And though Nymphs, to some, are considered cross-breeds," it sounded like it pained him to say such things, "they are a type too. Though technically they and their God came *after* Fairies and Witches."

"No," Natalia said, less powerful this time.

"There are then those who say there are Demons to match the Angels, but there is no proof to their existence so they aren't recognised."

Natalia tried to stand. "I'm not hearing this."

James locked his hands onto her shoulders, holding her. "You are."

From somewhere, Peri's voice called, "You have too, amore."

"I don't have to listen to nonsense!" Natalia cried out.

"It's not," her father whispered. The tremble in his voice stopped her. "It's not nonsense."

James backed off, allowing Natalia to face her father. A snake was slithering around her innards. When her father nodded, her chest became tighter. She wanted to run, to hide, to *escape*, but with her leg damaged she knew there was no chance.

"You saw the lights go off in our house," her father continued, almost woefully. "I thought it was a power cut too."

"It wasn't?" she challenged.

"You said nothing had tripped."

"So?"

"A magical impulse." Natalia blinked at her dad. "It means that a spell was cast and interfered with the lights for a moment."

She shifted her focus back to James, her eyes welling at this madness, and he continued as if her silence was a sign of surrender.

"A Creature's entire life's Purpose is to rid the world of Monsters. There are thousands of Monsters, from many lands and Hells. Some types have been met time and time again over years like pests. There are then those that theoretically have never been discovered or haven't been seen in millennia and therefore are unknown potentials. As a general species, they are hard to track and observe patterns for.

"But wherever these Monsters come from, whatever shape they take, it means the Veils between their space and ours is breaking. It's said that they began to tear at the beginning of time but Creatures are trying to repair them." James paused.

"The Purpose of *all* life is for the soul to live. Creatures must see to it that Monsters don't disrupt that. And all Monsters want is to destroy. Most have no higher needs or wants than to ruin, turning worlds into their new Hell and home. It's an endless war, and while sometimes it's unfair, it's our Purpose. To protect life and souls.

"As I said, Creatures are trying to repair the Veils, which might buy us forever, one hundred years, or mere months. *Nothing* so far has worked. Piece by piece they're tearing, a slow fracturing as Monsters slip through the cracks from their worlds to ours - it seems no Monster naturally occur here - wreaking havoc.

"We do not know why we are one side of a Veil, why we are here and are letting them come to us. It just seems to be the order of things. We have the power to save and protect.

One day, there *will* be an end. As least, we hope. The Veils will be sealed, we will lose the eternal fight, or we finally will rid the worlds of Monsters forever. But, until then, we fight."

When Natalia spoke, breaking the silence that had fallen like a curtain, her voice was small. "That's what happened," she whispered. "Last night." She wanted to faint, but some part of her seemed to register James' words like she'd already known it all. "A Monster slipped into our world. I was in the wrong place at the wrong time."

James nodded slowly. "You're fast."

Natalia didn't feel fast. She felt slow. Slow that she didn't realise this wasn't a joke. Slow that she got injured with no escape. They were telling her stories she'd left in childhood, stories that *couldn't* exist. And yet...

"However," James said, gaining Natalia's attention again. "Things go deeper."

She sucked in a breath. How was there more?

"More Monsters than ever are coming through. It might've taken thousands of lifetimes for the Veils to get *this* bad, but we think it's a loop, a catching point. Monsters are coming through because the Veils are breaking but the Veils are tearing more because the Monsters are forcing their way through.

"That's why my family moved here. We were reassigned to help protect this Island. There had never been a disturbance here before, but they sensed something coming – we have ways of guessing, but nothing specific. We know where disturbances might happen, but it's always an eventually, so we wait until the when. And that happened to be the Scorpio. They hadn't anticipated the Calefaction."

"Scorpio? Calefaction?" Natalia wondered if she *was* stuck in a dream.

"You saw the giant scorpion," Alex piped up, head popping round the side of her father's body. Natalia had almost forgotten the others were there.

"That was *real?*"

"So was the, I guess you'd say, giant polar bear. Remember?"

"The one that went to kill me," Natalia blurted. She peeked at Sarah and James, and Sarah flinched. Natalia forced out her next words, not believing what she was about to say. "I know there's more."

Sarah touched her husband, as if to gather strength from him. "In this family, we're Witches." Natalia waited to sink into the pit she was facing again. "Peri's a mermaid. Alex, a Werewolf."

Natalia bent to look round James. "You're the wolf." It wasn't a question. "The one that was running up and down the street."

Alex's eyes lit with pride. "The one and only. And *not* a pet dog." She growled.

She then looked to Peri and Archie. "You were the group I saw in the storm?"

Peri nodded, but it was Archie who spoke gently. "My brother spotted you. He casted the spell that hid us, Monster included, from you."

That's why it all just disappeared.

When she met her father's eyes once more, his gaze watched her in return. His expression meant she needed to prepare for even more and, worst of all, whatever else there was, it would be the hardest truth.

How much harder could things be?

She already didn't want to believe what she'd been brought to face yet how could she deny it? Her head and heart believed too much, some secret hidden part of her already accepting.

This can't *be happening*, she thought. To break out of this torment, she tried moving her leg, expecting pain. There was nothing. She didn't wake up because she wasn't asleep. This wasn't a nightmare. This was happening. But how much more could she take? What would be the limit? No one was forcing this into her, not when parts of her were willingly digesting pieces like they created the end to a puzzle she hadn't known she was doing.

James jumped ahead anyway. "Your cheeks must've shimmered," he said. Natalia felt her cheeks heat at the accusation. "Have you ever wondered why? You can't have not noticed them."

Natalia looked at Peri desperately. "Can I have that bath now?"

Peri stepped from Archie's arms. "One last thing first," she promised.

"What is it?" she asked. "What can there *possibly* be left?"

"You acknowledged that your last name was your mothers," James reminded her.

"Dad?" She swung to him.

"I'm Human," he answered before she'd even asked.

"Mum?" She spoke no louder than a hollow whisper.

"Before you collapsed," Peri took over, "I saw you. So did Jasper and your dad. There was this moment, this *beautiful* moment, where your dad was holding you and a bronze edged, transparent, shield appeared around you both. It was like your body went into protecting itself *and* your dad, even though you weren't mentally present." Her smile was small. "You didn't pass out because of your leg. You collapsed because of the shield. You *created* it and it took all of your energy."

Natalia could see the darkness of the pit yawning before her.

"Witches can't create shields," Archie said.

"Only one Creature can," added Alex.

"Dear, there's a reason your last name is Whitebell and how you made a shield," Sarah said.

"I didn't see a shield," Natalia told them. At the time, she'd only felt her leg and her dad's arms before they'd both been taken away.

"Amore, I can promise you, there was a shield," Peri said.

"I don't know what you're talking about," Natalia replied truthfully.

Everyone was as silent as the dead.

It would've been blissful if Natalia wasn't waiting for the next assault. What would go first over the edge? Or would her heart simply give out to spare her?

She wanted to plea, to beg as if her life depended on it. She'd heard and seen enough. Did she *really* need to know whatever else there was? And right now? Couldn't it wait? This last thing was going to be the biggest after all.

Gingerly, she turned to her father and his mouth was already open.

"You're a Fairy."

That was it. The final smack.

Though she never physically moved, her soul felt like it was thrown from her body. Nausea swept over her and her head dropped between her knees. The ground ebbed and swayed. Her leg throbbed and her body whined with exhaustion.

"Fairy?" she spluttered out.

Her father nodded, eyes cast down as if ashamed. "Your mother didn't want you to know."

"Why?"

"She wanted you to live a Human life."

"For how long? When was I going to be told? If this is true, why was this hidden from me?"

"I don't know."

"Isn't it important for me to know?" Her father didn't reply. "You," she pointed an accusatory finger at James, "said all Creatures have the same Purpose. That includes me too, right?"

"Some don't follow it," he immediately stated. "There are those who disregard it—"

"As if it doesn't matter?" Natalia's chest bubbled as her voice rose. "By the sounds of things, with there being no alternative to the Veil situation yet, you need every pair of hands! I've seen two Monsters in two fucking days! That might not be an outbreak, but what if the Veils suddenly collapse? I don't know a lot, but even I know that that's not good. So again," she looked at her father, eyes stinging, "when was I going to be told? This is my life, isn't it?"

This time, his green eyes wavered as they held her brown ones. "Your mum wanted you to have a normal, Human, childhood."

"Why?" The tears fell. Betrayal wormed into her chest. She knew her mother would've had her reasons, but still, it hurt. And pain couldn't just be washed away, even if it was no one's fault for it existing. "I was going to find out somehow! I was going to be in this life eventually! But like this? After being attacked?"

From the other side of the room, Peri told her, "You were in the wrong place at the wrong time, amore."

"Doesn't make me feel better!" she shouted before lowering her voice. "I was always going to be a Fairy because I've always been a Fairy. But I was kept from that. I was kept from a whole life. A whole Purpose! Here I was, worried about nursing, when life could hold *so much more* than that."

Her father jumped from his stool and went to her. "I'm sorry," he said, sounding honest.

"I know." She deflated, all her energy sapped. "I'm sorry too."

He kissed her forehead. "You have *every right* to be angry."

He withdrew and Peri was suddenly *there*, her one hand out. "How about that bath now?" she offered. "It might calm your heart. It'll certainly give you peace and time to think."

Natalia nodded, submitting. For how she'd imagined her week going, even just her birthday, this wasn't it. Still she was conflicted. Everyone had spoken with conviction. Even her father. But could it be believed?

She wrapped her arm over Peri's shoulder. James gave her a sympathetic look as Natalia was hauled up. "What does this mean?" she asked meagrely. "For me, now?"

"You're untrained," James told her flatly. "You threw up a shield by accident and then passed out."

"But I *could* be trained?"

James looked to her father, who in turned looked at her. "Is that what you want?" Her father asked.

"Isn't this my Purpose? Aren't I supposed to want it?"

Natalia thought of her nurse training. Was she supposed to put that behind her? It'd taken her a lot of work to get here, even if she hadn't been actively doing it long. Could she work on the side, or was being a Creature a full-time thing?

There was no space in her brain for anything to be processed. Not now, anyway.

Sarah walked over and touched a small hand to Natalia's tear-stained face. "It doesn't have to be," she said. "You can walk away while the Council are unaware of you."

Natalia zeroed in on her father. "Can I think about it?"

He nodded. "Of course! You have a lot to think over."

She unhooked herself from Peri to fall into her father's embrace. They hung onto each other for a moment. Then he guided her back to Peri who waited patiently near the doorway.

What do I want? Do I want this life? Am I definitely *not in a dream?*

The idea of peace and quiet had never sounded better.

When they at last made it to the bathroom, Peri aided Natalia in undressing. At first, it was embarrassing. But soon the nerves faded, especially when Natalia realised she needed the help. Peri seemed unfazed, even when she had to heave Natalia's sore leg out of the water once her body was submerged.

The water was warm and bubbly. Peri left, promising to be on the other side of the door if Natalia needed anything. Natalia was sure she needed nothing except loneliness. Lying face up to the ceiling, she sighed heavily.

Two days ago, she'd had no thoughts of stories filled with Creatures and Monsters. Yet here she was, dumped right in the middle of a reality she couldn't quite grasp. It was like she'd become a rock repetitively being thrown against a cliff, wearing her down.

A Fairy.

She tapped the surface of the water in sync with her heartbeat. Could she believe these people? They'd only just become acquainted. How could Creatures and Monsters exist? It seemed illogical. And yet she'd *seen* proof to say otherwise.

Even more bizarrely as the fact that she could somehow *tell* they were being truthful.

She pinched herself and bit her lip at the pain. *That* seemed real enough.

Natalia sank below the water completely.

Peri heard her name being called. She opened the door, expecting Natalia to need help being lifted out of the bath. When she got there, however, she struggled to hold in her laugh. Natalia wasn't in the bath. Instead, she was face down on the floor, a towel haphazardly thrown over her back.

"Why didn't you yell *before* you ended up in this mess?" Peri asked, amused.

"I thought I could manage." Natalia groaned as Peri shifted her into a sitting position.

"I told you. It'll take days for you to heal."

"Can't you use magic or something?"

At that, Peri did laugh. "*Amore*, in case your brain turned to water, I'm a Mermaid. If you want magic, you'll have to ask the family."

Natalia's cheeks pinked with a near missable bronze sheen overtop. "Sorry."

"Anyway, they *have* used magic on you," she expressed. "That's why it'll only take you days to heal. Without it, you probably wouldn't be this well off already." Peri put her arms out, tucking them under Natalia's armpits. "Now, let's get you sorted."

With minimal effort, Peri got Natalia up. Natalia winced with nearly every step and Peri could only sympathise. She'd never been struck by a Calefaction's claws, and hoped she never would be. Though Calefactions were low ranking Monsters, according to the incomplete records - files the Council kept of all known Monsters, which Creatures were taught about growing up - they could still issue pain and punishment from Hell.

Calefaction's claws were made of fire which could transfer into the target via broken skin. The cut on Natalia's leg had been sustained as a result of clawing and it was deep enough that fire had indeed been transferred. It was just a blessing Natalia hadn't been bitten. *That* didn't have a recovery time. There wasn't one. A Calefaction's mouth was hotter than any Human furnace; they could expel a fire their bodies created, and it burned unlike any known heat source.

Peri sat Natalia at the crooked writing desk; it was the closest point to the en suit and she didn't want the girl to struggle further. She handed Natalia some underwear and clean clothes. Tony, Natalia's father, had brought them over when he'd raced round in a panic.

"I'll do your hair once you're dressed," Peri announced.

"Oh, no, you don't—"

"I *will*," Peri insisted, not about to take a no. "It's the least I can do."

Peri turned her back to give privacy, even if she had seen the girl's body already, waiting to be called for assistance. There was silence until Natalia called for help with her bra claps and the zip of the dress. Her father had chosen a simple mint green dress and white leggings.

"It's February," Natalia mumbled, glancing down at herself. "What was he thinking? I haven't even seen these clothes in years."

"Practicality," Peri answered.

"I'm sure freezing is practical."

"With leggings, we can monitor your leg without having to tear or cut them off. Plus, your wound can be left to breathe easier while it heals."

"That won't save my arms from their inevitable falling off."

Peri went around the bed, lifting up a thick white cardigan she'd brought from Home City despite never having plans to wear it. She wondered how it'd come to be in this room when it wasn't her space. But in moving, everything had gotten jumbled. She handed it to Natalia, who slipped it on and buttoned it, and she picked up the nearby pink hairbrush.

"I know it sounds like I'm complaining a lot—"

"You are," Peri cut in.

Natalia dropped her head. "I don't mean to. I'm sorry."

"You have every right to complain."

In the small mirror on the desk, Natalia looked at Peri. "I do?"

"You don't know who we are. You have our names, nothing else. Not to mention the whole thing of what you just found out about yourself." Peri started brushing Natalia's long hair. "I imagine it's like the world crashing around you."

Peri couldn't begin to imagine what that felt like, to not know about the biggest part of who she was, the part that was entirely *her*. She'd always been a Mermaid. It'd never once been hidden from her.

"I still don't need to be rude about it," Natalia argued, tilting her head forwards. "You've all been nothing but kind. You and that boy helped me when I was first hurt—"

"Jasper."

Natalia nodded. "And then I was brought here to recover and heal," she continued. "You all just spent time out of your lives trying to explain to me how your world works, what I am, and how I might fit into it. And how do I repay you? By being a Class A bitch."

Peri stopped brushing. "Does that mean you accept it?"

There was nothing at first.

"No," Natalia finally answered.

Peri left it alone. Natalia had all she needed for now, all that she could cope with. What she needed was time and space to grow accustomed. The girl had to figure out what *she* wanted and what she didn't, what she believed or didn't. No one could force such thoughts or decisions onto anyone. There was no knowing how Natalia was doing, but to Peri, she seemed to be handling a lot better than she knew she would if the roles were reversed.

Whatever the eventual choice, Natalia had the right to make it for herself.

Peri finished Natalia's hair and dragged the chair against the carpet so Natalia could face her. The girl looked up anxiously, bronze now lining the edge of her brown irises.

She went to speak when the door burst open.

Jasper halted, clocking the girls, eyes searching over them. Peri tapped her fingers against her stump, waiting for his next move. If he was smart enough, he would've suspected them being in here.

His eyes finally rested on Natalia. "I love it when women invite themselves into my room, and here I have two!"

Peri rolled her eyes. "I'm your *brother's* girlfriend."

Jasper smirked. "Fine. But did we play musical bedrooms while I was out?"

"Your bedroom was the closest," Peri half-explained.

"I knew it! A guy takes *one* walk and suddenly his private space is invaded until it's no longer his. The tragedy."

"You're a drama Witch."

Jasper's attention went back to Natalia, his smirk softening to a smile. "How's the leg?"

Natalia glanced down then up again as if the sight of her injury made her sick. "Sore," she said. "Like there's fire contained inside it."

"In case you missed it, you *were* mauled by a Monster *made* of fire."

Peri wanted to hit him.

Natalia didn't blink. "I have two questions."

Jasper launched himself onto his bed facing them, stomach down, his head in his hands, his feet in the air with his ankles crossed. Peri thought about hitting him harder now. She had no idea what he was doing, like always.

"Things are finally getting juicy," he proclaimed. "I'm down for playing twenty-one questions."

"Only two," Natalia insisted.

Peri forced Jasper to move over and sat beside him. "Ask away," she said.

Natalia's eyes flitted between Peri and Jasper. "Did you stop that thing yesterday?" was her first question.

"Yes," Peri answered immediately.

"How?"

"That's question two," Jasper unhelpfully pointed out.

"They're parts A and B," Natalia retorted.

He grinned approvingly, and Peri curiously watched him as he spoke. "Calefactions are low ranking. You just keep hitting them, so to speak, until they're gone. Magic doesn't work on all Monsters, and neither do weapons. But Calefactions can be brought down by both."

Thank the Gods for a short and sweet answer. Maybe I won't hit you now?

"I saw it choking," Natalia said. Peri was sure her brain was fizzing but then again, Natalia had asked for answers.

Peri touched her stump. "That's how you get rid of them. It sounds worse than it is but you have to make them choke on their own fire. It's the easiest way to kill them. As Jasper said, there are other ways, like weapons, but this is less drawn-out."

Natalia looked surprisingly calm. Sunlight beamed in through the window, the bright day not quite reflecting this conversation.

"After they've turned to ash," Peri continued, "the remnants of their existence goes back to the layer of Hell, or world, they crawled out of. They're never seen from again."

"So they say," Jasper mumbled.

Unfortunately, Peri couldn't disagree. There was no proof anywhere that the Monsters didn't reform and come back. They had no way of knowing if they were fighting the same damned Monster over and over, or if it did turn to ash forever once dealt with and there were simply thousands of that type that kept cropping up. It was just an assumption that they remained ashen.

"You had another question?" she asked.

Jasper seemed to notice something Peri hadn't picked up on because he said, "You don't have to ask if you don't want too."

Natalia's eyes glistened. There was an unexplainable sadness hovering in her gaze and Peri wanted to take the girl's hand in support.

Natalia took a shaky breath. "No, it's ok."

"*Amore*," Peri pressed, "you really don't—"

"What exactly does it mean to be a Fairy?"

4

Improbable Belief

*N*OAH COUGHED WHEN HE APPROACHED. The woman, Katherine, turned to him – whether because she'd heard his lame attempt to draw attention to himself or just suspected someone was close. When he stepped beneath a lamp, Katherine smiled.

"Noah," she greeted.

They weren't well acquainted but she'd seen him enough with Natalia over the years.

He fiddled with the bottom of his jacket. "Sorry ma'am. I know you've just finished work and…"

"What is it?"

Noah looked up and Katherine's eyes were wide and questioning. *Just ask,* his chided himself. "Have you heard from Natalia?"

From the day they'd become friends, they'd been inseparable. Whether they were tagging each other in things online, playing games, or sitting in the same room watching movies, not much time usually passed between them talking.

But for the past week, Natalia's messages seemed flat; like something had been taken from her, some great energy sapped from her being. Not just that, but Natalia hadn't invited Noah round and had declined his invitations as well. It wasn't like her.

That was why he found himself here, in the middle of a dark Main Street, at ten o'clock at night. He'd meant to find Tony, but had seen Katherine first. He was just worried about his best friend. So much so he'd bitten down his nails.

Katherine shook her head, dangly earrings bobbing. "She's not been to work all week, calling in sick every day."

"Sick?" *She's ill?* But then, why wouldn't she just say so?

"She should be back in the morning." Katherine stepped from her café door. "Come on. You can walk me home. We'll talk on the way."

Noah obliged, not finding an excuse to deny her.

Archie kissed Peri's forehead, the smell of apple shampoo wafting up his nose as he did. She snored softly. Rolling the covers off, he stood on the dark wooden floor. Peri didn't stir. Barefoot, he crept from the room.

He nearly yelped once the door closed behind him.

Jasper was propped against the stair banister, one leg crossed over the other casually, eyes turned towards the shared bathroom. He was dressed in dark jeans and, more notably, a ripped t-shirt. His hair was wavier and there was salt in the air around him.

Archie edged towards his brother. "Where are you hurt?"

"Nowhere," Jasper murmured.

"I may not be a Fairy but I know when you're lying."

Archie's gaze lingered on Jasper's right shoulder which drooped slightly. He lunged for it. Jasper winced as they collided.

"Fucking seven Hells," Jasper hissed, holding his bicep as crimson seeped through the otherwise white t-shirt. "That *hurt*."

Archie surveyed him. "Why lie?"

"I wasn't hurt *that* bad before."

"You're bleeding."

Jasper pulled his hand away, red smears covering his palm. "I am now!"

"You were before."

"It'd stopped until you forced yourself on me like a wild bear."

"I didn't force myself on you."

"What did you do then? Trip? Come in for a hug?"

Archie's patience was wearing thin – he was the most patient out of the siblings too. Not even the birds were singing yet; he'd only come out for water. "I'll bloody hurt you twice as much as whatever hurt you in the first place if you don't open your trap and tell me what happened," he warned, though far too tired to actually follow through with the threat. "And why are you even out here? Your room has an en suit."

"There's no medicine cabinet in there."

The bathroom's door opened and their mother blinked at them. She turned and yanked the light cord; white light burst behind her, casting her as a silhouette. She said nothing and left. The truth would come by morning, it always did, so she needn't ask now for it.

Archie dragged Jasper into the bathroom, giving him no room to reply and forced him onto the toilet while he rifled through the medicine cabinet. Jasper sighed heavily and Archie peered at his brother's reflection in the mirror. Jasper's eyes were half closed, his lips dry, and his cheeks flushed faintly. He looked exhausted.

"I went for a walk," Jasper admitted. "I wanted to understand this place, to see its possibilities."

Possibilities meant something different to this family. They meant all the ways a Monster could come to be here, on this side of the Veil, in this spot. Whether that meant swimming, appearing by their own portal – it wasn't noted anywhere that any could do that, but just in case – by following a Witch, or simply sneezing to this side – Jasper had sworn he'd seen that once. But possibilities also meant ways Creatures could defend themselves, and the world, or escape if the situation became dire. Witches, for example, could create portals but only in certain places.

Archie handed over a damp cloth. "And?"

Jasper took it and slid it under his top to his shoulder. "The Island has enough of both." Confliction crossed his face. "But this Island is big, as big as a mainland city. It's a six hour round trip on foot."

Archie took the cloth when Jasper handed it back and gave him a square white gauze patch. Jasper raised his t-shirt gingerly. A gash, no bigger than a couple of inches, stretched along his right shoulder. Violent pink shading surrounded the wound, but at least the bleeding had stopped again.

Jasper applied the gauze. "This place will be no different than any other place on Earth." He winced as the centre touched the gash.

If Jasper did fight something that got through from another World or another Hell, this place could easily be an equal target for Monsters now. This place needs protection, just like any other.

He didn't want to admit to the Council being right aloud.

Archie narrowed his eyes at his brother. "And your injury?"

Jasper grinned at him. "I ran into a Jij and Gold helped me stop it." He rose from the toilet and the door creaked as he left.

What is Jasper doing?

Archie feared he'd never get an answer to that question. Jasper had always been here and there and everywhere at once. But, at the end of the day, he always came home. Who cared what he did in between to keep himself busy or entertained? As long as it was safe. But now he truly had his Purpose to think of.

Climbing back into bed once he'd finally had his drink, he kissed Peri's hand as she held it out to him, mumbling something about his absence. Only then did Archie remember something Jasper had said. The name. *Gold.* What was the most infamous Vampire doing here on Venderly? That was, if Jasper had been telling the truth about it. Archie wasn't convinced either way.

Darkness surrounded Natalia and she wore the cold like a blanket, her feet crossing concrete to grass.

Her new headphones blasted classical tunes into her ears to get her motivated as she walked. It was before dawn. She knew this would be her only chance of the day, and she hadn't been outside for days.

With her blood pumping, she heard Peri's voice. *Don't try and do anything more strenuous than walking.*

But Natalia had no time to wait. The world wasn't going to pause for her to catch up. She'd already given herself a week to heal and recover. She was only walking the neighbourhood, trying to build up her strength again. She was on her second lap of the houses now, about ten minutes in, but her leg was already aching.

She gritted her teeth and tried closing her mind, but it wouldn't comply.

Creatures and Monsters were *real.*

The thought should've sparked joy, and maybe years ago it would've. Now, the whole idea now only made things darker. She'd been harmed by the latter, close to being killed. Monsters wanted nothing more than to destroy, and a Creature's entire Purpose in life was to stop them. They had to let life prevail. It was complicated. The world was no longer simple.

But has it ever been?

Drenched in sweat - despite the fact she hadn't done anything strenuous - and with a mind refusing to be set free, Natalia decided she was done.

Tony had gone to work hours ago, leaving her to move through the empty house. She showered in burning water, securing her towel about her body before sitting on the toilet lit to inspect her right leg. Examining it, she frowned.

"Stupid bandage."

She untied the knot, then used nail scissors to cut through the rest. Why did she even need the bandage anymore? Peri had said she'd heal and that it would take days. Those days were up. It was about a week old now.

With the bandage gone, Natalia inspected the white gauze patch stuck inches below her knee. Due to the extent of bandaging, she hadn't been sure on the exact site of the injury. She pursed her lips, scratching at the corner where the gauze was already peeling until she could yank the entire thing off.

She wished she hadn't.

The smell of burnt flesh hit her instantly and she gagged. She had to hold her breath to look down, and found her skin scorched black. A yellow and green bruise formed on the outside of the wound, the centre furiously red.

Again, acid rose in her throat. And again she had to force herself to look on.

The two gashes she'd initially spied in the garden had torn to become one, the affected area now matching the size of her palm.

Natalia's hand shook as she gingerly touched the ashed skin along the side of the wound. Instantly, she yelped and pulled away, string down at her fingertips. They were red, raw. Were they... *burnt*? How?

She continued to stare and watched a red-orange substance flicker inside the wound, pulling the skin closer together.

There was still fire *in* her.

But if that was true, was her leg ever supposed to heal?

There came another lick of fire and the wound sealed a millimetre more. Was the fire that had damaged her now healing from the inside out? Or was it trying to shut itself inside to kill easier?

Regret sank in.

She bent awkwardly, trying not to wretch as she rummaged through the cupboard under the sink until she found a large white patch and a roll of bandage. That would have to do.

She bit her lip as she attempted to sterilise the wound with a wipe, but the wipe ended up burning and she started sweating. Sweating turned to swearing. Frustrated, she slapped the white patch over the wound and covered it with the bandage to hold it in place, then wrapped her entire leg and tied it off in a knot.

Because she now knew what was underneath, she knew not to remove it again. Someone else could have that burden next time. Preferably while she slept.

Natalia and her dad had returned home three days after the initial incident – four more days had passed between then and now. There'd been no talk of Creatures, Monsters, or any of the craziness revolving around them. Natalia had stayed in bed, more under her dad's instruction than her own, until this morning. She'd phoned in sick at work and had barely said more than a few words to Noah.

She wiped her forehead on the nearby towel and puffed out a breath, heart thumping inside her chest like a drum. She grabbed the sink for support, hauled herself up, and staggered back to her room. She changed into the first clothes she saw and tied her hair into a ponytail before putting her precious star earrings in and shoving on some shoes.

Her leg protested at the staircase. Maybe the walk *had* been a bad idea. Natalia descended anyway, wincing the entire time but refusing to give in. She left her house as quickly as she could, mostly so she couldn't turn back.

As crazy as the world seemed now, she carried on through its storm, hoping that it would calm and mould around her.

Peri snagged some fluffy pancakes, smothered thick peanut butter on top, and licked the knife as she walked to the table.

Archie sat beside her as she took her first, gooey bite. He touched her thigh with his hand, warmth spreading through her at the contact. She smiled to herself as she ate.

Creatures had the same average life-span as Humans – Vampires and Fairies excluded. However, most of the time, the nature of their Purpose cut their lives short. That meant a lot of Creatures sped through life. They tended to fall in love quicker, deeper too – not just because of their fleeting time, but something in their genetic make-up was wired differently. It made their connections stronger, and though that didn't mean they would only ever fall in love with one person, most seemed too. And so, a lot of Creatures married and started families earlier than Humans too, because they wanted to live while they could.

Peri had fallen long and hard for Archie, and he'd fallen in return. Every time he was near, her heart raced and her smile grew. He was her everlasting love and her home.

Peri and Archie had met back in Home City almost four years ago. She'd been fourteen, Archie seventeen. They'd been paired for a project in City School and by the end of the week, Peri had realised her feelings and had taken a chance. After asking if it was alright, she'd kissed Archie there and then in the empty classroom after their presentation. From there, their relationship had blossomed like it'd always meant to be.

But when Peri had told her parents, they'd been less than pleased. They didn't agree with their only child wanting to be with someone not of the sea. Peri had argued endlessly, saying that it was her choice, that her heart wanted this. In the end, her parents had finalised the conversation without much resolve.

So when Archie had announced he was moving to Venderly and asked her to join them, she had gladly accepted. Sarah and James were elated when she'd accepted. Her own parents threatened to disown her if she moved out. They had mostly stuck to that promise, barely talking to her now – only ever sending a card and a small letter on her birthday, never anything more.

Archie squeezed her thigh to gain her attention. "What are you thinking about, darling?" he whispered.

She smiled. "How glad I am to have you."

He pressed his lips to hers. While she knew she tasted of peanut butter, he surprisingly tasted of strawberry jam. They came together like two pieces of a puzzle that wouldn't normally be interlocked, becoming more beautiful combined than the original picture.

"Do you mind?" They broke apart, Peri meeting Jasper's scowl opposite them. "We're at the dinner table. You have a bedroom for that sort of stuff."

"You wait," warned Peri. "You wait until you meet someone."

"I meet plenty of people."

"No. Wait until it's someone you *completely* connect with, someone that will hold your heart inside their chest."

"Maybe," Jasper agreed, acting like he was considering her words. He flicked his head, displacing his waves. "So, do you two have plans today?"

"Way to change the conversation," Archie commented.

"I agreed, didn't I?" Jasper's eyes flicked to Peri. "I'm not going to wait around for something to bite me on the arse. If it happens, it happens."

Peri accepted his answer and gracefully changed the subject back again. "I was thinking of going for a swim," she answered.

For days she'd been thinking about touching her fin to the sea, dreaming of the waves cascading over her skin and scales, of salt coating her tongue and lips, of the seaweed tangling between her fingers and of the fish that would swim beside her. As much as she loved the land, she couldn't deny the call of water.

"And after?" Archie pressed, continuing to eat.

"Training, maybe?" she said, pushing away her empty plate.

"Is everyone invited?" Jasper asked through a mouthful.

"Sure."

"That reminds me." Jasper stood suddenly, his chair screeching against the floor. "I need to head into town."

Archie's eyes narrowed on his brother. "Why?"

Jasper tapped a shoulder. "In case you forgot, I ripped a perfectly good t-shirt, and now it needs replacing."

Peri looked between the brothers. "What did I miss?"

Jasper ignored her. "While Peri's swimming, you might want to keep an ear in this house."

"Why?" Archie asked, resigned. "What have you done?"

"Nothing."

"If it's *nothing*, why do I need to keep an ear out?"

"Gold said he'd be popping over."

Jasper dashed from the room, the front door slamming in his wake.

Peri's heart pounded. She twisted her whole body towards Archie, a perplexed expression written across his face. What had she missed?

Katherine's Koffee and Kakes was relatively busy for a Wednesday. Only when Natalia took a break halfway through her shift did she realise it. Her feet ached and her left leg shot constant shocks along her nerves every time she moved. Groaning, she eased onto the bar-stool in the kitchen. A breeze entered the room through the propped open back door, a welcome comfort against the burning sensation along her healing wound.

Being on her feet for two hours made her appreciate what Peri had meant by "taking things slow". She'd committed now, though was grateful she was halfway towards the end. After, she could climb onto the sofa and not move all night. Her dad had already said he'd cook.

"Are those poppy seed muffins cooled yet?" Katherine asked, stepping down the mini-step into the kitchen. She reached out, touching the hot tray and pulled back quickly. "Maybe not." She rounded on Natalia, eyes narrowed.

So far, Katherine hadn't brought up her absence so neither had she.

"What?" Natalia bit into the marshmallow bar her boss had forced into her hand. Katherine's eyes fell unsubtly to where Natalia had rolled her trouser leg up, the white bandage peeking out from beneath the fabric. Natalia tugged at her jeans. "I—"

"Tried dancing again?" Katherine prompted.

Natalia's stomach twisted. "Yeah."

The light shimmered against Katherine's pink lips. "Must've lost some of your elegant touch."

"I didn't warm up properly."

"You'll get back into it." The bell out front dinged and Katherine sighed. "I better get out there." She looked wanted to say more, but didn't, instead dashing away and taking the still-hot muffins with her.

Natalia ate her bar, remembering her last ballet recital since Katherine had brought the whole thing up.

At the time, there had been a flurry of blue tutus, Natalia's being the fullest. She'd been the lead. Both her dad and Katherine had come to watch, both being the first to applaud in the crowd, and they were so proud that they'd taken Natalia for ice-cream after, a nine at night.

Her heart ached with loss. There was no stage, no music, no tutus, and certainly no ballet anymore. After that recital, her dad couldn't afford the class fees, so she had to give it up. Her eyes stung and she blinked to chase away the tears. Those days were long gone now. She would hang onto the memories with fondness but those moments would never be in her future.

Finishing up her snack, she peered into the store. People were milling about, sharing gossip or simply a drink. No one glanced her way. Before she could change her mind, Natalia kicked off her shoes, double checking the main store.

She raised her arms parallel to her body, tilting her nose and chin upwards, and breathed.

Rising onto her tiptoes, she brought her sore leg up, her sole skimming the length of her other thigh, as if in a tree yoga pose. She felt lighter instantly. Then, she swung her left leg back, toes pointed upwards. She tipped her body forward until she faced the floor, her toes reaching for the ceiling in a familiar, comfortable stretch.

Lowering her leg again, she stood with both feet on the ground, shoulder width apart. In dancing, her left leg had always led – she was left handed after all. So when she rose onto her left, forgetting the injury, it gave way.

She collapsed with a *thump*, hands slamming against the tiles.

So much for dancing again.

Natalia scrambled up in time to notice the backdoor being nudged. Pulse quickening, she snatched the first time within reach and crept towards the door against her better judgement.

Behind the frosted glass, a figure appeared. While she had the upper hand, Natalia swung round the door and latched onto the intruder's t-shirt, dragging them into the store area tucked into a secluded corner of the kitchen.

The person grunted as their back cracked against the shelves, knocking a few unbreakable things off. A grown followed. "The *fuck?*"

Natalia blinked in recognition.

She immediately let go, staring at the boy with dark wavy hair and green eyes. The boy who had *saved her life*. Peri had called him Jasper.

Natalia gave him a once over. His black t-shirt and coat were dusted with flour but otherwise, he seemed fine.

"What the hell are you doing sneaking in here?" Natalia snapped quietly.

"Not trying to get attacked," Jasper replied, shaking off the flour. She noticed the freckles dotted underneath his eyes when he looked at her directly. "Though, I doubt a wooden spoon would hurt *that* bad."

Natalia glanced at her "weapon" and her cheeks heated. In her rush, she'd armed herself with a wooden spoon. She threw it onto the nearby counter.

"I guess we can say we were *both* pleasantly surprised by this experience," he said.

"Pleasantly surprised? I nearly attacked you."

"Nearly, and with a wooden spoon no less."

"You haven't seen how well I can hit someone over the head with it."

"I have a thick skull." He smiled.

Natalia sighed, resigned. "What are you doing here? And why didn't you just come through the front door?"

"Why aren't you wearing shoes?" Natalia glanced down and curled her toes as if to hide them. She looked back up and Jasper's smile grew. "Seems we both have questions."

"You can answer mine first."

"That's fair since you asked first," he agreed. "I was in town, buying clothes, and decided to come and find you after. Nice t-shirt by the way. Very appropriate."

For the second time, she looked down at herself. "*I'm a Fairy, bitch*" was on full display across her chest. She folded her arms, attempting to obscure the words.

"My t-shirt choice doesn't matter," she grumbled. "What matters is why you decided to find me. How did you even know I was here?"

"Natalia? Everything alright?" Katherine's voice cut Jasper off before he got a change to reply.

Natalia poked her head round the corner to see Katherine at the far end of the kitchen. "I'm fine," she said. "Just trying to organise back here since I have time."

Katherine laughed. "You *know* it's a mess. It always has been and always will be."

"I thought I'd try."

"You're on a break. Sit and eat. You've earned it *and* need it."

"I will. One minute?"

Katherine shook her head, mumbling something, and walked away. Natalia turned back to Jasper as he tried unsuccessfully to flick the flour from his hair. Giving up, he met Natalia's gaze. Tension hung in the air around them but it faded quickly.

At last, Jasper said, "Your dad told us where you worked a couple of days ago."

"My *dad?*"

"Something about us knowing in case of emergency and he couldn't get to you in time. I think it made him feel better knowing you'd always be safe, that if he couldn't get there, someone would."

Her head pounded and her shoulders sagged. Her dad had *never* failed her and she would swear on anything that he never would. She welled up uncontrollably and sniffed to try and keep herself together.

"And I *did* want to find you for a reason," Jasper continued. Either he saw the change in Natalia's expression and was politely ignoring it, or he saw nothing. Natalia didn't know why, but she guessed it was the former.

"That would be?" she asked, giving him a measured stare.

"To see if you wanted to train with me and the others."

Natalia's tears faded into nothing as if they'd never come. "What?"

"It's not a difficult concept to understand."

"Let's pretend I've been hit on the head recently and it *is* difficult."

He gave her a sweeping look. "I doubt anyone else has asked you yet, but I'm sure they will. It's clear how little you know of our world. I wondered if you wanted to learn and train with us. Up at the house."

She wanted to hold her own heart, to will it to calm. "What would that include?"

"I'm glad you asked." He grinned, stepping from the shelves he hadn't really been trapped against. "You would learn who you are as an individual and as a Creature, see you can do, all about your Purpose and how to fulfil it."

She raised a critical eyebrow. "You mean like learning to fight Monsters?"

"That is our Purpose."

"What about your training?"

"Fairy, we've done nothing *but* train for this since we could first walk. For us, this is the real world, the bit where we fulfil our Purpose by actually fighting the Monsters with our gifts."

"But..." Natalia trailed off, unable to keep up with her own crashing thoughts.

"You'd be learning from the best of the best."

She narrowed her eyes at him. "Who?"

"Me." He smirked. "I'll put on a good show to prove it."

"I expect nothing less than the best! It's the only way I could get a clear and concise study done. I'd also need comparisons. Especially if you want me to be combat ready to actually fight and fulfil this duty too."

Jasper gave her an approving nod. "You don't seem *so* bad."

Natalia threw her arms in the air. "I'm glad you have that settled," she said, stepping away. Joking with Jasper seemed easy. It was like he'd known she needed a moment and this had been his way of giving her that without allowing her to sink to the ground. She rubbed her temples. "As to your offer," she continued, "I don't know."

"What part are you struggling with?" His voice was smooth, as if her answer genuinely intrigued him.

She removed her hands from her head and saw the bronze that coated her fingers. "Like this." She shoved her hands towards him. "What is this? How can I be doing *that*?"

He touched her wrists, fingers wrapping carefully around them to hold still. "That's Fairy dust."

"See," she pulled from his grip, "you're saying all this stuff, but I don't think you realise how it sounds to me."

Jasper cocked his head to the side. "How does it sound?"

"Nonsensical! Fairies... I *can't* be one."

He nodded slowly. "I know it's a lot to understand all at once, especially since you had, what? Eighteen years," Natalia nodded so he continued, "without *any* of this being in your life. But, the thing is, you're not Human. As much as it might seem unreal or wrong or nonsensical, it's quite the opposite. You can spend your time wasting away in disbelief, but I can swear on anything you want that this *is* real."

She stared. He was being patient, more patient than she thought he would've been - a clear misjudgement on her part. His hands were in front of him, leaving his body was unguarded, though his eyes watched her cautiously.

There was no gain for Jasper on this. There would be no reason for him to lie or make this up. The only gain to be had was hers.

Natalia's heart and body jolted. *They* were the walls Jasper was trying to break through, the walls that would allow her mind to open and accept herself. Accept a life that was more complicated than just being Human, a life where stories of Creatures and Monsters were real - A life that *should* be exciting, but would also be dark, for their Purpose in being born to kill the evils of the world made it so.

"I have no evidence against it," she said. "But—"

"But nothing," he argued, stopping her mid-track. "You're just trying to contradict everything because a Human life is all you've known and it's been cosy. I know that if you start to believe your world will shift, you'll feel like you're giving up control, but that will be momentary. All I can say is that it'll be for the better, in the end."

"Can you be certain?"

"No." He grinned. "But it'll be the truth. *Your* truth."

Jasper waited for her reply but there wasn't one. Natalia had nothing to fight against. If she was being honest with herself, there hadn't been anything for a while. She'd seen the dust on her face. And there was no denying the wolf, the giant scorpion, or the fire-breathing polar bear any longer.

She'd lost track of how many times she'd tried to ruin the images now burnt into her brain. There was no more time for denial. As Jasper had called it, it was the truth, and in her gut she'd always known it.

"Those things really happened, didn't they?" Her eyes locked onto Jasper's face as she said it, searching for a lie she knew she'd be able to sense somehow.

"All of it," he confirmed, nodding.

"I'm really a Fairy?"

"Yes."

She breathed heavily. "There's no going back, is there?"

"To your Human life? No. That was a false existence anyway."

She glared at him. "That's *not* helping."

Jasper held up his hands in surrender. "I'm not here to upset you."

"I know." She dropped her gaze.

"You're not blindly believing in anything. Somewhere in you, you can sense I'm telling the truth."

"How?" Her eyes once again flicked to him questioningly.

"Fairies have this thing where they can tell if someone is lying."

"My stomach squeezes," she blurted.

Jasper's green eyes illuminated. "See! What more proof do you need when you already feel it? Do you need a skeleton to jump out of the ground and tell you all in interpretive dance? What about a plane writing in the sky? Another Calefaction? I'm sure I could arrange for most of those things if it meant you gave in."

She couldn't help herself, she laughed. "I don't want *any* of those things."

"Are you sure? They sound awfully fun. Except maybe the Calefaction."

She smiled slightly, and he returned it. "I might not understand, but I think I do believe. I think I have for a while. Since that storm.

When I first saw you?"

"Alex saw you that day," Jasper admitted. Natalia remembered the brown wolf - Alex. "She was convinced there was something about you. She wanted to come get you. I suppose we did, just a day late."

I'm a Fairy! Her mind screamed. *A Fairy! Of all the things!*

She knew, if she asked, Jasper and his family would help her to understand everything.

Her heart thumped at the thought of their acceptance. A calm melody ran through her blood, singing along her veins, and dancing all around her body in a tune only she could interpret.

Jasper hugged her, albeit a little awkwardly, but he let go quickly. "Welcome to the real world, Fairy."

"It's *Natalia*," she smiled. "Witch."

He stared at her and she wondered if she'd done something wrong. Soon enough his smile returned. "I know this isn't going to be easy. You have a life to leave behind. But you won't be caught in a lie any longer."

Natalia pulled a face. "I have a lot to learn, don't I?"

"Better late than never."

"Even eighteen years late?"

"Even eighteen years late," he confirmed. "So, how about you come over after work?"

"My dad—"

"I'll speak to him." The way Jasper's face morphed, Natalia could've sworn he was excited. "Peri and Mum will want to look over your wounds anyway. Though, you should be able to do that on your own."

Natalia's face contorted as she remembered the rancid smell and state of her leg. She swallowed back the rising bile. "I should?"

"Fairies are excellent healers. Or so I hear."

Is that why she'd done so well at school, why her exams had felt like they'd gone by breezily? Was she really a natural in more than one way?

Jasper walked past her to the door and she stepped under his arm to block the exit. "What other things can Fairies do?"

He grabbed the handle beside her hip. "Those powers, or gifts, will be explained."

"Not now?"

"You're at work," he reminded her. "This isn't the time or place."

"And later will be?"

He nodded and Natalia relented when her stomach didn't squeeze, moving aside. Once Jasper was outside, he turned to her. "You smell, by the way," he said charmingly.

"Walking a fine line there, Witch boy."

Jasper laughed. "I think it's your dust. You smell like burning wood."

"Is that good or bad?" She tried to smell her clothes and found nothing.

"I'll talk to your Dad and meet you at the House later," he replied before walking into the streets without looking back.

Natalia closed the door after him. Her chest and shoulders felt lighter, higher even. But she still needed to understand – what she was, what gifts she had and what she could do with them, what this Purpose meant *exactly*. A whole other life full of beautiful and devastating Creatures and Monsters awaited her, *if* she wanted it.

What have I gotten myself into?

5
Bronze, Gold, and Green

THE JIJ CRUMBLED INTO A HEAP WITH A SQUEAK. The little bugger had jumped Jasper who was unprepared for an unsolicited attack. Its arms had wrapped tightly around his neck, choking him, so he'd fought back.

Though Jijs were similar in size and colour to lawn flamingos, they had three legs instead of two and the physique of a garden gnome. Despite being agile, they weren't usually the climbing type – according to the open records, they hated heights. Mostly they groaned and moaned from the ground, spitting wherever they went. Biting was this particular Monsters' tactic; a way to transfer venom to their victim. It wasn't toxic enough to kill Creatures, or even Humans, but it did give a killer headache and flu-like symptoms.

How this one had gotten the better of Jasper was unclear, but it annoyed him nonetheless.

Blood the colour of wet mud slid from the Monster's chest, pink smoke dissipating from the wound. Jasper's magic had popped its heart on impact.

No one wanted a prolonged death, so Jasper gave mercy. Flexing his fingers, he slammed another small bolt of pink magic into the Jij. The Monster squeaked, then took one last breath and disintegrated into a pile of black ash.

The smell of blood clogged Jasper's nostrils. It didn't matter how long he'd been doing this – though he had little "real world" experience, more classroom theatrics and teachings – he still didn't like the smell of a Jij.

The walk home was short. Jasper had been minutes away from the door when he'd been caught unawares. He climbed the short stone steps and knocked on the front door, eyes drawn to the patterned glass.

His mother's face appeared when the door cracked open. "And *where* have you been?"

"I went shopping." Proving it, Jasper raised the bag he carried. "Then I stopped at a bar, did some body-shots, and drunkenly signed up for a sky-diving class."

She sighed, her resolve melting, and stepped aside.

He closed the door with his foot once in the warm. For February, Venderly seemed unnaturally cold. Was it like this everywhere on this plane, and world, of existence? Jasper was used to the year round warmth of Home City – though it was part of this plane, it wasn't part of this world, it was sealed off from the inside, separating it.

Jasper's mother grabbed him to kiss his cheek. "Never change," she said. "Not for anyone."

Smiling down at his mum, he still felt like a little kid. Would that feeling ever stop? "I wasn't planning on it," he assured. "Not a *full* personality change."

"Might do you some good."

Jasper whirled round to see Peri gliding down the stairs. "I see you didn't drown this morning," he quipped.

"Shame, isn't it?" she quipped, winking.

Peri disappeared into the living room, Jasper's mother on her heels, and Jasper made for the creaky oak staircase. He shut himself in his bedroom, throwing his bag onto his bed.

From the beginning, Jasper saw how juxtaposing this house was; the newly refurbished kitchen and dining area below contrasting the bedrooms that seemed to have been decorated two centuries ago. His especially.

Dark green wallpaper met dark wooden panels halfway down the walls. A four poster bed, complete with tied back rich red curtains, though missing a "roof" segment, was pushed against the wall so Jasper could see into the hallway. An old writing desk sat against the adjacent wall, opposite the en suit – the only other one in the house besides his parent's. In the far corner was an out-of-order stonework fireplace and between it and the en suite, a dark wooden wardrobe.

After changing out of his sweaty clothes and into something better, he ran downstairs. By the time he touched the bottom step, noises echoed from the living room.

Curious, he followed.

The door swung open, unhindered. Gold stood in the centre of the room proudly flashing off his new gold-lined blue jacket. When he spun, the setting sun caught the precious metal in blazing glory.

Meeting Jasper's eyes, Gold broke into a grin. "My boy!"

Jasper didn't even blink as he was yanked into the room. He was put beside his mum, whose eyes flickered between them. Jasper cursed his breathing for probably being what caught him out, but what was *her* problem? He'd warned them of Gold's arrival.

"I didn't get a proper look at you last time," Gold said, unsubtly eyeing Jasper up and down.

"I'm sure I felt your eyes on me," Jasper replied, grinning. "*Especially* my arse."

Gold returned the smile, showing off the golden gem stuck to his right front tooth. If cats were perceived as mischievous then Gold was devilish. "What can I say?" he joked. "Though you are a *little* young and pert for my tastes."

Jasper's mum cleared her throat. "You didn't tell me Gold was stopping by." Her eyes narrowed on him, the message clear; she wanted to have a word with him about inviting guests into *her* house without her knowledge.

"I told Archie," he admitted.

His mother blinked, stunned.

Peri cut in, "We didn't believe you."

Jasper remembered Peri being there when he'd told Archie at breakfast. But he had no doubts she knew about the first time he'd mentioned Gold to his brother as well. Jasper sighed. There were no secrets between those who shared hearts.

Gold took Peri's hand. "What matters, dear one, is that I am here now."

Jasper's mum looked at Gold sternly. "Why are you here? If you don't mind. Not that we don't love having you—"

"I do not take offense to your words, my dear," Gold said, offering his other hand to her. "I am here," as they touched, the doorbell rang, "because of that."

Natalia nearly started pacing along the porch. Had coming here been right? Was she making the right choice? Did she really want this?

Before leaving her house she'd binged on her entire box of Malteasers and had gone for a run, hoping it'd clear her mind. If anything, she'd made it worse. She almost considered turning around but the door opened.

Too late to go back now.

Sarah, Jasper's mother, stood there with a smile as bright as last time. "Natalia," she cooed, though there was an air of shock in her tone.

"Did Jasper tell you I was coming over?" Natalia asked. Sarah's face didn't change. "If he didn't, I can go. I'm sorry." She started to leave. This *had* been a bad idea after all.

"Wait!" Sarah called, Natalia paused before reaching the steps, turning back to Sarah leaning out the door. "He didn't tell us, but that doesn't mean we're going to send you away."

"Are you sure? Please, tell me if I'm over-stepping or intruding."

"Dear," Sarah smiled. "You're too good."

Natalia didn't know what that meant exactly, but didn't ask.

Sarah pulled her into the house where it was marginally warmer.

"Fairy," Jasper greeted. Natalia spotted him as he entered the hall, windblown hair strewn across his forehead. He turned to his mother. "Are you going to say I neglected to inform you of the Fairy's arrival too?" Natalia ignored the way he called her out.

"This time, you did," Sarah answered sternly.

Natalia relieved herself of her coat. Sarah offered to take the item but Natalia hung her garment herself. She might've been a guest, but she didn't want or need someone to wait after her.

Her heart pounded with energy, her body cold *and* warm all at once. "I... wanted to know more," she admitted. "Jasper offered to help. He said he'd tell and teach me what I need to learn and know."

Peri poked her head around the corner, raising her hand and thrusting it toward Natalia in an obvious high-five. "That's it," Peri encouraged. "Another female in the clan."

"This isn't a clan," Jasper said.

"This definitely *is* a clan."

"Not yet it's not."

Peri rolled her eyes at Natalia. "What did he promise you to come here? His charm couldn't have enticed you." Natalia only smiled.

"Excuse me." Jasper sounded hurt, but it was clear he wasn't. The grin gave him away. "My charm is fine and has gotten me far in life, thank you."

"Let's go into the living room instead of standing in the hallway, shall we?" Sarah suggested, taking control. She fixed her eyes on Natalia and she shivered. "There is another guest with us today."

"Way to *not* make it sound suspicious," Jasper whined.

"Who?" Natalia asked as her shoulder blades started itching.

Sarah walked away without answering. Peri took Natalia's hand with her own and they followed.

The evening sun dropped toward the horizon outside. Pinks and oranges livened up the cream walls and the black corner sofa appeared shiny. In the centre of the dark wooden floors was a giant, fluffy, cream rug.

Someone was stood *on* the carpet, facing her.

Natalia stared. He was tall and slender with slicked back blond hair. Around his left eye rested a monocle. The monocle itself enhanced the eye's bright golden colour, contrasting the other's royal blue. He wore a blue jacket with a white handkerchief in the breast pocket. The golden insides of the jacket made it seem like it was rippling.

He smiled and the air vanished from Natalia's lungs.

Fangs extended from the corners of his mouth, long ones that could graze his jaw if he closed his lips. His tongue flicked out to lick the fangs.

"Vampire," she half-whispered. Her shoulder's itched more.

"I'm *the* Vampire, dear Fairy," he said. His whole demeanour was composed.

"I don't want to seem rude, but do you mind if—"

"You take a minute?" He shook his head calmly. "Go, little one."

Natalia power walked from the room; a spritz of air burst inside her lungs as if she'd escaped from an air-less bubble. She aimed for the stairs and crawled up them on all fours. At halfway the banister changed into solid wall, and Natalia folded in on herself, hugging her knees.

Of all the crazy things she'd experienced so far, somehow *this* topped them all.

Every other moment was blurry because of a distraction at the time but this one was happening in quiet. No Monster was breathing fire or cracking lightning and there were no fast-paced explanations she had to accept like her life depended on them. This was a slow moment, one she had time to face.

There was a damned *Vampire* in this house.

Natalia touched over her chest, as if her heart might flee at any moment, her palms and forehead slick with sweat.

"You alive up there?"

Natalia broke out of her staring contest with the steps as Jasper crawled up towards her, sitting a few steps lower to give her some space. He pressed his back to the wall, one leg to his chest with the other dangling.

"Gold won't think you're being rude," he promised. She grimaced but he didn't notice. "In fact, he's impressed you asked to be excused."

Natalia hadn't worried about then, until now. She stared as she continued to shake. "He said that, did he?"

Jasper looked up at her then. "Which part?"

"Any of it."

"He knows you're new to this and knows you need an adjustment period. He was just having fun with you."

"*Fun?*" Natalia screeched. It rang through her ears like a bird's cry.

"But he didn't know how little you *actually* knew."

"Before the other day, I knew nothing!"

"Exactly. Which is why he won't take offense to you running off."

"I didn't run. I walked."

"Power-walked. We all saw."

Natalia groaned, "Really?"

Jasper laughed heartily. "If I didn't know you were a Fairy, I would've assumed you were a Vampire because of how fast you moved."

Natalia dropped her head into her hands.

"He didn't mean any harm by what he did and he accepts you're new," he continued. "But Gold's the best you could hope for when it comes to meeting a Vampire for the first time. Someday, you'll have to be introduced to *everything*. And they won't all be that nice, or playful."

She raised her head slightly to stare down at him; an odd action since she had to look up at him before. "Is that a professional or personal opinion?" she asked, noting how his smile vanished and his green eyes shone despite the lack of light. "I could easily lock myself away and never meet anything again."

"You could," he agreed. "Will you?"

Could I really give this up? She thought. *Could I run from it all?*

After all she'd already been through, Natalia sensed there was no turning back now. As much as coming face to face, teeth to fangs, with a Vampire had made her heart stop and her mind see blood, she supposed it *could've* been worse. Maybe some Vampires weren't as nice as Gold but Monsters were worse still, and Natalia had already met her fair share of those.

She realised then that Jasper was staring. He seemed to be waiting for an answer while already knowing what she'd say. There was a twinkle in his eye, a curiosity, but she couldn't pinpoint what he was curious about exactly.

Without warning, she stood. Jasper watched her and she matched his gaze in return. He must've seen something because he smiled and stood too.

Despite being shaky and sweaty, she accepted the hand Jasper offered. They descended together, Natalia retrieving her hand once they were off the steps.

Crossing the threshold into the living room had everyone turn their watchful eyes distinctly to her.

The Vampire stood, glided over, and touched Natalia's hand without a word. She was too scared to do anything and waited with baited breath as warm lips pressed to her skin.

"To second beginnings," he declared to the room like a toast.

Natalia avoided looking directly at him, thinking she'd rather not face his fangs again. "I'm sorry," she said, guilt winding through her body. "For running out. I was—"

"Overwhelmed?" Gold, as he'd called himself, provided.

He threw a defanged smile in her direction. His golden eye glinted and she was mesmerised by it. She blinked and suddenly it seemed less appealing, like it'd lost its magic to her.

"It's not because of you," she said. "Until the other day, I didn't even know what *I* was, let alone what else is out there."

"My girl, you need not explain yourself. This world is new, freshly birthed to you unlike your favourable, I imagine, Human one. That in itself is awfully fascinating. Something we *must* discuss if you will allow me to offer you tea some time?"

Natalia managed a smile. The way Gold spoke, it was like he belonged in a different century. Maybe he did, something *she* would have to ask *him* sometime. *Maybe indeed over tea*, she thought. *Just never say "freshly birthed" again.*

Realising she hadn't verbally replied, she said, "I think I can do that."

"Excellent!" Gold cried. He lowered his voice again. "But if you don't mind, for the time being, I need to speak with you. Preferably alone."

"Alone?"

"I will not bite." He smiled and Natalia double checked for fangs, but they hadn't reappeared. "The idea that brought me here was about talking to you, and not about tea. If you wish to have those you trust remain, then I see no reason why they cannot. There is nothing that I have to say that they cannot hear. I would just have thought that being alone with me would make you feel more comfortable in my presence over time. Settle the differences, shall we say, together, between two parties."

Natalia looked to the others. While they were here, guiltily, she *did* feel safer. But was that just because she didn't understand what she'd been forced to confront? Would she feel better about Gold by giving him the chance?

She caught Jasper's eyes and he offered her a single, subtle, nod. She trusted Jasper, and so if Jasper trusted Gold she could try too.

Settle the differences.

"Ok," she agreed, facing Gold again.

"Cross my undead heart," Gold promised as he drew a cross over his chest. "I will not harm you. The minute you wish to stop, or you wish to have company, I will respect it. Everything is in your hands."

There was no issue with her stomach – no pinch anywhere. She gave him a nod, not trusting her words, and he gave one in return.

Peri launched to her feet, ushering everyone out, saying that they should get dinner started. She threw Natalia a lasting look. Natalia knew exactly what it meant; the very minute she felt unsafe, Peri would be there.

Once the room was cleared, Gold directed himself and Natalia to the sofa. Natalia sunk into it, shuffling to face the Vampire who now held her undivided attention. She tried crossing her legs for comfort but with Gold's intense eyes staring her down like he never needed to blink, and with the memory of his fangs fresh in her mind, she figured she wasn't about to feel any less on edge.

Gold clasped his hands together. "The beginning is always the best place to start. Unless it's a horror story. Then working backwards is more effective."

"Is that why you're here? To tell a horror story?" Natalia fiddled with her trouser leg. She tugged on a loose thread, fixating on it until it pulled free.

Gold touched her face, guiding it up, his fingers warm pokers under her chin. When their eyes connected, he let her go, the warmth gone with him. "No, my girl," he lulled. "There is no horror story."

"I'm sorry." She let go of the thread. "I don't mean to be rude, I'm just curious why you're here. You said you came to talk, but why? How did you know I was going to be here? How do you know who I am?"

Gold laughed and it sent a shiver down Natalia's spine, the kind of shiver that only came when something beautiful was sung. When he stopped, the air settled. "One question at a time, I think," he said calmly. "I didn't know you were going to be here until you made the decision to come." Natalia went to interrupt but Gold held up a hand to silence her. "Vampires have ways of knowing things. They can use certain Crystals—"

"Crystals?" Natalia blurted, unable to contain herself.

"They come from this world and plane, the layers of Hells, and sometimes other planes in general."

"Other planes?"

Gold smiled, kindness lighting his eyes; the gold vaguely disappeared, but the blue one never faltered. "It's easy to forget how little you know. You are so ready to accept this world."

"I'm sorry." In reality, she wanted to argue how she hadn't yet fully accepted this world because there was so much to accept. But an apology sounded better.

"There is nothing wrong with wanting to know more or simply wanting more. Never apologise for trying to understand, my girl. Knowledge is power and the highest kind. It will get you the furthest if you're smart enough to master it."

Natalia cast her gaze down. "I'll try to not interrupt."

"Save your questions," he agreed. She glanced back up, her eyes wandering along his unaged face. How old was he? He could've been one thousand or twenty. "I may explain and answer what you want to ask as I talk." He nodded, seeming satisfied. "By *planes*, I meant planes of existence. But before that, where was I? My poor old brain cannot simply be stopped. Ah, yes! Us Vampires, if we know how, can connect to another life. To be quite honest though, most Crystal work is considered old fashioned now. But anyway. I saw that you were debating coming here over staying at your residence. When you decided, I knew where to find you and arrived ahead."

"To talk?"

"This is where it gets a little more complex," he tipped his head, his monocle unmoving, "or interesting."

"I don't know if I like the sound of that."

"The Council?" He phrased it like a question. "They wish to speak to you."

Her brown eyes swam in the dusk light. "The Council?"

"Apparently, they have no records on you. That is nobody's fault," Gold added quickly. "They are merely interested in amending their files."

"Like a *thing* to collect? And they sent you?"

"I owe them a favour or two."

He glanced away for a split second. Natalia saw it then; a glimpse into a soul that was very old. But when he looked back, the youth returned, though his eyes seemingly held centuries of secrets in their depths. Natalia couldn't help but wonder how much the Vampire had actually been through.

Gold cleared his throat. "They asked me to come, to see if I could convince you to go and see them."

"Seems like an awful lot of trouble for one person."

"One *Fairy*," he emphasised.

She shook her head to free it from cobwebs. "It's easy to forget."

"Or you still wish to forget." Natalia stared at him, open-mouthed. Gold took her hand and patted it. "I'm not here to judge. I am only here to offer my services as a guide for your journey and as a friend on your side. They want to add you to their system, not a collection, *especially* if you're considering joining the Purpose of our kind. It's standard procedure for them to have records – birth's, marriages, deaths."

The silence Gold offered engulfed her. White noise burned inside her ears. If hadn't been opposite her, clasping her hand, she would've forgotten he was her company.

Natalia sat like stone, as much as her hyper breathing allowed.

There wasn't a choice here. Gold was probably under instruction to drag her screaming if she disagreed. Why else would they send a Vampire she'd never met instead of a letter of invitation?

That made up her mind.

She nodded once.

"We shall leave tomorrow," Gold announced.

Natalia paused. "My dad? Can he come?"

Gold's eyes narrowed. "Is he a Creature?"

"Human."

Gold abandoned her hand. "I can ask."

"Tell the council that if he can't come, I won't be either."

Her words circled inside her head, her heart pounding to their fierce tune. When had she become so brave? Brave enough to challenge an entity she had no grounding with when she barely believed who she was?

Gold grinned. "I will," he promised. "And if I may make a judgement? You'll make a fine Fairy."

She didn't know she needed the approval, but her eyes welled. She tried to blink them away and thankfully managed too.

"You still have questions," Gold surmised as he stood. "Ask them."

Natalia stood alongside him. "Why would the Council have no records on me?" *Where had that come from?*

Gold adjusted his monocle as if to get a clearer perception. "Probably because you were brought up in the Human world from birth," he answered. "Would you be surprised if I told you that, though it was and is uncommon, it does happen? A few Creatures every few years are found to be undocumented."

"Do you collect them all?"

"There is no collecting. And no. I only search for the special ones."

"Special?" Natalia's shoulder blades itched. "What makes me special?"

"I do not know. Perhaps they have seen potential in you? Or it might be because of who your mother was?"

Natalia inhaled sharply. "My mother?" she whispered.

"Your last name. I doubt it was explained to you *how* important it is," he said, straightening his jacket. "The Fairy Kingdom, which is an entire land that exists on its own inside this plane, the same way Home City does, has a royal family. Their last name is Royal, for obvious reasons. The Queen of the Kingdom had two daughters. The oldest was to receive the Throne. She has had no heirs, and has not yet married either. Though Fairies, unlike other Creatures besides Vampires, have extensive life-spans compared to other Creatures. But that's off topic.

"Because the eldest daughter took the Royal name, and is meant for the Throne, the other daughter was given another name. Yet it was not spoken. She asked everyone who called on her to use her first name only.

"One day, however, she left. It was said she didn't want to have a life in the palace, and instead wanted to fight Monsters and save lives, and the Queen let her go as it was her daughter's right to choose.

"That daughter, the second heir, had the last name *you* carry, Natalia. The name of Whitebell."

The second heir was my mother?

A lump formed in her throat and her blood ran cold. Did her mother really leave a Kingdom and being a princess to live out her Creature Purpose? And then she'd gone on to hide Natalia from the very Purpose which she'd now chosen for herself? That didn't make any sense. Natalia covered her face. Just when she'd thought she was free of surprises, here was another, ready to pierce like an invisible blade into her sanity.

It sounded plausible, but it didn't make sense.

"I did not mean to displease or upset you," Gold said solemnly.

Before she could respond, the door was kicked open, sending it smacking into the wall. Natalia jumped and turned to the noise.

Archie and Jasper were by the door's frame, but Peri was ahead of them, already in the room.

"And what's going on in here?" Peri asked harshly, her brown eyes lingered on Gold. Natalia noticed Peri was holding a golden three forked trident. "I sensed a change."

"Mermaids," Gold huffed, turning to Natalia, "can sense people's emotions and notice when there's a change. Though they can't always tell *what* the change is."

"I'm ok," Natalia said, sending her stomach reeling. Archie's green eyes bore into her as they narrowed on her and Gold.

"You have lots to discuss," Gold told them all. He flurried past to the doorway. Still cast in the light of a sunset, he exuded confidence; Natalia wished to be equal in what Gold seemed to be. He gave Jasper a sweeping glance as if interested in him in some way, and then returned his gold and blue eyes to Natalia. "I shall meet you on the dawn. Be packed and ready. Rest well."

Gold left.

Peri zeroed in on Natalia. "What's going on?"

"Can you promise you won't stab me if I tell you?" Natalia asked, pointing. Peri glanced down at her still raised trident and she lowered it eagerly. "I have to go see the Council," she said, not bothering to waste more time. "Apparently, they have no records of me and now need some."

"*Have* to?"

"I think I'll be dragged kicking, screaming, or unconscious if I don't go willingly."

"What about drugged?" Jasper piped up. Natalia's eyes found him; his blazing green eyes matched the mischief in his grin. "Was there a chance of you being drugged if kicking, screaming, or being unconscious weren't viable options?"

Natalia wanted to laugh, thankful for the change in pace and how easily Jasper made her feel comfortable despite the situation. It was like he knew what she needed and was providing it – had he been in this situation, the roles reverse in some ways, for him to know?

Peri, however, took the situation more seriously. "Why don't they have records on you already?"

Natalia hesitated. *Should I tell them?* But she shook the unease away. There was no harm. She trusted them with her life, a life they had saved already.

All of them were patient and quiet while Natalia spoke as softly and concise as she could. She told them everything – why there were no records, how unusual it was, and who her mother could potentially be. Once she'd finished, it felt like a weight had been lifted. She hadn't noticed the pressure before, but now that it wasn't there, she could breathe without restraint.

Archie was the first to talk. His gaze was nervous, unsure. "I don't want to upset you," he said. "But we'd guessed *who* you were."

"Your last name." Natalia looked to the doorway. James stood there. Clearly no one had seen him come in, because they all looked equally stunned. Like the last time Natalia had seen him, he wore a suit and his hair was well-kept. "I told you when we first met that your name was interesting. I'm just sorry we didn't tell you *how* interesting."

"I understand why you didn't," she said, smiling weakly. "There was already so much inside my brain, I'd have been overloaded if you'd told me this too. So thank you for thinking of me, even if I didn't appreciate it at the time."

James smiled back, like a father looking at his sweet new child. "You are more than welcome."

"Does my father know? About my mother, I mean?"

After a moment, James nodded. "He told us when we first met. Don't be angry with him, either. He didn't tell you for the same reason we didn't."

Natalia could never be angry with her father. "Thank you again. For everything you've *all* done for me." She searched the faces in the room. "I don't know what I would've done without your help."

"Probably cried," joked Peri.

"I can still do that," Natalia countered.

"You won't," Jasper argued, grinning. "We're officially the lights of your life. We make everything better."

"Speaking highly of yourself again, I see."

"The best only speak of the best."

Natalia smiled at him and he returned it. His entire self gave off a welcoming pulse that she wanted to gravitate towards. Though he joked, it was his way of lightening the mood, of taking the weight out of things, and Jasper had a habit of doing it at the right time. It made her feel comfortable, like she really did belong here.

Jasper turned on his heels and left, followed by James, and Natalia faced Peri and Archie.

When she was certain the others were out of ear-shot, she spoke again, keeping her voice low. "I just don't know what to think," she admitted. "There's so much I have to learn and want to know. So many secrets about this world and my family. Even about *myself*!"

"We'll help you," Peri declared.

Archie's expression was kind. "That's what we're here for. Self-appointed guides who will help you through this mess that has become your life."

A mess? That was too nice of an explanation of what her life had suddenly become. From her birthday, to where she'd been almost killed by a fire-breathing polar bear thing, her life had been completely ripped out from underneath her until she was standing among the sky.

"You think we have a better idea of what's going on?" Peri asked in return. "We're learning all the time."

Natalia could believe that. Still, she frowned. "But you have a trident," she countered. "You at least *look* ready."

Peri shrugged nonchalantly. "It's just a little weapon I keep with me sometimes."

"Liar," Archie said, laughter in his smile. "She hangs that bloody thing above our bed. The second she hears a noise, she's ready to grab and stab." Peri grinned without a hint of an apology.

Natalia laughed at them both. "Is that a technical term?"

"We'll teach you how to do that too," Peri promised, flicking the ends of her black bob. "If we're all going to see the Council—"

"Wait," Natalia cut in, stunned. "*I'm* going with Gold."

"Do you really think we're letting you go with him? Alone? We trust him enough, but…"

"I'm not alone. My dad's coming."

"I don't know much about the laws on letting Humans in," Archie said, scowling. Because of his size, it made him look a little menacing. "It's a grey area, but if they say he can, the more the merrier."

Peri gave him a stern look. "Including us in that equation, I hope."

He kissed the back of her hand. "I was, darling."

Peri's eyes made a motion and it seemed to be a signal. Archie left a second later, leaving the girls alone, and Natalia noticed Peri staring at Archie's behind as he walked. When Peri caught Natalia watching her, she grinned mischievously. "It's the simple things," she mused. "Now, how about we start your training?"

Natalia blinked. "What?"

"Not the physical training," Peri assured quickly. Natalia, honestly, hadn't expected to start *any* form of training for a while. "That'll come later. Your leg is still healing. Maybe in a few days we'll get you doing simple stuff, like balance training?" Peri tossed the ends of her hair. "What I meant was how about we start training you on the basics of what Creatures are and their gifts and abilities? Help you settle in before you meet the Council." She stepped closer. "Where do you want to start?"

Natalia's cheeks flamed. She touched the skin and pulled her fingers away, twinkling bronze dust coating the tips. She wasn't aware she needed to know anything for the meeting with the Council, yet

Peri was making out like she did.

Peri stared intensely at the dust as if she'd never seen it up close.

"At the beginning," Natalia said, wiping her hands on her clothes. "That's always the best place to start. Unless it's a horror story."

Peri's expression shifted. "What?"

"Nothing," Natalia dismissed. "I'll eventually need to know everything anyway, so why don't we start somewhere and fill the gaps as we go?"

"Are you sure?"

Am I sure?

The answer was easy this time. There was no more running and hiding and wishing all this gone, because she no longer wanted to send it away. This was her life and, like her mother, she would accept it. Her heart and head were in agreement over what she wanted at last.

"Yes."

6
Where Blood Lies

ERI CROSSED HER LEGS UNDERNEATH HER. "Ready?"

"How're we doing this?" Natalia asked.

"There definitely won't be essays," Alex established. "How about a pop quiz? That's what *they're* likely to do, *if* they do anything remotely like this. Which there's no chance they will."

Natalia nodded, swallowing her nerves. "I think that sounds best."

Alex lowered onto the other barstool so she and Peri sandwiched Natalia in.

The last few hours had been spent going over all Natalia might need to know. To Alex, it didn't sound like they'd fed her enough. But it didn't matter to the Council how extensive anyone's knowledge was. Every meeting was about what the Council wanted to know and hear at that time.

Whatever the Council wanted from Natalia was guess work. Hopefully it was just as she'd said, that they wanted basic information on her.

Alex only hoped the Council would be less cold with Natalia than they had been with her. They were known for their welcoming tones or kindness on any count. However, Natalia wasn't seemingly in any trouble, unlike Alex, who had come to their attention by picking a fight with a Werewolf - the very Werewolf that had turned her as a result.

"Archie?" Peri called.

He wandered into the room seconds later and stopped round the opposite side of the island counter, leaning on his elbows. "You rang?"

"Pop quiz," Alex explained loosely.

Archie looked taken aback. "On me?"

Alex didn't try muffling her laughter. "No, you Kifflegger," she said. Peri snorted.

"Kifflegger?" Natalia questioned.

Archie narrowed his green eyes at Alex, causing them to darken. "A rather low level Monster. They have floppy tails and scuttle on six legs. They're blind and usually deaf. Mostly harmless. It's an insult, like calling us dumbasses or brain-short," he answered. "Thanks, sis."

She winked. "Always, bro."

"Are not all Monsters dangerous?" Natalia asked next.

Peri pulled a face. "Not in the way we think. But just because we don't see the damage, it doesn't mean there isn't some in other contexts. They might not hurt Creatures, but they might hurt Humans, animals, or something else."

"Monsters," Archie moved his gaze to Natalia, "want to take life and souls. Ever since the Veils opened, they've had a taste for this world that they can't seem to ignore. A taste that has them craving it and others that flourish. Most seem to have no purpose other than destroy. Actually, I've never seen any with a bigger purpose. They seek nothing more than destruction; a world they can destroy and turn into their new Hell. They live off it."

"And it's our Purpose to ensure life lives on." Natalia's voice was quiet, but in the silence of the kitchen it was clear.

Alex nodded. Though she'd not grown up for the first fourteen years in this life, she'd learnt enough since.

Souls deserved to live. To thrive. To prosper. Monsters were incapable of allowing such things, purely for their own greed and need to ruin. And they never went down without a fight. But neither would the Creatures. They'd been gifted a higher Purpose by the Gods eons ago; to *kill* Monsters and ensure souls lived.

It seemed odd that Creatures had a Purpose only because Monsters lacked one, yet here they were. They would fight until the last breath was taken, until the war was won for good.

"Except," Peri continued. "There are a few who seemed to have broken free from their mental absence."

Natalia blinked, shocked. "What?"

"Some Monsters work with us, help us to learn about their kinds, even fight *with* us. They're vetted by the Council and are kept under strict rulings."

In the absence of sound, Alex could hear every heart in the room.

"About that quiz?" Archie prompted.

Natalia sat straighter. "Right."

"You've got this," promised Peri.

"Does she need a cheerleader?" Archie responded, grinning. "Are we *all* going to have to get those short skirts and pompoms?" He looked like he was imagining it there and then, though who he was picturing inside his head was unclear. Alex was just glad her *sight* didn't include mental images – at least, not with those outside her own kind, if at all.

Peri's grin was devilish. "You'd pull them off spectacularly, *amore*."

Archie laughed like he'd never heard anything more ridiculous. When he was done, he focused his attention and energy on Natalia, though laughter remained in his eyes. "We'll call out Creatures and you tell us what you remember," he said, keeping his tone as serious as he could. "We'll fill in the gaps or correct you as we go. *Only* if we have too."

It's better than what I had, Alex thought.

Alex had gotten no preparation whatsoever before her meeting with the Council and at the time she'd been freshly torn to pieces. She'd looked like she'd bathed in blood. Now she carried the scars along her back and chest. At the time, she hadn't immediately changed to a wolf. Nor had she been adopted into an accepting family. A lone wolf caught in a shine of a new moon.

But she had her pack now, even if they weren't all the same, and it was time she helped someone else enter.

"Let's start easy?" Peri suggested. "Fairies."

Alex watched Natalia's chest rise and fall slowly. "Fairies create their own dust. It usually either trails behind them or shines on their cheeks as a Human might blush. All dust has magical properties. It can be used to create shields that can protect the ones creating it or others." She sounded like a robot reading from paper.

"You don't always have to be together to do that," Archie intersected. Natalia flashed him a quizzical look, and Alex copied it. "Say you're separated from us in a fight, but we're in the more immediate danger. You can throw a shield around us without putting yourself inside it."

"Oh."

"It's not easy to do," he told her frankly.

Natalia took another deep breath and continued. "Fairy dust can also be used to dismantle some Witch's spells and reverse some of the effects of Monsters. It can even reverse some injuries *caused* by them. The colour of the dust depends on the individual and it doesn't run similar with others in the same family. Furthermore, the colour of the dust is usually the same as the individual's wings. In my case, they're likely to be bronze."

Alex stood from her perch, moving to click on the coffee machine. Archie instantly seized the opportunity to sit beside Natalia.

No one mentioned what was left unspoken - that none of them had yet seen Natalia's wings. They were meant to look like a butterfly's; four sections completely coloured with the same colour as her dust. All Fairies were born with them, but Natalia's hadn't presented themselves. Was it just taking time? Would they then arrive naturally once she was comfortable with her true form?

Whatever the reason, Alex couldn't deny her concern at Natalia's current lack of wings. They'd come eventually. They had to.

"Some Fairies have the ability to turn invisible," Natalia continued, still speaking as if reading from a text book. "It takes skill, practise, and power."

"I don't know of *any* Fairy that's capable," Alex commented.

Archie narrowed his eyes at her. "You haven't been in our world long," he said, not unkindly.

"Alright Mr I've-been-here-all-my-life," Alex mumbled, pouring the coffee. "Tell me if you've seen or know of anything different."

"I can't say she's wrong," Peri said honestly.

After a moment, Archie agreed. "Neither can I."

Alex faced them again, using her mug to hide her grin. Her eyes landed on a patient Natalia. "What do you know of Werewolves?"

Natalia's brown eyes gazed directly at her. "They can be created—"

"Made," Alex cut in. She'd always preferred that word – it made it sound like there was a choice behind the action.

Natalia accepted the change and begun again. "They can be *made*," Alex nodded approvingly, "two ways. They can either be bitten or scratched enough that their blood or saliva is transferred, or they can be born into it. However, if they're bitten, the change will be less controlled throughout the first few months. Eventually, they shift entirely by their choice. Except on a fully moon. No one can escape a full moon unshifted. Even those born that way."

"Those random initial shifts tend to happen when moods change," Alex expressed. She sipped her coffee, finding it sour despite the amount of sugar she'd spooned in. "Angry, sad, even hungry. I sneezed once and it happened. It's pretty painful at first too." She sighed, remembering all too well how her bones cracked in and out of place as they lengthened or shortened or, worse, fused. "It *does* get easier, and yeah, you do get to choose eventually when you want to change, but even after a full moon as a newly made, you still shift uncontrollably. For *months*. It takes a while to settle."

"Aren't there Crystals to stop it?" Peri asked.

"Vampire Crystals?" Natalia chirped. Incredulous eyes flew to her and the poor girl seemed to shrink into her seat. "Gold mentioned them when he was here," she explained. "It was how he found me, or at least knew where I'd come to be."

"Different Crystals have different properties," Alex said. "Moon Crystals, if worn by a wolf, can hinder the change on a full moon, or even a first transformation for some turned younger. That's *if* you can pay the high price for one."

Alex had learnt about Moon Crystals too late. *After* her first transformation. And the second on a full moon. After she'd completely thrown care to the wind, paving the way for bloodied revenge. By that point, a Moon Crystal wouldn't have suppressed her rage or confusion. There was no Crystal on *any* plane that could've done that.

It was her fault after all. She'd picked the initial fight that left her bitten and turned, and then she had been the one to seek revenge. So, to Alex, the Crystals were pointless. Especially now that she was comfortable in her ever-shifting skin.

"What else?" she asked, wanting to rid her mind of the terrifying memories.

"You have heightened senses: hearing, smelling, tasting," Natalia continued. "Once you're a wolf, you can communicate with others through your mind. They can be in your pack but they can also be random individual wolves with practise. Your body temperature is naturally higher than all other Creatures and you can heal most injuries instantaneously, except when attacked by some Monsters and silver. Silver wounds don't heal, nor do they kill instantly, but the element burns and *can* kill if not treated." Alex shuddered at the thought.

"As for the Monster thing?" Peri added. "Make a note that *most* Creatures take time recovering from their injuries."

Alex caught Natalia glancing down as she said, "Right."

"Though, it hadn't been in a dire state like I'd expected."

Natalia looked like she wanted to contest that, but Alex stopped her. "Though Werewolves *can* heal quicker when Monsters are involved, Creatures in general heal faster compared to Humans. However, sometimes Humans are completely unaffected by certain Monster attacks when us Creature's aren't, and vice versa."

The Fairy grabbed the sides of her head. "Talk about brain ache."

"Say the word and we'll stop," Archie told her.

"Please," she half-begged.

Just then, Natalia's phone began to ring, buzzing along the counter. She picked it up and hobbled out of the room. Alex followed the girl with her eyes. Her heart reached out for her, knowing how hard and confusing learning all of this nonsense could be. *Especially* after a trauma. Out of everyone, Alex could sympathise best.

"She seems to be doing better," Peri surmised, also looking out past the doorway.

Alex turned back round, rubbing her head and messing her hair up further. "She's still not walking on that leg properly."

Peri's eyes met hers. "It'll take a while."

"I won't be at work tomorrow," Natalia said from down the hallway, having a conversation that only Alex could hear beside the caller and herself.

"It's not an overnight fix," Peri continued. "But considering what I thought the damage *would* be like, based on what happened, the wound's in remarkably better condition already."

Natalia's voice dropped. "I'm not sick, Katherine."

Archie looked to his girlfriend. "What were you expecting?"

"For her to be off her feet for *weeks*."

In the hall, Natalia sighed. "Dad already knows what's going on and why I won't be there," she stated. Alex caught the *thump thump* of the Fairy's heart as if it were her own. "I texted him. Noah knows too.

I'm seeing him tomorrow night if all is well. No. What?" She laughed shortly. "I *promise* I'm not contagious. Bye."

Alex heard the phone click off and Natalia reappeared, crossing the kitchen to her previous spot. What had the phone call been about?

"What did I miss?" Natalia asked, laying down her phone.

"Nothing important," Archie said.

Natalia seemed to accept it, though Alex caught the look Peri gave him. And that got her thinking. Why *hadn't* Natalia's injuries been worse? Going against a Calefaction, with no training, should've resulted in almost irreparable damage.

Natalia had gotten lucky. But Alex didn't believe much in luck.

"I feel like someone's talking about me." Jasper came bounding into the kitchen, hair swept off his face. He smelt of cold nights and Alex sensed his heart racing. From the black stains on his shirt, he'd been chasing something and had clearly caught it. He sidled up to Alex. "So? *Were* you talking about me? If you weren't, I'll be sad."

"Were your ears burning?" Alex teased.

"Like the fiery pits of the Seven Hells," Jasper winked. Natalia yawned in response and Alex followed her brother's eyes to her. "Sorry, but are we boring you? If you say yes, I *will* be deeply offended."

"Now, would I admit to something like that?" Natalia teased back. "But I do think I should leave soon—"

"Not before you tell me what you were talking about," Jasper demanded.

"They were teaching me," Natalia explained at the same time Peri said, "How it's a miracle the sky hasn't fallen on you yet for all your devious deeds."

Jasper grinned. "It's because I'm charming."

"Charmingly annoying," Alex mumbled, knowing it was loud enough.

"You love me though, don't you?"

Alex scoffed. "They tell me I have too."

Jasper laughed at that, his facial expression settling to neutral. "Is the practise trial over?" he asked.

Alex flinched. "She's not going on *trial*."

"If it *was* a trial," Natalia came in, "I would be ready."

"You haven't done anything wrong for it to come to that," Alex told her. She had first-hand experience on what a trial was like.

Jasper's attention was focused on Natalia. "Think you've learnt enough?"

She blanched. "If I don't know it by now, then I won't know it in time."

"There are *always* things we forget or learn later on," promised Peri.

"If you want to leave," Jasper moved back round the counter, "I'll walk you home."

"You've just come in," Natalia argued.

Jasper pulled at his jacket. "And so I'm the best dressed to go out again."

No one said anything, so Natalia promised everyone she'd meet them in the morning.

Alex wandered to the living room in time to see her little brother and Natalia leave, peering out the window. They walked side by side down the stone steps and as Alex pressed her hand to the cold glass, she could feel their hearts at her fingertips.

A low fog rolled in from the sea, wrapping around Natalia's ankles. She walked briskly to keep up with Jasper and hoped she wouldn't trip over her attempts.

"What's the Council like?" she asked, needing to fill the silence.

Gold had said the meeting with the Council shouldn't be a long one, so Natalia and Noah had arranged for a movie night. She was excited to see her friend after so long, but Noah's text seemed *off* like he was hiding something when really she was hiding from him. It made her uneasy.

Jasper's gaze didn't deviate as they pushed on. "It depends. There's one Council member to represent each of the seven Creatures. In my experience, they all seem pretty emotionless and void of hearts."

That didn't install much confidence.

She wrapped her arms around herself to expel the chill that surrounded her. Hearing the Council weren't the kindest had nailed home the idea that she was somehow facing a trial no matter how many times the Darby's told her all they wanted were records.

Out of nowhere, Jasper stopped. Natalia almost ploughed into him, managing not too just because she'd neglected to blink in that second. Jasper's arm flew out in front of her, holding her back, and her body went rigid with tension. Hesitantly, she bent round his arm and saw the ground break apart.

Black sludge surfaced from the cracks. It circled like a gloopy tornado; the smell of damp dog wafted towards them. Jasper motioned once with his arm and together they both stepped back, forcing Natalia up against the nearest garden fence; the wood pressed uncomfortably into the back of her legs, making her left leg twinge.

From the side of his mouth, Jasper whispered. "Now would be a *perfect* time for a shield."

"I can't," she whispered back. Making the previous one had been by fluke and she'd passed out after, which he seemed to be forgetting. The chance of creating one now, without practise or training, was highly improbable. The black sludge twisted together until it towered over them both. There was nothing Natalia could do to protect them without it being an accident. "What is that thing?"

Jasper was using his own body like some sort of shield, blocking Natalia. The streetlight's glow cast half his face into shadow. "Do you really want to know?"

Do I?

As if any sudden movement would be a bad idea, she shook her head and Jasper turned away again.

He does that a lot, she thought. Jasper often accepted her answers or questions without pressing. She appreciated it, since half the time her statements were rhetorical; she didn't know why she wanted to understand things, she just did.

The black sludge groaned. The noise was reminiscent of when a large amount of water was sucked through too small of a pipe.

The Monster groaned again and this time, with a *pop*, a hollow green mouth appeared, followed by two matching eyes and arms sprouting at its side. Then the sludge receded off the ground forming something resembling feet. A thick tar-like substance dripped from its increasingly humanoid physique.

"Try not to let it hit you with its drippings," Jasper whispered.

Despite their best efforts to remain near silent, the Monster's eyes found them.

It flew forwards.

Jasper shoved Natalia. Her knees buckled and she tipped over the fence, landing hard, her wrists taking the brunt of the force. She sat up on the lawn just as the Monster lunged at Jasper.

He dodged effortlessly, raising his hands.

The Monster twisted, its eyes faced him while its legs pointed in the opposite direction. The Monster screeched as it began to tear apart in the middle until there was a hole Natalia could see the houses on the other side of the road through. Witch spells were mostly silent these days, Natalia had learnt, and seeing one performed was unnerving.

Natalia looked between the Monster and Jasper. Jasper *controlled* the Monster. The way he circled the Monster was predatory.

Instinctively, Natalia scrambled back. Jasper continued circling and twisting the Monster. There came a grunt from Jasper, like he'd hit a blockage. But with one last forceful push, the Monster ruptured.

Black sludge launched everywhere.

A cold feeling spread along Natalia's shoulders, then subsided.

"Are you ok? Did it get you?" Jasper lept over the fence with ease and landed beside her. When she peered at her shoulders, she found them covered in black dots. Jasper brushed at them frantically before his eyes focused on her face, searching over it. "Does it hurt?"

She looked at his hand. "It feels cold."

"Did you get hit anywhere else?"

"I don't think so."

He let go and waved his hands. At his command, the sludge around them rose into the air. The droplets hung like dead stars, each turning slowly into fine ash with the blow of the wind.

Once gone, Jasper slumped back onto the grass. Natalia looked down at him. His eyes were heavy, his lids near shutting, and sweat had beaded across his forehead and top lip.

"I did warn you about not letting it hit you," he muttered. It wasn't unkind, but it wasn't particularly nice either. "The sludge might feel cold at first but it becomes freezing, deadly so."

"Like freezer burn?"

"*Exactly* like that. Siltapolia kill by wrapping their victims in their slime. It gives a calming effect at first. Slowly, the cold damages nerve endings. Then, the Monster's burn their victims alive. There's usually just enough feeling left in the poor souls that they can feel their end."

Natalia grimaced, anxiously avoiding looking at her left shoulder. "I'm glad you didn't tell me what that thing was *before* it was dealt with."

"Siltapolia are still low level Monsters. Quite mindless and the type to do as they please. They're relatively blind and so are directed by noise. I think they've been known to kill other Monsters mistakenly."

"Saves us a job."

Jasper put his arms behind his head and smirked. "Us?"

She turned away, feeling her cheeks heat. "I'm considering it."

"We better hope that tomorrow goes well then, yeah?" He sighed, hauling himself up. "Speaking or tomorrow," he brushed his trousers free of grass, "let's get you home."

Natalia took her time standing. Coldness clung to her neck though she knew there was no sludge or ash there. "Is it really going to be that big of a deal?" she asked him as they walked.

Jasper considered it. "They just wanted records on you, right?" When she nodded, he continued. "Then no. It won't be much. You might even get the chance to see the City."

"Gold said it wouldn't take long." At least, she hoped it didn't, she had plans with Noah.

"Hopefully not."

"Is the City pretty?"

He slowed. "What gave you that impression?"

"The way everyone talks about it." She shrugged, recounting the conversations that had taken place around her as she'd been learning the gifts and qualities of Creatures. "It seems like everyone sees it as this special place."

"It *is* special. It's the home of all Creatures. Just under half of the entire Creature population live there. If we don't have residency there, we still go back for celebrations throughout the year. Most Creatures are married there and the burnings of our bodies at the end of our lives happen there too, unless under special request."

Natalia touched her earrings. "But everyone talks about it like it's magical."

Jasper grinned. "Hasn't everything you've come across been magical so far? What makes you think the home of all Creatures would be any less? It's *more*." He stooped into an effortless bow. "And it would be an honour to show it to you."

She spoke steadily, "I might take you up on that offer."

"Then it's settled. I'll be your personalised guide once all the Council nonsense is done with. I will admit I haven't had time to prepare hats and collectable badges for the tour. But I know the City well enough and won't get you lost."

"It would be your responsibility to find me if I was to get lost." The space between her shoulder blades itched and she fidgeted to free the irritation. When it was gone, it was replaced by a twinge in her leg. She studied the ground. "Why are you so willing to help me?"

Jasper ignored her question as if he'd not heard and began knocking on a door. Natalia glanced at him and blinked, realising it was *her* door he was knocking on.

For a few beats she was dumbfounded. How did he know where she lived? Then it twigged. He'd been here before. He'd fought off the Calefaction here, saving her life. That had been mere days ago.

So much had transpired since then. Now it was hard for Natalia to know where she stood exactly in the world, caught between the Human life she'd had and the Creature one she was being given.

The door swung inward, revealing Natalia's dad. Tony smiled, looking them both over and moving aside so they could step into the always cold hallway. She slipped off her shoes and jacket which, upon removing, she noticed had tiny holes burnt into the right shoulder.

"Drink?" Her father asked from further down the hall.

"No, thanks," Jasper answered. "I'm just here to help pack."

"I'll have my maltesers hot chocolate?"

Her father smiled and left.

Natalia shuffled past Jasper, brushing against him by accident in the narrow hallway. The contact sent a zap up her arm where they touched. She half ran up the stairs to hide her face full of bronze and dived into her room.

"You'll only need the essentials," Jasper announced from behind.

Natalia spun to see him rooting through her wardrobe. Besides Noah and her father, and one person she'd had a relationship with before, no other boy had ever been in her room, but then, nor had any girl – she didn't have many friends who visited.

Jasper drew out an overnight bag and threw it into the centre of the room. "That should be big enough," he decided. "Unless you plan to bring the kitchen sink and a horse?"

"Does it look like I can afford a horse?" Natalia replied, holding out her arms. She didn't think she'd be staying overnight. It was only meant to be a couple of hours, right? Would she have to cancel her plans with Noah after all? Or was this to bring a change of outfit?

Her walls were painted dull orange, the same colour that had been there since she was a baby. The peach window curtains were the same too, as was the flimsy wooden furniture that the room could barely contain. The double bed was the newest piece.

She gathered up socks, dumping them into the bag, and glanced at Jasper as he reached into the wardrobe, only to pull back like he'd been caught doing something he shouldn't.

She went to ask what he was doing when her father appeared with a steaming mug in hand. Natalia collected the drink, forcing Jasper further into her room. "Thanks dad," she said.

"Is Gold meeting you here or..." he trailed off, confusion written into his eyes. Natalia blinked, realising they'd specified a time - dawn - but not a place.

"We'll work something out," Jasper declared.

"You're coming too, dad," Natalia added.

He tipped his head and Natalia saw the faintest grey at the roots of his hair. "I wanted to talk to you about that."

"What, dad?"

"Katherine."

"Oh?"

"She was here earlier. I didn't know, but—"

"Dad," Natalia cut in. She placed her mug on the closest cabinet top and dropped her voice, hoping Jasper couldn't hear - Jasper began to whistle as if to block himself out of the conversation. "If you're about to tell me that Katherine is some kind of Creature, I don't want to hear it. That sounds horrible, I know, but I already have *so much* to process. If I have to learn *one* more fact or detail about someone right now, I'll scream that I've gone crazy."

He surrounded his daughter with his arms, surrendering her in a bone crushing hug. "You're *not* crazy," he whispered. "But I do understand. It was a lot for me too."

"Whatever you have to say, can it wait?"

"Of course it can!"

He kissed her head and moved away. Natalia nodded and her father kissed her once more before leaving, pulling the door as he went.

She immediately collapsed onto her bed, defeat hammering inside her head and heart like a drumbeat she didn't want to become familiar with.

Jasper's face appeared above her. "Do you need a minute?"

"I think I need more than a minute." She fixed her eyes on him. She could only imagine what she looked like at this angle, but Jasper looked no different besides some tangles of hair dangling into his face. "Can I ask you something?"

"I'm sure you're capable of doing so."

"What was it like when you first learned about this life?"

Jasper tapped Natalia's legs so she sat up, allowing him to join his side. "It was different for me," he said. "I was raised around magic and Creatures, seeing Monsters when I was still being carried by my mother." His green eyes roamed over her. "I can see it in you, you know. That you don't really know what's real and what's not. All I can say is that you'll get there. I had my whole life to learn, to get where I am now, and I'm still learning. You just need time and a little confidence, and you'll come around to believe."

"It's not that I don't believe," she argued, dropping her gaze. "It's that I have too much to suddenly believe in when before I thought the sun rose in the morning and set at night, and that Humans were the only beings beside animals to exist."

Life kept throwing new directions at her and she didn't know which way to turn. There was an up, down, left, and right. But now there were diagonals too.

Yes, things took time. Time she'd barely had. She knew eventually things would settle and then she would have the freedom to understand more.

But for now, what she knew and what she was already trying to believe in was enough.

The Council was her focus. After that, she'd have time to grasp everything else; what it meant to be a Creature, how she might become a better one, what her powers really were, and how exactly her Purpose worked if she decided to follow it.

Natalia stood and started packing. Jasper mirrored her in silence.

The world would keep falling and rising. And she should too. Even if her head hadn't come around yet, it would. She would figure it out, like Jasper had said. It would just take time.

7
A Court of Creature Law

HE SIGHT OF GOLD STANDING IN BROAD DAYLIGHT caused shivers to run up Natalia's spine, the feeling congregating between her shoulder blades – an odd feeling despite it happening on and off for years.

"My dear girl!" Gold exclaimed enthusiastically upon seeing her. He stole her hand and kissed it. She flinched when his cool lips touched her skin. As he let go, his monocle fell from his eye, but the golden eye, along with the blue, remained focused on her. "I will not bite you," he promised, adjusting the monocle back into place. "Unless you ask." He wiggled his eyebrows. "Nor will I harm you, or your friends, in any way."

"I'm sorry," she said meekly.

He laughed, sounding genuinely amused. "I understand. You are not yet used to the likes of me. My mere presence has upset people in the past. But that is penance for the type of Creature I am. There are stereotypes, like how we wish for nothing but blood and to drain life from souls. Over time, you grow accustomed to people flinching or being uneasy in your wake."

"I'm not uneasy." Her stomach twisted a notch. "I was surprised."

"By what, may I ask?"

Natalia avoided his gaze. "Last time we met, you were warm."

"You must know that Vampires can change their body heat? We can collect the cold or the warmth, and we may pass either on if we choose."

He touched her face gently and warmth spread all the way to her toes. When Gold removed his hand minutes later, she shifted her coat tighter around her. The brisk wind lashed at her face until all she felt was ice.

As her father locked the door behind him, Natalia feared what else she might've already forgotten. Mentally she recited all she knew about Creatures and hoped that the Darby's efforts weren't in vain, that they hadn't wasted time trying to help.

Natalia wanted to prove herself capable, to *everyone*.

She wanted to prove she belonged.

That was what she wanted. In a dreamless sleep, she'd come to realise she wanted to be part of this crazy, unbelievable, magical world after all. Even if it didn't make sense. She wasn't sure it ever would.

This meeting had to go well. It *needed* to.

"Are we ready?" Gold asked as he pulled out a sapphire-encrusted pocket-watch from the chest pocket of his white suit. "Time is running from us and I was hoping to stroll around the City beforehand." He snapped the watch shut and pocketed it again.

Natalia went to speak but was interrupted by noise.

Out of a swirling and pulsing green tunnel, six figures emerged. It vanished behind them the second they were free of it.

Peri wore a pastel yellow summer dress despite it being winter, her body neatly tucked into Archie's side with her trident in her hand. Archie's light brown hair waved in the wind, as did his t-shirt, emphasising his broad shoulders. Alex stood off to the side with her full fringe parted in the centre and her skin a deep gold under the sunlight. Jasper's hands were tucked into his jean pockets, his freckles obvious in broad daylight. Sarah and James stood together, their hands touching as they conversed quietly.

"*Witches*," Gold said in a dramatic sigh.

"Mermaid," Peri corrected, holding up her trident.

"Werewolf!" Alex half-yelled at the same time.

"Apologies," said Gold, not sounding apologetic at all.

Without a word, James separated from his wife and lifted his hands, waving them in circles. From where the swirling tunnel had been moments before, a scoring wing, powerful enough to compel everyone to step back, rose up. Natalia shielded her eyes with her arm until the wind subsided. Where the previous tunnel had been a new one stood, this one brown and darker inside, and the smell of burning wood wafted towards them.

Gold, with his fangs exposed, peered down at Natalia. "Ready?"

Natalia looked back at him. "What do we do?"

"It's a portal," Sarah explained, stepping up front. "All you have to do is follow the person before you. The course we're taking has been set so you won't get lost inside." That wasn't a reassuring notion to Natalia but Sarah didn't seem notice, taking her husband's hand, and slipping into the portal with him like they were walking through a doorway.

Natalia peered at her dad. "You don't have to come," she whispered.

His green eyes watched her. "When did you get so old?" He smiled. "Plus, your mother, for *ages*, talked about The City. We never got to go together."

"Humans are rarely let inside," Archie said matter-of-factly as he passed. Peri marched into the pulsating tunnel at his side.

Natalia returned her father's smile, adding, "You're allowed in. We have permission."

Her father nodded. "Then this is my chance. I have to come."

Natalia squeezed his hand for a brief moment, if only to reassure herself, and then let go. As much as he was her rock and would always be her father, she needed to find courage in herself. If she wanted to be a Creature, she needed to stand on her own. He wouldn't always be with her, though with him at her side now, it gave her to confidence to start trying to stand alone.

They walked in unison, father and daughter. As Natalia's toes crossed over the threshold, she felt her heart beat inside her throat. It was like the entire tunnel was *alive*.

"Natalia!"

Stunned, she turned. Alex and Jasper were rushing forwards. What had she done? In an instant she realised they weren't coming for her. There was someone in front of them. Natalia narrowed her eyes as she trotted backwards.

Noah.

Natalia couldn't call for him, or for anyone. She couldn't even scream.

Like a hand had curled around her heart, she was snatched away by it.

It felt like she was falling; through air, through water, through space itself.

Instinctively, Natalia prepared her hands for the fall. But she didn't land on any ground. She was suspended, stuck like a plank of wood and her face pointed to the blue sky above.

Whoever had frozen her in time lowered her, righting her too, until she stood on two unsteady feet, blinking ahead. Archie stared at her, carefully scanning for injuries or anomalies. Up this close, Natalia could spot the beginnings of freckles along his cheeks.

"Thank you," she said in a single breath.

"You would've fallen with grace, I'm sure," he said, smiling – it was the same, borderline cheeky smile Jasper had. She smiled back, thankful.

Suddenly she remembered the tunnel and, more importantly, who had been chasing it. "Noah?" She whispered his name, rotating in circles as her stomach dropped further and further with each movement. "Noah? Noah!"

Natalia found him.

And he was falling.

Rushing to his aid, Archie caught him mid-air, suspending him like he had Natalia. It was odd to see it from this angle, one body wrapped in green mist. Then Archie clicked his fingers and Noah's body crashed down into his waiting arms. Noah's eyes were closed, his mouth agape with a sweat along his forehead.

"Noah?" Natalia's reached out for him.

Sarah came to her, stopping her in her tracks. "He'll be ok," she promised. Natalia didn't trust it. "James?" Her husband turned his head at the call of his name. "Get the boy to our house. Tuck him in and answer his questions when he wakes. Take Archie and Alex. I'll handle the Council."

James nodded, his slicked-back hair staying in place. Archie went first, Noah still cradled in his arms like a child. James and Alex rushed after them. Natalia wanted to call for her friend, wanted to hear him yell back, but her words tied in her throat.

Sarah touched Natalia's shoulders in a motherly gesture. "I promise he'll be fine," she said. "The walls of portals are treacherous for non-Creatures. They whisper things. Your father was protected because we were prepared for him to accompany us. Your friend was not. Thankfully he was out quickly. He looked exhausted but otherwise fine. I don't think there will be any damage done. The voices wouldn't have gotten to him in that short time." Her face creased. "But I will warn you, dear, he now knows of this world."

Natalia's eyes stung. "What—"

Sarah cut her off. "James will explain to your friend all that he wants and needs. He won't be able to walk away from this world as if it were a dream."

He'll be like me. That was Natalia's first thought, but she came to see the truth as she blinked back tears. *He* won't *be like me. He'll know about me and the others but he won't be one of us. He'll still be on the outside.*

Natalia blinked back her tears. "Will he be safe?"

"Yes, he'll be safe."

There was nothing Natalia could do. Noah was in the best hands. The Darby's had cared for her after her unfortunate introductory circumstances, so she trusted them with her best friend. That didn't quench the urge to run to him though. She wanted to be the one he saw first when he woke, allowing her to spill her own secrets before the others could.

But she couldn't. It couldn't be her.

Natalia looked away from Sarah guiltily and rested on Jasper. He was smiling. The gesture seemed like it was meant to be comforting and Natalia tried to return one of her own but her smile faltered.

"I am sorry for what has transpired," Gold said, cutting in. Natalia glanced at him. "Your friend will have knowledge not many on the outside are privy too. I know you worry for him, but he *is* safe. After the meeting, you will be able to go to him. First, we have an engagement."

Peri held Natalia's hand, her trident shoved under her armpit. Natalia knew Gold was right. She could see Noah after, he needed rest and time, just as she had, so she shifted gears in her brain.

"I shall lead," Gold insisted.

Peri squeezed Natalia's hand and whispered close to Natalia's ear. "Once this is done, we can go home and you'll be able to see your friend and how fine he is."

Natalia's heart sank. "I hope he won't be mad."

"You didn't drag him through the portal. He made that choice on his own."

"No, not that."

"Then what? What would he be mad about?"

"Because I haven't told him anything about this life yet. He doesn't know about me."

Peri shook her head causing her black bob to bounce. "If he's a good friend, he'll understand."

Natalia only hoped Peri was right. She didn't want Noah to be mad. She'd not told Noah because she'd never found the right words. Nor was there a good time. How could she just bring up she was a Fairy? It sounded like lunacy. It had to be her. So she'd avoided him. The plan *had* been to tell him this evening. Now that was out of the window.

Natalia took a shuddering breath and let go of Peri. Turning, she squeaked.

Stretching before her was a city. A city that truly *did* appear to be made of magic.

Grand brick houses had golden doors and wooden beams and, in some cases, massive plants outside the front windows. Black and white unlit streetlamps were positioned on either side of the wide grey stone path that went both forwards and behind where everyone currently stood, leading onwards in both directions. The fountain at the end of the row of houses was glistening with water that changed colour each time it spurted out from the simple three tiered vase centrepiece. Scripture was carved into the wall of the fountain but it was too smoothed over, and Natalia was too far, for it to be readable.

The sun beaming above was hotter than it had been at home, and Natalia understood why Peri had worn a dress. It felt like summer here; Natalia instantly regretted wearing a jacket. A vibrant blue rippled above them, occupied by a few white clouds. Birds dived and swooped overhead, their calls cawing out into an otherwise clear sky.

Natalia spotted draped vines along fences and twisted flowers in nooks. Brilliant colour flashed all around her. Bunting connected from house to house. There were even chalked flower designs on the ground, some delightful while others simple.

She touched the petals of some orange tulips and wanted to question why they were here, why any of it was. But the over-sized white marble building ahead pulled her attention.

The building stood behind the fountain, complete with an archway over the open, heavy looking white doors. The entire place stood out in gross grandeur. Natalia would rather spend her time in the bigger city she assumed was behind her than be near *that* building too long.

"What is this?" Natalia asked, facing her friends again.

"This place?" Jasper had been so quiet, Natalia had almost forgotten he was there. She nodded, pushing all thoughts of whatever was happening around here away for now. "It's *the* City," he said. "It's Atlantis."

She narrowed her eyes at him. "That can't be right."

"Why can't it be?" She had no reply and he smiled. "Creatures and Monsters are real, so why can't Atlantis be?"

"In the myth, it sank."

"It never sank," Peri jumped in. "It was just hidden from Humans."

"For safety," added Sarah.

"We had to be kept safe," Gold corrected. His miss-matched eyes glinted. "Back in my time, Humans hunted us. They hunted all Creatures."

Nothing's changed, she thought. *Humans still hunt and hurt what they don't understand, usually out of fear and hatred of what they're ignorant and naïve of.*

Gold fiddled inside his blazer. Seconds later he pulled out a black velvet headband and held it out. "This is for you," he offered.

She took it. "What for?"

"To wear."

"Why?"

"You don't look much like a Fairy."

In her state of confusion, Jasper approached. She held her breath as he reached up. He tugged on the band holding back her bark-brown hair and it tumbled about her, falling to her elbows. He smiled and tucked the front pieces behind her ears, then took the headband from her. Obediently bowing her head, Jasper pushed the band on, assuring it rested nicely.

Without a word, she raised her head. Jasper's eyes were on her hair still. Tantalisingly slowly, he reached out and let a strand slide through his fingers as he stepped away.

"Better," Gold said approvingly to Natalia, though his eyes remained on Jasper.

"It would be a bigger statement with flowers," Peri said, and shrugged when Natalia looked at her. "It's the Flower Parade, a Fairy festival, *this* week. Right now." She swung her arm wide, indicating to the flowers. Natalia nodded, more so because she now had some answers to her questions from earlier. "You'd look much more the part with flowers since Fairies are known for them."

"And stars," Natalia said, and then doubted herself, adding, "right?"

Jasper's face lit with pride. "You'll do just fine inside."

Natalia's chest constricted. She'd thought herself ready, but as Gold hooked her arm through his, her heart kicked up a storm. *Was she ready?* Each beat was giving her different answers.

As she went to confront the conflict, her feet tapped against marble floors. Being inside her mind had allowed her body to be guided without her knowledge.

I have to be here, she tried to encourage herself. *If I want to be a real Creature, I need to be here.* She had the genetics. She just didn't yet have the approval or validation to truly become what she should've always been.

Sarah, Jasper, and Peri, sidled through a pair of double black doors before Natalia could say goodbye. Natalia's father at least stayed, only to stop Natalia and Gold two paces later.

He kissed her forehead. "You're brave and smart," he whispered. "And you're a Fairy. Keep calm and do as they instruct. I'll be here. I love you, my Natalia." He gave her another kiss and then followed behind the black door, also not waiting for Natalia's words.

Closing off her mind from invading thoughts, she again linked her arm with Gold's. His fangs extended; though it was only the third time Gold's fangs had appeared, Natalia felt more impending doom from the unexpected meeting awaiting her.

She wasn't awarded time to dwell or panic about anything as the white doors ahead swung open. All eyes turned to her. It would've felt like a mock wedding if a sense of dread hadn't nestled inside her chest.

Gold lead on and Natalia kept her gaze ahead, trying to pretend her heart wasn't crying out, urging her to run in the opposite direction. Eyes were watching, attempting to slice her down the middle to see what was written there.

The further she got down the white walkway, the more she wished she was insignificant. She was just a girl who hadn't known she was really a Fairy. But that's *exactly* what these people found so intriguing. This kind of news demanded attention. She was real-life gossip being paraded before them.

Flickering candles illuminated the church-like setting, despite the sunlight outside. Beautifully depicted pictures of Creatures were animated in the lofted glass windows – there seemed to be a Mermaid, a Fairy, even a wolf. Though the windows didn't sit as high as the wooden beams that stretched towards the white ceiling that might possibly be out of reach of even magic. The gaping audience themselves sat on matching wooden pews split in two halves on either side of the walkway.

Before Natalia could ask for more time, or a longer walkway, she was forced to stop. Gold detached their arms and kissed her hand with warm lips. He wandered away to stand by a long marble table.

Natalia twisted her head to find someone familiar, someone comforting, and caught Jasper. He shook his head once, slowly. Natalia's shoulder blades itched and she grimaced. Immediately she turned back to face the front.

A door beside where Gold stood creaked. Exactly seven figures emerged. All were dressed in black cloaks, hoods pulled over their heads. Gold kissed their hands one by one as they swung past to take their seats behind the large table. Natalia had been told the Council was made of elected members, one from each faction of Creature, and they would serve out their terms until they left on their own accord, were killed in battle, or were wanted to be replaced.

"Natalia Whitebell," one of them called; it was hard to discern *which* one. "Step onto the platform."

A white platform, about five feet squared, lit up in front of her. With a deep breath, she climbed onto it. No one would miss what happened now; she wanted to curse at whoever would listen for displaying her like some freak as the platform ascended, raising her. The only thing giving her the confidence to stand was the knowledge that there was support at her back.

"Female," another voice from the table rang, though rather nonchalantly, "Recently turned eighteen. Father is Human. Residency on Venderly Island. Mother is dead." Natalia's heart-rate increased at the mention of her mother. "Mother was a child of the stars, as is the child here."

"The Fairy was lost from us." This voice sounded feminine. "She was discovered by the recently relocated Darby family after a Calefaction attack. She sustained a leg injury as a result."

Another voice chimed in. "She has been learning the ways of our world. She has considered the possibility of training and following our God-given Purpose."

How could they read every part of her? It was disconcerting. What magic was it? Yet she remained like stone. The growing murmur behind her back was silenced with a flick of one of the cloaked figure's hands.

The Creature at the far left end of the table moved their hood and Natalia could see their pale lips move from beneath it. "Natalia Whitebell, Fairy. Can you confirm these facts?"

Gold faintly nodded. "I can," she said, her voice airing a confidence she didn't exactly feel.

"I can *Council*," one of the hooded barked.

"I can, Council," she repeated.

"Everything said is correct?" asked another.

"It is, Council."

"You are a Fairy, your mother a Princess to the Fairy Throne," another murmur rose from the crowd, again hushed by a raised hand, "making you an heir?"

"So I've been told, Council."

"And you wish to join our cause? A Purpose, a *destiny*, given to each Creature. A Purpose which in our hearts we all know and must follow. A Purpose that means stopping Monsters from taking our Worlds for their own selfish devouring. A Purpose that will last a lifetime, and beyond after you're gone."

"I think I do, yes."

"*Council.*"

"Council," Natalia added. Each question showed the weight of her answers.

"You wish to see each soul as a precious force, one that must be saved and given a chance to live?" asked the smallest figure at the table. "You wish to see all evils from the worlds gone? Even if that may mean some of your own kind being ashed?"

Natalia didn't understand. Someone at the table seemed to sense her unease because they explained. "Creatures may become infected by a Monster given injury, or other means, making them mentally vulnerable and susceptible to evil. If it meant saving the rest of Creature kind, would you rid the world of that evil? Would you rid the world of any Creature that promises death against their own kind whether there may be Monster provocation and influence behind the act or not?"

Would she really have to take out her own kind? Would she have to kill those who turned against Creature kind, whether Monster's had caused the change or not? She imagined stabbing Peri with her own trident, strangling Archie with wire, locking Jasper away in a coffin to rot, pushing Noah from a great height.

Natalia knew certain Monsters would have ways to hurt others, ways of causing injury - after all, she'd been a victim. Their main motivation was to wreak havoc and destroy whatever they could. But she'd never considered that there would be those who could infect a Creature until they were no longer themselves. Their very *essence* taken. How often did that happen? And so she *certainly* hadn't thought about Creatures turning against the world on their own volition. Why would a Creature, maybe even a Human, choose to give in to the dark when there was so much light?

"Yes, Council."

This time, they allowed the whispers to be heard. Natalia tuned them out on her own. Her mouth had moved independently, her heart overtaking her head.

She searched her mind for a reason to why she'd agreed but also for a reason for why she wouldn't have. Everyone here would've agreed to something similar, the terms and conditions couldn't have changed. They all knew and followed their Purpose. They had all accepted. And now, so had Natalia.

Having to end a darkened life, one that threatened the sanctity of others, whether through Monster influence or not, *had* to be rare though. How often could a Monster turn a Creature to become one of them instead? Surely the Council just had to specify it in case there *was* the tiniest percentage of a chance an occurrence came - they'd merely covered their arses.

In the end, Natalia settled on hoping it wouldn't happen in front of her if it *did* happen. Because while she sounded brave, she didn't know if she would match up if faced with the situation.

"Natalia Whitebell." Natalia looked up at the figures and silence fell around her like a curtain. "If you were given the opportunity to train, would you move to our City or any other in finding the aid you need to learn?"

That was easy. "Not permanently, Council."

"You wish to stay on your Island?"

"I do, Council."

One with a deeper voice asked, "Who would train you there?"

Natalia restrained herself from turning. "Hopefully, the Darby's, Council."

"They were the ones, were they not, who taught you of whom and what you were?"

"Yes, Council."

"They have been teaching whatever you ask of them thus far?" asked the feminine one.

"Yes, Council."

"What would happen if they were relocated?"

Commotion kicked up behind Natalia. Her eyes caught Gold's and saw him shake his head firmly. She was getting awfully fed up with playing a statue.

However, Natalia's head did turn when Sarah appeared to the right. Sarah didn't stand on the platform and her face was rid of emotion. At this angle, she appeared older while also firmer and stronger. This was her element, after all.

"Council," Sarah addressed politely. "As your documents will provide, I filed for a non-relocation order several days ago. I received the acceptance this morning before arrival. That means, unless my children decide they wish to in the future, my family won't be moving. Our home is now on Venderly Island."

The Council member on the far right nodded. "I assume these documents however do not stretch to Natalia?"

Sarah blinked but her gaze didn't reach Natalia. "She is not part of our family."

"And the mermaid girl?"

"Peri? She *is* covered since she is living with us and is in a committed relationship with my eldest child."

"Well," said the deeper voiced member, "You may be seated, Sarah Darby."

"Thank you, Council."

Sarah looked at Natalia as she passed, flashing a smile like she'd somehow won the biggest toy at a fairground. Natalia couldn't return her gesture. Her heart was pounding inside her ears like a warning.

"Natalia." The voice that spoke was one Natalia didn't think she'd heard yet, though it was hard to distinguish exactly who had previously addressed her and who hadn't. Still, Natalia focused her attention to the Council. "As you are over eighteen and have a Human father, we cannot just relocate you. Well, in theory we can. However, because of the circumstances, if it is your wish to stay on your Island and be trained there, we shall allow it."

The smallest wave of relief hit her. "Thank you, Council."

"That is, if the Darby's are willing to train you? If they are not, you may have to leave behind what you have, then move back after completion."

The words sounded like a challenge, a test that Natalia needed to pass. She could almost sense the Council members grinning behind their cloth shields. Was she willing to give up what she had, her father and her friends, for any amount of time, to become a true Fairy?

From behind, Sarah's voice boomed around the chamber. "We will train her, Council."

Natalia reached for her star earrings as her shoulders itched, praying the motion distracted people from the faintest of gasps she'd made.

It was as if the Council were measuring her will. She didn't know how many more near impossible questions she could answer. Every Creature surely counted, so wouldn't the Council want any Creature they could on their side in the fight against the darkness when they'd probably lost so many to the cause already?

"Very well," one member said, drawing it out. "There is one more matter we must discuss before we get to the final test."

Test? Natalia's mind reeled but she stayed silent, eyes forward.

"A Human followed you through the portal. An *unsolicited* human."

"Oh." The word escaped her mouth *too* quickly.

"You don't deny it?"

What should she do? If she admitted it, she could potentially put Noah's life at risk. But would it be worse if she denied it? Panic spread through her chest like a wildfire.

"He followed me through," Natalia admitted seconds later, though it felt like hours. "He showed up as I was entering the portal."

The smallest looking Council member nodded. "We understand. That is what we thought. Since you were honest, and since your friend seems to be no immediate threat, we have agreed to let it go."

"But it mustn't happen again," said another member. "Next time there *will* be consequences."

Natalia's heart skipped a beat entirely. "Yes, Council."

"I'm guessing he is currently being taken care of?"

"James Darby and two of his children are kindly watching him," Natalia answered, then wondered if that was the right thing to say. "Council."

"Is he to learn of our world? To be given information on us? He *is* Human." The way Human was said, Natalia would have thought it was some sort of curse-word.

Natalia took several shaky breaths. This had to be another test, but some things were more important than passing. "Noah's my friend, Council. If he is awake, James might already be telling him want he wants to know."

"He may remain in Atlantis then, for as long as you are."

"Thank you, Council."

Natalia remained still and unblinking, her stomach flipping, as the Council members all nodded at once.

"One last thing," one of them said. "Reveal your wings, Fairy."

Natalia's heart was ready to leave with her soul detached.

She'd barely seen her gifts at play before; the one time they *really* had come out, besides the occasional dust on her face, she'd been passed out. Forcing her wings out was going to be a problem. She'd never seen them and didn't physically know *how* to get them out.

"Is there an issue?" a snide voice asked.

"No, Council." Her stomach twisted.

Her frantic eyes found Gold's. He didn't move and neither did she, fighting every fibre of her being that was telling her to escape now. Her breathing became strenuous as she searched for anything that would indicate she had wings at all. A cacophonous mess of thoughts inside her head rattled and screamed at each other.

As if the self-shouting was paying off, a wicked twitching began between her shoulders. She closed her eyes in hope.

Nothing flurried out.

"There seems to be a problem," noted one member.

"She looks pained," said another.

"She is new to this. Maybe she hadn't done this before?" presented another. "She's only recently discovered who she is. If the notion and the wings were suppressed for years..."

"Then why would she say she was fine?" asked someone else. "And how can we tell either way?"

"Natalia Whitebell?" one called. It drew Natalia's attention until she stood straight. Her back seized, like glass cutting her skin on the inside, and she cursed. "You have passed everything so far. You need only reveal your wings. Then we can accept you. You would be free."

The smallest member, who Natalia now recognised as the most feminine sounding one, spoke. "We understand this is new, that you were taken into the Human world and lived there, but we need to see them. We have run tests, that is what the platform you are standing on does, but it cannot reveal your most previous thing to us. Only *you* can. And then you will be a Creature. You can live among us, fight alongside us, follow what your birth-right is."

That didn't encourage Natalia much. Had someone not revealed themselves before and therefore had been thrown away, or worse?

Natalia doubled over. She tried feeling for her wings or at least for some sign inside that suggested possession of a pair. Again there was fluttering between her shoulder blades. And again nothing sprung to life.

The moment of surrender came when she stood. There *was* something there, she could feel it. She just couldn't reach it. Someone said something to her but Natalia didn't hear what. The platform was lowering but she couldn't move. She was drowning in a sea of her making.

Appearing from nowhere, four people surrounded her.

A paralysing purple spark slammed into her chest, hitting like a blow from a hammer. Blood rose in her mouth, but try as she might she couldn't spit it out. Seconds passed before another purple spark shot into her back, one that made her entire body run cold. This time, she tipped forwards helplessly, her body limp and useless, landing in the arms of two people.

She was dragged from the room, the tips of her feet scraping against the floor.

8
Carved in Stone

THE ROLLING STONE LOCKED INTO PLACE.

A single candle hung on the wall inside a black metal casing, the flame unmoving. There was no window for extra light, only grey walls. The dim light showed nothing, not that it needed to.

I've really pissed off the Council, Natalia thought with a groan.

She was stuck. Alone. In a stone prison.

There probably weren't even any guards outside. Why would there be? Who would have the strength or power to try and escape? She certainly didn't. She wasn't even convinced anyone would hear her scream and shout through the thick walls and solid door. At least whatever magic had incapacitated her before seemed to be wearing off. An acidic taste lingered in her mouth and her head was cloudy, but there was nothing she could do, and she knew how much worse things could've been. She could feel her body again, though stretching ached still.

Not wanting to give in to the solitary confinement, she tried to stand and instantly lurched sideways, crashing into the wall.

She glanced up at the candle as she reached for it. After several grunts and groans, Natalia seized it and slid it from the casing tentatively. Hot wax dripped across the back of her hand and she winced, but refused to stop.

Once the wax was dripping to the floor and she could see clearer, she inspected the cell. It was a six foot square box with a low-hanging ceiling. Luckily she wasn't big enough to need that much space, however it was still claustrophobic.

Tears swelled in her eyes and she dropped to the floor, the candle light revealing yellow and black straw beneath her. If this wasn't a dire circumstance, she might've found the breath to laugh.

Her head fell against the wall. As it did, she noticed the dents in the stone. Blinking curiously, Natalia guided the candle along the wall, her fingers grazing the lettering. G. M. The further she went, he more the letters repeated.

Pain gripped Natalia's heart like a vice. What dark desperation drove people to engrave walls in the hope it would allow their voices to be heard?

The Council had her thrown in here for not presenting her wings, wings she wasn't entirely convinced she *had*. For disobeying, she'd been cast aside like she was nothing more than the straw she now sat on.

Stroking the letters on the wall, finding all the cuts and grooves, she hoped there would be no need for her to leave any desperate messages behind. But a tear slipped down her cheek and she found herself wondering if her headband was strong enough to carve into stone.

Noah's view was beautiful. The sun was setting beyond serene waves and the most wondrous lamps were being lit in the streets below.

What was at the heart of this place, or was it the heart itself? Maybe it was both. Maybe the magic kept the heart beating and the heart's rhythm kept the magic alive in an endless cycle of self-dependency.

When he was younger, Noah had dreamed of Vampires and

Werewolves and Witches. He even remembered asking a shopping mall Santa one year to send him a Creature he could go on midnight adventures with. Now that wish had been laid before him. Those downstairs were telling him that the things he'd dreamed of were *real.*

Should he believe in childish dreams all these years later?

The man with the miss-matched eyes, one gold and one blue, had elongated his canine teeth on command until they'd touched near his jaw. The girl with the curly brown hair had cracked and morphed until there was no Human body left, a wolf in her place. The older man, the father figure with a kind smile, had taken time to explain everything to Noah, answering his questions, concerns, and quandaries.

And what Noah could deny least was that Natalia was here. She also wasn't. Tony had come back to this house nearly in pieces, the whites of his eyes red, claiming Natalia had been taken from him.

Was waking up here the same for Captain America when he was woken up seventy years later into a world he didn't know? Was this how he felt about not having his Bucky at his side?

Noah scrambled from the window when a knock echoed through the room. A girl with cropped black hair entered like she wouldn't have stayed back even if asked. She smiled, the door closing behind her.

Can I trust her?

"D'you want to talk, *amore?*" she asked. Noah noticed the slight accent. *Italian?*

"I think that man explained enough," he answered honestly.

True, it *had* been explained, and there were things he couldn't deny, but the whole premise of its reality made Noah dizzy. He'd thought about applying a damp cloth to his head. Was someone playing a prank? Was this Natalia's doing? Should he go throw up?

Though Noah hadn't said much, the girl's smile said he's shown plenty. "Natalia acted the same," the girl told him. "She was lost and confused at first too."

Noah licked his lips, his braces making them dry. "And now?"

The girl sat on the loveseat at the bottom of the bed. "She didn't have much of a choice. She's one of us. For you, it's different."

"Creatures and Monsters being real?" Noah's own words sounded wrong, like his own voice was being echoed but they'd been twisted on return. "It's not—" he cut himself off then tried again. "I heard the whirling wind—"

"Portal," she corrected.

"I heard the portal."

Her voice turned gravely serious. "You shouldn't listen to those voices."

He slumped down beside her. "I'm not," he assured. "But I *heard* them, only once and only briefly. And then there's all the things I've heard since. My whole view of life has shifted. Knowing my dreams and nightmares are real is a little," he indicated "little" by holding his hands several feet apart, "life-changing." He put his arms down.

"You're doing better than expected."

"What?" His stomach certainly wasn't agreeing.

"Not many people take this very well. You only passed out from the portal ride for a short time." A playful glint entered her dark eyes. "And you're dealing with all this information rather well, even if the Human part of your brain is trying to convince you that Creatures and Monsters don't exist when you can clearly see they do."

"Should I be proud? Proud that I'm dealing well and my *brain* is changing?"

"Natalia would want you to be."

Noah swallowed the lump in his throat. "Where is she? I saw her moments before stepping through that," he swallowed again, "portal. I haven't seen her since. Is she ok? I thought she'd be with her dad."

"She was," the girl said.

Past tense didn't sound good. "What's going on?"

The way the girl pressed her fingers against her stomach as if she was about to be sick sent a ripple of unease along Noah's spine. "Natalia had a Council meeting. But things didn't go to plan." Wetness brimmed at the edge of her eyes as she looked at him. "She was supposed to reveal her wings."

"Wings?"

"It was their last request. After that, she would've been free."

"What happened?"

The girl's voice was sorrowful. "She didn't show them."

The worry inside him was justified and hit peak levels. He was sure he was *seconds* from needing the bathroom now. "Why? Why would she do that? Or, *not* do that?"

The girl shook her head. "We don't know. But we're sure the Council will hold another meeting in the morning with her. They usually do in these situations, to give a second chance. Maybe she'll have better luck this time."

Noah didn't want to think about it but asked, "And if she doesn't?"

"There's a back-up plan being cooked up."

Noah asked no more. What even was there to ask? Plenty, he realised, but no questions he wanted the answers too right then. Without Natalia, he was left in a limbo debating whether this was real or not, and it didn't sound like she would be there any time soon to help him.

For all he'd seen, for all his heart wanted to jump at, having Natalia at his side to show him the path to the truth would be the guiding hand he needed. He'd spent eighteen years believing one thing, so it would take a near magical miracle to change. If those things really did exist.

"Do you want something to eat?" the girl asked, standing.

"What about Natalia?"

"Until the morning," the girl's eyes dropped, "we can't do anything."

Noah stood up but it was a mistake. He raced into the nearest bathroom and barely made it to the sink before all the churning acid and his breakfast came out.

Peri crept stealthily down the stairs, but despite her silence, a shape sprung before her at the bottom. Thrusting out her trident in panic, it collided with something with a *clang*.

The hall light flared, illuminating Gold's silhouette. His hand gripped the end of Peri's trident; one spike rested inches away from his collarbone on a broach decorating his jacket. Gold uncurled his grip as Peri withdrew her trident, folding it to fit back into her dressing gown pocket.

"I wasn't expecting anyone to be awake," she stated. She moved away down the hall. Though she heard no footsteps behind her, she somehow knew Gold was following.

He zipped past and appeared in front in the kitchen doorway. "Have you forgotten what I am? We roam the night."

"You *can* walk in the light fine, for now." She ducked under his arm and went to the fridge, pulling out a carton of orange juice. "Want some?"

He raised his neat eyebrows. "Are you alright, dear girl?"

Peri poured two glasses. "Yes," she cocked her head. "Why?"

She picked up her glass and the smell offered some relief to the pent up energy coiling in her stomach. The drink itself slid down her throat coolly. Before she knew it, she was finishing the glass and pouring another.

"I'm just drinking," she justified when Gold remained silent yet poised.

He pushed his untouched glass away. "How long have you been drinking that like that?"

"Not long." She put her cup in the sink. "A couple of..."

Her voice trailed off. Her mouth dropped open with realisation over what he might be implying, his unsaid words smacking her brain as if he'd told her outright.

Though her trident was no bigger than a garden folk, she brought it out and pointed it at him threateningly. Her heart hammered in her chest and a cold sweat brewed along her skin. She fought the urge to jump into the nearest body of water and swim away in its current.

"Not a word," she demanded in a whisper. She pocketed her weapon again. "*Please,*" she begged.

Gold crossed a finger over his undead heart. "My word."

"This might be nothing," she continued, trying to assess aloud. "There's a lot going on. We have Natalia and the Council to worry about. And we're in Atlantis."

Gold circled the counter until Peri was tucked into him, his arm over her shoulders, her side pressed into his ribs. Warmth rushed over her like a blanket and she knew what Gold was doing. It worked too because her shoulders relaxed and her stomach stilled.

"Perhaps Atlantis might be the best place?" Gold suggested. She tilted her head at him like he'd grown three heads. Even without his monocle, his golden eye was intense – where was it? "If not," he drew something from his silky blue pyjamas, "you may come to my place." Gold tucked a card into the pocket she stored her trident in. "All you have to do is shake the card. The rest will be managed according. Just, please, phone ahead first."

Peri removed herself from the Vampire, instantly missing his warm touch. "Thank you."

"I understand," he said.

And she believed he did.

He left the room silently, his drink untouched. Peri downed it quickly, only partially because she didn't want it to go to waste, and put the cup in the sink after.

She tip-toed all the way back into her room, shutting the door behind her and placing her trident onto the dressing table. Her gaze shifted to Archie as he rolled over in bed and rubbed his face until his eyes cracked open. He swung an arm above his head, propping it up, the blankets slipping downward to expose his bare chest. Peri grinned, a mischievous glint entering her dark eyes.

"Oh, my *amore*," she whispered.

"Darling?" He watched her through barely open eyes. "Are you alright?"

She dropped her dressing gown and moved the duvet aside. She slid on top of Archie, pulling off what little she'd had on and pushing against the nothing he had on. One of his hands instinctively touched her thighs, drawing patterns into the skin, while the other snaked upwards to hold the side of her neck, his pinky against her collarbone. She bent forwards, pinning her hands against his firm chest.

"How are you?" she whispered, kissing the corner of his mouth.

"Kiss me properly," he groaned.

Again, she kissed the corner of his mouth and giggled. Archie shifted his hands and suddenly Peri was captured beneath him, his hand still touching her throat. The pressure wasn't crushing, it was merely a hold, one Archie knew Peri liked.

"I did tell you," he said, grinning.

"I wasn't listening," she replied, sliding her hand up his thigh.

He bent to her neck, kissing just below her ear. His voice was soft and sensual against her skin. "I'm going to be listening to you."

"*Ti voglio.*"

Peri gasped in surprise when Archie bit her ear then resumed kissing down her throat to her breasts. She loved the gentle kisses and the way his hands moved the opposite. And when he took the lead, Peri didn't mind at all.

Jasper was halfway to the bathroom when a booming roar rattled his bones. He huffed. "Can I piss in peace?" Another roar. "*Please?*"

Seconds later, another came.

Jasper dashed to the bathroom, did what he needed, and waited. Nothing. But Jasper knew that sometimes hearing silence was worse. He threw on a shirt and jumper despite Atlantis' usually warm climate.

Running downstairs while shoving on shoes wasn't his smartest idea, but he managed to descend without falling. He stopped on the bottom step to tie his laces, his family joining him a moment a later.

"Is something out there?" Alex asked, untying her messy hair only to put it back up. Jasper decided to not point out her screwed up t-shirt or the sleep still evident in her eyes. "Are we going to check?"

"I don't plan on leaving it to the Council," Jasper remarked coldly as he stood. He hadn't liked the Council much before and now he had an even more burning hatred for them. "And I don't plan on waiting for them to throw us in a cell for *not* being out on the streets."

Alex crouched, putting her palms to the floor and bowing her head. Peri extended her trident with a flick of her wrist. Archie straightened his jacket and with a snap of his fingers, the tips glowed green. Their mother gave a nod, saying that she'd watch on but wouldn't be joining, while their dad was tying his shoes.

They flung themselves out the door. Jasper paused as a voice called out for him to wait. He whirled round, coming face to face with Natalia's friend, Noah the Human. His clothes were a crumpled mess as if he'd slept in them, and his lips were dry and cracked.

"You're not coming," Jasper told him sternly before he could utter a word.

Natalia wouldn't want you to go, he thought. *And she wouldn't forgive me for letting you.* He had no idea why he thought it, yet he did.

Noah stood taller. "Excuse me?"

Jasper moved his body to block the exit. "You're Human."

"And? I know you're all Creatures."

"Whatever is out there, what we're heading towards, *won't* be."

"Oh." Noah took a sinking step back. "It's not a Creature?"

A piercing, howl-like sound tore through the open door. Noah jumped backward and Jasper took his chance. He lept back, grabbing the door's handle on the way and slammed it shut.

He turned to the empty street, his family long gone. To no one, he answered Noah's question. "I don't think it will be."

A roar, one so familiar in Natalia's brain, dragged her from her dreary slumber. Questions filtered through her subconscious with rapid efficiency. How long had she been asleep? How had she even managed to sleep in such an uncomfortable place? Had a noise at all woken her, or had a memory leaked into her dreams?

She reached for the candle in the dark. The flame was long gone, dried wax plastered to the floor holding it upright.

Yanking it free, the flame burst to life. Natalia almost threw the candle in surprise at both the magical flame and the second roar that ripped through her cell, echoing over the stone. Natalia gulped. A noise enough to penetrate solid stone had to be powerful. It had to be close too.

She stood, waiting for someone to shunt aside the stone from wherever the doorway was.

She counted to one hundred before it sank in. No one was coming. Who cared about a prisoner? What did it matter if what was coming came for those convicted of a crime?

Bile rose in Natalia's throat when she heard the bone rattling noise again. She gripped the candle like a weapon, clenching her jaw. If no one was coming to recuse her, then she was going to save herself. She faced the direction the roar sounded strongest, holding the candle out before her like it could ward off whatever was coming. The subduing magic that'd been used on her earlier was still dormant under her skin, a weakness inside her body, and so she still couldn't tell which wall was the moveable one to escape.

As if someone or something was listening to her jittery thoughts, the wall behind her began to grind and shift until she was staring as a body-sized gap. But the stone seemed to stick in its movements from there. Taking no chances, Natalia scraped through the opening.

Once on the other side, the stone slammed back into a place.

Natalia glared at it. *How did the stone move?* she thought. *Would I have been left to rot if it hadn't? If I hadn't made it through fast enough...*

She pushed the thoughts aside and inspected the narrow corridor. Water, a couple inches deep, drowned the stone floor. Natalia's feet sloshed in it as she moved.

Turning, she found another cell sitting opposite hers. From this side of the door, it was clear what parts of the walls were cells, the doors of solid round stone easily recognisable even in the dim light. This particular door had a large triangle ridge broken away. Natalia crept closer and an arm poked out. She dropped her candle by accident but sank to her knees on purpose, grabbing for the hand.

A girl squirrelled her way out, breathing audibly despite the darkness of the corridor. Though the lighting was dim, only a few candles linking the walls, Natalia could see the terror controlling the young girl's gaze.

Natalia wasted no more time. She took the girl's hand again and ran.

Ascending steps loomed before them. Natalia pushed the girl ahead, wanting to be sure she escaped. If something happened, Natalia could find another way. But the girl stopped.

"Keep going," Natalia encouraged.

"I can't," the girl whispered. "There's stone."

Climbing up to her side, Natalia reached out, brushing her hand against solid stone. The girl was eight. But it didn't make sense. These steps couldn't have led nowhere. This *had* to be their way out. Without any light, it was hard to see if they had any other options, but would it even matter? What was going on?

Natalia bent so she wasn't as close to the ceiling. "What Creature are you?" she asked, wondering if it would be any help to their current situation.

"Werewolf," the girl said. "I was bitten a week ago. The Council found me two days ago and locked me away because I'd been bitten by accident. Apparently, I needed a trial to find what happened and who'd bitten me."

"*Fuck.*" Natalia glanced at the girl. "Sorry." The girl offered a weak smile.

Just as she went to speak again, her body grew hot. She stood and forced the girl back down a few steps. Cautiously, Natalia reached up, her fingers barely grazing the ceiling before she pulled back like she'd been burnt.

Everything clicked.

Her throat clogged and her tongue felt like sandpaper. The sweat that broke out wasn't heat related. Her stomach flipped and her heart both wanted to stop and run faster all at once. Her entire soul rolled like waves washing out to the ocean and not to the shore as if nowhere, in her mind or in reality, was safe.

Natalia forced the younger girl back even further, relieved when she didn't protest. If this stone was burning, whatever was above must be too. The situation had suddenly been raised from extreme to near deadly.

Fairy dust can break and dismantle some Witch spells.

The thought hit her like a bolt of lightning. Natalia closed her eyes. Her dust usually came intermittently, more frequent however when she was nervous or embarrassed. She needed a moment that would set her on edge now to bring forth the dust.

She touched her hair, where Jasper had slid the band into. He'd been helping her, she knew, like he'd done plenty of times before. And while meant nothing except offering aid, it still sparked something inside her, something she'd never felt before; her head spun at the memory and her face heated.

She touched her cheeks as she opened her eyes. Dust coated her fingers when she pulled them away.

Over her shoulder, she yelled, "Close your eyes and cover your head!"

She didn't wait to see if the girl had done as asked and began to mark the stone above, smearing her hand and subsequently the dust across its warmth. Moments later, she covered her head with her arms and fell flat against the steps.

The ceiling burst like it was blown apart dynamite.

Rock and rubble rained down. Natalia choked and when the shifting stopped she dug herself out. Fresh air filled her lungs as she observed her handiwork. The damage was more expansive than she'd thought she was capable of. Ten people could easily climb through the hole at once. Though the result was bigger than predicted, her dust had done the desired job. But how had she done it?

How was I not crushed?

She wondered if she'd managed to throw up a shield accidently, but had no time to ponder it as the rubble beside her began to shift.

She dug around until her hand contacted something solid, the girl's head appearing above the surface after several forceful tugs. Her face was coated in grey ash but she was breathing.

Under the glow of the streetlamps that beamed on them, Natalia took in her companion. The girl couldn't have older than twelve. Her black hair hung in several braids, there was one golden earring in each ear, and her dark brown skin matched her beady eyes, alive below curved eyebrows.

Together they scrambled up the last few steps until they were safely outside. Natalia frowned, noticing they were outside the Council building, the fountain still spraying. The girl pointed at something and tried to pull free, and Natalia's gaze settled on a man and woman. They searched frantically, over-turning the rubble of fallen house tiles and crashed out wall.

Natalia let the girl's hand go but she didn't move away. Instead, she turned to Natalia. "Thank you for getting me out," she said. "I hope I see you again."

"You're a Creature now." Natalia tried to smile. "I'm sure you will."

"Kiva?"

Natalia looked over to the two who had been searching rubbish. Now their eyes rested on her and the girl.

"Bye, Fairy," the girl, *Kiva*, said and ran off.

Natalia nodded and ran in the opposite direction.

The air was hot and sticky. Natalia had to slow down to gather her bearings. Her eyes widened as she saw trees in the distance burning, plumes of smoke rising into the starless sky.

Natalia quickened her pace. Her legs stung and her feet slapped the floor, yet she didn't stop. The closer she drew, the more it seemed everything was shaking.

The next roar was so loud Natalia had to cover her ears with her hands, willing her heart not to shatter like glass from fear.

What Natalia had been hunting arose before her.

The air all but left her lungs. She staggered backwards and tripped, falling to the ground, rough cobble digging into her palms. A Calefaction. Her leg twinged and her mind threatened to show her the memories of the last time she'd met a Calefaction but she blocked them out.

Natalia remembered Jasper saying that Atlantis was surrounded by a magical shield; like the type she could create with her dust but on a grander scale. Atlantis was locked away like a limbo of sorts, though it was within the same plane of existence as Earth. The forests surrounding the city lead to nowhere except back to itself, or at least, that's what Natalia gathered.

She frowned. The whole point of Atlantis being sealed was to keep things in and to keep other things out.

So what was a Monster doing here? How had it gotten in? Natalia thought the only way in or out was via portal. She didn't know much about portals or Monsters, but she was certain Calefaction's couldn't produce portal magic on their own. But then the Darby's *had* admitted to there being pieces of information missing about all Monsters, known and not – whether the information had been removed from records, whether it'd never been discovered because the Monster hadn't been seen ever or for a long time, or because it'd died out.

The Calefaction reared its head, stood on its hind legs, and blew into the air. The fire blazed orange and gold; a mix of beauty and death. When it stood down, the ground rumbled. Compared to the last Calefaction, this one was larger, as if it was more mature in age. Desperately, she searched for another sign of life without moving her eyes too far from the Monster.

But no one was there, just her and the Calefaction.

A Creature. A Monster.

Finding what courage she had left, Natalia wiped her face and adjusted her headband. She tried to remind herself of her dad's words; she *could* be strong. But the words floated away like a child's unrelaxed hand on a balloon string. Facing a room of her own kind was entirely different to facing a Monster alone.

It began circling her, clearly sensing something in its vicinity. Mentally, Natalia ran through what Fairies could do, what gifts and skills they had that could help her, all while knowing there was a clock hanging above her head counting down. Making things worse, there were very little resources at her disposal. No weapons – not that she knew how to use one – and certainly no wings. The best and *all* she had was her dust.

The Calefaction's head whirled, empty black eyes locked onto Natalia. She let out a small gasp, a shiver trickling down her spine. If the Monster's hadn't previously sensed her, it had now.

It stalked towards her. Natalia knew she couldn't outrun or overpower the beast. Did she stand a chance of keeping it occupied until help arrived?

Smoke puffed out of the Calefaction's nose and she gulped. Could the Monster smell fear? Could it hear her heart ticking away like a bomb? As if answering, the Monster's mouth slid open, grinning almost, teeth on full display.

There was no time to curse.

The beast lashed out. The flat side of its paw collided with Natalia's side, smacking her into the air. *Now would be a perfect time to appear*, she thought, calling to her wings. They didn't come. Nor did a scream.

Unable to stop herself, she went arse first through a glass window.

Landing with a *thud*, she scrambled, despite the hazardous glass, for cover beneath the window that was now only a hole. She pulled her knees to her chin, an ache spreading through her bones. The room darkened further and smoke wove through her lungs. She sucked in breath, holding it, swearing it wouldn't be her last.

She nearly screamed when a large white snout poked through the window. The fur brushed Natalia's hair and it took every ounce of her nerve not to react. The snout sniffed around, taking it's time. She shoved a hand over her mouth to try and subdue the whimpers she felt bubbling in her chest.

Slowly, the snout retreated.

To kill a Calefaction you have to choke it.

She didn't know where the stupidity and burst of adrenaline came from, but she jumped up from under the window, revealing herself. The Monster's eyes locked onto her, its mouth opening. All her panic swam to her chest and face, and she touched them. Once the mouth was wide enough, she blew as much dust as she could into it.

A horrid gagging noise filled the silence. The Monster thrashed and retreated hastily. But Natalia refused to back down now. She climbed through the window, instantly aware of how badly her body was singing as she gave chase.

The Monster only made it to the end of the street by the time Natalia caught up. It spasmed uncontrollably, its oversized body shaking like a leaf in the winds. That was when it jolted to the side enough to unveil two shapes running towards her and it.

Fire raged from the Calefaction's mouth.

One person screams were transformed into sounds of popping and cracking. The other person dodged the fire but the Monster didn't relent. It slammed its paw into the person's chest with a direct hit of its claws. Natalia ran for them, to help, and stopped halfway. The person was already on the ground, pinned. The Monster raised its paw a few feet and then it came down again, stabbing right through the Creature's body with vicious black claws. The Calefaction pulled back its claw, flinging red into the air and onto its fur.

The Calefaction turned and lowered to be at eye level with Natalia once more.

"Fairy?"

Natalia didn't move until the Monster grinned again.

Then, she threw herself under its belly. The ground nicked her arm and she bit down her curse, rolling sideways to free herself from under the Monster. Jasper looked equally impressed and confused to see her as he helped her to her feet with a strong hand.

The Calefaction stomped the ground furiously, drawing back Natalia and Jasper's attention. Jasper pushed Natalia aside just as the Monster's head snapped towards them. Its jaw opened, yet it jutted like an animatronic running out of charge. Natalia turned to Jasper, seeing his arms spread wide as pink light and mist poured from him.

Unsure of what exactly compelled her, Natalia walked to the Monster's side. One of its black eyes followed her. Natalia made a show of wiping her dust from her face.

And stuck her entire hand onto its eyeball.

The Monster howled but Natalia didn't relent until her dust turned the whole eye red. Her heart jumped in feverish excitement at its agony. This was her revenge for what had happened, for this time and the last time she'd met a similar Monster, and she didn't care. It felt *good*.

She blew the dust off the back of her hand, scrunching her nose at the white slime that dripped to the ground in globs when she pulled away. She took one look at it and wretched.

"Natalia?" She turned towards the whisper. Jasper had a scorch mark through his shirt and along his shoulder but was otherwise unharmed. His arms were still raised, his body lightened by a pink glow, but his green eyes focused on Natalia as if she was all he could see. "Are you alright?"

She walked to him. "Are you?"

Compelled to touch him, Natalia moved aside the burnt edges of the shirt with her fingertips, making a conscious effort to be gentle.

Natalia was about to inspect the damage, Jasper watching her, when a tearing noise stole their attention. The Calefaction was writhing and twisting behind them. It couldn't properly do it, but it tried shaking its head. Clearly Natalia's dust was leaving a lasting effect. Its face was even drooping on one side now.

Natalia gasped as the Monster combusted.

When she stopped feeling ash raining, she uncovered her head, only to find Jasper's body covering hers. And she was twisted around him too; his head was tucked in and covered by her arms. In the same moment they'd tried to protect each other.

By the time they uncurled from one another a crowd had surrounded them. A few people were fighting tree fires, but most were clustered around Natalia and Jasper.

"The *Fairy* is out!"

The crowd split. Seven figures concealed by cloaks came to be front and centre. From the way they were angled, Natalia suspected they didn't see Jasper at all.

"What are you doing above ground?" one asked.

"Saving my arse," she hissed, blinking in astonishment. Adrenaline coursed through her. She'd almost been killed. Twice. Once by rocks underground and once by a Monster above ground. And these people had the audacity to question her motives as if she was a common criminal? "The door to my prison moved aside enough for me to get out. If it hadn't escaped, the ceiling would've collapsed on me. I *also* got Kiva out, by the way, not that you were asking. Forget me. You left a *girl* down there. Then I found the bloody Monster terrorising this sealed city and fought the damn thing! Two other Creatures tried and lost their lives. Where were you?"

A collective gasp ran through the crowd and she knew instantly that no one normally challenged the Council. But all she focused on was Jasper's snort. She didn't dare look at him, knowing she would've fallen apart either crying or laughing, so her focus remained on the Council.

"We were getting everyone to safety," said the smallest member.

"That takes all six of you, does it?" Natalia bit feeling her stomach twist at their response - something wasn't right. "You're the all-powerful Council. I'm sure three of you could've led the people and the other four could've coped taking on the bloody Monster instead of leaving it! I was alone until those two," she paused, pain stinging her chest and mind, "and Jasper arrived."

One of the members turned to Jasper. "Where is your family, Witch?"

Jasper pointed to the smoking trees. "Putting out fires." His tone gave away nothing. "We saw Natalia fighting the Monster in the streets, so while it was distracted, we divided."

"You helped, alone?" someone sneered. Jasper ignored them.

The tallest member, who stood the furthest away, spoke next.

"Due to these circumstances, I see no further reason for you to prove yourself to us. It has been seen you are one of us. For this, you will not be reincarcerated and you will be allowed to return to the Darby's house."

The member with the deepest voice added, "You may stay some days if you wish, or return home now? The choice is yours?" They bowed their head slightly. "For what you did with the Monster, thank you, and we can only apologise for what happened, that we didn't arrive to help you."

"I had Jasper," Natalia told them, holding back what she really wanted to say, just like they seemed to be.

"The boundaries will be enhanced," confirmed the smallest member. "And an investigation into how that Monster got in will be conducted immediately."

The Council swanned away as fast as they'd come, the crowd dispersing with them. Natalia hadn't been expecting an apology, but she'd gotten recognition that she was right, which was more than she'd expected from the Council.

Jasper smirked. "I don't think I've *ever* met someone who's made the Council apologise. *And* they didn't make you address them. I'm impressed."

"You shouldn't be," she said, guilt worming through her stomach. "I feel bad."

"Why? They did *you* wrong."

"Still," she slipped off her headband and a few shards of glass fell from her hair, "I shouldn't have snapped like I did, no matter how many times I nearly died today." Her eyes went to the extinguished trees. "Are your family really over there?"

Jasper didn't press her on what she'd first said. "Mums at home, Noah too." When she went to speak, he added, "But the others are over there. Plus others. Most of the residents had cleared their houses before the Council showed up."

Exhaustion filled her body like lead. She yawned. "I've had enough mayhem, swearing, and near death experiences for one day."

"Are you sure?" he joked, grinning.

"I'm sure. Where's your house?"

Jasper wiggled his fingers. "How about a lift?"

"I've had enough magic for one day too."

"Old fashioned lift it is."

Natalia didn't ask what he meant or try to fight him as Jasper swooped her up and cradled her against his chest. She wrapped an arm around his neck instinctively and his lips curled into a smile; she didn't ask why.

Natalia tucked her head against his collarbone, a little awkwardly at first, but eventually she settled. She breathed in his cold night's scent and silently began to cry.

For the two Creatures who had had died trying to stop the Calefaction – even if it was their Purpose, and they knew death was a possibility, no one deserved it. For Kiva, who could've been crushed as if she were nothing. She even cried for herself and how she risked everything to help, despite not being received here. She cried for all she'd been through and hadn't yet had time to think about.

And Jasper let her. He didn't complain, even as his shirt grew wet with salty tears, her grip on him growing tighter and tighter. He didn't press for an explanation either, just offering silent comfort and support.

It would've been obvious to anyone who looked closely – though no one was around except Jasper, who kept giving her brief glances – that her heart was breaking while also trying to re-form and re-shape.

They wove through the streets. As they passed by more of the edge boundary that touched land, a silver sheen-like wall hummed beside Natalia's ear. Through blurry eyes, she spied the boundary wall glisten and how, about six foot off the ground, there was a red handprint pressed within it.

9
Dance of Daisies

"**A**RE THE COUNCIL STILL OUT SEARCHING?"

Her mother nodded. "Dad's out there now."

"He didn't come home to sleep?"

Alex sat at the round table and realised how much she missed their new home on Venderly Island. It didn't matter that she'd spent more time in Atlantis and Seattle. Venderly felt more like home than anywhere else ever had. Or maybe that had something to do with the family she'd come to be loved by? Too many bad memories were attached to her past, except from her adoption, and that's really where her life began.

This house was smaller than their home, barely enough room to house the six of them, not then including Natalia, her dad, and her friend who had all crashed here last night. But the décor was oddly similar with wooden floors and accents, and green or cream walls.

Sarah sat opposite her, holding her cup with both hands. "He came home for a few hours and went back out at first light."

"Have they found anything?"

"They're still trying to figure out how the Monster got *in*. We know that Calefactions can't teleport—"

"But it got in somehow."

A bare-chested Archie moved into the kitchen, cutting off their conversation. He yawned, running a hand through rumpled hair. Alex didn't need advanced sight to see the red marks on the top of his back when he turned to fill up a mug with coffee. Alex smiled to herself – Peri surely could explain how they got there.

"Gold left last night," their mother announced, staring into her mug like there was something quite interesting at the bottom. "He said he had no other business here and he'd done all he was needed to do."

Alex's hand went to her hair and began loosening a knot. "How much longer are we staying?"

Sarah raised her eyebrows in question but didn't ask. Alex loved that about her; she waited for her children to go to her with their concerns or reasons. "A day or so more," she answered. That hadn't been the original plan, but now they were here...

"Peri needs to repair her trident," Archie said as he took a spot at the table. "We might stroll around the City and get it done today."

Alex scowled. "I thought she was going to the Flower Parade?"

Archie's eyes opened. "I forgot about that! It's the last day, isn't it?"

"March first. Same day every year."

"What about you?" their mother asked. It took Alex a moment to register that her eyes were locked on her.

"Have you ever been?" asked Archie.

Alex shook her head, the knots forgotten. "Eight years down the line."

"Why don't you join Peri? She's taking Natalia."

"And Jasper?"

Archie shrugged carelessly. "Who knows what our brother's doing." Alex enjoyed how he looped her into being "our", making them of shared souls.

"Even he doesn't know sometimes." Alex smiled.

"We'll have a party here tonight anyway," their mother announced. The Darby's always held a garden party on the last night of the Flower

Parade. "And stop worrying about what everyone else is doing." She put her mug down. "If you want to go, ask the girls. I bought their dresses. I can buy you one too."

"This late?"

She nodded confidently. "This late."

Do I want to go?

She'd never experienced it before, simply because she'd never felt like she'd fit in. She had been an orphan and a murderous one. Pasts like that were held against people. Even Alex held it against herself. Never going to the parade was less about not wanting to go and more about not wanting to be accused of something whilst there if something went wrong.

Alex left her breakfast. She was fed up playing the victim *and* the monster. Today was the last day and if she didn't join it this year she feared she never would. This year she was going to bite the silver bullet and say fuck it to the world.

Natalia's wet hair dripped down her back and her body ached the more Peri combed through it. Her cuts and scrapes had been patched but with every brush, the sensation sent electric shocks around her body.

A knock at the door. Peri yelled, "In!"

Noah's head poked round the door. Natalia was so startled and excited at seeing him that she lept from her seat and flung herself at him before Noah stepped into the room. She wrapped into him, relieved he was safe.

Remaining in his arms as she pulled back to look at him, she said, "You're here."

Noah grinned, braces shining. "No thanks to you, princess."

Peri closed the gap between them and pointed the comb towards Noah. "How do you feel?"

Noah tucked the neck of Natalia's dressing gown back into place at her throat. She snorted and Peri glanced between the friends. Noah dropped his hand and his tone grew serious when he asked, "Can I have word, in private?"

"Whatever you have to say, you can say to me too," Peri insisted.

"She's a good friend," Natalia assured him.

Noah seemed to accept that. "Is... all of this real?" His dark eyes were wide, *wild*, desperation visible as he waved his arms as if trying to physically grasp onto something tangible. "Is *everything* real? Are Creatures and Monsters really real?"

Natalia's heart sank through her body. She was well acquainted with the slippery slope Noah was trying to navigate. In fact she was *still* there. Even now, she didn't have a firm grip on the cliff edge she dangled over. But she had the truth now, *her* truth, despite not fully understanding it.

Without warning, Natalia thought of last night and how Jasper had carried her home. She couldn't remember entering this house. Had she fallen asleep in his arms? The memory was unsettling. Her cheeks flamed in response and when Noah gasped, she knew the bronze dust had appeared.

"It *is* real," he whispered.

Her dust had been her best option of proof. Explanations were all well and good, but Natalia remembered words had only done so much for her. It wasn't until she'd had undeniable proof that she'd begun to accept things. Meeting his eyes, she nodded.

Noah's face softened. "This is your life?"

She took his hands in hers. "You're part of this now too," she told him. "You're not a Creature, but you're a Human blessed with knowledge."

"Those people don't come along often, amore," Peri said behind them. At some point, she'd walked away. "We call you Watchers. You're not one of us but at the same time, you are. You can see us, be part of us, without sharing our Heavenly gifts."

"Maybe I should get myself bitten by a Vampire or something? *Really* join you."

"I'm sure Gold would like you *too* much," Peri commented, wiggling her dark and well-shaped eyebrows.

"Gold?" Noah questioned.

"The Vampire who brought me here," Natalia answered.

Noah sighed and removed his hands from Natalia's. He smiled. "So, what's the mission? Are we strolling around this City? Is everyone going to show off their powers in a talent contest?"

How is he handling this so well? "No. There's a Fairy festival—"

"The Flower Parade," Peri cut in, closer.

Natalia turned and Peri was at her side again. She was dressed in a lengthy two strapped, white to blush pink ombré dress that sat beautifully against her golden brown skin. Her cropped black hair was pinned up with pink rose clips. At her throat hung a pink necklace and a stack of bracelets clung to her left arm.

"It's the last day," Peri continued. "And *I'm* taking the Fairy."

Noah pulled a face. "A parade? That's *not* my scene."

Peri smiled, her usually blue painted lips swapped for a gold and pink lip-gloss. "They'll be a smaller party here tonight. The Darby's always hold one for friends and close family as a conclusion to the Parade party. Maybe you'll dress up for that? Who knows, you might meet someone cute."

Noah threw Natalia a wink – she knew that to mean a "no thank you" signal on the last thing Peri had said – and then slipped out the room. He appeared comfortable, much more than Natalia had been.

The second he was gone Peri shuffled Natalia back to the chair and resumed her work.

By the end, Natalia barely recognised herself. Her long brown hair was pulled behind her shoulders, curls pressed into the ends, and a thick band of daises held it out of her face. Her lips were painted a subtle mauve, and the strapless bronze dress clung to her curves, daises stitched throughout the length of the skirt. Her heels were simple, not too high or low.

She looked beautiful.

Was this what being a Fairy meant? Was this how Fairies were supposed to look? She remembered stories of how Fairies were enchanting - what Mermaids could do with their voice, Fairies could do with their faces.

"Yes," Peri said.

Horrified, Natalia realised she'd spoken aloud. "I meant—"

"Don't you *dare* back-track!" she scorned. "You *do* look beautiful." Peri's smile was kind and warm. "And yes, Fairies do tend to be the best dressed at any event."

Peri wasted no time and snatched Natalia's hand, dragging her along. Archie waited at the bottom of the stairs. As the girls descended, he smiled and started snapping pictures with a camera he pulled out from his jacket - candid, action, and overly laughing shots where the girls couldn't hold a serious smile. It all reminded Natalia of prom.

At first, she hadn't wanted to go to the Parade. It'd taken hours of arguing to give in, mainly as Peri wasn't about to relent. Natalia had argued because it seemed unfair for a Parade to happen after the city being ruined and lives lost. But Peri had reminded her that things like this happened all the time. Creatures constantly put their lives on the line and things didn't always go according to plan. Everyone knew what they were getting into when they took up their Purpose - it was their *life*. This was no different. Life was continuing on as intended. And these festivals helped celebrate life and living.

Still, it was one of the hardest things Natalia had to accept.

Peri gave Archie a swift kiss and sashayed past, leading Natalia out onto the streets. Someone shouted their names as a light breeze brushed their skin, and Natalia glanced back to find Alex chasing after them.

Her one-shoulder dress was a deep green, shorter in the front. A stem of pink gladiolus flowers were woven into her wavy brown hair, green leaves and all. Natalia didn't know *how* she knew the flower type, she just did, as if it were natural for her to know.

Natalia turned to the city as the other girls hugged.

Banners of bright flowers were strung up between houses and streetlamps. Fallen petals were scattered along the ground and the walls were decorated with even more vines now.

"Every flower has meaning," Peri explained as they joined a gaggle of similarly dressed people. "We wear what we want to represent or have."

Natalia eyed the crowd. Some wore flowered dresses, some posh suits, and others in between wearing whatever fancy garments they had. They danced in what had been the City's square, though the fountain was absent.

The girls stopped together and Peri took a white ribbon from the large pole that stood in the fountain's place. She passed one to Natalia and another to Alex. As one, they started swinging. Somehow Natalia knew the music and the dance like it had been built into her bones.

Natalia's heart steadily rejoiced. Her soul was living, as if for the first time she understood this was who she was meant to be. The night before washed away, taken to the clouds by the musical rhythm. She wondered how long this bliss would last, selfishly hoping it would be for a while.

"You're wearing roses," Natalia said at Peri.

"Pink roses," Peri corrected as she twirled.

"What do they mean?"

They came together in the dance, their ribbons twirling round one another. "Things like grace, gentleness, joy."

"My daisies?"

Peri smiled sweetly. "Innocence and new beginnings."

"Oh." Natalia looped round Peri and collided with her, their backs touching. "And Alex's flowers?"

Alex danced with another girl, their laughter inaudible but evident on their faces. Peri answered, "The gladiolus represents strength."

Peri was right. The flowers didn't just have meanings for what they were. They had meaning to each person.

The music changed. Natalia unhooked herself from Peri to twist and twirl round other Creatures as the dance required, holding her dress so she wouldn't trip or rip the material.

Innocence and new beginnings, she thought, *how fitting.*

In just over a week, Natalia had come so far. From seeing a giant scorpion, a wolf, and a dead body in the rain, to being attacked by an over-powered polar bear, to dancing in a City she'd been locked away under. Her mind almost couldn't keep up. So many things had happened in so little time, *days* in fact. It was like the world couldn't wait to bring her into the fold, and right now, she was flying through it willingly.

Natalia wanted to be a part of this despite knowing there would be hardship like last night. But, what life didn't have something? This was who she was. Her new beginning. She was a Creature – mind, body, heart, and soul. She wanted this *life* and it belonged to her.

Eventually, the dance ended. Thunderous applause broke out. Peri moved through the dancers towards her, pink-cheeked and grinning. From all her years of dancing, Natalia's heart was elated to finally be blessed enough to do what it loved again, though her injured leg ached in protest.

"Have you done this before?" Peri asked, fanning her face with her hand.

"I used to dance ballet," Natalia admitted.

Peri stopped still. "You never told me!"

"In case you've forgotten, we've had other things to worry about. Dancing was at the bottom of my list of things to admit."

"Speaking of admissions." Peri's demeanour changed. Her left hand went near her stomach while her right stump lay against her chest where her heart was visibly beating under the skin. "I need a drink."

Natalia could've sworn Peri was about to say more, but when she didn't, Natalia didn't press her. "What about Alex?" she asked instead.

"I'm fine," Alex said, appearing out of the crowd. She indicated to the girl at her side. "This is my friend, Farai. We met back when we were orphans here."

Farai grinned, her gaze showing no shame of her past. Natalia smiled back, as did Peri. Natalia couldn't help but admire the girl's white-silk dress and the way the fabric hung off her curves, complimenting her rich onyx skin perfectly. Her black hair was tied up into a sleek ponytail, white earrings and silvery white eye-shadow matching the gown.

"We're just going to spend the afternoon dancing and catching up. I'll meet you at home later," Alex promised. Farai waved and then they were rushing off, their fingers tangled together.

Natalia took Peri's hand and led the way through the crowd, pretending to know where she was going and pushed through anyone in the way. Peri bumped into a young girl, who she called Kei – Peri didn't explain who she was exactly, only that she was a family friend, though Peri didn't look too pleased to see her – and apologised before they made off.

Eventually, the girls approached a wooden stand occupied by an older woman and a young boy. Natalia asked for two drinks as Peri wandered off. When the young boy handed over what looked like cloudy lemonade, Natalia realised she had no way to pay them. What even was the currency in Atlantis? Regardless, she'd foolishly left her money at home. But the boy wouldn't let her refuse. He handed over the large cups and smiled, saying thank you for the service.

Open mouthed, Natalia walked away searching for her friend.

Peri was perched on a wall belonging to someone's front garden. Natalia passed her a drink and sat beside her, careful not to fall backwards, and wondered if the homeowner would find and scold them.

"They wouldn't let me pay," Natalia told her.

Peri laughed, sipping her drink. "They wouldn't. Everything's free when there's a party." She sipped again. "Can I ask you something?"

Music flared up in the background. String instruments and what sounded like a flute were playing away. Natalia's heart pulsed. "Of course. You've done enough for me. It's about time you asked for payment."

"There are conditions," she warned, putting her drink down beside her.

Natalia drank. The liquid wasn't too sour or sweet yet there was something beneath the surface that made her face and body buzz, not like alcohol did. She tried another sip and still couldn't identify what it was.

Peri took Natalia's silence as acceptance. "I'm not going to give you all the details yet and I also don't want you telling anyone about what I'm asking of you."

"Who have I even got to tell?"

"Your dad? Your friend?"

"Promise," Natalia drew a cross over her heart. "I won't."

"I know we barely know each other, but I consider you a friend."

Natalia agreed, not just because Peri had saved her life, but because she'd been there afterwards. Friendship wasn't about how long someone had been in a life for, it was about how that time together was spent and how that person came to make the other feel and think. Peri had made Natalia feel accepted and wanted and equal.

Now was Natalia's turn. Not just to return the favour, but to be a friend.

"What can I do?" she asked.

Peri smiled, her eyes gleaming. "When we get home, I need you to come with me to something."

"Go with you where?"

"I told you, I'm not explaining everything, *amore*. *Non ancora.*"

"Are you sure you want *me*?" Natalia lowered her drink and reached out for Peri's hand with the other as the other girl stared in silence. "Okay," she agreed. "Wherever you want me to go, I will. But how are we going to get to wherever this thing is?"

Peri's smile turned devilish. "Magic."

"Just some old hocus pocus?"

"All *you* have to do is show up. The rest is on me. I'll explain everything later."

Natalia wanted to ask more, but Peri had already said there would be no explanations yet. She only hoped she wouldn't wait too long for answers.

"How about another dance?" Peri downed her drink and stood, holding out her hand. Natalia accepted it.

They were halfway back to the dancing when Peri stopped. An older man and woman came strutting up to them. Both wore royal blue, but neither of them donned flowers, and their eyes were narrow, unseeing.

"Peri," the woman addressed.

"*Madre*," Peri replied. "*Padre.*" The man nodded once.

"I'm surprised to see you here," the woman said, not sounding surprised at all. "And *chi è questa?*"

Peri's grip on Natalia tightened. "This is my friend."

"A *Fairy?*" The woman scoffed. "Speaking of other *types*," she raised her chin, "are you still with that wretched boy?"

"*Wretched boy?*" Peri's voice leaked with acid. Natalia wondered if she'd have to step in the middle of something soon and prepared herself. "Yes. That *boy* is still my boyfriend."

"And we still don't approve," the man replied, his voice gruff as if he hardly ever spoke.

"I don't need your approval."

"Until you have some respect for us and yourself, *buona giornata*." The woman pushed her nose into the air and the pair skulked off.

Once the couple were out of earshot, Natalia asked, "Who were they?"

Peri loosened her grip. "My parents."

Natalia blanched. "*What?*"

Peri sighed heavily. "They don't approve of Archie. They never have. To them, it's beneath me to love someone who isn't of the sea. To them, marriage is nothing except keeping a bloodline and following the Purpose as if they'll receive some sort of crown and payment from the Heavens for being the last ones standing. But no one in the family, except me, really fights because once again, that's beneath them." Peri shook her head with disdain. "That's the first time I've seen them since moving in with Archie."

Peri closed off and Natalia didn't bring it up again.

Until night fell around them, they danced and sang and danced some more – mostly forgetting what they could. Each rhythm Natalia knew the steps to, the tunes familiar, and Natalia couldn't help but wonder if her mother had influenced her knowledge somehow. Had she taught or hummed them to Natalia when she was a baby? But how could she have memories of them when they'd spent so little time together? Natalia's mother died just two months after giving birth.

When the majority of the crowd began to disperse, Natalia and Peri linked arms. They found Alex along the way to the house, and she assured them she would be fine with Farai and would make her way home later.

The girls' swayed their hips as they walked, music still riddling their bodies. If Natalia could take one thing with her from Atlantis, she wanted it to be the music. How the instruments made her very soul feel alive, how each note was like being summoned by a pied piper that she longed to dance over the hills with, how every end came with a new beginning.

They passed a house with wooden boards instead of windows. Natalia gasped.

"Is that..." Peri trailed off.

Natalia's eyes travelled along the devastation. "I think so."

"It's no bother," came a calm, suave voice.

Natalia twirled, finding a man wearing a black suit standing slightly off to the side. A large purple iris was pinned to his shirt – Natalia knew it meant "wisdom and royalty". Natalia would've guessed he was mid-twenties at most, the street-lamps illuminating his handsome face. He smiled and it made him appear even younger, his eyes alive with some sort of awareness.

"Is this your house?" Natalia questioned.

"It is," he confirmed, his accent definitely English.

"I'm *so* sorry," she said, knowing no apology could reverse what she'd done.

"Don't be silly," the man waved her off. "I'm just hoping you didn't hurt yourself on the glass." He watched her intently, waiting for her answer.

"I'm fine." Natalia's scratches had been patched and there really hadn't been anything worse. She took her eyes off the man and rested them on the blocked-up window. "Were you inside?"

"No, actually. I was out of town. I came back this morning to find it boarded." He touched his iris. "I was told what happened, and I know it was an accident. Don't worry yourself over it. Creatures get into messes all the time. I remember a friend got slammed into a car back in London once." The man took his hand from the flower and pulled keys from his jacket pocket. "Now, if you'll excuse me, it's been a long day. I hope to see you around, have a lovely evening." He unlocked the door but turned back to add, "Those that didn't make it to today's sunrise will not be forgotten. Nothing was your fault." He ran his eyes over Natalia's face as if seeing something there, then slipped inside.

Natalia's mind flashed with the images of the fallen Creatures but she shoved them away, knowing the man was right. Those incidents weren't her fault. While they were tragic, that any loss of life was unfair, all Creatures had the same Purpose: to rid the world of Monsters. They'd simply been fulfilling theirs. It just hadn't gone to plan.

The girls didn't speak on their walk, they didn't need too; all between them had been said.

Peri barely knocked on the door before it swung open. Archie laughed as he watched Peri sway, promptly helping her inside when she tumbled into the doorframe. When Peri was seated on the stairs, Archie offered a hand to Natalia. She accepted despite clearly not being as buzzed as her friend. But how? Had three cups of that lemon drink been too much? What was even inside it? Natalia had forgotten to ask. Whatever it was, Peri was feeling the effects more than Natalia was.

Once Natalia was inside, Peri and Archie quickly became distracted with one another. Natalia hid her grin as they walked away, then jumped at an unexpected arm around her waist, a hand brushing her cheeks gently.

She was spun in their arms and Jasper smiled down at her, tracing his thumbs along her cheekbones. The green of his eyes was enchanting, an encapsulating spell only they could create. His wavy hair seemed longer, not enough to disturb his eyes and cover his entrancing stare, but long enough that it came down to touch the top of them, more so when he grinned.

"Are you alright?" he whispered.

She searched his face. "I've been worse."

He let her face go and surveyed the dust, *her* dust, coating his palms. "Are you sure?" he questioned. He stepped closer until the tips of their shoes touched. "You seemed flushed."

"I don't think I would be if you weren't so close."

Jasper smirked and Natalia was relieved, like things between them were still normal. After being carried last night, she'd feared what he'd say or how he'd act, as if it might've given him an excuse to no longer be around her. Clearly her assumption about the situation had been wrong. And she was glad for it.

"Daisies," his eyes left her face for her dress, "for new beginnings."

She noticed the flower he wore on his black jacket. "A chrysanthemum," she commented, running her fingers over the delicate petals. "For joy and optimism. They're my favourite."

"Are they really?"

"Which bit are you asking about?"

He smiled, illuminating his entire face. "If they're your favourite."

"My mother liked them too apparently."

Jasper brought his hand up to hers, a spark igniting under his fingertips. He guided her hand around his neck, weaving her closer, then did the same to her other hand until her fingers interlocked behind his head. Natalia's heart stirred like a caged lion, or like a chick waiting to take its first flight; the nerves and the power raced through her until it was all she had to hold.

"We should dance," he suggested.

Natalia's cheeks dusted again. "Should we?"

"This festival is about dancing."

Jasper slipped his hands around her waist, holding her as if she would hurt him, not as if she herself would break. The entire time his gaze flitted between his hands and her face, making sure she was ok with his actions.

"*Actually*," he continued, "it's about letting go of your past year and going into a new one with a full heart and desire to reach for what you want. The flower, or flowers, you choose are supposed to represent your ambitions for the new year."

Her eyes travelled down her dress briefly. "A new beginning."

"Is that what you want?"

His smile was infectious, so she returned it when she answered. "Yes."

"Then you understand your own kind. You understand what you

desire and what you want to see this year, making it yours, and so you'll reach to the stars for it."

They began to dance with ease, moving in time to their own cadence without music to direct them. They held one other as if the other completed their secrets and thoughts, ones that they harboured separately yet made complete sense when together.

"I didn't know you could dance," Jasper said. He spun Natalia away and back again, catching her hand on return, holding it to his chest. She could feel his heart pounding.

Natalia's stomach squeezed. "You did."

"Just an inkling."

Her stomach pinched. "It's more than that."

"You are a Fairy," he said, looking at her approvingly. They stopped dancing but didn't move away and Natalia's heart drummed frantically. "I saw your ballet slippers in your room."

She unhooked her hand and moved away. Jasper's hand lingered in the air for a moment before he pulled it to his side. His look of disappointed quickly changed to curiosity when Natalia started undoing her shoes. Her dress skimmed the floor and she threw the shoes into the corner once they were completely off.

"You're going to have to help," she half demanded.

He visibly swallowed. "What?"

"You didn't ask, but you want to see me dance." She stood taller, her back straight, legs ready to start at a moment's notice, her arms poised to guide her.

Jasper's green eyes glimmered. "It would be my pleasure."

She tip-toed to him, putting her hands on his shoulders. "I haven't tried this since the day you broke into work's kitchen."

She waited for him to say he'd never broken in, but Jasper only grinned.

The hairs along her arms stood on end the same way they used too. She sucked in a lungful of air, heart hammering, and focused on control. This wasn't a performance for a stage and that was more nerve-wracking.

She bobbed to flat feet and then back up to tip-toe. As she stood tall again, she threw her left leg back at a ninety-degree angle from her body – a left leg arabesque. Her skirts rose and she twisted herself around. Jasper's hand grabbed her ankle while in motion, and she stopped, her body facing away from him.

When she bounced her left leg, Jasper let go, and she rolled her body. Three times she twisted herself over. Then, she stopped. She spun on her right foot in a pirouette, her hair whipping her face as she went three times round. She drew her left leg to her right, and then pushed it out in another upward sweep, motioning for Jasper to join the dance.

He pulled her towards him, his hands clawing up her leg, and, as her body flattened against his, he lifted her, spinning; he had one hand by her bent knee that was sticking out and the other at her waist. Natalia was his arms, his face in her neck, his breath bewitching her heartbeat.

Natalia bent her arms around Jasper's head, gliding down as slowly as he lowered her. When her feet were grounded, she spun round. She saw in his eyes that if she were to jump, he'd catch her.

So she jumped.

Jasper indeed caught her in his arms and she glided through the air. She was a dove above an endless ocean, her mind among the stars as she floated through space, and her heart was not done playing the game she couldn't lose.

They repeated the same move twice; both times Natalia spun then jumped, her arms wide, her face to the ceiling, and her body at Jasper's mercy.

The third time was different.

That time, he wouldn't let her fly above him. She straightened out, wondering suddenly if she'd hurt him. Peering down, there was an incredulous smile on his face, one that said he couldn't believe what was happening. Natalia shared the smile back.

He lowered her with incredible mastery, his hands guiding up her legs, her skirts rumpling around her body. Her body pressed against his until her face was inches above his.

She rested her hands on his face. Just like she'd wanted to since the first moment she'd seen them, her fingers delicately traced his freckles. The more she danced across his skin, the more he seemed to smile. His eyes wandered over her face, like he couldn't believe what he was seeing and wanting more of it, and they lingered on her lips. Her heart thudded like it was struggling to keep up.

"You're not bad," he whispered.

"Is that all you have to say?"

"There's a lot I want to say."

A sliver of hair fell near his eyes and she brushed it aside as he lowered her further.

When at last her feet touched the ground, Natalia drew herself to him, tilting her head. Jasper mirrored her; his eyes continually danced to her lips as if checking something. As their eyes began to shut, their faces, nearing, the door banged open.

Their faces sprang apart. The lingering touch of his hand against her back sent sparks along her skin, the origin of an explosion bursting inside her chest which had been left unignited.

Dust sprang to Natalia's cheeks when Alex, grinning like the devil, appeared in the doorway. "Did I interrupt?"

"Would you care for my answer?" Jasper retorted, an underlying annoying coating his tone.

"I wonder if that's the work of Lemonspark," Alex wiggled her eyebrows, "or not?" She walked off whistling without explaining what she'd come for.

Natalia looked up at Jasper, finding him stone faced. "What's Lemonspark?"

He broke from his trance and stared back at her, pushing his hair from his face. "It's a Fairy drink served at the Flower Parade," he answered. "There are few Crystals that Vampires and Witches can't use, and the Spark is one of them. Only Fairies can use it. Its magic is added to lemon and other ingredients to make the drink. For Fairies, it's not so bad. To other Creatures, it gives them drunk-like symptoms without having alcohol, but worse. More intense." The hand on her back slid up, drawing her closer. "Natalia—"

"It's ok," she cut in.

Had the moment they'd shared been a production of Lemonspark? She knew she'd had some, that must've been what her and Peri had drunk. Had Jasper had a share of some? Had what happened been nothing more than a drunken scene? It stung to think about and tears readily formed in the corners of Natalia's eyes. But *why* did it sting so badly? Uncertainty rested inside her heart, a beat she'd never felt before. It was like her heart knew something yet wasn't telling her head. What was it?

Once again, there was too much to try and understand. And, once again, Natalia found herself stumbling blindly on a path she couldn't see the ending of. She blinked away the tears.

"How about a drink?" Jasper asked, changing the subject. He took his hand off her back and held it out like a gentleman.

She accepted it. "That sounds like a good idea." Natalia tried to smile and wondered if it was cracked.

"Drinking nearly *always* sounds good. But it takes some of us longer to actually get drunk." As they reached the doorway, Jasper frowned. "I hope that didn't make me sound like an alcoholic."

"I'll keep an eye on how much you consume," she promised.

"You might have to organise an AA meeting."

"Because I have them on speed-dial."

He grinned and she descended into laughter. Moments later, Jasper joined in. She ignored the part of her that ached as they moved again.

When they stopped laughing, Natalia could sense something was biting into Jasper's mind; his smirk didn't sit the same. But she didn't ask. He respected her to come to him, so she would offer him the same leniencies. She trusted that he would talk to her when he was ready.

The kitchen and garden – which flowed much like their Venderly home – were both full of people laughing and talking pleasantly. Jasper took Natalia to the cupboards and offered her several options before she settled on a glass of wine. Sipping it, she allowed herself to fall into the drink, letting it wipe her mind of her aches and worries.

For the rest of the night, Natalia carried on. She danced with Noah – who now wore a smart shirt and a gerbera flower for innocence; he said it was because he is innocent of the world he now was in. Peri and Archie had twirled her around several times too, sometimes it was the three of them together in a chorus of joy. Her dad even tried to entertain her, managing to stand on the ends of her dress in doing so, but he never stopped smiling.

She did give in and dance with Jasper again. This time less intimate than the last. They still had fun, evidence written into their smiles, but something remained between them, an essence neither seemed willing to break open over them.

10
Minds That Wonder

ATHERINE'S KOFFEE AND KAKES was calmer now that the Island's children had returned to school for the summer season. Adults still came and went, so did the business moguls, but the families would only come on the weekends now.

Natalia was thankful for the dwindling numbers. The few days she'd taken off had been during the half-term, and when she'd come back, the slog was nearly over. Nearly three had passed since her short-notice trip. Three weeks of running around the neighbourhood at night to build her strength and stamina, and baking in a sweaty shop or reading her nursing notes during the day.

Mid-March was Natalia's favourite time of the year. Full bloom spring was near. As she baked in the back of the café, she could peer out the window and watch birds dive over the island cliffs. There was mowed grass to smell when a door was propped open and the sun would constantly feel warm the breeze.

"How're you getting on, Nat?"

"Fine!" Natalia called back.

Katherine came into the kitchen anyway. She smiled, her new pink lipstick rich on her lips. "I'm glad you're back," she said, sounding honest.

Natalia took the tray of cooked white and dark chocolate cookies from the oven and let them rest beneath the open window. "I was away only for a few days," she said. The trip had meant to be a few hours but it'd turned into a mini vacation she'd not packed for, but thankfully Sarah had given her a few things so tide her over at the time.

"You better not be planning any more last minute road trips for a while."

"I hope not," Natalia half mumbled.

"In case you *do*," the way she said it made it sound inevitable, "I've hired another hand."

Natalia spun on her boss. "What? Really?"

For as long Natalia as had worked here, Katherine had gone back and forth about whether hiring more help was necessary. There *had* been another temporary worker, but they'd left before Christmas without notice.

Katherine stepped aside. Noah stood there, braces showing as he flashed a dopey grin. Natalia glanced between the two of them. "Hey, princess," he laughed.

"He's been begging me for weeks," Katherine said, clearly faking being annoyed.

"*Noah!*" Natalia cried.

"*Natalia!*" He chimed back.

"There's something I need to discuss with you both." Katherine's voice was solid, almost grave sounding, catching Natalia and Noah's full attention. She closed the door to the café, obscuring the view of the few customers. "When you left, Nat, I knew where you were going. And why." Katherine spoke steadily, taking great care with how she worded things. "Not because your dad told me, but because I know the Council."

Natalia's heart froze. "The Council?"

Katherine nodded. "I told your dad that I wanted to be the one to tell you. He knew the real me. He wanted to tell you before you left, he admitted that. Only because I'd waited and he thought you could do with someone else to talk to. So this is me telling you now."

Katherine touched the tops of her ears and snapped them. Noah gasped loudly. All Natalia did was watch, her mouth agape. Instead of clean rounded edges to her ears, Katherine had ears that reached a point.

"I wanted to tell you before." Katherine fiddled with the fake ear-tops. "Now things are calm enough, it was time I told you the truth. It's what you deserve."

Natalia started. "You're a—"

"Nymph."

"Of?"

"Water." Katherine offered a sad smile. "I'm still Katherine, the woman from Brazil, the boss of this café, the lover of life, the woman who appreciates and loves a pink lippy. I'm just not Human."

Natalia let the words wash her, waiting for them to consume her. They didn't. She released a breath, launching herself at Katherine and wrapping her in a hug. The woman laughed, though Natalia was sure she heard a sniff.

As she pulled back, Natalia said, "Thank you, for thinking of me and for not adding to the pile I was already burning through. I just wish you *had* told me sooner. You're my boss but you're also my friend, Katherine." Natalia managed a smile, hoping it was certain and steady. "I would've been able to handle *that*."

"I'm not going mad, am I?" The girls turned to Noah. He was fanning himself with his hands as if he might pass out. "Did my new boss take off her ears?"

Katherine chortled. "I did."

"I've been here," he looked to the clock, "not even five minutes and the world's gone weird again."

"The world's never *not* been weird. The difference is you can see it now."

"I think I want a refund and to be sick." He went over to the sink and splashed some water onto his face, coming away with droplets stuck to his lashes.

"Speaking of seeing," Katherine turned her gaze to Natalia, "have you seen the Darby's recently?"

Truthfully, Natalia hadn't. Since coming home from Atlantis she'd only seen Peri a handful of times, Archie and Alex in passing once, and had heard from Sarah and James when they'd rung up to announce there was still no news on her application to train and become a full Creature.

Despite having been judged a Creature at heart, clearing the Council's stupid trial, she wondered if shouting at them for their lack of care hadn't been her best move. All she wanted now was to be validated and deemed viable enough to become a Creature like she was meant to, and according to their rules she couldn't train until the papers were cleared. The Council wouldn't withhold her application as a way of punishing her for testing them, would they? Everything still seemed so out of reach, her fingers slipping through fog as she tried to grasp onto what she wanted, what her birth-right was.

Katherine took Natalia's blankness as her answer. "You should go see them," she suggested. "Even if you haven't heard anything, it might be good to be around them?"

"Maybe after work."

Natalia went back to her work. Several moments passed before footsteps echoed softly through the room, and she spied the door closing behind Katherine. She sighed, shoulders dropping.

Noah cleared his throat. When she faced him, Noah had closed the gap between them. She turned away and picked up the icing bag. Whatever he was about to say, because he *would* say something, she didn't know if she wanted to hear it.

"Katherine's right," Noah began. "Seeing them might be good."

She began to make the icing swirl. "How? How exactly would it be good?"

Noah pulled her round, icing squeezing across the counter and onto her shoes. He didn't look at the mess, his eyes focused on her face. "Because *you*," he indicated to all of her, "need to settle everything. They're your friends too, aren't they?"

"Of course they are!"

They'd all done more than they ever should have for her. She considered them friends. They'd taken her dancing and had readied her for the Council. They'd saved her life. But what actually had she done for them? Did they think of her as a friend or just someone to feel sorry for?

"Whatever is going on, you need to sort it out." Noah's eyes showed no signs of a jest. "Why not start training early, on the basics that you don't need clearance for? The Council might have already phoned or sent a letter? You might be approved now!"

"As it regards me personally, they can tell *me* if I'm approved or not," she barked.

Noah ignored her outburst. "You'll be with these people all the time. They offered to train you, remember? So sort out whatever is going on before you get accepted and things become tenser."

"*If*," Natalia felt like she was spitting venom, "*If* I fucking get accepted."

Noah let her go, face dawning with realisation. "Is that what this is about?"

Natalia put her back to him, placing the icing bag down, blinking to rid her eyes of the sharp tears that threatened to spill. Did all Creatures have to be vetted before they accepted? Natalia doubted it. What would happen if they *didn't* accept her? She'd still be a Creature, but wouldn't be able to follow her Purpose. But how could they stop her if she went after a Monster? What happened to those who *did* choose to leave over the years; why would they leave? Did they sometimes follow their Purpose despite probably not being allowed too? What happened then?

"I'll see them after work," Natalia promised. The longer she kept away, the longer things stewed. She turned back to her friend, giving him a weak smile.

Noah eyed the door to the café. "How about now?"

"After work is fine."

"But what if this was the only chance?"

"I need the money and I'm not disrespecting Katherine like that. Plus, they'll be there when I finish."

"You'll be paid in gold by the Council soon."

Natalia scoffed. "I doubt that."

"Quit acting up. You have a short window of opportunity here."

Natalia tried thinking of more excuses, stalling for more time. "It's your first day. I can't have you covering for me already."

"Did you hear Katherine or not? She's *expecting* you to run out every now and again. And if you become a fully-fledged Creature, you'll have to run out of here if there's a Monster attack," Noah pointed out.

"I can't."

"Can't or won't?" he challenged.

Natalia blanched. She felt a pull towards the Darby's, her heart yearning for them as if they were tied by strings, but she didn't know if she was ready. She hadn't been accepted. In her mind, she was still partially Human because she wasn't a fully accepted Creature yet. It was as if she was stuck between two worlds, a limbo. She felt like a failure, and she couldn't face them with pride until she'd been accepted into their life.

Noah grabbed her and marched her to the back door. "You *can*," he insisted. "And I'm making sure you will."

He threw her coat at her and opened the door. Before Natalia could stop herself or argue, Noah pushed her out. She nearly fell and as she steadied herself, the door slammed shut in her face. Her fists pummelled it several times, to no avail. Noah was silhouetted behind it, his body propped up against it to prevent her from getting back in.

Like it sensed her frustration, the sky surrendered too, releasing the looming storm. Rain pelted down from grey clouds as the howling, warm wind shifted the air. So much for a perfect spring.

Natalia huffed and shrugged on her jacket. Now she was locked out of work *and* it was raining.

Gradually, she made her way from the café, no more excuses left to avoid what she'd been putting off. Thunder rumbled across the sky and inside her chest.

Peri slid down the embankment, not taking care as she went. Really, it didn't matter if she fell in. She'd just transform faster and maybe lose some clothes in the process.

This part of the Island, this beach in particular, was separate from the rest – it was its own private space. The path to the diving point on the cliff was steep but someone over the years had had sense, putting wooden steps from the top to the mid-way point. In the weeks Peri had been living here, she'd come to notice that there wasn't much beach; only an area below she currently was had a patch of stony sand. It wasn't much but Peri rarely came to the beach for its sand.

Peri slipped off the flip-flops and tucked them into a cliff nook then removed her dress, leaving her in plain black underwear. Her feet padded against the wood and stopped at the diving-point as she turned to face the cliffs.

Lashing wind whipped her hair into her face, her body tipping. She raised her arms and took a lasting breath.

The thrilling chill of the water sent a spark across her body as she crashed into it. She sank, not as an anchor, but as a willing victim to the waves. As her toes curled into the sandy bottom, a familiar sting rippled throughout her nerve endings.

Her feet seized until they joined together as a single fin. Her legs fused from ankle to hips; bones twisted and warped as her skin was replaced by shiny dark grey scales extending up her waist and covering her bellybutton. Where her bra had been, two equal patches of dark grey scales now concealed her breasts. Her neck pinched, sending a spasm rocking through her entire body, but she didn't dare move before it was over.

Then, she breathed in.

Cold water rushed in and out, air moved slower. Despite being alone, she grinned. Land was welcoming enough, but water encompassed every part of her soul. The water made her what she was; her given home while land was her found home.

Her fin swayed rhymically in the small current. Peri glanced up and noticed she wasn't far from the surface. Her fin twitched. She knew what it wanted. What *she* wanted.

Weaving through the water, she raced upwards. The sunlight drew nearer the harder she pushed. Before she could scream, or laugh, her head burst above the surface. Mid-air, she tried flipping. It had only worked a few times before – she needed the momentum and the right angle.

Her body indeed dived round on itself until she hung upside-down, facing the water. The air pricked her skin and she tried to breathe it, but pure air did little in this form. Then gravity kicked in. She crashed back into the water, a lot less gracefully than her original dive from the cliffs.

She stayed by the surface, only her eyes above the water. As she searched surroundings, a string-like trail caught her attention.

The attachment was on land, high above the cliffs, the source moving. The grey tone of the string was easy to identify. Drawing her face from the water more, she caught a hint of smoke in the air.

Peri darted for shore and heaved herself out, lying with her back against the sand. Her neck spasmed as her gills shrank, her legs descaled and separated. The remnants of a tattered bra covered her chest, and slowly, her hands and feet appeared too. For good measure, she wiggled them; last time she'd transitioned, she'd gotten up too early and had been stuck face down in the sand as a half Mermaid half Human for a while. She cringed at the memory.

"Need some help?"

Peri looked up to find Alex grinning down at her, and she moved her umbrella to cover Peri's half-naked form. Not all water could make Peri transform, and since she'd been a Mermaid her whole life, she could control her shift the same way Alex could control hers. She could dive into the sea and keep both legs, or she could sit on the edge of a paddling pool and transform. But regardless, she was thankful for the cover now that her Human skin was beginning to shiver from the rain that had begun.

Alex handed a bag of clothes over and Peri stood, nodding gratefully. Alex turned her back to give Peri privacy but kept the umbrella raised between them.

Peri changed swiftly, wondering how Alex had known where she was. As if reading her mind, Alex threw down Peri's flip-flops at her feet.

"It's like you're stalking me," Peri joked.

Alex turned, her face giving nothing away. "Maybe I am."

Peri narrowed her eyes. "Did Archie put you up to this? Is he making you spy on me? I *can* find out," she warned. Alex didn't flinch and Peri was a little disappointed but not surprised; it took a lot to shake Alex these days.

"No, he didn't. I was feeling cramped inside the house and saw you dive off the cliff. I got your clothes when I saw you break the surface and then came down to meet you." She pointed to the second set of wooden steps that led down to the hidden stony beach.

Peri's gaze went over Alex's head, clothes forgotten. "Did you sense—"

"The smoke?" Alex shifted the umbrella, though it wasn't raining anymore. "I don't have the ability to sense it in the air as wiggly lines like you, but I can smell it."

Peri fought the urge to roll her eyes. If she tallied up every time people assumed her mood sensory appeared as wiggly lines in the air, she'd have covered an entire house with scratches. "It's more like a string tied to a person's chest," she tried. "I'd see an aqua blue string if you were sad. A deep sea blue string means confusion."

Alex groaned. "Sounds complicated."

"It is, and we don't always get it right."

"What? What do you mean?"

Peri's chest prickled. Though the girls lived in the same house, they'd always respected each other's spaces. Before, they'd barely talked about their gifts or powers; the middle of battling Monsters was hardly the best placed to explain one's abilities. Outside of battle, Alex rarely asked for specifics and unless she did, no one brought it up to avoid overwhelming her.

Peri smiled weakly. "We can confuse emotions, like sadness for pain, or happiness with anger. Sometimes we get it right, but other times, emotions get wrapped and become crossed. Mainly because people feel more than one thing at a time, unless it's overpowering, which it can be in Creatures."

"But you can tell that it's happening? That there's something?"

Peri peered up at the cliff-top again, watching as the grey-string drew closer. "At least your senses tell you things more accurately."

"Like how someone smelling of smoke is heading towards our house?"

Alex was right. The person smelling of smoke, who *had* to be the same person as the one with grey string around them, was heading right towards their house. Curiosity and protectiveness wrapped around Peri, and the girls said nothing as they marched up the wooden stairs together.

Archie went to the door after the fifth consecutive knock. The rain had subsided for a while, but now a full blown storm with high winds and lightning had come. Who could be outside in this weather?

When he opened the door, he tried to put a smile on his face.

Natalia, drenched through so bad that her layers of clothing were doing nothing to keep her warm and her hair was dripping down her face, stood before him. She shivered, her arms wrapped around her body in an attempt to keep her warm.

"Come inside," he told her, ushering her in. She stepped in and shivered in the heat of the hall. There was no time to think, he only had time to act. Turning to the stairs, as loud as he could, he yelled, "DAD!"

Archie fumbled around in the downstairs bathroom. He grabbed a hand-towel and came out, catching Natalia's hair in it, tying it up into a twist on top of her head without a word. She seemed too numb to do anything for herself but gave him a single nod of consent before he peeled off her jacket, throwing it onto the bathroom floor. As he pulled off her soppy cardigan, struggling to make her elbows bend, James bundled through the doorway. Archie hadn't asked for more towels, yet his dad had a stack of them in his arms. Archie took one and wrapped it over Natalia's shoulders.

What had possessed her to walk here during a storm? Creatures weren't susceptible to things like the common colds – though they had their own variation of the flu – because they healed. But that didn't mean they were invincible all-together.

Archie guided Natalia upstairs, leaving his dad to fuss with the sodden clothes. They made their way into the bathroom and Archie sat Natalia on the toilet so he could turn on the shower. She took some encouragement, but finally went beneath it, sitting down as the stream poured down on her.

"You just sit and warm up, okay? There are soaps and stuff if you want to wash and clean." Archie indicated to the shelf stacked with bottles of shampoos and body-washes. "I'll be right back," he promised her. "I'm just going to get you a drink."

"Okay," she mumbled.

Shaking his head, Archie raced back downstairs and into the kitchen. He flicked on the kettle and grabbed a mug, shovelling chocolate powder into it.

Footsteps padded against the floor as the kettle pinged off, and Archie was aware of someone behind him. Years ago, his heart may have stirred wildly at the thought of something at his back. But he'd had years of dealing with Monsters and what they'd come to do, and years of dealing with mischievous siblings. So he finished making the drink and then turned with it in his hands.

Jasper sat on the kitchen island, legs swinging, his damp hair dangling long he too had been in the storm. "What's all the commotion?" Jasper's eyes searched his brother's face before locking on the mug. "Is that for me?"

"Natalia's here," Archie answered.

Jasper didn't shift his eyes from the mug. "Is she?"

"She came through the storm."

"I wonder why."

The phone rang in the other room and Archie wondered if that was his mum. She was back in Atlantis, only for the day, to hopefully finally close Natalia's deal on becoming a Creature. The application was taking a while, so Sarah had gone to "see what was wrong."

Archie held out the steaming mug. "You could go find out?"

Archie heard their dad down the hallway picking up and answering the phone. Jasper jumped off the island. "Seems like dad's now busy," he said. "Maybe I should go and be the good child of the family, and finish sorting the washing I saw him dealing with?"

Jasper dashed off before Archie could utter a word. He rolled his eyes though his brother could no longer see it.

Archie walked back upstairs and knocked on the bathroom door. He cracked it open an inch and heard Natalia call out that it was ok.

Carefully, he nudged in to find Natalia perched on the edge of the bath, a green towel wrapped around her body - the rest of her soaked clothes were now piled in a heap. Her words, about being ok, had been strong, but her head was in her hands and she was sniffing. Archie put down the mug he carried and went to her. Bending in front of her, he put a hand on her bare shoulders, moving his fingers in a circular motion in the hopes of offering comfort. Peri always enjoyed the motion when she was upset. Natalia didn't push him off so he took it as a sign to continue.

"Natalia?" Archie kept his voice low. "What's wrong?"

"The storm crept up on me," she mumbled.

"You're upset because of a storm?" He studied her and eventually she shook her head. "You don't have to tell me why you're upset, but it might help you if you do. I can a keep secret if you want no one else to know. Even from Peri."

Archie didn't want to keep anything from his girlfriend, but this wasn't about her or him. If the roles were reversed, Peri would do the same. They trusted in each other that they'd be keeping secrets for the right reason - not to hurt one another, but to help someone else.

"Why haven't I been accepted?" Her voice was shaky and quiet, her breaths shallow and sharp. It was like the floodgates inside Natalia were breaking and Archie sat there as her ears. "Why is the Council taking so long to come to a decision? Was I wrong for shouting at them? The situation was *fucked*! Do you think making me wait for their ruling is punishment for what I did? Because that's how it feels.

"I didn't even know that I wanted to be a Creature. Not fully. I thought it was fanciful, a joke, a lie, when you all told me of who and what I was. But the idea grew on me. The more I understood, the more I wanted to be part of it. I wanted, *want,* to be *present* in it all. And I don't want to think about what will happen if I don't get accepted." She sniffed, wiping her nose with her forearm.

"Can the Council just not accept me?" She continued. "What will I do? Will I still be a Creature? How can they monitor me to make sure I'm not following our Purpose, the one that's buried inside of my blood and body? What happens to those that choose to leave this behind? Why do they leave?" She took her head from her hands, meeting his eyes. Hers were red and puffy and mascara ran down her cheeks with a mix of snort and tears, but she was unbothered. "I just don't understand what's happening and what's not happening. But I want to be a Creature."

Twice. That was how many times Archie had bared witness to this kind of pain before. Just like those times, his heart sank until it felt like it was beating inside his lower abdomen. He was on the outside looking in on her pain but unable to take it on himself. He felt his own lungs struggle to breathe.

He wanted to help, but there wasn't much else he *could* do. Listening and being available was sometimes the best kind of aid because it showed care. And despite not knowing Natalia well, Archie *did* care. Because she was Peri's friend and slowly becoming his, and that was enough.

Archie sat on the floor and took Natalia's hand, dragging her down too. They sat crossed-legged in the tiny space. The light in the bathroom was dim, but Archie could see how pale Natalia was.

"Would you be alright if I answered things slowly?" he asked steadily.

Natalia either didn't hear him or his words didn't register. In her moment of distraction, he let her hands go and clicked his fingers. At once her shoulder slumped and she raised her brown eyes to his green ones. He hated using magic to change someone's attitude in circumstances like this; it was a last resort. But this was one of those times it was needed, for Natalia.

"You used magic," she said. It wasn't quite a question. There was a glimmer in her eyes and seconds later, bronze appeared on her cheeks. "Thank you."

Archie took a deep breath and saw Natalia do the same. "Mum's in Atlantis," he began. He kept his eyes on her, making sure she was alright. If things changed, even by a small margin, he would stop. "She's trying to establish what's going on with your application. I won't lie. I've never seen or heard of this before; where the Council validates a Creature before letting them begin training."

"Can they do that?" Her eyes glassed over. "Can they stop me from following my Purpose?"

"In theory, they can do what they like. They're the Council."

"So, do you think they're making me—"

"Wait to punish you?" Natalia nodded and he took her hands again. "I don't think so. I think this is more about curiosity and safety. They're curious about you, the Fairy Queen's granddaughter and a woman who was raised as Human. And they want you, as an heir and Creature, to be safe, as well as us, though it might be hard to see considering how they act. They don't want us dying to protect you if you can't even try to protect yourself. Our Purpose is to make sure life lives. That includes our own. Royalty doesn't always take precedence over our Purpose."

Natalia's face livened with understanding. "They want to be sure I want this. That I'll train and protect life, not make people end theirs because I'm incapable."

"And the whole not accepting you thing, I don't know much about it. It's highly unlikely they'd turn you away. Right now, the worlds need all the help they can get."

"But if they *did*."

"Again, not that they will, but if they did, I wouldn't know what would come after. You'd still be a Creature at the end of the day. They can't cut that out of you."

"There are those who don't follow their Purpose, aren't there?"

Archie's heart thumped hard. "There are."

"What do they do? Can they ignore their calling? Do the Council monitor and punish them if they go against the walls put in their way?"

"There are those who don't follow their calling, usually not through their choice." He talked slow in hopes that what he was implying would hit Natalia before he had to spell it out. Unfortunately, she didn't pick up on what he was aiming at. "I don't think anyone actively leaves it. Those who leave are made to."

"What?"

He nodded. "The Council banishes them."

Natalia blanched. "*Banishes?*"

"I don't know much about this," he admitted. "But it's usually because of misconduct. *Serious* misconduct."

"Like what?" Her voice was barely above a whisper.

Archie tried to think of an example, clicking his tongue as he thought. "As I said, I don't know much. The Council keeps everything like this under magical lock and key from the public. Very few know anything. But the best I can think of is if you attempted to get hurt by a Monster to ensure a transfer of their powers for your personal gain."

Natalia was silent a for moment. "That can happen?"

"There are very few Monsters that *can* transfer their powers."

"Why would someone want them?"

"To harm other Creatures or to be boosted to be heralded as a hero." He let go of her hands then and picked up the cooled mug of hot chocolate, passing it to Natalia. "Imagine if you had a Monster power and it allowed you to wipe out hundreds of the bastards at once. It would raise you up and you'd get commended for it. There are also some that just want the power for power's sake, not to be a hero."

"Oh." She sipped her drink.

"But it's unjust and unlawful. It all goes against what the God's gifted you. Our Purpose may be hard and unfair, but it is a gift in itself and we have been given enough to fight with."

Again, Natalia remained silent for several heartbeats. "Wouldn't it damage you? To take on that other power?"

"The Creature part begins to die."

"Begins?"

"In the process, a lot of Monster's transfer more than just powers, like blood, but that's where it starts. If the action is stopped, the Creature is saved but banished. If the action *isn't* stopped, then that Creature becomes more Monster and must be killed like one, whether it was once your neighbour, mother, lover, or child."

Natalia's face held fast but Archie could read the uncertainty in her eyes. "I won't get banished," she said, trying to sound confident. Then it faltered. "Will I?"

"Have you done anything to upset the balance of the law so much so that banishment is the only acceptable punishment?"

"Does shouting at the Council count?"

"I doubt it." Archie smiled. "Now, how do you feel? Any better?"

The bronze on her cheeks shimmered. "Thank you."

"It's my pleasure. And as I said, Mum's in Atlantis sorting it all out, and she's damn good at her job. So if you've done nothing scandalous, you'll be one of us in no time."

"I don't want you to hide this from Peri." Natalia's tone was steady and sure. "Same goes for anyone else. This isn't a secret and I don't want it to become one."

A knock came at the door before he could respond. Archie stood and offered a hand out to Natalia who accepted. He unlocked the door as she slurped her drink.

Jasper stood there, grinning. "One pile of clothes, delivered by a very handsome young Witch," he said as charmingly as he could muster. He was indeed holding a pile of clothes, the socks hanging out the sides and threatening to jump out. "Where's the patient?"

Natalia's head appeared below Archie's arm which was holding the door. "Patient?" she challenged, putting down her now empty mug on a shelf.

"If I've offended you, you won't want this." Jasper began to turn.

"Ah!" Natalia lunged for the clothes and caught them.

Archie gave his brother a studying look, who then spoke to Natalia. "Don't you need to get dressed?"

Natalia glanced down at herself then raised her eyes again, bronze dusting her cheeks. She ducked behind Archie and shoved him away, locking the door.

Jasper's eyes focused over Archie's shoulder as he asked, "Everything ok?"

"I'm sure she'll tell you in her own time," Archie answered. Though Natalia had expressed that there was no secret, they were her thoughts and feelings to share. "She wanted answers on a few things."

"Bad enough to walk through a storm?"

Archie nodded once. "Bad enough that she had a wobble."

Jasper's mouth made an "O" shape. In this house, having a wobble meant someone was having an extreme personal meltdown, though it was a nicer way of explaining it.

"Is she ok?" Jasper whispered after a few moments.

Archie nodded again. "She will be."

"You explained everything? You answered all of her questions?"

"To the best of my ability." Archie gave his brother a curious look. What was going on in his head? He'd never seen him act like this before. "Instead of asking me, ask her yourself."

Jasper opened his mouth as the bathroom door opened. Either Jasper or their dad had found some of Peri's old clothes, ones she wouldn't miss: a white vest, a black shirt, and an old baggy pair of grey jogging bottoms. The sleeves on the shirt and legs of the trousers were shorter on Natalia, and all of the clothes were a little tight, but they did the job.

Natalia held out her mug and Archie took it. "Thank you," she said, smiling softly at Jasper. Flecks of bronze were stuck to her lashes and her bottom lip.

Jasper grinned. "As much as I want take the credit, dad got the clothes for you and Archie made the chocolate." He moved closer and jutted his arm out, elbow first. "Does my lady require a guide?"

Archie expected her to challenge Jasper calling her a lady, *his* lady. Instead, she asked, "What for?"

"You won't be getting home tonight; the storm's getting worse, so you might as well make the most of being here. We might as well start some part of your training. If you have the energy?"

Natalia appeared uncertain. She quickly shook her head and rolled her shoulders. Her face turned from a canvas of confused sadness to one of confident wondering. Archie knew Fairies were confident in most of what they did - it was a trait they all wore on the surface. He'd just never seen it. But, in that moment, he did.

Natalia accepted Jasper's arm and they walked off. Archie watched them go with curiosity before turning to clean the bathroom.

As he did, arms wrapped around him. They snaked over his body until the hand and stump rested against his muscled chest. He smiled and pulled the girl from him, twisting them both round and dipping her lowly in his arms until she had to peer up at him. Peri giggled. The smell of the sea was pressed into her skin. His heart leapt like a deer in spring.

"Are you going to kiss me?" she asked, a devilish smile on her face.

He bent his head and their faces met. There was salt on her lips and Archie licked it off. He felt Peri melt underneath him, and he melted against her, too. It was a charming kiss, unlike any other. None of their kisses ever seemed the same; all of them were fresh and passion-riddled and powerful as if it were the first time.

Pulling back, Peri's grin remained but weakened. "I saw a soul string," she announced.

"That was Natalia," he said, certain.

Peri blinked. "You sure? Is she alright? Has something happened? Who do I need to fight?"

Archie tucked Peri into his side, ignoring the dampness of her hair. Because Natalia had given him permission, though he had refused to tell his own brother - only because Jasper should've asked himself, he seemed interested in her enough, yet it was like he was avoiding something - he began to tell Peri of the girl who had walked through a harrowing storm for answers.

11

Honesty Hours

"**HOW ARE YOU?**"

Natalia tried to not lose her footing as she walked, her right leg twinging. She'd started to wonder if it ever would heal. It had only been around a month since she'd sustained the injury, but a month was also a long time too.

"My leg's playing up," she admitted.

Jasper reached the bottom of the staircase first and stopped there, turning to her. "Is that the one that was clawed?" His eyes travelled down her legs. "Dancing the other week probably didn't help if it's still not fully healed."

"I honestly don't remember if it hurt at the parade or not."

His eyes met hers. "I meant, do you think you agitated it when *we* danced?"

Her face reacted, coating in the bronze dust that never rested too deep from the surface anymore. How had she only made it appear once or twice before? Now it seemed to shine every other minute. She wanted peace from it. More often than not, it gave away how she felt in that moment.

Avoiding his gaze, she said, "I actually think it did some good."

Jasper gave no warning as he reached up and snaked his left arm around Natalia, his palm and fingers splayed across her upper back.

Jasper's other hand wound around her middle. Before she could protest, she was pulled flush against him and lifted off her feet. She was twisting in the air. Her heart pounded though her body relaxed.

After a moment, Jasper lowered her. "If you ever need a dance partner, I'd be happy to lend myself. For the purpose of physiotherapy, of course."

Natalia's lips curled. "Of course," she agreed, face shining, "All in the name of healing."

"Will you be requiring my services?"

"Not right now." Natalia's eyes trailed the empty hallway, all too aware of how she remained in his arms. "Maybe in the future." She slid her arms back to her side, away from where she'd rested her palms against his chest.

Jasper smirked. "I'll keep an open diary for you."

He removed his higher hand from between her shoulders, but left the other in the small of her back as they walked on, side by side. His hands were gentle, delicate, not belonging to someone who handled magic or killed with it.

A jolt shocked down her spine as his fingers moved ever-so-slightly.

A burst of white light lit the hallway, followed by a crashing of thunder. Natalia could see out past the glass kitchen doors as they walked. It was dark until the sky livened again.

The storm was getting worse indeed. Natalia was thankful she'd made the choice to stay at the Darby's. Right now, she admittedly wanted nothing more than to be here, where she felt safe and around people who understood her. The weather just gave her an excuse to stay.

"I think you'll be with Alex tonight," Jasper announced. He peered sideways at her, his hair falling across the tops of his eyes, half shielding them. "If that's alright?"

"It'll be fine, thank you." She paused as another crash came. "I texted my dad to say I'm here but whether he gets it or not..." During storms, most phone signals on the Island died.

"I'm sure he'll be fine and I'm sure he knows you're fine too. You're a Creature. You can look after yourself."

"I have a few injuries to the contrary."

Jasper laughed and held out his hand. "And that's why we're here."

Natalia accepted, almost jumping as another shock raced along her skin. Was Jasper using magic or was something else at play? Shaking her head, she looked to see where *here* was. A wooden door with an ornate golden glass handle was built into the back of the staircase.

With his free hand, Jasper opened it. Dim light shrank downwards. He urged Natalia ahead of him, her heart racing nervously. Her right hand touched the sloping rail and she clung to it, leaving her more dominant left hand free to defend herself against whatever awaited her.

"What's down here?" she asked, turning back. Jasper didn't reply.

I hope it's not spiders. She could almost feel phantom cobwebs around her neck.

The steps creaked and groaned like the wood might snap at any moment. The lower Natalia went, the more warm air brushed against her, wrapping around her limbs with a grip of a ghostly hand. Her palms grew sweaty and her right leg pulsed in anticipation.

The stairwell opened.

Wooden flooring touched all four reasonably lengthy grey walls. While spotlights were switched on, showing how sparse the rest of the room was besides a small dark grey corner sofa.

Natalia kept expecting the room to change around her. "What is this?"

Jasper passed her, strolling directly to the centre of the room. He clapped his hands and raised them above his head. The sound of rushing win blew through the room. Natalia blinked and when she opened her eyes, everything *had* changed.

The floor was sandy instead of wooden; Jasper was barefoot at the centre of it. Three white circles were drawn into the sand, one where Jasper stood, and two on either side of him about five feet away.

Jasper looked pleased with either himself or the change. Or perhaps both. "It's a training room," he said joyously.

"Training room?" Natalia stepped further inside.

"Like a gym, but for the supernatural."

"A gym?"

"A home gym," he added.

"I can see it's a home gym since it's in your *house*."

He laughed and then explained, "It's how we keep our fitness up. We learn to harness both our abilities and skills, sometimes even against each other. Sometimes physical weapons, like swords, come out to play too. We use them in fights sometimes," he shrugged carelessly, "like Peri with her trident.

"We train what we can do, and learn about what we can't. We prepare for the unexpected. Everything we do is to make *ourselves* a weapon."

Natalia eyed the room, waiting for something else to shift. "Training, gym, yeah," she mumbled.

"Does that, *at all*, make any sense?"

"Surprisingly, yes." She tucked her hair back as her pulse hammered in her throat.

Natalia watched him grin and didn't like it. *He's going to do something,* she thought. He said nothing, but flicked his wrists in a snappy flourish.

Ropes sprung from the sand. Natalia squeaked in surprise and somehow managed to leap over the first one, only to fall right within the grasp of the next. It tagged her left ankle, forcing her to the ground, face down. Groaning and rubbing sand from her chin, she rolled onto her back. Her following breath was knocked out of her as her body was yanked upwards.

Hanging upside-down from the ceiling like a bat, strung up by one ankle, was unfortunate to say the least. It got worse when Natalia's borrowed clothes began to rise, or fall depending on perspective. She slammed her hand against the vest as it started to rumple.

How long could she hold this for? Her arms were already beginning to wobble and her face burned with embarrassment.

Jasper stalked into view. "Monster's won't wait for permission to attack."

Natalia glared at him. "Does this happen to everyone? You break them in by tying them upside-down?"

Jasper drew closer, two more ropes wrapping around her; one took at left wrist, and the other at up her waist. She was righted, able to see properly again, but her head throbbed as the blood rushed away.

"We haven't had fresh blood around here for a while," he said, grinning like an idiot.

"Oh. So not only am I now a Human—"

"Fairy."

"*Fairy*," she mocked, "piñata, I'm also a fresh bag of bones to play with? That *does* make me feel better."

Jasper held himself as he laughed, letting the rope at her wrist snake away. Natalia giggled too, an idea fluttering through her mind as she did. *Dust can break a Witch's spell.* The ropes were a spell, weren't they?

Giving herself no time to doubt, she rubbed her hands against her cheeks and then bent with what little give the waist rope offered. Her palms planted on the leg rope and it went *ping*. Confetti actually burst out. Quickly she went for the rope at her middle. Natalia could've rejoiced when that too went *ping* if she hadn't been falling.

To her surprise, she didn't land in the sand, but hit something that groaned beneath her. Pulling up, she realised what. *Jasper*. Her hands were beside his chest, her legs mashed with his, their faces inches apart with her long brown hair falling like a curtain around them. He smelt of grass after rain.

"Monsters won't wait for permission to attack," she repeated, trying to not draw attention to the compromising position they were in.

Jasper's surprise melted into approval. "You're learning." In a swift movement, he put his hands on Natalia's sides and sat himself up, leaving her in his lap. He reached up and tucked her hair behind her ears, his touch lingering on the side of her face. "I should've used a more complicated spell. One a bit of Fairy dust couldn't have broken."

"Then how am I supposed to escape?"

He smirked. "That'd be something you'd have to figure out for yourself."

"I better start researching."

"Start with how to land."

She stared. "What?"

"I've never been used as a crash mat before. Though, I'll admit I'm to blame. I *did* get in the way to stop you falling."

Once again, Natalia became aware that she was still on Jasper's lap. If she wanted, she could trace his freckles, and so she did, with her eyes, mapping out the sky on his skin. She absentmindedly leaned forward and brushed aside the waves of hair dangling close to his eyes with her fingertips, uncovering more stars.

"Thank you," she uttered, pulling her hand back, trying to find somewhere else to look. "But I didn't ask you to do that."

"Maybe not. But I didn't want you to get hurt."

Natalia's heart stopped. And then started.

The silence between them was hers to fill. The question had been hanging since he'd ask, since before they'd come down here, and she was yet to respond. Now that she was face to face with him, with nowhere left to run.

"When you asked earlier, about how I was, you didn't mean my leg." It wasn't a question, it was a statement. Jasper said nothing, only watched with a calm indifference. "You meant how I *really* was, how I felt inside my head and heart, not my physical health. And honestly?"

"Always honestly between us," Jasper whispered.

She took a deep, unsteady, breath. "I'm a little all over the place."

Jasper waited a moment. "A little?"

"I had questions. Ones I couldn't type into the internet for answers. Most of them Archie had the answers for." For the first time in a while, she touched her starry earrings, not knowing what else to do with her hands. They gleamed under the tender lights of the room. "I know he told you."

He didn't argue. "He didn't tell me how you felt."

"Do you *really* want to know?"

The smile was genuine. "That's why I'm asking."

"Noah pushed me out of work, into the storm, to come see you all. He knew I was avoiding you."

"Why?"

"Why did he push me out?"

"Why were you avoiding us?"

Natalia looked down. She didn't want to see pity or agreement in his gaze. Her already tender heart-strings felt like could snap at any moment. "Because I felt like I was letting you down."

Jasper reached up and brushed the backs of his fingers against her face, then rested his thumb below her bottom lip with his forefinger under her chin. His eyes burned. "You haven't let us down," he promised. "How could you even think that?"

"Because I haven't been accepted."

"Whatever game the Council is playing, it's *their* problem. I won't let you, for one second, think you're letting us down because of their inability to see how good you are as a Creature *and* as a person."

Natalia welled up. If her emotions weren't written plainly on her skin, Jasper made sure they did by pulling her into a bone-crushing hug. He no longer seemed to care about either of them hurting, because neither of them would break. They weren't made of glass. They were made of magic and stars.

Jasper's lips brushed against Natalia's ear and the hairs on her body rose. "Natalia?"

"Mm," she mumbled.

"Hold on."

Natalia just managed to hold onto him before he rose. Jasper laughed beneath her. Seconds later she unlatched herself from his neck to stand, a sneaky grin brushing his lips. The lights above cast him in an eerie glow. He could've passed for being a Vampire in that moment, with his dark hair and green eyes and his dark clothes. Yet there was something else lingering in his smile, an air of regret. Natalia didn't understand. Regret, about what?

"This time, I'm going to warn you," he said, grinning again. "We should practise, so when you *do* get the all-clear, you can show the Council how stupid they were for making you wait."

She stood firmer, stronger. "Right."

"And Natalia?"

Hearing him say her name sent a flutter through her heart. "Yes?"

"I can speak on everyone's behalf when I say we're proud of you."

"What?" she croaked, trying to hold back the tears she could feel building.

"We're giving you our help because you deserve it. You're one of us and you're our *friend.* We care about you. So you haven't let us down. You never will. It's impossible. Trust me."

She blinked fast. "I do trust you."

His responding smile was kind. "Now, let's change the pace. Ready?"

After a breath, she replied. "Yes."

Ropes lashed around her. This time, she dodged backwards.

The clock in the hall upstairs chimed eight times.

Her paw slipped and her head bowed.

Instantly Alex woke with a jolt. The room smelt of smoke, the type she'd come to associate with Natalia, who was currently sleeping in her bed. Alex herself had taken the seat at the end of the bed; she often ended up curled there as a wolf, the feeling of hiding within her fur offering more comfort than her Human skin sometimes, so didn't mind the arrangement.

The storm was gradually leaving, though it hadn't completely gone yet. Rain still poured from the sky, but there was no more thunder and lightning. Grumbling, Alex tried to rest her head back on her paw, repositioning them one over the other.

Then the smoky smell was replaced with a cold, frozen vanilla.

Alex lept from the seat and padded to the window. As she did, the clock downstairs chimed for midnight. Her nose hit the cold glass as the last chime rang.

She sniffed and bounded back to Natalia, jumping on the bed. The Fairy stirred but didn't wake, not until Alex licked the side of Natalia's face, tasting the brassy tang of dust.

"What is it?" Natalia mumbled, rubbing her groggy eyes. Alex nudged her cheek. Natalia shuffled and Alex nudged her again, her head twitching to the window. Natalia watched her. "What's going on? Is something wrong?"

Alex nodded. In response, Natalia's brown eyes finally flew wide and her mouth opened. She didn't bother to see the state Alex was in and scrambled to find some socks. Alex watched her, her pierced eyebrow – which stuck, like her nose stud did, even in this form – raised.

Barking the whole time, Alex pounded down the stairs, Natalia on her heels. The house needed to wake. When they hit the ground floor, everyone was forming a shoulder to shoulder line around the top of the stairs, their sleepy eyes not quite registering what was happening.

Alex rolled her shoulders until her bones crunched and cracked. Limbs groaned as they slid around. Pain tore across her body until she was screaming and howling consecutively; every shift asked her body to fracture and break to rebuild into something else.

The worst came when her face changed. Her nose shrank, cracking on its way, and when she could no longer see a snout, she *could see* the red stain on her chest. Her teeth moved and shrank but the taste of squirrel didn't disappear – a tang of metal lingering on her tongue. Her eyes grew larger, watering as they took in the halls light. The fur slithered away to leave her shivering and naked; she could've shifted with clothes on, they would've made her fur shorter and thinner, but she'd morphed after a bath.

Without so much as a word, Natalia stole a long coat off the rack and draped it around Alex's shoulders, though Alex was sure it was too late for any modicum of privacy.

"What's going on, girls?" her mother asked, rubbing her temples as she normally did when tired.

Jasper yawned. "I need my beauty sleep."

"We don't have time for this," Alex forced through gritted teeth. "Something's outside. I'm not sure what, it was in the distance. But I could smell it. It was like winter, like ice and snow."

Her father snapped to attention. "A Monster?" Alex nodded. "Can you be sure?"

"I can be sure that it's not a Creature and doesn't seem like any Human I've ever met."

"Everyone," Sarah took charge, "get changed."

"We don't have time," Alex insisted. Could no one hear the urgency?

Her mother's eyes landed on her, nervous desperation written into her gaze. "Is it really that bad?"

Shrugging off the coat, Alex crouched to instigate the shift again.

"Yes."

Running down the slippery hillside of Opal House was one thing. Doing it in pyjamas and bare feet was another.

The rain drenched Natalia in seconds, her hair flopping over her shoulders in clumps. The clothes she'd borrowed from Peri to sleep in were stuck to her body.

"It's up Main Street," Peri announced, staring off, as they reached the bottom of the hill. What could she see? Alex had explained her piece, but it was as if Peri could see something else. It seemed though that either way both girls had come to the same conclusion - it was a Monster.

Natalia glanced at Jasper, finding him already staring at her. His normally wavy hair was plastered to his face and he ran a hand through it, scraping it back. His grey jogging bottoms hugged his legs and he was missing a shirt, the rain running down his chest. As if knowing where her eyes had been last, Jasper gave her a smirk and withdrew a blade from his trousers before breaking away from the group.

Alex, now a wolf again, raced after him, a throaty growl resonating from her chest. Peri flicked out her trident; the gold flashed in the dark like a beacon of purity. She gave Archie a smile and charged off. He mumbled something Natalia didn't catch and ran after them all.

Being alone made a voice appear in Natalia's head, one that told her to turn back and seek safety. But what kind of Creature would she be if she ran and hid? Creatures were meant to face danger, to fight, to charge head-first into it all.

Natalia flicked her hair from her face and started running harder. The more she pushed, the more her feet stung and the more her right leg burned.

By the time she caught up, everyone was already in a chaotic mess.

Archie and Alex were double-teaming a Scorpio. Its tail lashed out and it swung its body. Alex ducked at the right moment and somehow bit the Monster under its head.

Peri was by Katherine's café, her back pressed against the wall as a sludge Monster – the name of which escaped Natalia's mind – came for her. The Monster flicked its head and black gunk sprayed out, coating the wall but missing Peri by inches. With a yell, she stabbed her trident into the Monster's inky body. Even standing far back, and despite the rain, Natalia could smell the damp dog odour the Monster gave off and she fought not to gag.

Jasper and Sarah were combating another Scorpio, this one larger than the other, and redder around the edges. Natalia neared them and gasped when the Scorpio's pincers snapped at Sarah, but the claws stopped before slicing through her waist. Natalia turned to Jasper, his arms out before him, and realised he was keeping the claw away. He jumped in time to avoid the free claw, just seconds away from being pushed over and seconds away from his magic being undone.

Natalia searched for a way to help, despite having no weapons or experience. As she did, a breeze unlike the wind blew along her neck. Coming to a halt, she didn't see anything, but felt something wrap around her hair. By the time she could react, the Monster yanked.

Natalia hit the floor with a thump, the back of her head colliding with concrete. A pained groan escaped her lips. She went to move, only to find an icy shudder run up from her feet. There was *just* enough effort left in her body to push herself up onto her elbows. The air vanished from her lungs and her heart searched for any escape it could to protect itself.

A Monster sat trapping her thighs, grinning with pearly white teeth.

The Monster wore the face and body of a Human, yet it wore no clothes on its light, powder-blue body. With the wind, its hair waved and Natalia could smell that frozen air now, with its undercurrent of vanilla, distinguishable amidst the rain. When it smiled, it was hard to tell that it wasn't a Human. But the gleam in its eyes told Natalia it wanted to harm her.

"You are a child of the stars," the Monster whispered. It crawled up Natalia's body and she wanted to kick it, to fight it, but the further the Monster came to her face, the more paralysed she became. The Monster stopped when its head was poised above Natalia's. "Aren't you?"

"Yes," Natalia answered through gritted teeth.

"And beautiful, you are." Natalia said nothing. She laid there, helpless, unsure of what to do as the Monster ran a long, deadly finger across her cheek. "But children of the stars are always beautiful," it mused. "The *most* beautiful. Gracious. Burning. Like stars themselves. That is where you get your name and why you have it after all."

Rain dripped into Natalia's eyes, making it appear like she was crying. "What do you want?"

"You are beautiful."

"That doesn't answer my question."

The Monster withdrew its hand and lowered its face further; Natalia could smell acid on its breath. "I want your pretty," it spat. "I want to be inside your skin. I want to walk within your body. I want your gifts and your powers and the way you make yourself look like the night's sky. But, I'm not here for that now."

Natalia's heart pounded a hateful rhythm through her ears. "What—"

"You burn brighter than your sisters and brothers. And I came here to find you."

Why has it come for me? How can I burn brighter than any other Fairy?

The Monster tipped forwards until its nose touched Natalia's and a whimper escaped her. The Monster lurched forwards then suddenly jerked back. Three golden spikes protruded from Monster's chest yet it didn't stop it grinning.

It snapped its blue fingers and vanished.

Peri appeared above Natalia, looking slightly frazzled with her black bob misshapen and a red scratch on her chin. "Need a hand?"

"Is that thing dead?" Natalia asked, searching for any sign of the Monster.

"Bloody hoped so." Peri pulled Natalia to her feet and then looked at her trident. The spike on the outer left side was bent. "That *bastard!*"

Natalia couldn't explain it, but she had a feeling that the Monster *wasn't* dead, like a cold shiver that lingered at the base of her spine. It was only an inclination, an instinct, but she trusted it. Something about this entire situation had been wrong, so why would its death be different? Most Monsters came to destroy, yet this one had intelligently talked, claiming it'd come to find her.

Without ash at its disappearance, there was no evidence that it really was dead.

Natalia shivered. If it *was* still alive, Natalia was certain that it would come again. But what did it want her for?

Peri walked a few paces off and Natalia watched her go, grabbing her hair in her hands as if to protect it.

Small piles of ash were sifting away, sinking into the ground or blowing in the wind. No living Monsters remained.

So much for helping, she thought guiltily.

Jasper came through the rain, tucking away his blade. He had no injuries or even scratches to prove he was in a fight, but there was a weariness to his gaze. "I'll walk you home," he offered. "It's closer that our house at this point." He pointed to the nearby cut-through.

"Take Alex," Sarah insisted as the family regrouped. "I don't want anyone walking anywhere alone for a while."

Jasper saluted. "Yes ma'am."

"I *will* magic you into next week, young man," she warned. James, grinning, wrapped an arm around his wife.

Natalia's lips twitched as she searched the others for signs of injury.

Sarah's hair was plastered to her face and the sleeve to her top had been cut into ribbons. Peri had her scratch and Archie winced as he looped an arm over Peri's shoulders, though he didn't have any visible wounds.

Natalia swallowed a grateful sigh of relief.

Sarah pinched the back of Jasper's neck, and he yelped. Rubbing it, he stuck his tongue out at his mother and walked away, approaching Alex and Natalia and motioning for them to follow. Alex nudged Natalia's legs, and Natalia's eyes were drawn to a patch of crimson-stained fur behind the wolf's right ear.

Gillingham Road didn't keep its light on, unlike other streets. The pitch blackness was hard to see through. Natalia blinked when the light above her front door pasted them, letting her eyes adjust.

Out of nowhere, a hand touched her shoulder. But when it did nothing vicious, like strangle her, she allowed herself to relax. She turned to see Jasper smiling down at her, like he was preparing to say goodbye.

"Both of you can come in," she said quickly, making it a decision she'd already made for them. "I'll get warm blankets and clothes and drinks."

The door swung inwards and Natalia saw her dad, back-lit by the hall light. It took him a few seconds before he fully opened the door. Alex and Jasper shimmied into the hallway, shaking and shivering.

Her dad looked between them all, offering a weak smile. Natalia gave him an apologetic look before running upstairs. She dived into the bathroom, where she discarded the wet clothes into the bath and wrapped herself in a dry a towel. It was strange to think that only hours ago she'd been wrapped in a different towel, in a different house.

Once she felt comfortable enough, she moved to the landing and opened the cupboard, pulling out what she could, and called for her friends.

Alex bounded up first, still in wolf form, and snatched a towel with her teeth before diving into Natalia's father's bedroom. Jasper was slower. He went to say something but Natalia shoved a towel into his arms and pushed him into her bedroom before he could.

When she shut the door, she thought about what a weird idea it was, to put him in her room. Her face sparked. So she opened the door to get him out, so he could change in the bathroom, but it was too late.

Though his back was to her, Jasper was naked. Natalia's face heated even more. Stretch marks spread along his upper back and close to his hips. Her eyes moved lower, taking in his pale yet firm bottom.

Jasper wrapped the towel around himself, tucking it at the waist, and turned. His eyes widened, surprised. "Is something wrong?" he asked quickly. "Has something happened?"

"No," Natalia shook her head, "everything's fine."

Jasper's lips quirked. "Admiring the view?" He even did a twirl.

She tried to keep the heat in her cheeks under control. "I just thought how odd it was for you to be in my room," she admitted. "I was going to put you in the bathroom."

"Why is it odd?" His gaze swept over the room feigning curiosity. "What are you hiding in here? Some weaponized spoons? I know you love the regular ones but maybe you're secretly working on an upgrade for battle?"

"I'm not hiding anything." She noticed her underwear drawer was open and swiftly kicked it shut.

Jasper eyed the drawer with intrigue. "Do you think I've never seen underwear before?"

"But this is *mine*."

Natalia was close to Jasper, and it was the first time she was realising it. With his bare chest exposed, she could make out faint white stretch-marks over it and the tops of his arms too. There was also a smooth, light pink scar just below his neck on the left side. How had she not seen it before? It was easily the size of her fist. Maybe bigger.

Jasper noticed her staring. "Remember when I told you to avoid the Siltapolia? I told you they'd cool you before burning? That might've been your first time seeing them, but it wasn't mine."

Natalia reached out tentatively, touching the old burn with the tips of her fingers as if she might hurt him further. "What happened?" she asked lowly, her attention fully invested on the mark.

"I got hit," he said simply.

"And it leaves a permanent scar?"

"Lots of Monster afflictions do if you don't treat them immediately."

She ran her fingers along the raised skin. "Is that what happened to you?"

"Yes."

"Does it hurt now?"

"Not really. When I'm cold it twinges sometimes, but I don't notice it much."

Natalia met his eyes and the irises were as green as summer leaves. "Could I heal it? With my dust?"

He stared back. "I would like to ask you to try."

"Do you want me too?"

"Not now." He wrapped a hand around hers. "Years ago, it might've worked. It's been too long now. It's permanently healed as it is. Otherwise, I would've said yes."

Jasper brought his other hand to her face, cupping her cheek. Her heart thumped; this time, it didn't want to run to protect itself, but instead wanted to jump out of her chest and into his. His thumb brushed over her skin and he smiled, bringing his head even closer until she could feel his breath.

"You know we're still in your bedroom?" he whispered.

She gave him a look. "I never would've noticed."

He laughed. "Would you mind if I—"

"Natalia!" Her dad called, cutting Jasper off.

Jasper smiled and let her go. Natalia's heart sighed as she walked away from him. "We're coming down," she promised her father, calling out from the landing. "Can you make three hot chocolates, please?"

Her father said, "Of course," and then disappeared from view.

Alex emerged from the other bedroom, back in human form. Her curly hair was dry and she'd tied it up, but her self-cut fringe remained, split in the middle like before. Natalia's gaze shifted to the small blood trail that trickled from behind the girl's right ear.

Alex touched the mark. "Don't worry about this. I'll heal," she said. "I gave that Scorpio what for." Natalia went to turn but Alex called her back. Alex drew closer as if about to spill a secret. "I will advise *you* on something though."

"What on?"

Alex's grin was wicked. "Next time, keep your voices down or talk where I can't hear you."

Natalia's face blazed and she dashed back into her room. She'd forgotten about Jasper and nearly jumped out of her skin when she saw him on her bed, his arms behind his head, his ankles crossed.

"I need to change," she announced. She pointed to the towel he wore. "So do you." His gaze swept over himself as if he'd forgotten. "Go into my dad's room and pick something. He won't mind."

Jasper moved quietly. But as he reached the door, he turned, and Natalia smacked into him since she'd been following. She took a step back, but he stopped her from moving further by putting a hand on either side of her neck, his thumbs against her jaw.

"Are you sure you're alright?" he asked.

Natalia thought about the Monster and what it had said. "Yes," she lied, causing her stomach to twist. She *was* alright. She was safe now; she hadn't been hurt. But how long would that last?

He dropped his hands, not looking entirely convinced. "It's getting late," he observed. "Maybe we should have our drinks and retire? It's been a busy day."

"Retire?" she mocked.

He grinned. "The old-age equivalent of saying 'We should go to sleep.'"

She smiled. "That sounds like a plan."

In a flash like lightning, Jasper bent and pressed his lips to the corner of Natalia's mouth. The moment didn't last long. Before she could say or do *anything*, he was gone.

She flopped onto the bed.

Once again so many things were circling Natalia, rushing around her as if she were the centre of a hurricane. Her head buzzed. She wanted to do as Jasper had said; to have her drink and then go to sleep. Her eyes were burning and her body ached, and her mind was simply done for the day.

Eventually, she'd have to confront that which circled her. *Again.*

The clock beside her ticked to one o'clock.

12
Skyless

THE NEXT MORNING, Natalia tip-toed down the stairs. Her fingers slid along the banisters as she attempted to keep her breathing steady, knowing full well that Alex could probably hear her. She made it into the kitchen alone, the door silent as it was pushed shut.

Turning, she inhaled sharply. Jasper stood over the stove. Natalia moved closer, wondering when he woke and trying to decipher *what* he was doing. Something sizzled and she realised he was cooking.

As if sensing someone behind him, he looked round. He hand a pan to hand, and a near perfectly round pancake inside. But his eyes focused on her. "Fairy," he sang.

"You've said my name before," she told him.

"Natalia."

It was like a whisper along her skin. She brushed it aside, ignoring how her heart pulsed dangerously inside her chest, and asked, "Why are you cooking?"

"Your dad wanted to make breakfast, but got a call from work."

"He's gone?"

Jasper nodded. "Left a few minutes ago. Someone's called in sick, apparently, so I took over here and he took over there."

Natalia switched the kettle on. "Coffee?" she offered, leaning back against the worktop. "Or are you a tea in the morning kind of guy?"

"Coffee," he said. "If you're making."

"I wouldn't normally."

"But for me you will?" He tilted his head to study her.

"If that's what you want, then yes. Just this once."

Natalia *just* caught sight of Jasper's smile as she turned for two mugs. She went about making him a coffee, hoping he didn't mind how she made it – she realised halfway through she should've asked how he wanted it – and then made herself tea.

What about Alex? Will she want a drink?

The second Natalia put the kettle down again, steam rising from the mugs, the doorbell rang. She half jumped out of her skin and then cursed under her breath. Was she going to jump at everything now? Is that what she was becoming, a scared little rabbit near a fox?

Natalia walked to the front door and yanked it, and managed to catch it before it smacked into the wall. She half expected Alex to come thumping down the stairs on all fours to complain about the noise. She didn't.

There was no guest beyond the door, only silence. This had to be some kind of joke.

No one passed by in the street, not even a bird tweeted from the nearby treetops. But there had definitely been a definitive knock. Was a local kid playing ding-dong-dash? Natalia knew of very few children living in this area though.

As Natalia gave the street another curious glance, something flapped beside her head on the door itself. Her hands tore the note down and she stared at it.

The cream coloured paper was thick and card-like, and the handwriting was unlike any Natalia had seen before. Written in gold and cursive, with a red seal of approval stamped below, were three words. She read them several times and still they didn't sink in. All they did was make her heart hit the roof and her eyes well until she was sniffing.

The Council accepts.

"Jasper?" she called. He didn't come, so she raised her voice. "Jasper!"

There was a flurry of noise. Natalia barely looked up before a giant brown wolf was knocking her to the ground; Natalia was careful to protect her head on impact, throwing her hands behind it to soften the blow. Alex spent minutes sniffing the air and searching with beady eyes for signs of trouble, using her body to keep Natalia down. Obviously finding none, she climbed off, gruff-like as if annoyed.

"You alright down there?" Jasper asked, peering over Natalia. "Having an impromptu nap?"

Natalia watched Alex retreat to the bottom step of the stairs and stood up. "I think Alex thought I was calling for help." She held the note out. "I wanted you to see this."

He took the note, read it, and then flung it in Alex's direction. He rushed at Natalia without a single noise. For the second time in a single minute she was hit by another person, but this didn't send her to the floor. His arms captured her, squeezing her.

Natalia was laughing. The *Council* wanted her, and now she could be a validated Creature at last. She really was a Fairy now. For the first time, this life had chosen her back.

The wet March turned into a sunnier April.

Peri was bored. Sarah and James were back in Atlantis and Archie, Jasper, and Alex were out for the day in town. She'd paced the entire house at least five times before calling Natalia. Thankfully, her friend had answered her phone.

She walked the length of the house a few more times, flipping the calling card between her slender fingers. Peri took a deep breath as the door rang.

Natalia held out a white box. "Trick or treat?" Peri yanked her inside with little care or consideration. "Hey!" she complained. "What's the matter?"

Peri bolted the door and marched into the kitchen, giving Natalia no choice but to follow her. "Nothing," she answered unhelpfully. Something *was* the matter though.

The house seemed so empty, and normally, Peri wouldn't be here to see it like this. She'd been asked to accompany the family but she'd elected to stay behind. Today was the perfect day to execute her plan. The rest of the doors and windows were already closed and locked, ready.

Natalia put her box down on the island counter. "You sure you're fine? You don't even want the muffins I brought?"

"Remember back in Atlantis, at the parade, when I asked a favour of you?" Natalia nodded. "This is me cashing it in." Peri held up the card Gold had given her over a month ago. She'd been putting it off, stalling seeing him, but now she was ready. She needed a definite answer, although she was pretty certain already. "We need to see Gold and this is how we're doing it," she said, her voice calmer than her heart. "I've already rung him to expect us."

"What's all this about?"

That's what I plan on finding out.

Peri licked her painted blue lips and shook the card. Blue sparkles, like glittery rain, fell from it. At first, nothing happened. Peri glared daggers at the glitter. She was about to swear and complain about having pinned all her hopes on this when the card leapt out of her hands and tore itself apart, little pieces vanishing into the air.

Peri barely looked at Natalia before it felt like her heart was being ripped from her chest.

Natalia's heart landed first. Her body followed.

She panted and dry heaved. The stress of travelling via magic was like a near death experience. It separated all that she was and then slammed every piece back together again.

Vowing to never do it again made her feel better, though she knew it was probably a false promise. She just hoped next time didn't come around quickly.

Natalia found Peri watching her curiously. Other than her hair being a little scruffy, she was otherwise unfazed. Natalia tried fixing her own hair. "How are you so ok?" she asked, finding it mildly unfair.

Peri smiled sweetly. "*Amore*. You need a portal to transport from anywhere within the same plane to somewhere locked, like Atlantis, or somewhere over a greater distance, like half a world away. *Jumping* allows you to transport with magic, but with limited range. We were on a long weekend break and Archie once tried and managed to jump us to Paris from Russia. Now *that* was retch-worthy. *Non è buono.*"

With the sickness subsiding Natalia peered around, blinking. They were at the new rooftop bar. She hadn't been here since her birthday. She could picture Noah drinking and storm clouds hovering in the sky. Her birthday had been a day she'd never forget, the day everything had changed.

"There he is!" Peri announced enthusiastically, and then marched off.

Natalia struggled to keep up. Eventually, Peri stopped, at the back of the roof and Natalia was thankful. Her gaze settled on Gold who was seated casually with one leg over the other, sunglasses shielding his eyes, and a glass of something brown in his hand. He didn't acknowledge the girls, not until Peri touched the table with her trident.

He put the glass down. "Are you *trying* to frighten me?"

Peri withdrew the weapon. "I booked an appointment."

Gold lowered his glasses, then pushed them back up. "So you did. And are you sure you still want it?"

"Sì."

"Are you sure you want the Fairy to come?"

"Sì," Per repeated.

"That *Fairy* has a name," Natalia bit at the same time.

Gold smiled, showing off his extending fangs to Natalia; it was easy to forget he was a Vampire. "You ooze confidence, and it's only growing," he said. "By the way, I am glad to hear of you being accepted." He raised his glass in a toast and swallowed down the contents in one.

Natalia wanted to question how Gold knew, but he stood unexpectedly, folding his glasses and swapping them for his monocle. No one on the roof turned their heads. Natalia was still unclear on what Gold could do, or what magic he'd stolen – she was sure the magic on his calling card hadn't been his alone, there had to be a Witch's influence – so maybe the public didn't turn to see them here because Gold didn't want them to look.

For the second time in five minutes, Natalia's heart was pulled from her body.

This time, she landed without seeing her life. Nausea engulfed her, and though Gold hadn't warned them the jump was coming, it had been smoother than the last.

A glass full of shimmering silver appeared under her nose. The smell of salt and mint wafted over her senses, as did the fizzing sounds.

Natalia searched for who'd brought it, but saw no one. Eyes widening, she glanced out the window at the scene beyond; skyscrapers and glass-buildings filled the far horizon, and people rushed about below, their bodies no bigger than small dots.

"Where are we?" she asked, gazing in awe.

"New York," Gold answered.

Natalia's head whipped round to find him but the room stole her attention.

Nearly every wall seemed to be a window that overlooked the city. Bright light was bursting through the glass and reflecting off the crystal chandelier sending colour dancing about the room. Rainbows spread over the black furniture of the otherwise sparse living room occupied by nothing more than a sofa, armchair, a black fireplace, and an oversized TV on the only solid wall.

"You should drink that." Natalia squeaked in surprise as Gold swanned past her. Walking backwards to be in line with her, his fangs on full display, he added, "It helps recover from the magical jumps."

Natalia took a sip, finding an unfamiliar tang on her tongue, just as Peri came into the room from somewhere else in the building. When had she snuck off? Where had she gone too? Natalia felt bad for not having noticed.

Peri had changed into a white shirt that was far too large to be hers, a nervous smile etched onto her face as she came to stand beside Natalia.

"Are you ok?" Natalia whispered.

"I will be."

Again Natalia sipped her drink and gave her friend a sideways glance. "What's going on? Is everything ok?"

Gold waved his hands. "Peri, dear?" he called.

Despite not knowing her long, Peri was trusting Natalia with whatever this was, and so she pressed a "good luck" kiss to Peri's cheek. Peri's eyes lit up and she sank away, holding her shoulders notably higher.

Natalia did nothing but watch as Gold instructed Peri to lie on the sofa. Natalia couldn't contain the small gasp that escaped her when he unbuttoned the middle of Peri's shirt to expose her stomach.

The Vampire turned to her at the sound, noting her unease, and offered a gentle smile. "She'll be fine," he promised.

The door that Peri had appeared through opened again. Before Natalia could object, a woman emerged and approached Peri.

The woman rolled out a tired red rug and knelt on it, putting her body sideways to Natalia and Gold. She wore a deep purple, old fashioned dress that somehow suited her petite frame.

Natalia didn't trust this woman. Honestly, didn't she trust Gold. She didn't really know them. So she kept her eyes vigilant, waiting for something to go wrong while keeping her fingers crossed that nothing would.

The woman raised her arms and shuffled until she hid Peri from view. Unhappy, Natalia shifted, moving to Gold's other side and watched the woman run her hands above Peri's body, refraining from physically touching. A concentrating scowl centred the woman's face as she lowered her hands over Peri's exposed lower stomach. It was then she pulled out a long, glowing white Crystal, circling it above the flesh. She then waved it above Peri's head before slipping it back into her dress pocket.

"Who is she?" Natalia asked, still not willing to take an eyes off Peri.

"Evangeline is an old and dear friend," Gold told her, his voice levelling with a notion of humour to it. He was enjoying this, Natalia realised. "She's someone who can work the Crystals better than anyone else I know."

"You trust her?"

"I would not have asked her here if I didn't."

Evangeline, as Gold had named her, pulled herself onto her heels and stood. She helped Peri stand and led her to Natalia and Gold. Evangeline and Peri could pass for being the same age, yet Natalia somehow knew they weren't. Evangeline was like a girl out of time; the age behind her eyes, in her careful stare, gave it away.

For the work with the Crystals, she must've been a Vampire, but there was something *more* about her. An essence about her that was different.

Evangeline touched her own necklace when they stopped. "You have seen what the Crystal said," she spoke directly to Peri.

Natalia's looked at everyone in turn. "What's going on?" she asked. Was something wrong? Was Peri *dying*?

Peri touched Natalia's hand and looked her in the eye. "I'm *pregnant*."

"Drink, my dear girl?" Gold offered, moving to his bar.

With the two young Creatures sent on their way, he poured himself a drop of whiskey. The first taste hit him like a bullet and he grimaced, but it wouldn't be enough to make him stop. Whiskey had always been his favourite, and this Van-Hook whiskey from 1869 was everything.

He gazed at the bottle, smiling, remembering the fire at the distillery that'd come months later, the one he'd had *absolutely* nothing to do with.

"No, thank you," Evangeline answered.

Gold turned to the ever young Evangeline. "Is something wrong?"

Many years ago they'd met in London, when trains filled the air with smoke and the world was not yet digital. Even now Evangeline looked no older than she had back then. She had collected some fashions over the years and cycled through them all; the purple dress she wore today was one of the oldest, with its long sleeves and slightly low neckline.

"It's my death day," she said as if that answered everything.

To Gold, it did.

April fifth, for Evangeline, was the same as his December second. Those days held emotions for them both. Every year that Gold felt like he'd overcome it, he found himself looking at his marks and fangs in the mirror while his undead heart – he was convinced – thumped, but only once. While it now held less powerful emotion, there was still part of him attached to that day, a part of his soul embedded in that time. And for Evangeline, her day was newer than his, despite still being over one hundred years past now.

"A drink may help?"

He raised a full bottle of freshly procured AB negative. Blood-lust was a constant thing for them now, and it had been for a hundred years, but on their death day that too seemed heightened.

She shook her head, smiling sadly. "No," she insisted. "I must be going soon."

"Must you?" She didn't reply so Gold refilled his drink and sipped it. "There was something in your eyes. When you were examining the girl."

"She is young."

"That wasn't it."

"You know me well." Gold would've been disappointed if he didn't since they had a century of friendship behind them. He'd been with Evangeline through part of her story, though he didn't know some of its complications, and it was not really his to know. But through these years, they had remained close. Evangeline put her hand on Gold's, their momentary coldness combining. "The baby."

"What about it?"

"You know what it's last name will be."

Suddenly Gold understood. How had he not realised before? "Young Eva—"

"I have not heard that name for generations." Evangeline touched the ends of her hair, as she always did when nervous or sad.

"Generations makes you sound old."

She smiled. "I am."

"Blood and family never stop being ours." His face and drink turned sour. "I think they will need our help."

"Because of the baby?"

Gold shook his head. "No."

She gave him the sturdiest look. "Was it the other girl?"

"I can't put my finger on it," he said, "But there is something in the air, and something in her heart."

The landing was smooth enough but that wasn't what upset Peri's stomach.

Natalia turned on her the second she could. "You're *pregnant?*" she whispered.

Not even Peri's abilities could help her decode what Natalia was feeling, let alone understand her own emotions. Peri touched her stump and then her stomach gingerly. Tears welled up in her eyes but they weren't sad.

"I think," Peri said slowly, "I've known for a while."

Since Atlantis she'd had an inkling; it wasn't a secret, yet she'd told no one at the time, only because she'd wanted to be sure. Gold had sensed it though, and had she was grateful for his help.

"What did the Crystal say?" Natalia asked, blinking fast. "Or show you? How does it even work? Couldn't you have used a normal test?"

"It said I'm four months gone. Human tests don't work on Creatures, they're inaccurate. We have to use pregnancy Crystals or have a blood test. Plus, periods for Mermaids are irregular, so I couldn't even tell that way."

"Then how?"

"The orange juice."

"Orange juice?" Natalia looked at her quizzically.

"I remember madre saying that she was attached to oranges when she was pregnant. That and I didn't feel *right*. Not that pregnancy isn't right but..." she trailed off for a moment. "I mean, I felt sick."

"Don't you think you need to tell Archie?"

"Tell Archie what?" Came a deeper voice.

The girl's eyes grew in each other's sights. Neither of them had heard the door close and neither of them had heard Jasper and Archie come in. Peri's heart wanted to disappear behind scales and under water. Natalia gave her a knowing look and grabbed Jasper's arm without a word, dragging him away immediately.

Archie came closer and took her face into his hands. "Darling? *Tesoro?* What have you got to tell me?"

"Darling?" Archie prompted.

He noticed how Peri's hand remained on her stomach, almost protectively, and how her eyes were downcast, but when he called to her again, she raised her sharp gaze. Her eyes shone with tears. He went to wrap her into a hug and she stopped him, putting her stump to his chest.

"Archie—"

"Yes?" he cut in, both nervous and eager to find out what this was.

"I'm pregnant."

Archie's heart stopped as he waited. When he wasn't torn maliciously away from the here and now, he felt tears along his lashes and cheeks. This couldn't be a dream, could it?

"You're..." he trailed off, unsure of *what* to say. He wanted to be sure, sure that this wasn't a falsehood.

"I really am."

Archie let go of her face and dropped his hands to her stomach. He went to touch her but hesitated. Peri smiled, and guided his hand to her. The overwhelming pulse that ran through him was like lightning. His girlfriend, the most beautiful Mermaid who could swim and sing him to his end, was carrying *his child*.

This was no dream.

"How do you know?" he asked next.

"Gold."

Archie met her eyes. He usually wasn't angry, and he wasn't now, but annoyance rose. "Gold?"

Peri's tears began to spill. "With everything happening, between Natalia needing us and the most recent Monster attacks, I didn't want to add to your pile."

"So you added to yours alone? So while your pile is five miles high, mine is only four?"

"It's not like that!"

"Isn't it?"

"No!"

"It looks that way to me. We're supposed to be a team. Our piles are meant to be equal."

"I wanted to be sure first! I was worried about working up to nothing."

He moved his hands back to her face, holding her like she was a diamond. To him, she was the utmost precious one. "It still *should've* been shared. I'm part of this too!" Archie sighed heavily, his annoyance easily melting. "How did you even get to Gold?"

Peri swallowed. "He gave me a calling card laced with magic back in Atlantis. He'd noticed me drinking orange juice." She waved a hand like she wouldn't explain that part now. "That's why I stayed behind today. I called Natalia so she could come with me. I wasn't sure and I didn't want to make you worry or get your hopes up for something that might not have been real." She looked down again. "Or for you to decide you didn't want this."

"Darling." His voice was strained. He tucked a finger under her chin, making her look at him. "I know you had Natalia, and I'm glad you had someone, but it should've been me. Whatever would've happened, whatever you had wanted to do, it would've been your choice, but I still should've been at your side."

"I want this baby," she said strongly.

"I want it too, Peri, and I want to be a part of all this. *Our* baby. *Our* future."

Peri's smile pierced his heart and he wanted to thank her for it. "Really?"

"I love you, Peri Sofia. With all that I am, I love you."

He encircled her body within his arms. Their lips met in a burning frenzy, with energy that spoke the language both of them knew but neither could speak aloud. Peri's tears washed over him, mixing with his. This was love; the most powerful emotion that only hearts alone could understand.

As their lips parted, Archie still held her to him. "I want this *so* much. Every part of it," he whispered though it wasn't a secret. Doubt, however, surfaced again. "But this is real? This isn't a dream?"

Peri shook her head, sniffing. "No dream."

"You really are pregnant?"

"About four months."

Archie's breathing hitched. "*Four months?*"

"I'm due in September." She wiped her face and replaced her sour frown with a smile so bright. "That's what the Crystal showed me."

"Is that all it showed you?"

She nodded. "No gender. No Creature."

"Our own little fish."

"It might be," she laughed. "But it might be a little Witch. We'll have to wait and see."

"September," Archie said in disbelief. "Who else knows?"

"Currently? Just Natalia."

"Your parents—"

Peri cut in. "We're going to hang off that one." He didn't push that; Peri knew what she was doing, so if she didn't trust her parents, then that was that.

Archie's hands slid over his girlfriend's body, his fingers feeling her edges and sharp parts and her curves. She sighed in content and leaned into his touch. When his hands came to rest around her stomach, he was sure he felt movement.

"Little fish," he mused, receiving what he thought was another push.

"*Our*," Peri touched his face, "little fish."

Archie grinned and kissed Peri again. In just a matter of months, two would become three, and Archie's heart swelled to twice its size. This was always inevitable – at least, he thought so, right from those first moments – just a matter of when.

"I love you too, with all that I am and will be," she whispered against his lips quietly, it meant to be heard by only him.

This was euphoria, and his love for Peri and their child was going to be eternal.

Jasper didn't mind Natalia dragging him down into the training area. But he was curious as to why. So he asked. "What's going on?"

"Family stuff," she brushed off.

Jasper raised a suspicious eyebrow. "Let me get this straight. There's family stuff going on and you know about it but I don't, despite me being part of said family and not you?"

Natalia whirled on him. "It was none of my business to know."

"But you *do* know."

"I owed favours and paid one back. But this..."

"This was you paying back a favour?"

"Yes. Well, the favour was to be company, not to find out anything."

"Those things sometimes go hand-in-hand though," he told her.

They stopped at the bottom. The basement walls were laced with magic; it was built to allow no noise or magic to leak out, or vice versa.

"What's going on?" he asked, trying again.

"Archie and Peri needed to talk."

"To talk?"

Something flickered in her eyes. *Uncertainty.* Jasper became conflicted on whether he wanted to know, but Natalia's eyes cleared and she sighed. "Peri's pregnant."

Of all the things Natalia could have said, Jasper hadn't been expecting that. After a few minutes of stretched silence, he cleared his throat. "They *definitely* needed to be left alone then."

At some point, Peri and Archie would've married and had children. The two of them were destined to be together, if things such as fate of the Gods were real. So for them to be stepping into that chapter of their life was normal. Besides, every Creature did things at a different rate. It didn't matter if someone was sixty, forty, or twenty. A lot of Creatures didn't see old age because of their Purpose and thus tended to fall hard and fast in love - sometimes only once - whenever it happened. So they often did the "growing up and old" thing whenever they could, whenever it felt right for them. That is, if it ever felt right - some never chose or wanted that kind of life, and instead lived to defend and to be free. Either way, there was no right or wrong as everyone was different with what they wanted, how much they wanted, and when.

Natalia grimaced. "I hope Peri won't be mad at me."

"For what?"

"Ruining the news for you."

Jasper laughed. "I'll try and act surprised. I'm a master of acting." He paused. "Speaking of surprises," he started walking to the back wall, "can you try and act surprised for me?"

"Are you going to hit me with something? Because I won't have to act."

He smiled. "Do you trust me?"

She didn't even breathe first. "Yes."

His heart jumped once. "Close your eyes."

He didn't wait to see if she obliged. He went straight to the loose panel in the wall - he and Archie had found it by accident a few weeks back - and pressed his hand upon it. A tingle spread from his fingers up to his wrist and the panel glowed a faint blossom pink until there was a click.

Jasper snatched what he needed and secured the panel again.

He turned to find Natalia swaying on the spot.

She didn't look out of place in the training room or around other Creatures anymore, not compared to when she'd first arrived. There was now more confidence in her bones, and though her cheeks weren't dusted with their familiar bronze, he knew she could call it forth. She wore her "I'm a Fairy, bitch" t-shirt, which was both ironic and hilarious.

Where she was, she belonged. Who she was, it was the truth.

Jasper smiled, knowing she couldn't see. There was magic to her that was more than her Fairy essence, and it made Jasper's heart beat stronger.

He cleared his throat again and held out his hands. "Open your eyes," he said, watching her face.

She did, and gasped.

Lying in Jasper's palms was a dagger. The thin blade itself was silver, no longer than eight inches, and the hilt was bronze, the grip a slightly darker shade. The only thing that was bland were the little stones encrusted on either side of the pommel.

"This is for you," he announced, offering it out.

Her brown eyes went to his, their colour drawing him in. "A dagger?"

"A *Fairy* dagger," he corrected. "See these stones?" He held the grip of the dagger and put the blade down, pointing to the stones with his free hand. "They're more like half shells of crystals. You need to pry them open, add your dust inside, and close them again. Then the *entire* dagger will respond to *you* and only you. It will do whatever you command of it."

"I just need to add my dust?" She pressed her finger to the blade and, as she tilted it, both of their faces were reflected in the metal. "Can you hold it while I do this, please?"

He obeyed as Natalia shut her eyes.

What did it take to raise her dust? He wondered. Sometimes it seemed to come on its own and other times she had to call it. *What does she think of?*

Bronze dust was sealed within in minutes and, as the final crystal was pressed back into place, the entire dagger rose to life in Jasper's hands. It thrummed against his skin, even as he held it out to its rightful owner.

Natalia touched the grip, curling her fingers around it, and looked up at him expectantly. "Now what?" she asked.

"You won't always have to hold it," he told her, forcing his gaze to the blade and away from her face. "You can command it to, say, stand on its own, and it will."

She narrowed her eyes. "How?"

"The makers of the blade were Witches. They enspelled it to respond to every command once your dust tied you to it. *Your* magic connects your soul to the blade while the makers' magic helps it listen and obey."

Testing the theory, Natalia whispered "stay" and opened her hand. The dagger sat perfectly in mid-air, an invisible force suspending it. Then she went about commanding it, not always out loud, to do other things. Every time, the blade complied; whether it was to fling itself across the room or to land against the ground, tip up.

Natalia brought the blade back to her grasp. "Thank you," she whispered. "But why?"

"I had it made for you back in Atlantis and it arrived the other day," he said. "Some Creatures have weapons. Like Peri and her trident. We have gifts, like our magic and your dust, but they're not always useful. They don't always work against every Monster, so weapons are a back-up."

"So this isn't meant to be decorative wall ornament?"

Jasper chuckled. "It could be."

"But that's not its purpose?"

"Not normally. Though, you *could* hang it above a cosy fireplace."

She looked down at the blade. "What do I owe you for it? It *is* beautiful."

"And deadly," he reminded her. "But you owe me nothing for it. It's a gift."

Natalia looked up at him and disappeared.

Natalia waved her hands in front of Jasper's face. She even waved the dagger, close but careful not to slice his nose off. Not once did he react. He barely even blinked. He only scowled, eyes moving around the otherwise vacant room.

Several times she looked between her dagger and Jasper, still in awe at getting such a gift, wondering if that was the problem. Had somehow something more than obeying magic that helped Natalia to control the blade been put inside?

She readied the blade at the end of her finger. "Natalia?"

She glanced up.

Jasper seemed to watch her. To be sure, she waved a hand in front of his face again. He caught her wrist mid-wave this time and she gasped. "You can see me," she whispered in surprise.

"*You may take my land and my sea, but don't leave me skyless. For all the beauty lies within the Heavens above our heads, of which belongs to Cupid.*" Jasper kissed her palm, his lips as light as butterfly wings. "It's an old poem. Gold told it to me when we first met. I think he had a thing for me."

Natalia laughed. "What does it mean?"

"People used to think the stars were the Heavens themselves. So when Humans saw you Fairies with your cheeks of glitter, they used to believe you had come from Heaven to take them back to Cupid, who owned it all since there was a desire to belong there. They were saying that anyone could take anything from them, but not the sky as that was their ever after destination."

"That's where we get our names." Natalia's body shuddered, remembering the strange Monster who had said something similar. She gripped her blade a little tighter and touched her earrings.

"I think most of our names, like children of the stars for Fairies, or children of the moon for Werewolves, came from Humans at one point or another for some reason. A Human interpretation of us Creatures. They aren't wrong, except in the case of Vampires."

"Because Vampires can walk in the daylight," Natalia said, recalling the training the Darby's had given her before the Council meeting. That was a distant, yet haunting, memory now.

"Though, as they get older, the less they *can* tolerate the sun."

"Maybe the Human that named them came across a *really* old Vampire."

Jasper smiled. His green eyes softened along with his face. His dark hair laid just above his eyes and the tops of his ears and Natalia wanted to run her fingers through it.

"But the poem stands in regards to you," he said, pulling her from her mind.

"How?"

"Beauty *does* lie in those Heavens. And I can see it."

"You can? How?"

The tiniest amount of pink flushed his cheeks. "I can see you."

Natalia breathed in, her head and heart finally connecting the dots of her subconscious like points and lines on a map.

She wasn't shocked as if she'd *always* known, because she hadn't – at least, she couldn't say so. Yet she *had* thought about Jasper, many times, and there *had* been sparks of some kind for her in those moments. The dots were those moments, and now string had appeared to finally connect them and show the bigger picture that had been painted. A picture of the possible *richer* type of connection they shared.

They both went to say something at the same time, mouths gaping together, when a terrible scream came from upstairs. Jasper and Natalia blinked, and ran upstairs, Natalia acutely aware of how she still held her dagger. As the word "pregnant" echoed in a high pitched squeal, they slowed to a stop on the steps.

"Immediate threat over," Jasper joked.

"I don't think I could deal with *any* threat right now."

He pointed to her weapon. "You have that now."

She looked down at him. "I do, and I can make it do fancy tricks. But I can't actually *use* it."

"Then we'll add it to the list of areas you need to be trained in." He smiled.

More squeals came and Natalia said, "I suppose we should go up."

"I suppose so," Jasper agreed. "And I suppose I better act surprised." He grimaced then. "I'm going to be an uncle."

"I suppose you better grow up."

He faked shock. "*Never.*"

"You're getting old now. *Uncle.*"

Natalia grinned and didn't wait for his response. She rushed up the last steps and pushed open the door to find a hallway full of teary Darby's.

She put her dagger down on a nearby cabinet and was invited into the giant cuddle circle by Peri and Archie. So she joined them all with open arms, though her heart still sang out for one person in particular.

13

Diamonds and Crowns

NATALIA CREPT INTO HER FATHER'S ROOM, grinning as she sand over his snores. "Happy birthday to you, happy birthday you! Happy birthday, Dad. Happy birthday to you!"

Her father blinked, groaning until he registered the chocolate cake and lit candles in Natalia's hand. He flashed her a surprised smile and blew, sending up three wafts of grey smoke.

"Hurry downstairs," she ordered him.

"Cake for breakfast?"

She grinned back at him from the doorway. "It's tradition."

Natalia managed to cut the cake before the door rang. She pulled it open, finding Noah and Katherine on the other side. Katherine had a black and silver balloon in hand, and a small and sweet present tucked under her armpit. Noah had brought over a white and gold balloon.

Natalia let them in, her gaze flickering to Noah. "Your braces!"

Noah beamed, proudly showing off his bare teeth. "All clear, Princess."

"Since when?"

"Since yesterday. I'm officially free. Well, for a week. Then I get my retainer. Plastic teeth for a year." He smacked his teeth together in a biting motion.

"Plastic teeth." Natalia shook her head and took his hand, pulling him through to the kitchen.

Her dad and Katherine were caught hugging, innocently enough, but they sprung apart, faces flushed. Natalia smiled. He deserved to find love again and this could be it, *if* he went for it.

"You two should go on a date," Natalia said abruptly.

Katherine laughed, though it sounded full of nervous energy.

Natalia kept her face stony and hoped it played off. "I'm *serious*."

Katherine glanced up at Natalia's father, her blush intensifying. "We could?" he suggested lamely. His eyes flashed briefly to Natalia and then back to Katherine. "For my birthday? If you want?"

Katherine didn't seem to know where to look. "What—"

"I'm at the Darby's after work to practise. So's Noah," Natalia said, elbowing Noah when he went to protest. "You can go on your date and meet us there afterwards? Only if that's how you want to *end* your evening..." She trailed, leaving the conversation open for the two more adult adults – though part of the idea grossed her out, since it was her dad she was talking about.

"I'd love to go," Katherine blurted. She met Tony's gaze again. "If you do?"

He was beaming. "Of course!" He coughed, attempting to hide the high inflection of his tone. "We can go for dinner and decide from there?"

Katherine gave him a swift kiss on the cheek, leaving pink lipstick on his skin. He and shook his head, turning towards his cake. Noah grabbed Natalia's arm and dragged her gently into the hall.

"What the hell?" he whispered harshly. "*I'm* coming to the Darby's?"

Natalia shrugged. "I'm sure they won't mind."

"You haven't asked? That was a spur of the moment decision that I'm being held too?"

"To get them two," she pointed at the kitchen, "to *finally* give in and go out. It's been *years*. I've spent most of that time watching the tension build and the lovey-dovey eyes being used."

Natalia's mum, Lavender, had died when Natalia was barely months old. Beside the memories her father had to share, Natalia had nothing. But she did have the sadness her father carried. He wanted to move on and be happy again, but he didn't want to feel like he was disrespecting Lavender, nor did he want to upset his daughter by being with someone new. Natalia knew and understood it all. But he deserved happiness. Her mum was gone, and there was no point thinking over what ifs. She'd made him happy once, but she couldn't do it now. Katherine *could*.

"Plus," Natalia continued, "You need to be around more Creatures."

Noah's dark eyes narrowed. "Why?"

"Being around me isn't enough."

"Selling yourself well there."

Natalia scoffed. "I mean, from what I know, there are very few Humans who actively know Creatures exist. Mostly because Creatures hide since Humans used to hunt them and some don't care to look, or something." She tucked her hair back. "My point is, you're one of the special few who have insider knowledge and opportunity."

"Don't the Monsters hide?"

"They want chaos. Why would they bother hiding? Though Creatures tend to go around making Humans forget they've seen a Monster or cover an incident up before anything happens. That's a Council rule, or something." Just like they'd done with Natalia and the Calefaction in her garden, she'd learnt – her entire street had never seen a thing because, to them, it'd never happened, thanks to some Council magic.

"Do I have a special name? Something superhero-like?"

"A Watcher."

"A Watcher?" he repeated, sounding unconvinced.

"A Human with the blessing to see into this world by some means or another." Natalia smiled to herself, relieved her private tuition, courtesy of the Darby's, was helpful after all. "So you might as well join us."

"You make it sound like a cult."

The doorbell rang. "Isn't it?" Natalia grinned.

Natalia reached the door and the ominous figure behind it sent a shiver up her spine. Her hands shook as she fumbled with the handle.

Natalia had to blink twice at the woman on the doorstep. Her hair was long and silver with flowers wrapped into its length. She had rosy cheeks on a circular face and wore a pink strapless dress. Her brown eyes were calm. With a straight back, she stood tall. The light of the hall perfectly illuminated the small silver crown upon her head.

Everything about this woman was familiar yet Natalia couldn't place how.

"Are you going to invite me in?" The woman asked curtly.

"Why would I let someone in who I don't know?" Natalia countered, using the door as a barrier.

The woman rolled her eyes dramatically. "Natalia Primrose, child, it's *me*."

Natalia was playing no part in anyone's game. "Who's me?"

"Queen of the Fairies and the entire realm? Your *grandmother*."

Natalia blanched. *That* was why this woman was familiar; part of her was part of Natalia. Those brown eyes stared back every time she glanced in a mirror. She touched that long hair every time she tied it.

"Oh." Natalia opened the door.

"I know you weren't expecting me. I should've sent something ahead." The Queen didn't sound apologetic and stepped inside gracefully. "And I had forgotten that you do not know me, as you never knew your mother."

Natalia bit her tongue and led the woman through. She knew the land of the Fairies was within this Veil but separated from Earth, like

Atlantis was, in order to keep it safe.

Stunned silence arrived when Natalia and her *grandmother* reached the kitchen.

Noah openly gawked, and Natalia slapped his shoulder to get him to stop. Katherine took a step back as if she wanted to move very, *very,* far away. And Natalia's father looked uncomfortable as if the last time he'd met with this woman it'd ended badly.

"This house," the queen scanned the cramped room, standing in the centre of it, "is perky and petite."

"It's *home,*" Natalia's father emphasised.

The queen's eyes sought him. "Tony."

"Primrose." Natalia looked at the woman she shared a name with and saw her sneer. "I see my granddaughter finally knows who she is."

He nodded. "She does."

"And she's following in her mother's footsteps."

"Natalia follows no one," he argued. "She does what she wants, and, as her father, I support her."

The Fairy Queen rounded on Natalia icily. "I know I wasn't at your trial in Atlantis, dear. My other daughter, my heir, was getting married. Schedules clashed. Most Fairies were there, so you might not have known. Though I hear you did fine on your own. But is this really what you want?" Her face softened, the sharp edge to her voice dispersing, and somehow that unnerved Natalia more. "You could come back with me?"

"Come back with you?" Natalia questioned.

"Primrose," Tony hissed.

She ignored him. "I can offer you a place in my castle. You are a Princess, after all. Gods forbid something should happen to my my daughter, *you* are the next heir."

Noah unashamedly started gawking again.

Natalia, however, didn't take her eyes off her grandmother. "No, but thanks."

The Queen pulled back. "You would rather fight those nasty *beasts*," she spat the word, "and slash with swords and get dirty?"

"That's my Purpose as a Creature."

"But you have a choice. A choice that the Council would abide by without stripping you of your gifts if you left it. Let someone else do the work."

Natalia tried not to let her annoyance show. "When I first found out I was a Fairy, I thought long and hard about what I wanted. In the end, I decided that *this* is it. I want to follow my Purpose, just like any other Creature. It's in my blood."

"You are also a Princess. That's in your blood too, child."

"If I decided to leave, that would pass the work to someone else. One other Fairy, or Witch, or Mermaid, would have to step up and fight those *beasts*. How is that fair? Why should I relinquish the responsibility to live in a castle? I fought hard for what I have. If everyone left to take the easy choice, there would be no one to fight back and the worlds would be destroyed. So, thank you, but no thank you."

Natalia waited. Her skin crawled with sweat though her mouth was dry. Her heart pounded so ferociously she worried it might stop completely.

She'd just defied her grandmother and the Fairy *Queen*. She didn't know which was worse.

"You are brave, like how a Fairy should be. Though you weren't blessed with charm." The Queen sneered and turned to Natalia's father. "This is *your* fault," she accused. "The child is confused."

Tony stepped forwards, a fierce look on his face. "You heard Natalia. She's anything *but* confused. And she is *not* a child."

The Queen shook her head in clear disgust. "How did my daughter fall for you, *Human*?" She said the word like a curse. Her eyes travelled onto Katherine. "And I see you're about to disgrace her further by being with a *half-breed*."

Natalia stepped around her grandmother, unable to conceal her anger any longer. "My father is the best dad I could've asked for. He's taken care of me for eighteen years with barely any help. He's done nothing but love and support what I want, constantly putting me first. And Katherine has too. She's baked my birthday cakes, talked me through periods, given me presents at Christmas, and has been there when my dad couldn't. Where have *you* been? Oh yes. Not here. Sitting in some palace with your still-alive daughter. So I suggest you back off because this is my family, and you *aren't*."

"Yes." The Queen's eyes locked onto Natalia, and there was more captured within them than there was any semblance of emotion on her entire face. "But if they've done so much, why have I not gotten word on your wings yet?"

Natalia's mouth opened and no words came.

There *was* one thing still holding her back. She could have all the approval from the Council she liked but it meant nothing. Not that wings could make a person, but part of her *was* still missing. They should've appeared by now, and though she was aware of the itch between her shoulder blades, nothing came of it.

The Queen smiled like she'd won a game only she'd been playing. "I shall take my leave," she announced. "My offer, young Fairy, remains. My castle doors will open for when you decide to choose differently."

Natalia glared. "I won't."

"We shall see."

The woman let herself out, the door clicking closed behind her.

Everyone in the room dropped their shoulders, their energy leached from their bodies. Natalia worried her father's birthday was besmirched by her grandmother's untimely and unwanted appearance, and then felt guilty as she came over feeling more concerned about her lack of wings.

Where are they?

Noah walked alongside Natalia, their pace somewhere short of a sprint, but in the sun, it was comfortable enough.

Katherine had sent them away the minute work was over, closing up herself. Noah hadn't been working there long but appreciated every hour. He'd struggled to find work before and now, thanks to Katherine, never had to worry again.

They walked up Main Street and down Opal Street. Opal House stood tall and proud upon its hill.

"Imagine if Zoe knew I was coming here," he said. Zoe was his younger sister. In the past, they'd thought and joked about what was inside Opal House. Now he knew, and definitely wasn't disappointed. "She'd lose it, completely."

"She loses it with everything."

A laugh left his lips. "I'll tell her you said that, so don't expect a Christmas card this year. Even if I *do* agree."

Natalia laughed as she knocked. The Mermaid, Peri, opened the door. The gentle breeze shifted her hair about her neck, a few strands sticking on her painted blue lips.

"Nice to see you again, *amore*," Peri said as she moved aside.

Natalia didn't respond and Noah looked up to realise Peri's eyes were on him. "Me?"

"Sì, *amore*." Peri's smile was warm. "And you're *sempre*," she shook her head and clicked her fingers several times, "*always* welcome here."

"Thank you," he said, unsure of what else to say.

Peri's attention transferred to Natalia. "Everyone's downstairs," she said.

Natalia shrugged off her jacket, hanging it up. "What about you?"

"I've been benched." Out of nowhere, Peri slid her arm around Noah's waist. "But I'll have this one for company."

"Why?" Noah looked to Natalia for help.

Natalia smiled, clearly enjoying this, and opened the door on the underside of the stairs. "I asked Peri to teach you some basics."

"We don't have too if you don't want," Peri insisted. "But it's better than being completely benched."

"Don't do anything I wouldn't," Natalia said before slipping away.

Noah hadn't really spent time around Creatures and only had Natalia for reference. That meant Natalia was right. That now he knew this *other* world existed, he'd need to know more. Why wouldn't he continue to be special when he was being handed the opportunity? He was only learning.

I'm not planning on actually fighting.

Peri steered him away. He hoped he hadn't just thrown himself into the deep end. But if he had, he supposed he better learn to swim, and fast, because this was his life now. And a Mermaid was pulling him through the waters.

Jasper sat cross-legged on the floor between his siblings. Their parents were due home in the next few hours, and by the sounds of the door to the basement opening, Natalia had arrived. A waft of smoke drifted to them first and Natalia appeared moments later.

Why the smoke? he wondered. *Why does she smell of it?*

"Who benched Peri?" she said by a way of greeting.

Archie made a face resembling a mi between a grimace and a frown. "Technically, I did," he admitted. He stood and brushed his jeans despite easily being able to rid the crinkles with magic. "I suggested it. Peri doesn't do anything she doesn't want to, but she agreed. She's still keeping up with minor training though." He looked to the ceiling. For a big guy, Archie easily became flustered and embarrassed. Jasper loved teasing him for it. "I just wanted her and our little fish to be safe."

Alex sighed. "I still can't believe I'm going to be an aunt."

Jasper flicked her hair. "You've got the greys to support your position as crazy aunt."

Alex swatted him, leaving a lasting sting. "At least I won't be the hagged old Witch."

"*I* still can't believe I'm going to be a dad." Archie rubbed the back of his neck.

Jasper stood beside him. "You have five months to get used to the idea, because it's happening." He turned to the girls. "But now that the Fairy is here, we can at least distract you for half an hour."

Natalia narrowed her eyes accusingly. "You're not going to tie me up again, are you?"

Jasper snorted as Alex demanded Natalia stand against the wall. The boys didn't need instructions; they'd planned what was going to happen.

Archie linked his hands with Jasper and they locked eyes. Some magic required two or more Witches to complete it. This was one of those occasions. This summoning spell wasn't exactly on the side of easy, and they weren't just summoning a new training space or equipment. And some spells, though rare now, needed to be voiced.

They spoke together, almost in the same voice.

"*I can show the Earth. I can hold you together. Come to us through space. We summon you here-ever.*"

The air around the brother's grew clammy, the oxygen seeming to disperse from the room, but they held on.

Pink and green light pooled around them, which quickly shifted to a dark brown. The force trying to tear their hands apart was immense, so much so that Jasper had to dig his nails into Archie's hands just to keep them attached. A billow of white smoke plumed and a smell of sulphur rose. Humans often associated the phenomenon with ghosts, but ghosts weren't actually real, there was no evidence for them. *This* was going to be something inherently more dangerous and less well-mannered.

"I feel it," Jasper announced.

And as he did, he was forced apart from his brother.

His body skidded against the floor, the wood tearing his exposed skin in several places. Alex rushed to him, helping him sit, and Natalia had done the same for Archie. But getting the brother's to sit was the least of their issues.

In the centre of the room was a Monster.

It smiled with teeth of yellow and black. Its skin shifted constantly, the blue like water, but there was a gleam to it, like diamonds were embedded within. To Jasper, it smelled like frozen ice, but some Creatures smelt vanilla.

Without a warning, as the Monster neared Alex and Jasper, silver raced towards its body. And missed. Jasper glanced behind him where the weapon clattered. He stood shakily and walked to it, picking it up, before approaching Natalia and holding her bronze blade out.

"Ten for effort," he said. "But a one for aim."

"There's no time for jokes," she hissed through gritted teeth.

Natalia seized the blade and jutted it out as if she could will it to become a long-sword. Some Fairy blades did allow for physical changes, like Peri's trident did, but his gift didn't have those abilities.

The Monster turned until the tip of the blade was pressed against its midsection, where the bottom of the ribcage would be.

"Why is no one else freaking out?" Natalia asked, her eyes unmoving. She shook with nerves yet she didn't bow or waver to them, and Jasper was impressed.

The Monster grinned the best it could. "We're acquaintances."

Natalia blanched. "What?"

Jasper touched Natalia's hand and forced her to lower the weapon. She obeyed reluctantly, even when he put his back to the Monster to prove he was in no immediate danger. He remained holding her wrist but not to keep her in place, his reasoning was more selfish.

"Sometimes," he said, "there are intelligent Monsters, high-level ones usually, who become aware and realise their actions are wrong, that more exists than needless destruction. It happens rarely, but when it *does*, they can appeal to the Creature Council. After tests, many hours in court, and investigations, the Council sometimes decides that the Monsters are genuine."

"And so, what? They join this side?" she questioned.

"Pretty much."

"But—"

"They're constantly monitored by the Council to make sure they really *are* being truthful and do see the error of their ways."

"It's annoying," the Monster said without malice, "but worth it."

Jasper still didn't move. "They can be helpful in training. Or in giving us information about other Monsters we may not be aware of or haven't seen for a long time. Sometimes they even fight the bigger fight with us."

The Monster stepped around Jasper, forcing Natalia to face it, and for Jasper to let go of her. The Monster held out its hand. "I'm Kei," it introduced.

Natalia blinked, almost in recognition. "You bumped into Peri in Atlantis, at the Flower Parade."

Kei shrugged, unbothered. "I might've."

Alex had met Kei first when they'd been going through their respective processes with the Council. After Kei had been cleared, because she'd remained in contact with Alex, she had said to call on her if anyone in the family needed. Archie and Jasper had been learning the summoning spell, coincidently at the same time – it allowed Creatures to bring forth Monsters that were within the same plane of existence – though they next to never used it in case they didn't tap into the right Monster's wavelengths.

"I'm a Geminis," Kei added. The blue of her skin transformed until she had olive skin, and was suddenly wearing a white body-suit.

Natalia looked briefly at Jasper, the confusion evident in her eyes. "Geminis Monsters come in two variations," he explained. "There are those who feel and look like ice and those who feel and look like fire, though neither of them can control these things. However, they *can* manipulate thin, sharp materials, like cut stone or glass, in the same way you control your blade. Some can manipulate rope and wood too."

Realisation dawned on Natalia's face. "I've met one!" she exclaimed. Her brown eyes dropped, her cheeks dusting with bronze. "I was attacked by one before." Jasper sensed there was more, but Natalia remained silent.

Kei unexpectedly ran a hand along Jasper's neck causing his hairs to stand. "Are we here to talk, or to fight?" she asked, her voice low and a little sultry. "I don't want to walk away without seeing *some* action."

Jasper smiled and moved behind Natalia. "Let's practise your throw," he suggested.

"Blades cannot hurt me," Kei said.

"Trident's can't either, can they?" Natalia asked out of nowhere.

"No weapon can. I can only be hurt by magic or Fairy dust," Kei answered. "If blown into my eyes, your dust will blind me. If I breathe it in, it will turn my insides to ice that will never melt, or it would raise the fire in another until they can no longer cool." She eyed Natalia's blade, placing her hands on her angular hips. "Though it could not hurt to use me as your practise dummy or target."

"What about us?" Alex said from behind, indicating to her and Archie who'd been waiting idly by.

"We can test her fighting skill without a blade after. *That* will be fun for all."

Kei's grin was tormenting, even to Jasper who'd seen it plenty of times. Natalia, however, shivered and Jasper pulled her against his chest instinctively, as if to keep her safe.

Jasper had been close to Natalia before, but never *this* close. It was almost tantalising. His heart shuddered. There was a want, a desire in him to be near her. It was a feeling he'd only ever felt once before, once he'd established a connection, and that'd been short lived. Natalia made him feel it again, and *more*.

"Do you trust me?" Jasper whispered into Natalia's ear. She shivered slightly.

She didn't verbally respond but her body reacted agreeably when he raised her arm for her, the blade in hand. He moved her grip around the handle, loosening it. Then Jasper let go of her hand, moving his hand to her hip.

Kei continued to grin and even clapped when Natalia threw the blade directly into Kei's chest.

The sight of pizza as a welcome one.

Natalia ached all over. She'd trained for about an hour with her blade, throwing it at the Monster, Kei. Eventually they'd moved onto practise fighting with it and then got rid of the weapons completely.

It was safe to say Natalia had gotten the short straw in that draw. While everyone else had magic or an ability, Natalia barely had her dust. The more she trained, the more she realised Fairies in general were down on their luck unless their dust could harm or their blades could work. Though they *did* have wings. Or, they should.

She grabbed a plate, loaded it with as many slices as she dared take, and slumped at the long table. Peri sat gently beside her, Archie opposite, and Noah across from Natalia. Natalia barely spoke to them as she ate, the dull aches keeping most of her attention.

"Do you know what you're having? Have you got any names planned?" Sarah asked as she sat at the head of the table, tucking her dress beneath her. She and James had just arrived home from Atlantis, but they'd received the news of the pregnancy over the phone. Apparently Peri and Archie couldn't wait the extra few hours.

"I don't want to know," declared Archie. Then his eyes lifted to Peri. "Unless you want to?"

"No," she agreed. "And we haven't spoken about names."

"Jasper's good," Jasper decided, sitting next to his brother. "Nice and strong."

"Or Alex," Alex suggested, taking up the spot beside Peri. "It's gender-neutral."

Archie bit into his next slice. "I'm sure we'll consider *all* options."

Sarah nodded, a piece of hair falling from her top knot. "I suppose soon you'll be looking for your own house too."

Peri grinned at Archie as she said, "One by the sea."

"Speaking of water." Jasper turned to his brother. "Is that baby going to *actually* be a little fish?"

Peri threw a pizza crust at him, but answered once everyone had stopped laughing. "We don't know. It could be either."

The rest of the table descended into conversation. Even Noah joined in.

Natalia stayed quiet, picking at her food, too aware of her pain and how Kei was mooching around. The Monster girl finally stopped and sat beside Jasper, seeming to find every possible excuse to touch him. Natalia's stomach wrapped itself in knots every time.

The doorbell rang and Noah offered to get it. Everyone became easily distracted again so Natalia took her chance and escaped.

She crept towards the basement. Hearing her father's voice, and then Katherine's, nearly made her stop. Nevertheless, she carried on, taking extra care with the door behind her.

The training room was exactly as it'd been left. Painted targets were at the far end and punching bags at the other, one now with a tear since Natalia's blade had nicked it.

Natalia walked to the target her blade was stuck in and plucked it out, knowing full well she could've commanded it to her. She walked away and then suddenly swung round, flicking her wrist hard. The blade sank into the target's edge. She repeated everything over. This time, the blade landed point centre. The next time, she completely missed.

She sighed in frustration. No matter how much she tried, she couldn't get a handle on anything. She couldn't throw consistently, and though she *could* just command her blade on where to land, it felt like cheating. Besides, one day the power may be taken, or she might have a normal blade to throw. She couldn't dodge attacks and nearly always got hit. She didn't have magic at her disposal, only her dust, and even that she couldn't aim directly enough. *If* she could even call on it.

The only thing of value, that would work every time as a defence, would be her wings. Wings she was yet to gain. The itch always came but nothing ever appeared. No matter what she did, whether it was calling on them or trying to force them out, nothing.

What's wrong with me? If she couldn't make her wings appear, there was only so much she could do. *How can I face Monsters when I can't even help myself?*

Her heart sank. The one thing she thought made her a *true* Fairy was the one thing she couldn't make materialise.

You burn brighter than your sisters and brothers. And I came here to find you.

Natalia let her blade fly and wanted to scream when it grazed the target's edge. The thought had caught her off guard. Clearly seeing Kei had caused the memory to resurface and she hated it. Kei was extremely unsettling. Was it because of the memories she brought with her or something else? Natalia couldn't put her finger on it.

"Princess?" Natalia called her blade to her hand as Noah edged into the room, the lights giving his umber skin a sheen over his forehead. "Are you alright?"

"I wanted to get more practise in." Saying the words made her realise how much better at lying without showing physical symptoms she was.

"That's not it," he told her. "Or you wouldn't have snuck away when everyone was focused on Tony and Katherine."

"I didn't *sneak*."

Noah pointed at himself. "I'm the only one here. And it took me minutes to realise you were gone and didn't seem to be returning. So, what's really going on?"

"When I get my hands on her—" Natalia and Noah turned to see Peri hobbling off the last step. Peri spotted them and marched over. The look on her face warned Natalia she better brace herself for a slap, but instead got a tight hug. Peri pulled back, touching her stump with her hand. "And where do you think you were sneaking off too, *amore*?"

"Told you," Noah said pointedly.

"I didn't sneak," Natalia argued. "And if I *had*, I haven't got very far, have I? I came here to practise."

Peri said nothing, but dragged Natalia into the tiny toilet room at the back of the training room. Inside, Peri forced her round to look in the mirror.

With frazzled hair, scratches over her neck and cheeks, and a dark bruise forming above her collarbone, she was a mess. Her upper lip was split and her cheeks were sparkling more than she'd ever seen them.

Scratch being a mess. She was worse than that.

"I think you're done," Peri said, using a tone that left no room for arguing. They re-entered the room. "Come back upstairs and eat more pizza. Or we can go into another room and play games? Maybe spar on the lawn, instead? We could even go for a swim?"

"Wouldn't it be freezing?" Noah pointed out.

"Didn't you ban yourself from some those things?" Natalia added.

"Keeping a fish from water isn't healthy for it," Peri said, waving her stump dismissively. She put her hand on her stomach. "Being in the water is kind of my thing, and it won't hurt the baby. Mermaids don't just let go of the water when they're pregnant. Mermaids *are* the water. Plus, it'll keep my overall fitness up."

"Maybe tomorrow? I really *do* want to get in more practise."

Peri folded her arms. "Why? What are you trying to prove?"

"Prove? I'm not trying to prove anything."

"Are you sure you're not trying to prove to Kei that you're capable of fighting?"

"What—"

"Because I think you are. And Kei isn't worth it. She's finicky and tricky and sometimes downright nasty. Archie was telling me how hard she went with you when she barely made any moves with or against the others. She probably saw you as a threat, as competition, and didn't like it. So she went out of her way to make you suffer and back off, which, because of your lack of training, is easy for someone like her."

Natalia was beyond confused. "Threat? Competition? Back off what?"

"Jasper," Peri and Noah said in unison.

Natalia's eyes flicked between them both. "What?"

"Kei has had a thing for Jasper for as long as I can remember," Peri explained. "She even thought *I* was a threat until she realised I was with Archie, and even then she thought I was going to snatch him."

Natalia didn't like this. She wanted it to stop. She'd barely just come to a conclusive thought about Jasper and how she felt about him – that maybe she liked him as more than a friend and that they maybe shared some sort of connection.

Noah and Peri smiled like Natalia's silence was enough. Natalia wanted to deny it, to refuse the unsaid accusations, but she felt her cheeks warm and dust coated them in seconds until it was even manifesting in her palms – she'd never done that before.

All three of them went to speak when someone called out. However, their words were muffled by a large, deafening, alarm.

"Shit," Peri cursed. "*Merda!*"

"What's happening?" Noah asked, holding onto Natalia for support.

Peri's voice wrapped around Natalia until her spine felt weak. "That's the alarm for a Monster *invasion.*"

14
The Waves Inside a Heart

ONY REACHED OUT and instinctively tucked Katherine to his side. Despite the noise and commotion, he heard her gasp. He forced them both forwards. He *had* to find his little girl. Love had been lost from him once. He wasn't about to lose again.

His chest constricted with every step, an invisible killer snake winding around the lungs. At the last second, Natalia barged through a door beside him. He snatched her and nearly tore her arm from its socket as he pulled her into a fierce hug. His heart became unbound and free once more.

The alarm shut off as quickly as it'd come, the Darby family congregating in the hallway as if awaiting instructions.

Sarah, the lady of the house, pulled on a jacket. "Okay," she said, demanding everyone's attention. "That was the Monster alarm. It means there is more than one out there, more than a handful. This won't be easy." Her eyes caught Noah in the small crowd. "Noah? Since you have little training, you're staying." Humans *could* fight the fight with Creatures, but it was rare.

Noah looked pale. "Fine with me," he agreed.

"I will too," said the mermaid, Peri.

Her boyfriend, Archie, went to her. He was much larger in both muscle and height but they fit together when he pulled her into hug.

It reminded Tony of himself and Lavender. And now Katherine, maybe. As if knowing his thoughts, Katherine put a hand to his chest, spreading her fingers over his shirt. Could she feel his heart and how it thumped at her touch?

"Tony?" James called, stepping forwards.

Before Natalia had ever met the Darby's, Tony had known of James John Darby. Lavender had introduced them years ago after a trip to Paris; they'd been travelling for fun while James was moving for work. Coincidence had meant they'd met then and now.

Tony shook his head. "I'm staying," he decided. It wasn't a hard choice to make. "I can't fight anymore." He'd done some training in his time, but it'd been minimal and he was way out of practise.

"I'm coming," Katherine said immediately after. She stared up at Tony shyly, not asking for permission – she didn't need to ask for permission, they didn't own or control each other – but in a way to reassure him that this was right and what she needed and wanted to do, and that she would be alright.

"Natalia," Sarah called, not in question. Natalia perked up. "You're staying."

"*What?*" Natalia's voice was shrill.

Kei, the Monster girl, whose skin was blue and curvy again, grinned, though it looked more like a snarl. "It's because you can't fight," she mocked. "We would be too busy looking after you and picking your pieces up afterwards." She shuffled her body to stand in front of Jasper, blocking him.

Tony looked down at his daughter. She was seething. "I *can* fight!"

"You've had *luck* before."

James pulled Kei away by her arm and Tony clutched onto his daughter, both girls being held to stop them before a fight ensued here in the hall. Tony looked at his daughter, more concerned about her – she'd never once gotten into a fight before. The look on Natalia's face gave away *exactly* how she felt; he could see that this wasn't exactly all about not being able to fight.

"You *can* fight," Sarah assured her as James continued to block the still-snarling Kei. "We've seen it. But this isn't a one-on-one situation. We'll be outnumbered. You've only just become a Creature and lack the training for this. And until you've had that training, it's not safe for you. I'm sorry."

Tony held onto his little girl but Natalia didn't seem to want to argue. He hoped Natalia knew these people wanted to keep her safe just like he did.

It had killed him to lie, to pretend for all those years that Natalia was Human, but it had been his wife's last wish. Tony had never known what from or why, but Lavender had wanted to protect Natalia.

He hadn't been inside the room for Natalia's birth, but Lavender had died nearly two months later, so something had been wrong almost from that poignant moment. Maybe before? No one had been sure. Had what killed Lavender been what she was protecting Natalia from? How had she known what to protect Natalia from, or had she been taking no chances?

Tony never understood but had respected Lavender's wishes, keeping Natalia away from *that* life until right moment. Except there hadn't been one. She'd been attacked before he could explain. If only he'd told her sooner, she wouldn't be so inexperienced and could be on her way now to follow the Purpose she was born with. Instead he had to watch her sink back like she'd been stung.

As the Darby's fanned out, shutting the door behind them, Natalia stepped away from her father, giving him a raised eyebrow before turning her back.

He went to call out that she would get her chance when he felt a sudden kiss against his cheek. Katherine pulled away but Tony wasn't about to let her go easily, and with so little.

He held onto her waist and tugged on the ends of her jacket until they were pressed together. *Years* he'd been waiting for this and it just happened to come before she would leave towards danger. Part of him had wanted to be free of this world, free of the life of Creatures and Monsters and the war, but the other part was glad he'd stayed.

With a heart burning with complications and conflictions, he pressed his lips to hers. The kiss was sweet and slow, her lips soft, as if they had time to spare for each other.

They parted too soon. Tony kissed Katherine's hand; a promise that when she came back things would move on with them, but first she must return. Katherine squeezed his hand and wiped the edge of his mouth, then left without looking back.

Tony sighed and spotted Peri, a smirk on her face. Noah, too, seemed a little impressed, his eyebrows raised high. Tony blushed. He turned to Natalia, but she wasn't there.

A gust of wind lapped his ankles and he spun, panic coursing through him. The doors in the kitchen were wide open.

The three who were left ran to the open space, their feet meeting grass. Tony spotted Natalia atop the fence at the bottom of the garden. He called to her, hard and loud, his heart pounding inside his head.

Not again. Not again. Not again.

I can't lose you too!

She didn't hear him and disappeared over the top.

Jasper nearly let out a laugh, and would've if the situation was different.

Scorpios, more than he'd ever seen in one place before, scuttled onto the beach from the sea, pincers snapping and tails thrusting. Two Kiffleggers were scaling down the cliff-side, the noise of what was below drawing them in. There was even a Poena climbing out of the water it lived in; sea creatures were mixed inside of its grey yet pellucid body – they absorbed anything they touched to gain energy, and they'd been known to snatch a bit of magic from a Witch if they touched one.

Jasper rubbed his hands together but not for warmth. He was about to mention how this wasn't an invasion when three Mitters –

Monsters that were as hard as rock, the colour of damp slate, and were seven feet tall at their smallest – burst from the cliffside. Jasper groaned. *Now* it was an invasion. Why did he even have to think otherwise? He should've known the Seven Hells seemed to listen.

The sand shifted beneath his feet, making it hard to run. He had to persevere. Gritting his teeth, his eyes found Archie being swarmed by the Mitters.

Jasper touched his fingertips of both hands together, and when he pulled them apart, two of the Mitters scattered. One was dumped into the ocean, its body seizing on impact – water was their one weakness, so it was odd to find them so close to it. The other Mitter collided with the cliff and seemed to become lost within it.

Twice more Jasper thrusted his magic and twice more he was successful. He wiped the sweat from his head and his heart pounded relentlessly as two Siltapolia burst from the ground, and Jasper tumbled into the pit they'd created. He frowned. For Monsters that preferred to roam densely treed areas, or would skulk around fresh water lakes, it seemed curious to find them on Venderly.

Something was going on, it had to be. Something *wrong*. It couldn't be a coincidence that Monsters who weren't normally found in places like this were suddenly sprouting here.

Wrinkling his nose at the damp smell, Jasper tried to find a way out of the hole. Though it wasn't overly deep, the dry sand shifted faster than he could grab onto it. But he had no other option. Just as he went to climb, one of the Siltapolias peered over the edge of the pit. Jasper cursed.

Black tar-like gunk dripped from the Monster. Jasper dodged it the best he could in the small space, relieved when it burnt the pale sand instead. He remembered all too well the last time he'd been touched by this Monster type, and wore the scar by his neck as proof.

Palms touching, Jasper raised his arms and breathed out. The Monster above him reacted, suddenly listening, knowing something was nearby. Then Jasper turned his hands, one going upside-down while the other was righted.

With a noise that sounded like a pipe draining, the Monster came apart.

The sand shifted, threatening to bury him alive. It took most of the strength he had to climb free.

"Fuck," he cursed, knowing how close to being burnt he'd been. One misstep and he'd have had a second scar.

"Jasper?" Archie's voice carried from somewhere.

Jasper looked for his brother but found only the torn apart beach.

He wasted no time, he had no time, and flung himself forwards. He clapped his hands together and tore them apart seconds later, repeating it over and over.

Two Scorpios split into ash. Three Siltapolias dodged his trap but fell into his mother's. Archie finally came into sight, nearly touched by the Poena, but his dad saved him, only for another Scorpio to spring from the sea. Katherine, who Jasper deemed was definitely misplaced running a cake shop, waved her hands and a cascade of waves attacked the Monsters closest to her at her command. Kei was even attacking one of her own; her face was a mask of fury as if she didn't want to be associated with what she had once been a part of.

Unlike all other attacks, this one seemed unnatural. The way these Monsters kept appearing, it was as if they were being forced to – like their need to randomly destroy and bring Hell to everywhere was being focused and narrowed on this one point. Jasper was sure he'd never seen or heard of this kind of coordinated attack before.

Monsters attacked each other; their need to destroy included themselves. So what was it here? Why were they attacking this beach?

Screaming erupted over all other noise.

Jasper turned towards the sound to find Archie pinned beneath a Scorpio, its tail inches from his neck, their mother trapped within a claw. Jasper went to help, but found himself face down and eating sand with something heavy on his back. A moment later the weight was gone.

He managed to gather himself onto his knees just as something slashed over his shoulder. Gasping in surprise, he shuffled to face the thrower.

Natalia? his mind cried. *She's here.*

She stood, one of her hands out, palm up, and her face mimicking Hell's anger – whether from being left behind or from the scene around them, Jasper didn't know. Her hair lashed out, curling into the wind, her eyes unblinking. She was covered in sand and had a rough look, as if she'd been running and fighting consecutively to make it here. She didn't look good – she was sweaty and panting and a little bemused – but she looked powerful. Like a warrior.

Like a Creature.

Jasper's heart skipped.

Her blade returned to her once called and then flew again. Jasper heard a thump behind him and turned to see a Scorpio with a Fairy blade stuck into its claw. It might've been a mistaken aim, since its claw was as high as its face, but it did enough.

The Monster appeared paralysed, enough so it allowed Jasper's mum to free herself. With no remorse, she made quick work with dispatching her captor.

In his peripheral vision, Jasper caught sight of a blur.

He turned back to Natalia and wanted to shout, to scream, but the words caught. He could only draw short, shallow breaths. The dread rose even higher when he noticed that Natalia had somehow created a shield around herself and was now dropping it.

Natalia stepped forwards, ready to receive her blade again, and a bolt of what felt like electricity shot through Jasper.

Monsters piled around him suddenly, locking him in a cage of bodies, and Natalia was gone.

Natalia groaned and when she opened her eyes, everything was blurry to begin with. Gradually it all came to focus.

She faced the sky, sunlight shining above her. There was a buzzing inside her head and she felt sluggish, even in thoughts, but slowly felt herself come back to normal. She tried feeling for her blade and found wet sand beneath her fingers. More worryingly, she realised, she was face up in water. The salty air told her it was the ocean, and it was soaking through her hair and caressing the edges of her face, just below the sides of her eyes. If she moved, she'd either be drinking or drowning.

How did I get here?

Something shuffled nearby. Natalia tried to raise her head, but searing pain split along her left wrist and forearm. She screamed and tears flooded her eyes. Pressure descended on top of her chest, and something pinned her wrist, like an anchor holding her until could no longer make noise.

Through the silent tears she could squint at a shape, one she wished she hadn't tried to see.

"Are we going to meet like this again?" The familiar Monster asked. It was the same vanilla scented Monster that had attacked Natalia last time. It smiled. "Did you feel my pain?"

A wave crashed over Natalia's head, causing her to splutter. *I've got to be more careful*, she thought. She was vulnerable to the water in this position and to the Monster who'd obviously put her there.

"Your pain?" Natalia asked, talking to keep it distracted while she thought.

The Monster's smile turned to a grimace. "The pain I'm giving," it said. "The glass I can raise slices Human and Creature skin alike, as if there was nothing thinner in all the worlds."

"My wrist," Natalia said aloud, realising what the Monster meant.

She tried to raise her left arm and pain spread throughout. Torturous screams left her mouth before she could stop them.

"I wouldn't move. It's buried beneath your skin."

"My..."

"Until I remove it, it is your pain, and your reminder that *I* am in control of *you*."

"You're *sick*. A real Monster." Natalia's head reeled, fireworks detonating inside her brain, but she couldn't see their pretty colours, only hearing their explosions. Her grandmother had been right about one thing, some Monsters were no more than beasts.

Jasper.

He'd been the last thing she'd seen as she'd come from within her shield, one she couldn't remember how she'd conjured it.

What of the others? She'd seen her blade land miraculously in the arm of a Scorpio but she'd never seen the repercussions.

Am I still near them? Are they near me?

Her heart told her she was nowhere close and she could neither hear nor see any signs of fighting. Even the water was mostly still.

Natalia needed to get back to the group. This time, they wouldn't be saving her. And they shouldn't have to. It wasn't their job. Their job, their *Purpose*, was to protect *all* life, not just hers, just like they'd said back at the house.

The Monster that sat on Natalia's chest now had already survived one attack and Natalia knew why, unfortunately thanks to Kei. These Monsters, the Geminis', couldn't be hurt by blades or weapons, so Peri's trident had done nothing except provide a diversion for its escape. But also thanks to Kei, Natalia knew she *could* hurt this Monster.

"What do you want?" Natalia asked. She needed the Monster to talk. How long did she have before she drowned or had something worse done to her? Whatever she was going to do, she needed to think fast.

The Monster waggled a finger in her face. "We have done this."

"Last time, you said—"

"You burn bright."

"Bright?"

"The *brightest*."

"Is that why you want me? Because I burn?"

"*I* don't want you." The Monster's grin was like staring into the jaws of a beast that life would be lost too. "And no one wants you because *you* burn."

"Then what?" she tried to move and rolled her left arm accidently. Pain intensified and she breathlessly gasped.

"I told you not to move." The Monster sounded bored, or that could've been due the difficulty in hearing it – everything was garbled. "And you are wanted because you *can* burn. You are special."

The Monster slithered like a snake from Natalia's chest to her stomach and leant sideways towards Natalia's arm. There was silence and stillness.

However, that stillness was a lie, a false hope, because in the next heartbeat, her arm was ripped apart.

Natalia screamed. Her legs thrashed against the ground in an attempt to throw this *beast* off. But the movements also caused the sea to ripple and sank her face further. In that moment she no longer cared. Maybe drowning would be better.

When she could no longer scream, her energy, air, and adrenaline stolen, her head lolled to the side. Half of it fell below the waterline, her mouth gaping and tongue tasting salt. At this new angle, however, she could see better, if only with one eye.

The Monster dragged a stone along Natalia's left arm. Her skin peeled back with ease. The pain shuddered up and down Natalia's body, vibrating her entire skeleton, but she could no longer react, a numbness taking over – all her nursing training told her she was going into shock.

Blood leaked from the gash that ran from her left wrist up her forearm. The wound formed a complete "T" shape when connected with the already dug horizontal slice by her elbow - she guessed that was the section where the glass was imbedded. The Monster then added thinner lines off the shape, making the cut become a bolt of lightning, but the colour of crimson and with the stench of death.

The longer she resigned, the more her urge to fight leaked into the sand. If she wanted a chance to save herself, she would have to take it. Now.

Natalia found something buried inside herself and dug for it. The shock was the main blockade and she had to centre the pain into her arm to overcome it, even for a brief moment. When she felt the throbbing, she thrusted herself out of the water.

Catching the Monster off guard, it hissed. Natalia didn't wait and threw her right fist forwards, hitting the Monster's jaw. Natalia touched her own cheeks. As the Monster lunged for revenge, Natalia blew her dust. It landed in the enraged Monster's eyes, who summoned a sound between a Human scream of pain and the howl of a lonely wolf.

Natalia pushed the Monster sideways and climbed away as it clawed at its eyes. The pain in her arm spread drastically to her heart. With a gasp, she fell back to the sand and her head landed in the sea again.

Though the Monster was blind, it still somehow knew where Natalia was. It staggered on top of her, its hands coming to her throat. The pressure in Natalia's head began to build as the spindly fingers squeezed.

"Just because they want you alive, doesn't mean I can't hurt you first," the Monster established, then squeezed harder.

Natalia began to struggle. Her arms wiggled and her legs kicked, but nothing got air through her mouth or nose. The world and her life flashed around her. She could see the sun, sea, and sand. She could see home. She could smell her mother's perfumed handkerchiefs and Katherine's cakes. She could see her dad laughing and Noah smiling without braces. There was Peri calling her "*amore*", Archie consoling her on the bathroom floor, and Jasper dancing with her as if they were all that the world contained.

Suddenly air flooded Natalia's lungs so fast she choked. She rolled over, face down, inhaling the air of the sea deeply, her lips inches from it. Her hands went to her throat, her fingers grazing over the skin. She kept her hands there as if to protect it and turned round.

The Monster was struggling with a giant brown wolf on top of it.

"*Alex*," Natalia croaked. She barely spoke above a whisper.

The wolf bit the Monster's neck, causing what Natalia assumed was clear, ice-like blood to spray down it's body. The Monster convulsed, gagging with its tongue hung out of its mouth.

The wolf nodded in approval at its own actions and ran off along the beach.

Despite feeling woozy, Natalia managed to stand, legs shaking, ignoring whatever was left of her attacker. She searched for Alex and saw how golden the sand was.

Natalia flung open her right hand as pain coursed through her left; she gritted her teeth as her eyes filled with tears. Though she was wet, tired, and beginning to falter again, she staggered forwards.

A weird Monster with fish stuck in its see-through stomach lunged at Natalia as if from nowhere. It caught her left arm and every nerve in her body that could still feel shrieked.

The Monster keeled sideways, its stomach spilling onto the sand like a popped water balloon. Natalia stared, stepping towards it and found a piece of glass about the length of her little finger sitting inside the remains. In a blink, the Monster turned to black ash, the glass disappearing with it.

What? What happened?

Natalia whirled round and snagged her own arm in the process. While there was pain, enough to curse aloud with a very loud "shit", it was nowhere near as excruciating or blinding as before.

Tentatively, she pressed her forefinger to her wrist.

A gush of thick blood leaked forth but there was no electric shattering of her body. She eyed the cut. It was flat, smooth. Had the glass somehow come out? Had it been her piece of glass that'd killed that Monster? How was that even possible? Maybe her dust had dislodged and flung it?

That felt possible and there certainly wasn't a lump under her skin anymore. Unless that other Monster had been lying, but she doubted it. So what had happened?

Energy and adrenaline had carried her this far but it seemed it'd run out, for she sank to the floor for a second time.

The pulse in her left arm became so intense it was all she was aware of. There were no sounds, smells, or sights. She couldn't even tell if she was breathing. Would she soon be able to reach inside herself and pull out her heart, to hold its unbeating husk in her palm?

She took what felt like the last breath her body could take and dropped down still.

Tony stroked Natalia's long, tree coloured hair. Like this, he could see how young and precious she still was - the little girl not too far buried beneath the surface. The girl that had struggled to ride a bike at age five, the girl that always wanted dessert before her meal, and the girl who never forgot to dress as a Witch on Halloween.

Natalia whimpered and Tony put the back of his hand to her head. Slowly, yet surely, her temperature was coming down. Though it still raged like an unchecked inferno.

Two days. That was how long Natalia had been in and out of consciousness for.

A knock at the bedroom door came and Tony shuffled round to look. Katherine popped her head in and then came to his side. He didn't cry but slumped his head onto her shoulder, exhausted.

"I brought food," Katherine whispered, pushing a container of something warm towards him.

"Thanks," he said, touching none of it.

"Tony, go and have a rest."

He raised his head again, dark circles visible under his eyes. "I can't leave her."

"You're no good to her tired and run-down. Go have a shower at least." She put a comforting hand on his knee. "I've looked after her for years. This will be no different. I won't move."

The argument went on for a few more minutes before Katherine finally dissolved the last of Tony's will.

Standing under the shower, he let the water pelt and scorch him. His skin burned more as he scrubbed at it. He stayed like that and to himself admitted he could've stayed forever. Guiltily, it *did* feel good to just take a moment.

Climbing out, he barely dried himself before dressing and returning to the bedroom. "How is she?" he whispered from the doorway, voice laced with concern.

"Better," Katherine answered.

"Better?" he repeated.

"She woke up for some water while you were gone." Her smile was soft and it nearly made him collapse. "I even got her to eat two chocolate biscuits before she passed out."

Tony sat beside Katherine again and she picked up his hand, holding it in her lap. "Good. That's good, right?" he asked, unsure.

She nodded. "How do you feel?"

"Cleaner," he answered, eyes still on Natalia.

Katherine sighed. "She should be walking in days."

Tony's attention snapped to her. "Says who?"

"You had a long shower," she said. Tony's stomach sank, the guilt returning, but Katherine didn't seem to be judging, only stating a fact.

"I managed to get Sarah on the phone. She said that if Natalia keeps waking at intervals, it's a good sign. The time she spends asleep will decrease until she can fully stay awake again. She's already eating and drinking."

"What else did Sarah say?"

"That it'll take weeks for Natalia's arm to heal." Katherine sighed again. "It helps she's a Fairy."

"Does it?" He tipped his head back, looking at the ceiling. He couldn't see how there were any benefits to anything right now.

Katherine kept it simple. "Like Werewolves, Fairies heal fast but use more energy."

Tony touched his daughter's duvet, running the fabric between his fingers. "Is that why she's sleeping?"

"She's using energy to heal her other injuries, yes. Which is why I insisted on her eating sugary things when she can. Just another thing that helps the recovery process." She shrugged like she didn't know why. She squeezed his hand. "She'll get stronger, Tony."

Ever since the attack, Tony realised how little he knew about all this. Lavender had taught him bits and pieces, but their time together was mostly a whirlwind and he never paid much attention to what was happening outside of it. When Natalia had been born, the entire world was hidden from her. Now, she was laid in a bed, asleep to heal injuries she never should've gotten.

Tony groaned and rubbed his eyes with the heels of his palms, pressing them in until she could see stars. How had let this happen? His eyes began to sting. Had she suffered because of him, because he hadn't prepared or protected her?

"This isn't your fault," Katherine whispered, peeling away his hands.

"She's barely been a part of this world for two months, and she's already suffered so much," he said back, his voice cracking slightly at the end. He breathed in a deep breath to steady himself. "Even her mother wanted to protect her from this world, I just don't know what from. I don't even think *she* even knew. But there was *something*."

Could Lavender, all those years ago, have seen or known something that was to happen? Had she wanted to keep her baby safe, more than the motherly instinct would've pushed for, because there was something more?

Tony didn't need to be any type of Creature to know there was something in Natalia's very essence that screamed she was different. Not just from any other Fairy, but from *all* Creatures.

Katherine squeezed Tony's hand as his heart raced. "She'll be ok," she promised. "In a few days, you'll see. She just needs time."

His eyes locked onto Natalia's rising and falling chest. "I know."

"She'll be Natalia again soon."

Tony dropped against Katherine, the energy at staying upright escaping him, and she held him.

Natalia flinched several times as Sarah ran her fingers along her bruised skin coloured in varying shades of purple, yellow, and green.

Once the extensive examination was over and Sarah was convinced there was no more need for concern, Natalia was free to do as she pleased.

For the last few days, Natalia had been cooped inside her bedroom. Her dad and Katherine hadn't left her side unless it was to eat, use the bathroom, or sleep. But they worked in shifts so Natalia always had eyes on her. It had felt a little unnecessary until they'd explained how many times she'd passed out or hadn't woken up, or how feverish she'd been.

This morning, Natalia had got out of bed and made it downstairs for breakfast by herself. Katherine had all but jumped out of her skin. Her dad had rushed Natalia to the Darby's so she could be checked out – he said to make sure she *was* healing.

She was. She ached and had the bruises, but they'd go. The same couldn't be said for her left forearm. It had to be kept covered in thick bandage for the next few weeks. Though she'd not seen it, she knew there was stitching sealing the "T" shape shut. Apparently no magic could erase all of this. She's tried using her dust, too, and failed, meaning she'd be left with a scar.

My first scar.

She edged towards the basement, the room she'd spent the most time in other than the kitchen. The door was ajar and smoke wafted up from below.

On shaky legs, Natalia descended, mostly out of curiosity, staring when she reached the bottom.

Lit candles gave off a resonating glow around the room. They were resting on the floor, floating in the air, and there were even some stuck upside-down on the ceiling. A very thin veil of pink smoke rested in the air. The floor was sand, the walls white, and there were mirrors on the opposite side, all which thrived in this ethereal light.

In the centre of it all was Jasper, on his back, arms and legs spread wide. Getting closer, she could see that his eyes were shut. His chest bounced with fast breaths and his forehead was drenched in sweat; his shirt stuck to him, giving him a slim outline, and his hair was plastered to his forehead. Every few seconds, he groaned softly as if to let pain out while trying not to be too loud for others to know he was hurting.

"Archie? Alex?" Jasper called, seeming to sense someone nearby. "Peri?" He sounded unsure.

Natalia swallowed her nerves and backhanded a floating candle out of the way to move to him. "No," she said, "The Fairy? Natalia?"

The smallest of smiles appeared on his lips. "You say that like I don't know who you are." He poked an eye open and in the dull glow Natalia could see the skin around it was bruised. "But I know *exactly* who you are."

"I didn't know your mental state."

"Perfectly fine, thank you. Better than most, I'd say. And that's on a bad day."

"You're here alone, using magic to do who-knows-what, and surrounded by hundreds of candles. Is that what you call perfectly fine?" Natalia wasn't convinced.

"Even if I was suffering from brain damage or memory loss, you're unforgettable."

She stopped. "Are you in pain?"

He closed his eyes and tapped the spot beside him, sending nearby candles scattering. Natalia sat to his right, facing him. "A little," he admitted. He turned his forearm up to her, a red welt visible on his flesh. "Remember when I said that Monster attacks and injuries have to be treated right away? That's what I'm doing."

"By lying in the middle of an ocean of candles?"

"For an hour, each day, for a week. There's a spell involved too, hence the pink ambience."

She remembered the skin below his neck. It was proof that Monsters *could* leave their mark. Just like the scar she was soon to wear forever.

Without thinking, she took his wrist in her hand. He gasped; whether from being shocked at her touch or because she'd caused pain, she wasn't sure. She breathed slowly. What *was* she doing? She didn't know, but also, she *did*. She raised his arm to her mouth, having to lower herself slightly, and then blew out wisps of air. Bronze dust danced along his skin until it settled onto the burn.

She replaced his arm and looked at him shyly, only to find herself now gasping at how close they were. She hadn't seen or heard him sit up and now their faces were inches apart. She couldn't see the green in his eyes, nor could she smell the sweetness she knew he wore. Control was lost and she reached out. Using a finger, she pushed away damp strands of hair from above his eyes.

They'd been this close before but each time they'd been torn apart, like two storms that were never meant to become one hurricane.

"Jasper?" she whispered. She could feel his breath on her face. "How's your arm?"

"You're like starlight itself, Natalia. You burn with all the power and shine of a star. To the Seven Hells with my arm."

He cupped her face with his hands, lifted himself, and kissed her.

Their lips met with finality – not that the moment was to be their last, but with a passion that *at last* ignited them. They were held captive in an everlasting blaze and Natalia wanted to burn within it forever.

Jasper touched his forehead against hers and Natalia snaked a hand to his chest, finding his heart beating equally as furiously as hers. She looked at him, and the nervous smile on his face that she knew mirrored her own.

"I'm sorry," he breathed. "I couldn't control myself. I should've asked. But I didn't want to let this chance pass. Not again."

"But you did ask, a hundred times you've asked. Maybe not with words..." She traced lines into his freckles, hoping to create her own sparks and stars along his skin.

He brought his face close again, eyes fluttering shut, brushing his lips against hers teasingly.

This time, she kissed him. He seemed surprised at first, almost as if he hadn't believed she'd want him back, but she wanted him more than anything. He wrapped an arm around her waist, the thumb on his other hand stroking along her jaw. Her arms snaked around his neck, her hands knotting into his hair.

"I don't think I'll ever get used to doing that," Jasper said, his voice a little scratchy. "It's a shame," he smirked, "it just means I'll have to keep doing it to try and get used to it."

She laughed. "Oh, what a shame indeed. Means I'll have to keep doing it to you, too."

"Of course." A smile worked onto his face, one that showed *him*

– kind and heart-warming, secure and fighting, sometimes cheeky and sarcastic, but all real. "You're special, Natalia," he whispered, like he was sharing a secret. "You are special to *me*. And I think you have been right from the beginning. You grew on me without me being aware of it. Like a fungus or infection."

Natalia snorted. "Charming, as ever."

He let go of her waist and played with a strand of her hair. "Lemonspark had nothing to do with what happened when we danced. That was all me and what I felt for you."

"Jasper—"

He fake gasped. "Here comes the rejection. I can feel it."

"Jasp—"

"I won't accept it. I will cry and pout and bury my head in ice-cream until I eat my weight in it. I will weep and write horribly sad songs and shout from the nearby cliff-top."

"I would *love* to see you pout and eat your weight in ice-cream."

"So you'll reject me to see if I follow through? That's fucking cold."

She rolled her eyes but didn't stop grinning. "No. I won't do that."

His smirk returned. "No?"

Despite her injuries and having a lot of things to think about still, Natalia had never felt better and her heart thumped as a part of it was set free.

15
Ties and Knots

OVER THE FOLLOWING WEEKS, Natalia was caught in a cycle of healing, working, and training.

The first Sunday in May was the first chance in a month that she was free. So when Peri texted her, wanting to go shopping, Natalia jumped at the chance of doing something different.

Peri, Natalia, and Alex, walked through the busy market place. They'd met early, when the sun had barely woken, coating everything in a pink haze. It had been Peri's idea; she'd said she needed a full day since she was beginning to slow up and Natalia hadn't believed it until she saw it. Peri now had a reasonable bump, even while wearing a floaty summer dress, and got out of breath just by walking.

After checking out a few stalls, and even searching a few shops, they decided to take an early lunch. Well, Peri did.

They took an outside, umbrella covered, table at the local Italian restaurant – Gordito's. Peri all but collapsed into a chair. Natalia groaned as she sat – all the training, no matter how much or how often she did it, always left her with some kind of pain. Alex sat without issue, giving the others judgemental looks.

Peri passed out the menus. "I'm fancying something meaty," she said, fondling the pages. "Nothing too creamy." Her face went pale despite the brilliant golden sunshine that cast a halo around her body.

Natalia grimaced. "Is there anything *we* should avoid for you?"

"Anything with mayonnaise. The texture and look..." She stopped, closing her eyes to breathe deeply. When she opened them again, she continued. "Everything else is fine. I think."

"Pasta it is," Alex decided, folding her menu again.

Peri folded hers and reached the best she could to take Natalia' hand. "I'm glad you came out today."

Natalia smiled at her. "So am I."

Being cooped up at work and just training was starting to drive her insane with its repetitive motions. There had been a moment where she'd considered resting at home with Noah and a movie. Though, Noah had been coming round some evenings to do exactly that. So she'd picked differently, for a change of pace.

"I couldn't miss out on buying all the fun baby things," Natalia added, and looked to Peri to find her with the biggest grin.

It was hard to believe that she'd only known these girls for a couple of months, and yet their lives were woven together. Soon, there would be a new life among them. Natalia turned back to Alex who was undoing her ponytail; Alex's curly hair fell into her face, and Natalia noticed how her fringe was slowly growing out. Like this, even though they weren't biologically brother and sister, it was possible to see how much Alex was like Jasper, their hair constantly dangling millimetres above their eyes, their smirks and smiles similar, the way they held themselves too, as if they would be the first line of attack or defensive if necessary, protecting what they loved and cared for most at all costs.

"How's the training?" Peri asked. It was hard for her, Natalia knew, since she'd been mostly self-benched. Archie had mentioned that she took longer swims, more-often. She'd even taken to cutting sandwiches with her trident a few times apparently.

Natalia groaned, her body and mind remembering all her aches and sores. "*Great.* It's just great."

"It can't be *that* bad," Peri argued. She let go of Natalia's hand and sat back, her hand rubbing circles on top of her stomach. "You train with Archie and Alex, but mostly get to spend sessions with Jasper." She winked.

Natalia's face heated as a young waiter came to take their order, returning within minutes to bring their drinks before they were left alone again.

"It's not like that," Natalia mumbled.

Peri sipped her iced lemon tea. "It's not like what, Natalia?"

"I don't know what you're thinking, but we train."

"In between all the make-out sessions, I get it." Peri's smile was deadly.

Alex cringed. "That's my *brother* you're talking about."

"Sure," Natalia nodded, "If you count beating each other with sticks making-out. Whatever works for you. Though, I think you have a strange thing going on." She sipped her cloudy lemonade.

Peri looked like she'd just silently choked. "*What?*"

"I told you. We train."

"With sticks?" Alex eyed her suspiciously. Though they had few training sessions together, they tended to use weapons or test agility and endurance by running or sprinting and sometimes by clambering through obstacle courses.

"Bamboo," Natalia confirmed. "Some kind of very basic weapons training, he called it. Since I'm new, I'm learning how to use and do everything. Plus Jasper said I can't always rely on my blade." She patted her hip; her Fairy blade tapped against her skin under her t-shirt where it was strapped around her waist.

Peri's look was unbelieving. "Are you sure?"

"I'm sure I would've noticed. *Especially* if it was Jasper."

Natalia had told the girls about the kiss a few days after, allowing herself time to let it sink in. They'd been so excited. Peri had nearly jumped up and down, and would've if Natalia hadn't told her to stop before she'd started. Alex had been a little revolted at first, but overall she was happy for her friend and brother.

However, since that first time, it hadn't happened again. There had been a few comforting kisses on the cheek or forehead, but nothing more. Natalia had been focusing on work and training, and Jasper had narrowed in to focus on helping her. He seemed to understand that she was serious about all of it, and though he never asked, he helped and they worked together like before, but somehow stronger.

She didn't want another situation like the one on the beach. She never wanted to be at the mercy of any Monster again unless she was dead.

Her hand clutched her arm, the calloused, ruined skin beneath her fingers. The lightning bolt scar was newly uncovered and deathly white. It was unmissable and Natalia hated it, but it was also a reminder of what she was fighting against.

It also reminded her that she had a secret; there was something deeper happening around her.

"I know you're trying to catch up on all the years you've missed," Peri said, sipping more tea, "but there has to be a balance. Don't sacrifice everything for this purpose, because, believe me, it's not worth your *entire* being."

It did feel like Natalia was trying to catch up on all the years she'd missed out on, so would it hurt, for once, if she let herself be a little free? She'd been hurt badly at the last fight, and it wasn't the first time nor would it probably be the last. Peri was right. Their purpose was a job from the Heavens above, a life-long war they had to fight, but their entire purpose revolved around souls living against beasts who wanted nothing more than to destroy without reason. Natalia would be a hypocrite if she didn't live a little herself.

Food came quickly and they were silenced. It was a beautiful meal and thankfully Peri tolerated the tomato and herby sauces. When they were done, they paid and left, heading to the general store.

Alex pushed the cart one handed, even riding it a few times, but

Natalia was too busy mulling over her situation to look at anything on the shelves. It wasn't until she bumped into a stack of ladders she snapped awake.

A familiar chuckle came from above. She glanced up gingerly. Her dad was smiling down, his arms full of soup cans. He smiled, put the tins on the shelf, and climbed down. "You need to watch where you're going," he advised, easily slipping into his 'dad voice'. "Next time, it might not be anything so solid."

"*Ragazze!*" Peri appeared, holding a cute little teddy bear onesie, complete with ears on the hood. "What about this?" She blinked, noticing Natalia's father. "Oh, hey!" She gave him a hug and a kiss on the cheek.

He chuckled and pointed at her item. "For the little one?"

"It gets better." She went over to the end of the aisle and returned with two larger versions of the onesie. "Imagine. All three of us, matching."

"Christmas card worthy," Alex laughed. Peri dumped the onesies into the cart as if Alex's words had convinced her to get them.

"Do you know what you're having yet?" He asked next.

Peri shook her head. "Not yet. We have an appointment soon."

"I thought you didn't want to know?" Natalia questioned curiously.

Peri smiled. "We didn't, but we're allowed to change our minds." Natalia smiled too.

"Well," Natalia's father interrupted, "there's a sale on in the baby section. Nappies. Bottles. Toys."

Peri rubbed her stomach; the small bump appeared bigger under the store's fake lighting. "Four months to go," she reminded them. "Can never be *too* prepared." She touched her stump, something Natalia had noticed she did when nervous.

Alex wheeled away with Peri in tow seconds later.

Natalia's dad sighed. "Seeing her like that, it reminds me of your mother."

Natalia looked up at him, eyes stinging. "Mum was like that with me?"

"She was proud to show you off, and always excited to buy baby clothes or toys."

Natalia hadn't thought about how her own mother had been when pregnant, but hearing about it made her smile.

"Make sure Peri doesn't go too wild," he advised, half laughing. "It might seem like time ticks, but there's *always* time. Plus, they'll get lots of toys as gifts when the baby's born. I can guess, anyway. It was like that for us." He dug into his back pocket and pulled out a note, slamming it into Natalia's hand. "Speaking of gifts, get yourself something. My treat." He kissed Natalia's head and scaled the ladders again before she could argue.

Natalia walked away smiling and shaking her head. Eventually she found her friends in the baby and toddler section. It was full of bright colours and the girls were pouring over the selections of nappies. All Natalia could think about was the money now stashed in her jeans.

After her attack, she'd received her first Council payment, as well as injury money. Katherine had explained it, once Natalia had stayed awake for longer than ten minutes. Apparently every Creature was paid every three months - Natalia's had been backdated to her eighteenth when it technically all began - since most Creatures didn't have "normal" jobs. Injury payments, however, were different. They were only given when the Council considered that specific Creature to be "out of action" for the foreseeable future. Thankfully, Natalia's hadn't been, and the Council didn't want money back so it was mostly a win all round this time - no serious injury, or worse, and a fair bit of income.

Now she had both her café wage and the Creature wage. She wanted to give the money her dad had gifted her back, but she knew he'd refuse it. So she consulted the girls on what she should buy, as her dad had put it, as a treat for herself.

"New clothes?" Peri suggested.

"A weapon?" Alex added, smiling.

"A weapon? In a supermarket?"

"You can buy a whole knife block," Alex said. Peri gave her a questioning look.

"I have the only weapon I can wield," Natalia said, jumping back in. "Everything else I've just trained with feels *wrong*." Most Creatures specialised with one weapon and her blade was it, the *one*. "I could do the clothes thing."

Peri shoved some packets of nappies into the cart and off they went to the clothes section, as simple as that.

Alex found some new tops, Peri got herself some comfortable shoes, and Natalia kept eyeing a top that said "Special Bee" on the front in black with a decorative bee beneath it. It was the sort of t-shirt Noah would buy her, but now the word "special" had different connotations attached.

Each time she read the word, her body shivered. She could hear the Monster calling her special, telling her that she was wanted. She could feel the glass cutting across her skin. It made her flip-flop between angry, weary, and confused.

I can't let that moment control me.

She grabbed the damned t-shirt and threw it into the cart. It was a cute top, connotations aside, and it was only her that was associating the word. Plus, there was also good attached to the word. Jasper had called her special, and special to him, and that overruled *everything*.

Alex suddenly popped up in front of her, her hair messier than ever. "What about a date?"

Peri arrived and put her stump on her heart. "Are you asking me? Because I'm going to have to let you down. I'm dating your brother."

"Not me." Alex waved her hands until they all stood in the dress section. "You're both lovely, but you're not *exactly* my type. Girls yes, but I prefer blondes."

"Blondes?" Peri snorted.

Alex grinned. "Not really. I prefer darker-hair. And that's not what I meant." She turned on Natalia. "What about *you* taking *Jasper* on a date?"

Natalia blanched. "What?"

"Give yourselves a night. No work. No training. Just the two of you."

Peri sniffed and wiped under her eyes. "I'm not crying. I'm just pregnant!"

When Natalia nodded once, it gave them the girls the permission they needed.

They rifled through racks and racks of clothes, eventually deciding on something that looked way above a grocery store grade dress. Natalia insisted that she had shoes and accessories at home when the girls tried to get her to buy some, so Peri demanded she at least did the make-up when the date was set.

Natalia kept eyeing her new dress and t-shirt as they went through the checkouts. How her life had changed in a short few months. And there was no turning back. This was the life she was always meant to have, with a few extra parts.

As the dress tallied, she realised that though she'd dated before, never had it been as exciting as even the *idea* of this was. Jasper was different. He held a place in her heart and getting to be close to him was something she couldn't describe, no matter what they were doing. The prospect of a date sent a bubbly energy all over her body.

So she *was* special, because she was special to him, as he was special to her. That was all that really mattered.

The Monster girl sprung to mind again. She tried to shut her out but the thoughts came anyway, uninvited and intrusive, like a tidal wave.

How am I special? Why would anyone want me? What for?

It didn't make sense. Nothing did. Why not go for a different

Fairy, one who at least knew how to hold a weapon? And if not a Fairy, then a different Creature entirely if it had to be a Creature at all. And if this *someone* really did want her, why hadn't they come back yet?

A startling thought occurred. Had the beach attack been a distraction formed to collect Natalia, knowing she'd show up? Only, Alex had saved her at the last moment, ending that plan.

Despite it all making no sense, Natalia knew somehow that there was someone, *something*, out in the darkness.

How long would they wait before trying again?

There were too many open ended questions, so much which was unanswerable. Natalia had a timer counting down inside her chest and was unable to see the clock. All she could do was wait for it to hit zero, if this wasn't all part of her imagination. She didn't think it was, which again left her with three questions; Why her; who wanted her; what did they want?

When her t-shirt was folded into a bag, she saw that one word that both brought joy and tormented her.

Special.

Archie stole Peri's hand, and his eyes looked down at her, not at her face, but at her stomach. It had been growing by the day. For Creatures, pregnancy was different than it was for Humans. No Human test could tell a Creature the good or bad news and not many of their equipment pieces could tell them if the baby, if they *were* pregnant, was healthy or not.

To say he was scared was an understatement. As they landed in front of the New York apartment that Gold had given them the address for, his heart-rate rocketed. His nerves hummed close to the surface until his hands shook.

Peri knocked on the door while Archie cursed at himself to get a grip.

For as long as he could remember, he'd wanted a family. When Jasper had been born, he'd cried nearly all night – so their mother said – but he did enjoy having a brother. Then Alex had arrived. She'd been a spur of the moment thing, one no one regretted. Their Mum couldn't leave her in Atlantis to go through life alone, and Archie had always wanted a sister, so the decision had been simple.

This wasn't that. This was to be *his* family, his passing of genetics and love. Archie had sworn he'd go to his grave before any harm came to his little fish. He already loved this baby with all his heart and he knew Peri did too.

The door swung open. Gold, wearing his monocle as usual, looked them over and moved aside so they could slip through. Gold slammed the door and slid a bolt across the frame.

"Evangeline?" the Vampire called.

For some reason that name sounded familiar. When a woman appeared, she looked familiar too. Archie just couldn't tell why.

Her long brown hair was swept back out of her face, revealing freckled cheeks. She had blue eyes and a smile that reached them. She was taller than Peri and held her back straighter, allowing the room to almost seem insignificant to her. The light made her appear young, no older than possibly twenty, but the measured look on her face said she was older.

"Peri," the woman addressed. Her eyes then switched to Archie. "And you must be Archie."

Archie couldn't help himself. "You are...?"

The woman, who Gold had named Evangeline, didn't blink. "Evangeline Morgan."

"Evangeline..." That name, this woman, it all seemed *so* familiar.

"I was a friend of the family," she said quickly, "A long time ago." Her eyes darted to Gold and then back and Archie suspected there was more, but that wasn't his business to know.

Peri stepped forwards then. "Can I ask something?"

The woman politely said, "Yes."

Peri put a hand to her stump, rubbing circles. "Are you a Vampire?"

On cue, fangs descended from Evangeline's top jaw. They seemed shorter than most Vampire fangs. As if hearing his thoughts, she held up a hand and clicked her fingers. Purple smoke and the tiniest of flames lit on her fingertips.

"Yes," she hissed, not unkindly, but because of the fangs. "And no. It's a long and difficult story. Maybe one day you shall hear it." Her voice sounded musical, like vocal magic. She stopped her flames and then her fangs receded. "Let's get back to you, shall we?"

Evangeline steered Peri to the sofa. They said nothing and Archie was left to watch on, unsure of what had just happened, the knots in his stomach returning.

"Order! Blueberry and chocolate muffins!" Noah half-yelled. A woman wearing a stupidly fluffy pink hat collected the bag of muffins and left.

Coming from the back, Katherine sidled up to him and said, "It's time you took a break."

"I'll wait until it's died a little," he insisted, going on to serve the next customer.

Twenty-six minutes later, Noah had been counting, he managed to get his break. He slumped onto the wooden stool, glad to finally be off his feet, and nibbled at the edge of a cherry muffin, his second favourite flavour.

Natalia flitted about in his wake, finishing bakes or starting new ones, and occasionally serving in the café, but when it went quiet she jumped onto the counter to sit. Even Katherine managed to escape for a cookie.

"Noah?" He peered up at Katherine, finding her looking over the calendar. "Could you pick up a couple of extra shifts next week? Or extend some?"

"Sure," he answered easily.

The bell out front dinged and Noah stood with a sigh.

Waiting patiently out front was a small gathering. They all seemed to be together, chitting or laughing about something. Noah started to take the order when they noticed him, relaying the information back to Katherine through the doorway.

As he pressed the total on the till, he felt someone come to his side, the air rushing up his arms. He turned wearily. Natalia was as pale as ice, and she glided around the corner toward the group as if she'd seen a ghost.

"Kiva?" Natalia whispered with a voice that didn't sound like hers.

A young girl twirled. Her hair was in two braids and she had glitter down the parting. The smile on her face was unmissable, right before she leapt at Natalia. Noah wondered where Natalia had met such a girl, and then he remembered Atlantis, the city of Creatures.

Atlantis had been weird. It had been the place where he'd first, *truly*, discovered that supernatural Creatures from stories were real. Everything had spiralled from there. Creatures, Noah could wrap his head around, but Monsters? It seemed even the Creatures didn't know the extent of them. Noah had tried not to think about it too much; it unsettled his stomach until he wanted to cut holes in everything he owned just to allow him some control over something.

Noah overheard Natalia ask, "What are you doing here?"

The girl, Kiva, responded, "There was a trip."

Natalia seemed to look at the rest of the group. "Family?"

"My parents are over there, but no. Mostly other Creature families we've connected with from Atlantis!" Kiva beamed. "They wanted to travel before the new school slash training year started. Half of them wanted somewhere warm, half wanted somewhere cold, and then there were those that overlapped that wanted something to see. So, they found here. It has the sea, which most people want. And it's not too cold! We went for a swim in it this morning."

The rest of the conversation was a blur. Noah served Kiva's family quietly and they sporadically went and sat at a table, taking up half the space in the café. When they were all there, Natalia re-joined him, and he asked, "And that was?"

A hard look fixed onto Natalia's face. "Kiva," she answered. "She's a Werewolf. A recently turn- *made*," she corrected, "one. I met her in Atlantis." She turned her body to him and there was strain in her eyes, like she was flashing back to a time he couldn't begin to imagine. "I met her down in the Council prisons."

"Princess?" His voice was soft, calm.

"When that Calefaction," she must've seen his blank look because she changed her wording, "that polar bear Monster," he nodded, "attacked, we were locked up. The whole ceiling nearly caved in. I got us out because the Council saw us as expendable and weren't about help us. And *then* I went on to save their sorry arses." Anger flashed across her face.

Noah remembered the ground shaking, him throwing up, and then being told parts of what had happened in the City, but never from Natalia. He took her hand. "You got out of there, and with her. That's what's more important."

Natalia seemed not to hear. "Kiva's here on a trip with her parents. There are a few other Atlantis families here too. Venderly is now a holiday destination for Creatures apparently."

Noah supposed birds flew in different directions; what one destination was to someone was different from what it was to the next.

"Do you know any of them?" he asked lower.

Natalia's face grew pale again. "They were at my trial. The whole room was a blur at the time, but somehow I *know* they were in the crowd."

"Just goes to show that the brain pays attention, even when we think it doesn't. Now that you're not trapped in that moment with those barrels of emotion, your brain can sort through everything systematically for you."

She smiled up at him and brushed his stubble – he'd been meaning to shave for weeks now. It was such a simple gesture Noah could almost forget they'd been talking about Creatures and Monsters.

The door dinged, the little bell chiming. Natalia withdrew her hand as the reflected light from the door caught her face, painting it in rainbow. When she blinked, it was gone, and in Noah's eye-line instead. He shuffled sideways and bumped into Katherine; she'd come from the back silently.

Two people were approaching the counter and Noah looked at Natalia in question. *Why are they here? For a nice cup of coffee and a treat?*

Natalia was grimacing.

"The Council wants an update in a couple of days," James stated. His usually slicked-back hair had a thick untucked strand on the right.

"On what?" Natalia asked.

"You."

"*Me?*"

"Yes, dear," Sarah said. She sipped at her caramel coffee, her freckles visible as her cheeks pinked at the heat. "They want to know how your training is going."

"What? Why?"

"They want to know if you've progressed."

Natalia's grip on her mug tightened. "Do they want to hear it from me?"

James nodded slightly, making his loose bit of hair bounce. "They'll want to hear your opinion on how you think you're doing, and then they'll want ours as your guardians."

Sarah added, "Your time off because of your injury will be included."

Natalia looked between them both anxiously. "Is that good or bad?"

Sarah used her hands as indicators on the table. "If they think you should be at point eight, and you're at point six, telling them of your injuries and recovery will give you some leniency, because the point you should be at will be dropped as it's taken into consideration."

They'd been sat at table off to the side for about ten minutes now, long enough for Sarah and James to explain the basics. They'd been to Atlantis for business and had been approached by Council representatives afterwards. A surprise review had been sprung on them with only a few days to prepare.

Natalia respected that Sarah and James would have to be honest, but she couldn't help worrying about what they had to say. Personally, she didn't think she was any better now compared to when she'd started. She could command her blade, and her balance and grace had improved, years of ballet paying off, but her dust aiming, healing, and the ability to sense lies weren't where she'd thought they'd be.

"Will I have to go to Atlantis?" Natalia asked.

James shook his head. "They'll simply call over the phone, but magic will be laced into the call so you cannot lie or cheat, not that you will, but others have tried to mock the system before."

Natalia drank and lowered the mug in time to see Peri and Archie walk into the store. She immediately rose from her seat and forced Peri into it, which received a grateful smile from Archie, and protests from Peri.

"And?" Sarah asked, looking between her son and his girlfriend.

Peri was practically bursting with excitement. She put a hand to her bump. "We're having a—"

Glass smashed behind them.

Natalia raced to the back of the shop. Noah and Katherine stood staring at where the window had been. The space was still there, but the protective glass was in pieces on the floor.

"What the hell happened?" she asked incredulously.

"You mean what in the Seven Hells," Katherine corrected, sounding like it was for her own benefit. "There was a Shadow."

Natalia glanced at Noah, who appeared equally as lost. What the hell was a Shadow? Shadows were attached to beings, caused by obstructed light, things that couldn't exist alone, right? She didn't know if she was missing the point, but how could a Shadow do this?

When the screaming started in the other room, the three of them ran.

What Katherine had meant by a Shadow and what Natalia had in mind were two *very* different things. Katherine had been talking about a pure and solid black being that took the silhouette and shape of an average Human or Creature. It wasn't see-through and had glowing red eyes that looked like they could peer into souls.

Four were chasing unwilling Humans and Creature alike around the café in a wicked game of cat and mouse. Katherine immediately picked up a broom and charged, making the best use of what she had to hand –Natalia understood then what Jasper had been doing by training her with bamboo sticks, because anything and everything could become a weapon.

Natalia turned to Noah, finding him already watching her. The reflection in his dark eyes was of her face and it looked stoic, not portraying how rattled she was. "Stay here," she said lowly. "Hide, if you have too." Noah nodded, clearly in no mood to argue.

With no plan, Natalia left him.

Sarah and James ushered everyone they could out onto the street. Natalia couldn't see Kiva or her family, or any of those who'd been with them, and she breathed a sigh of relief. Hopefully not seeing them meant they were out of the way.

A Shadow floated up to Natalia in the time it took her to blink.

She nearly screamed as a mouth snapped open on it but swallowed it down. Unlike the fiery redness of a Calefaction, this mouth looked like blood had pooled inside of it. It smelled like it too. Its eyes stared hollowly at her.

Natalia drew her blade and lunged. Her hand went through the Shadow as if the Monster had suddenly unsolidified. She pulled it back out, gaping. Without facial features, it was hard to tell if the Shadow was grinning or snarling.

"I'm not here to harm you," it said. Its voice was monotone and scratchy like it rarely spoke. Two arms suddenly popped out at its sides. Then a third appeared from its front. "We are here to collect you."

"Like Hell."

She lunged forwards. This time, she caught the Shadow unawares. It burst apart in a flurry of black ash which rained to the floor, oddly sounding like rice hitting tiles.

Screaming erupted from the far end of the room. Natalia spun, eyes searching for the source. Under a table, cowering in terror, was Kiva. Natalia's heart pounded inside her head. At Kiva's side was her mother, her *Human* mother, and a Shadow was approaching them both.

Natalia ran and threw her blade, hoping with all she had that it would land in its target.

She was already too late.

The Shadow snatched Kiva's mother with its third arm, its hand somehow inside her chest. Her face paled and Natalia couldn't see her chest rising and falling as she was dragged along the ground. Her head collided with the wall at the wrong angle and there was a sickening crack. A shiver ran along Natalia's spine. The shadow looked at the woman and cast her aside easily. Kiva's mum laid limp on the floor, her neck bent too far back on itself.

Kiva screamed and the Shadow turned to her. Natalia's blade hit it then, thumping hard into the side of its face. Though it hadn't stopped its first attack, it diverted its second attack *away* from Kiva.

"*You* are the Fairy," this Shadow spoke at Natalia as it rounded on her.

"Human," she lied, her stomach twisting.

The Shadow attempted to pull out her blade but it seemed to wince. As Natalia looked harder, a few of its "fingers" were now missing, a small pile of ash collecting at its feet. "This blade says otherwise," it said.

"I borrowed it."

"Fairy," it judged. Then tilted its head. "But not."

The Shadow crumbled to ash, Natalia's blade clattering to the floor.

Natalia lept over it all. Kiva hands covered her ears, her sodden eyes, red and blotchy, fixated on her mother's broken body. Natalia knelt in front of her and Kiva dropped launched into her arms, sobbing hysterically.

Before Natalia could speak, she was torn away.

Her limbs failed in their attempt to stop herself as Kiva screamed again, clearly able to see the attacker Natalia couldn't. She called on her blade as she passed it, a horrible feeling arising in her stomach. A lump formed in her throat and then in the next breath it felt like something was restricting her airways.

She tilted her head back and saw a Shadow had her by the scruff of her t-shirt and was dragging her, with extreme force and strength that it didn't seem like it should've possessed, across the café floor.

"We are here to get you," it said, noticing her watching.

Keep it distracted. Natalia swallowed the lump and went to stab at it but it was out of reach. She lowered her arms. "If I'm that important, why haven't you come before?"

"You are the Fairy."

"There are plenty of others."

"Not like you. We didn't know where you were. You were lost."

Daylight casted itself upon Natalia. For a moment, she couldn't see, and wanted to call out for anyone who could hear. Finally, when her vision cleared, she noticed she *was* outside. *Where is everyone? Have they escaped? Where's Kiva?* Her body was covered in sweat and her stomach was knotted. The scar on her forearm twinged, as did her ankle, as if the wounds had been re-opened.

This time, Natalia didn't care about consequences. She slashed her blade at the Shadow but cut off the fabric of her t-shirt instead. It was good enough.

Natalia clambered to her feet and lashed at the Shadow before it had the chance to face her. Black ash stuck to her face and hair as it incinerated. She spat it out of her mouth, and headed towards the café door, towards Kiva.

She made it a few paces before stopping dead at the sight of the reflection in the one remaining glass window of the shop's front. Three things flared inside of her; anger, revulsion, and horror.

A Calefaction had Peri's arm clamped in its jaws and was beginning to drag her away.

16

Starlight

AVE THE GIRL WHO WAS COWERING ALONE?

Save the pregnant woman who was being dragged by her arm?

Natalia's feet moved.

The café was a disaster. Broken glass was strewn across the scratched floor. Tables were overturned, some with broken legs. Chairs were bent or snapped. There were even a few dents in the walls and the main counter had a saggy middle as if something had been thrown into it.

But Natalia kept searching; she had no time to waste.

She turned everything over; tables, chairs, even a few fallen ceiling tiles in case she missed something. The more she rummaged, the more she split – not seeing anything felt good, it meant there was hope, but also finding nothing left the air open.

Natalia heaved another table out of the way, and let out a cry of relief when she saw Kiva huddled in the corner. She rushed to the girl half bent over her mother's dead body. Noah was at her side, an arm slung over her shoulder, holding her to him as she wept.

Natalia crept to their side, her lungs struggling to grasp onto air, but her heart finally at rest at finding them both. She knelt down in front of them. "We'll burn her," she promised. The Creature custom was to burn their dead so their ashes would be set free and their souls could be sent to guard Heaven's gates.

"In Atlantis," Kiva decided, her voice wobbling.

"Yes," Natalia agreed.

Kiva's eyes found Natalia's, reflecting back the gorgeous light of the sun. The connection was broken when Natalia remembered her friend still needed saving. "Noah?" He turned, his own eyes wet with tears. "I have to go after Peri," she told him, already letting go. "Stay here. It seems to be safe in this area now. Hide in the bathroom. Do whatever you can to stay safe."

She kissed Noah's forehead slowly, finding her own eyes stinging. She couldn't bring herself to look him in the eye and hoped this wouldn't be their final goodbye.

With a part of her heart left behind, she ran away.

At least two people she cared for were safe. Now she had to find the others.

If these were the choices a Creature had to make in order to follow their purpose, Natalia didn't know if she wanted to make them. The only reason she'd be able to make a call this time was because wherever Peri was, Archie was bound to be, meaning she already had some kind of support. For Kiva, there had been none. But if she was forced to choose again, to split her heart another time, could she?

As she'd told Noah, the area *was* clear. No signs of life bustled around, which was odd for a usually busy area. Main Street nearly always thrummed. Now, even the birds were silent.

Natalia ran past houses and down streets, her lungs and throat burning. She could see people behind the windows, and when they caught sight of her, they shut the curtains or visibly held up knives that reflected light back at her. She understood and dropped her head. All they could see now was danger, not help. She urged herself on.

Roaring came from up ahead and Natalia knew she was on the right track. She neared Venderly hotel, barely a road away from Opal

House. The smell of burning rubber stuck to the insides of her nostrils first, her brain trying to comprehend what she was seeing.

A Calefaction thrashed its head, something pale dangling from its mouth. Was that Peri? Was she dead too? Natalia's heart threatened to stop, but she shook her head.

No, she thought. *I won't believe it. I refuse!*

The hotel itself was burning, fire cracking on the top floor. All the magic in the world couldn't cover this up now, could it? Surely too many had eyes seen too much already.

A Shadow glided across the street and Natalia dived behind a car. If these Monsters were intelligent enough to talk, then they could spot her, even in a crowd, and right now there was no crowd. She was solitary.

Natalia needed a way out. She spotted her best chance to her right and bent her body awkwardly, running in that crouched position; it was easier said than done, and within seconds the strain had her forehead breaking out in a sweat. But she made it round the other side of another building, where she slammed her back to the wall and used a large dumpster to hide her body.

The sound of a hiccup startled her. She drew her blade and aimed it, and leapt round the dumpster. Arms surrounded her swiftly, like a bird flying into a waiting net, and fear gripped her harder. However, it subsided as the familiar scent of a cold night came next. A kiss was planted to the top of her head.

Jasper forced them behind the dumpster again, shrinking to their knees to use it as a shield. "I came as soon as I heard," he said, touching her face gently. "But when I didn't see you—"

"Where's Peri?" she cut him off. She didn't care about herself.

"I... I haven't seen her."

"They..." Natalia's breathing became rapid and she felt those tears rise a second time. "They... they attacked the café. Katherine called them Shadows? And there's a Calefaction. It had Peri between its teeth. And I had to choose. Peri might have Archie, but Noah and Kiva were defenceless."

"The Werewolf girl from Atlantis?"

"Her mother's dead and her father's missing." The weight crushed Natalia suddenly, burying her under invisible stone. "Noah's with her. They're safe. But Peri... we need to get to Peri. *Now!*"

She sprung up, calling her blade, and raced round the side of the building; a muttered "bollocks" told her Jasper would be following. Hiding would do neither of them good. Plus, it backed them into a corner; if they were going to be spotted, it would be better if it happened in an area they could control, in an open space where there was options, not hiding behind trash with their backs against the wall where they couldn't fight.

Natalia darted to a strewn car, and realised it had crashed there. She peeped over the bonnet as Jasper skidded to a halt beside her.

Though the fire in the hotel seemed to be dwindling, Shadows, *too* many Shadows, were pacing about the front doors like soldiers waiting for orders. Whatever the Calefaction had been chewing, it wasn't anymore, and raised its back leg.

Huddled together, on the other side of the beast and surrounded by a ring of Shadows, was Peri and Archie.

"Shit," Natalia cursed. "I can't tell if they're hurt." She turned to Jasper, and gasped.

A Shadow had its hand wrapped around Jasper's throat and was grinning down at her.

Anger coursed throughout her body like an out of control inferno. She gritted her teeth, her eyebrows knitting together, before she pushed off the ground and dove for them.

The weight of her body knocked Jasper free of the Shadow's grasp. He fell with a thud and she jumped over him, throwing a collection of her dust at the Shadow. It landed. The Monster jolted and fizzed, a smell like sizzling bacon wafting towards her, before it burst apart. She dropped to her knees and turned to Jasper, shaking her head above him.

Her dust was sniffed up his nose and sprinkled into his eyes. He sat up spluttering like he'd nearly drowned. His eyes were red, a somehow beautiful backdrop for the green irises. His dark hair was a wild mess and swept aside, a single ringlet touching on his forehead, and his cheeks were bright pink, but at least there was colour in them.

Nothing else immediately came rushing at them and Natalia straightened.

Jasper touched his neck and then pulled his hand away, looking at how it glittered. "Your dust?"

"Yes," she managed.

He rubbed the bronze into his face more. "To Creatures, if Shadow's go see-through, you can pass through them, which is poisonous. Your dust stops the poison, and—"

She kissed him. The tang of bacon – which she'd now been put off for life – mixed with his sweet scent. Using her dust had been a spur of the moment thing, nothing taught. Pulling back, she grinned. The kiss had settled part of her and saw that Jasper seemed to be thinking the same; his eyes were nearly all green and white, and they were flicking between her eyes and lips.

Natalia went to kiss him again and stopped midway. Peri and Archie were still trapped. There was a time and place, and this wasn't it. As if remembering their danger, guilt wormed through her stomach. This was *her* fault. If she'd just told someone her fears, her worries, and what the Geminis had said, that they wanted her, they might have been better prepared for this attack. But who trusted what Monsters had to say? The problem was, she knew they hadn't been lying; she just hadn't been willing to admit it, even to herself.

Natalia looked to Jasper desperately. "Can you jump us out?"

He closed his eyes and then opened them a breath later. "I can't sense a magical guard or barrier that'd stop it," he said.

"If there isn't one," Natalia peeped over the car, "why hasn't Archie jumped out?"

"There might be something we cannot see."

Someone, Natalia mentally corrected. Whoever was after her, if they'd gone through this much trouble already, *they* were bound to be here themselves. Otherwise, what would be the point?

"So we might have a fight the second we drop in?" she asked.

"We will no matter what with all those Shadows. It just might get *worse.*"

"Worse, we can handle. As long as it's not impossible, we stand a chance." She tried sounding optimistic but it came out flat.

Jasper swiftly kissed her cheek and said, "I wasn't planning on having a lazy day anyway."

He closed his eyes again; lines grew along his forehead as he started muttering words. A humming gradually built until Natalia felt the crescendo inside her skull. She grabbed Jasper's shoulders and peered over the car, just as four Shadows turned in their direction. She bobbed down and went to urge Jasper on when pink light spread around them, sucking them in.

Natalia was thrown. She landed in a tucked roll, only stopping when her body hit something. Groaning, feeling a hand on her chest, she looked up.

They'd both landed below the Calefaction.

Natalia and Jasper darted apart. How had they landed so far from their targets? She turned to see Peri and Archie, the latter using his body as her shield, but they were still too far. Either Jasper has misjudged his magic or he'd misjudged what was protecting them.

Grabbing for her blade, she realised it was gone; it must've come loose in the transition. She called it and took what was closest to be her weapon as she clambered to her feet, looking for Jasper. He stood a few paces away, a horrified pale look upon his face. Natalia didn't understand until she looked down at what he was *actually* staring at.

In her hands was a bloodied arm. One that had no hand.

Natalia threw it, holding in a scream. It landed by the Calefaction's head and it snatched it up. Had that been what she'd seen it with before? Was that—

Jasper rushed forwards and Natalia, gagging, had no choice but to follow. They dived back under the Calefaction. Natalia called for her blade but again it didn't come.

As they made it to the other side, four Shadows came to meet them. The ground vibrated when the Calefaction stomped its feet, and the Shadows looked at their companion as if unnerved by it.

"We are here for the Fairy," one Shadow said.

"Don't think so," Jasper argued. He drew a silver long sword off his back; Natalia hadn't noticed it before.

The Shadows ignored him and advanced. The Calefaction stomped its feet again, sending the Shadows scattering, and Natalia saw a break.

She pushed through them, careful not to touch, and landed on the other side. Throwing her hands in an arch, dust rained from her. She flashed Jasper a brief look, and he gave a curt nod, then ran, four Shadow in tow.

The shield closed. The bronze shimmered and kept Natalia, Archie, and Peri protected inside. As if wanting to test it, the Calefaction roared and spat fire. Natalia covered her head and waited to be burned alive, to feel her flesh melt away from her bones. Her heart hammered painfully as if this would be its last rhythm.

But the song carried playing.

Knowing her shield was safe when there came no pain, she untangled herself, and turned to the couple.

Archie's face was pale and wet with tears. Silent sobs escaped his mouth, but he was otherwise unharmed. Peri was not. Her entire right arm had been ripped off, though thankfully the shoulder joint wasn't exposed. The teeth marks around her shoulder were clearly from where the beast had tried sealing the best grip, and had then bitten straight through the flesh, taking the upper arm bone clear out of its socket too. Deep red blood poured from the wound. Her remaining arm was tucked against her stomach, her entire body hunched in a sweaty, shaking ball of shock and pain.

Natalia fixed her eyes on Archie. "Can you jump?" He said nothing, his eyes vacant. She clicked his fingers several times and that got his attention. "Can you jump out of here?"

"From this shield?" he asked, and Natalia nodded. He looked at the bronze shield with contemplative wonder. "I think so."

"Get her to Gold."

Peri began to hyperventilate, and then screamed. She was losing blood, her baby was probably hurting, her mind would be wakening from its shock by now, and the pain spreading throughout her body would be deadly. Natalia shook her head at Archie when he went to open his mouth; they couldn't waste time, she could read the thanks on his face at being giving the chance to save his love, and hopefully his baby.

They collapsed into a vision of green.

Alone again, Natalia stood, shuffling from the blood-stained ground.

Bile rose in the back of her throat until she gagged. She'd looked at Jasper before casting the shield, and he'd nodded, telling her that he understood and agreed to what she'd been about to do, that it was best to save what could be made safe. That had left him to fend off the Monsters. Once again, she'd had to choose between two impossible things – which life to save, and in that moment, Peri's had been more desperate. Where was he now?

The Calefaction she'd momentarily forgotten decided to make itself known by lighting the sky with fire. It took seconds for its attention to switch to the store across the road. Glass shattered and the roof began to melt.

This Monster *had* to go.

Natalia threw out her hands and the shield shrank; she realised her control and ability *was* getting better – if only the Council could see her now. The beast's eyes instantly found her, and she flung up her arms as if to somehow tame it.

Something brushed against her wrist and before she could find out what, she was yanked sideways, landing on her knees behind another crashed car, leaving the Calefaction to blast fire at no specific target.

Natalia cursed, turning to what had pulled her. Blue skim shimmered and hair waved in the breeze.

Kei.

"Bit messy, aren't you?" Kei mused.

Glancing down, Natalia realised Kei was right. She was covered in dirt, dust, and sweat. Kei was untouched by it all; her body was free from clothing, though she still seemed prepared to fight. Natalia hadn't seen Kei for a while – she'd been avoiding her when she was around if she could.

"You owe me," Kei announced boldly.

"For what?" Natalia watched the Calefaction stomp and focus on igniting another building, forgetting about her since she was no longer in its direct line of sight.

"For saving your life."

"You stopped me from killing that thing!"

"Could you have killed it after being burnt to a crisp? I've heard that Fairies are quite flammable."

"I could've ended it with my dust, and this would be over."

Natalia caught sight of someone dashing down an adjacent alley. She straightened. Two Shadows followed beats after. *Jasper.*

Before Natalia could call out to him, Kei wrapped her hand into Natalia's hair and was forcing her back. Natalia's back popped as it arched, pulling her low enough that she was staring up at the Monster.

"Let me go!" she shrieked, not caring if the Calefaction heard.

Kei surveyed her, eyes wandering up and down Natalia's body judgingly. "I don't get it. What's so special about you?"

Natalia froze. "*Special?*" She spat it like a curse.

"I just don't see it. There's nothing about you that's interesting."

"What do you want?"

"*I* don't want anything except to go home." She sighed somewhat longingly. "I never thought I'd miss it, but after being here for so long, I want to see it again. Here, there are too many rules that I cannot be free within, and after signing that treaty with the Council, I could never leave. Not unless death took my ash, but then how would I see the endless sands with no eyes? That's where I come from. A Hell with a landscape of sand dunes."

Natalia swallowed. Her scalp was burning where Kei clutched her hair. "What have you done?" Fear leached out of Natalia's voice, wobbling her words.

Kei's mouth twisted into a grin that the devils, demons, and Monsters of the Hells would be proud of. "I chose the side that would give me what I wanted, a life here and a life at home too. All I have to do is give you up."

"I never trusted you."

"I know. But you never saw through my lies either."

Kei let Natalia's hair slide through her fingers, only for her cold hands to surround Natalia's closest wrist. She forced Natalia to stand; her knees were weak from where she'd landed on the ground. Of all the things to be twisted round on her, Kei took the biscuit.

Natalia was made to march. "Who wants me?"

"You'll see," was Kei's response.

"Why do they want me?" Natalia tried.

Kei laughed.

The Calefaction stared as Natalia passed, but then turned its head away as if understanding she was off-limits.

Multiple times Natalia considered punching Kei, but as she

thought about it for the fourth time, Kei stopped and twisted both of Natalia's wrists up her back until she winced. Cold metal cuffed her skin and she wondered if Kei had commanded it or if the Monster had used real handcuffs she'd stolen from somewhere.

"Where are we going?" Natalia demanded.

Kei still didn't fall for her questions, though they weren't part of some distraction technique. Natalia just wanted the *full* truth. Kei's silence however told Natalia that she wouldn't be talking again, so she shut herself up too.

It wasn't until they neared the locked docks that Natalia could feel her heart again. When she saw the cranes and metal containers of the combined shipping and transport port - it rested on the West side of Venderly - her lungs filled with so much air she thought she might pop. With so much metal around, there was bound to be loose and broken bits. Kei could control and use it against Natalia. She would have to think very carefully and choose her *moment* perfectly.

Kei lifted one hand and the metal lock broke, falling to the floor in three pieces. Kei replaced her hand after pushing open the gate, and shoved Natalia on.

They walked through the yard; their footsteps echoed, making it sound like hundreds of people were marching together. Natalia tried to remember the twists and turns they took. Her heart screamed with every step and she longed to touch her earrings for comfort.

As the sky overhead darkened, she realised that she could no longer see any Shadows, and could no longer smell anything burning. Had the other Monsters been sent away?

When the island edge came into view, they stopped. Natalia faced the waves, breathing in the salty air, wishing she could dive into it. Kei kicked the backs of her legs as if seeing into her mind, telling her that she would be doing no such thing.

"Kei. My beautiful assistant." A voice, so horridly sweet and deep, came rattling round the containers. A body followed.

A figure shrouded in a black cloak, like the ones the Council had worn in Atlantis, came into view. This cloak, unlike those belonging to the Council, had gold and silver embellishments over it, and when they caught the sun, they seemed to shine not so differently to how Natalia's dust did. Were the designs laced with magic?

"I brought the Fairy," Kei said in a sing-song voice, dropping her vice-like grip on Natalia.

The person held up a hand and moved forwards. Their cloak caught more of the light, a cascade of colour surrounding them all. It was blinding, but Natalia refused to cover her eyes. If she wanted to escape, she needed to see *everything*.

Once reaching her, the hooded figure put a finger below Natalia's chin and tilted her head. She wanted to resist, to pull away, but held her emotions deep inside herself.

"You *are* beautiful," the figure cooed in such a familiar voice. Where had Natalia heard it before? "Like the brightest star in the sky." They released their grip and Natalia lowered her gaze; she could get no inclination of what this person was. "Only, you are on the ground and shining in daylight."

They clicked their fingers and two Shadows appeared. Natalia gasped. "Please," she begged, shattering her silence, turning her eyes to the cloaked figure.

The figure seemed not to hear as the Shadows approached her. Natalia backed up until her back hit something solid. When she searched for what, Kei was grinning and pointed. Natalia dared look.

One of the Shadows lunged and Natalia squeezed her eyes shut. A cold breeze captured her skin and she wondered if that was how death felt. *Cold.*

Something trickled over her neck and arms.

Natalia opened her eyes. The Shadows were gone and when she put her arms to her sides, she found no resistance. Her handcuffs, make-shift or not, were gone. She whirled round in fear just to see that

Kei was also missing.

Something fell from her body, and she gawked. Black ash covered her skin and clothes. She squealed and threw herself around to be free of it, and then remembered who she was in the company of. She froze in the figure's direction.

"The Geminis is gone," they said candidly.

"Gone?" Natalia peered at the ash.

"Gone. Dead. What difference does it make? I was only trying to spare your heart a little."

"She was helping you," Natalia said, confused. As much as Natalia tried to feel bad, she couldn't help but feel relief that Kei was gone.

"For her own gain. She wanted to go home, and I have given her that."

"You *killed* her!"

"This line of talk is going nowhere. It's not what I want."

Natalia reigned her anger in and fear took its place. "What *do* you want?"

The one word answer was simple yet devastating. "You."

Natalia fought to stay standing. "Why?" Her voice was barely above a whisper.

"You are special, and special to me."

"If I'm so special, so *wanted*, why have I never been taken before?"

The figure stepped back. "I have tried," it said, sounding honest. "When I first sent my Geminis to you, she was to confirm you were here. The second time, she was to collect you. She failed." The scar on Natalia's arm began to sting. "It seems you are stronger than even I could've anticipated, and the people you surround yourself with are well trained, though not as powerful. They could've been dealt with easily but you were also not ready."

"Not ready?" Natalia's voice rose. "Not ready for what? If I'm *that* special, wasn't I born ready for whatever you need?"

"In a sense, you *were*. But I had to make sure you knew you could control yourself and your abilities."

"Abilities? I'm a bloody Fairy! I can barely control my dust."

"Until your birthday, you didn't even know you were *that*. That's why I had to wait, until you had accepted your truth." The figure shook its hidden head. "And even then there's more to you than being just a Fairy." His voice sucked her in.

A shape tip-toed around the edge of a container behind the figure. Natalia wanted to scream but kept her mouth shut. She didn't want to draw attention.

The hidden figure before her seemed to sense something was happening anyway and turned, their hand whipping out. The shape made no noise as they fell to the floor. Lying there, Natalia realised she knew him and sucked in a breath.

Kiva's father. He had followed Natalia and for it he was now bleeding out, a deep slash to his throat. The cloaked figure kicked Kiva's father onto his back, making the blood pour and spurt faster until there was nothing else flowed. He hadn't even stood a chance. Natalia fought down the nausea.

"You are quite safe with me," the figure declared, turning back to Natalia.

Her face flushed. "I see no evidence of that. You wanted to spare my heart, but *twice* now you've killed in front of me!"

"Then take this and feel safer."

They threw something and it clattered inches from Natalia's feet. She bent and picked it up. *My blade,* she realised. She'd know that bronze glimmer anywhere. But one side of the was dripping red. This was her blade, but it'd been tainted.

"Do you feel safer now you have it back?" The figure taunted.

She raised it. "Will it hurt you if I try?"

"It depends."

"How can you even use it?" She stared down at the weapon as a thick droplet fell. "It's infused with dust. My dust."

The figure folded its sleeves together to stand how Natalia imaged a monk would. "Your dust has more to it than Fairy essence."

She blanched. "*What?*"

"I told you. You are special."

"That's all *anyone* keeps telling me and they never explain it." She raised her blade again, this time feeling more confident in her stance as she remembered her training. "You all keep saying that I'm special and needed and wanted, but you never explain why. *Why* am I all these things?"

Natalia sprung forwards. She was done listening to riddles.

Her blade tore through the side of the figure's hood. The sound of ripping material was music to her ears. But when she turned, the rip was healing itself. She gasped, heart sinking through her chest. How was that possible?

Maybe it really is infused with magic, she thought. So how was she to fight her way out now?

"I told you," the figure said, its voice remaining level. "Your blade works with more than just Fairy dust guiding it, and wanting to harm me depends on how you try using it."

Again, Natalia burst forwards. When she thought she was about to land a solid blow, her wrist was caught mid-air. Breath tickled the back of her neck causing her hairs to stand on end. She hadn't seen the figure move, but they were no longer in front of her.

She yelped as her wrist was forcibly lowered. Both her shoulder and elbow popped in protest. The figure didn't let go. Instead, they pushed her arm up her back so her hand reached for the opposite shoulder. Natalia kept struggling, but it was useless.

"You aren't like any other Fairy," they said, so close, "because you're not *all* Fairy. And you're enough of a Fairy to know I'm not lying."

Natalia indeed searched for the lie, distressed when her stomach didn't squeeze to any degree. She immediately stopped struggling, confusion walking her to a familiar pit's edge. The pain in her shoulder was released but the figure didn't completely let go, circling her wrist with their hand while applying pressure with the thumb.

There's no lie.

But that meant they were right, that Natalia wasn't all Fairy. How was that possible? She couldn't be only *part* Fairy.

Suddenly, the grip on Natalia faltered.

The figure was thrown to the floor in front of her. She went to smile in triumph at the wolf pacing and baring its teeth, but her relief was short-lived as the wolf was lifted into the air and hurled into the water. An orange container followed.

The figure stood effortlessly and Natalia felt the blood rush to her head. Though she couldn't see their eyes, she could feel an intensity that suggested they were glaring, hard.

"I *will* have you," the figure announced, venom woven into their tone.

Natalia's chest heaved with every breath. "What for?"

The figure pointed.

Broken shards of metal hovered mid-air. Natalia looked back to the figure. He was controlling these pieces, she knew, warning her to stay; she was in no position to ask or do anything.

"You are important." They extended a hand, got halfway to Natalia's face, and then drew it back. Metal clanged to the floor beside her, but she dared not look at it. "Are you going to hide in the shadows or come into the light where you belong?"

At first Natalia thought they were talking to someone else, then realised they weren't. "I have no reason to," she replied strongly. "And what does that even mean? Come into what light?"

"You were made to be important. To do many things. You are part of a plan that's been in motion for years."

"What sick game are you playing?"

"It's a game of chess," somehow, she knew they were smiling, "and you're the queen."

As she went to respond, a flurry of motion happened and the figure was wrenched back by something snarling, rupturing the silence between them.

Natalia managed to break the trance she'd been in and spotted a sopping wet Alex, her jaws gripping the figure's cloak. James lunged toward the figure next, lashing out with the sword in his hand. The motion sent the figure backwards, though its movements were janky and stalling. James kept his sword upright and pointed, but if the figure was fearful, they didn't allude to it. Natalia wanted to know who was under the cloak that protected more than just their identity.

Apparently, Jasper had the same idea as he launched off the top of a container.

He landed a second too late.

In front of their eyes, the figure faded into a black cloud of smoke.

No sooner than they vanished, fingers covered Natalia's mouth. She didn't need to turn to know who it was. "I will come for you," the figure said. "And I will have you, my queen, because you are important, not just to me, but for what you can do to and for the worlds."

Cold and warmth occupied the same space around Natalia. The hand over her mouth slipped away. Blade out, she spun. The figure was gone. She had no time to contemplate what they'd said as six Shadows materialised out of nowhere.

Natalia searched the port and somehow caught Jasper's eye. He was covered in dirt, a chunk of hair had either been cut or burnt away, and there was blood coming from where the fist-sized scar on his chest resided. But he was smiling; it said he was alright, that breathing was the best thing he'd ever done, and seeing her was the best thing he could image ever laying eyes on. It morphed into a smirk, like he was about to do something stupid or dangerous.

He rushed at the Shadows.

James followed.

Alex after.

Natalia raised her blade, her heart clenching at the dried blood encrusted on it. *How am I going to tell Kiva?* she thought.

Six more Shadows arose, stopping Natalia from contemplating it further.

Natalia had no doubt this was the figure's doing. They were playing this scene as if everyone was no more than puppets to bend and shape at will. But was it trying to unbalance them or trying to distract them from something else? Before she was left to find out, she ran with as much effort and energy her body had left.

Jasper and James cut through several Shadows in unison. Alex couldn't get a bite on one of them – probably not daring in case of poison. Natalia threw her blade from her hand and it caught enough of a Shadow for it to crumble. Four more took its place. Then another four.

The group were forced to converge. Natalia's back hit someone else yet she didn't turn to apologise. Instead, she remembered what she'd done for Peri and Archie.

Desperately throwing out her arms, bronze dust scattered along the floor. Her eyes caught Jasper's and when they locked, he was telling her he also had a plan. She nodded, trusting him completely, and called to her dust.

The shield closed around them as metal flew into the air. The Shadows soared too.

Only when the ash had settled did Natalia release the shield. They all stepped from it wearily, yet unharmed. Natalia looked around. No ash seemed to want to reform and no new Monsters seemed willing to take the old one's place.

"Look at you." Natalia searched for the voice, but no one was looking at her. Where was the voice coming from? It sounded like *her* voice, but they weren't her words. She gulped. Was it inside her head? "You are free now, and I will come for you, my queen."

Natalia whirled and still found nothing but ash. When she looked up, everyone's eyes were locked onto her. "What?" she asked, confused.

"Look at you," Jasper said, mirroring the words she'd just heard.

A chill ran up her spine. "What?"

Like a secret, he whispered, "Your wings."

Natalia gasped and spun round in circles to see them. She couldn't *stop* looking. Like a butterfly's, they had a left and right side and then them sides were split in half to make four sections – the bottom two sections on either side were larger than the top ones.

After all this time, they'd finally come out.

And then she noticed what was wrong, what sent her heart quivering.

They weren't an opaque bronze like she'd been led to believe they would be.

They were glass with bronze specks.

 THE END OF BOOK ONE

Acknowledgements

For this novel, there are quite a few people I owe the words found within too. So instead of waffling on, I think I need to dive in the deep end.

Firstly, to my mum. Thank you for supporting me, whether that's by giving me a word I need when I shout at you from the other room, or for simply listening to me prattling on and on and on. I know it's not been easy watching me do this self-publishing thing, but I know you have my back. For that, I'll forever be grateful. And I do love you more than Hula Hoops, I swear.

To Sophie. My "little" sister. You write too, so you know how challenging this whole process is. It's a mess. *We're* a mess. I know you pretend not to care, but I know you do – somewhere deep down, at least. I know you're proud – again, somewhere deep down – as I'm proud of you. Ew, right?

To Hannah. My personal screaming cheerleader bestest friend. We've had some adventures out in that big, wide world and I hope we have more soon. In writing, you clear my mind-fog and laugh at me whenever I say I've written 7,000 words for a chapter, and the loving insults in general are just class. You're brave to have read every version of this damned book, and I'm sure you'll read the sequels in all their forms too. Also, I'm so proud of you and of everything you've become! Here's to more gin and wine writing sessions, and to more of us sharing one brain cell.

To Kirsten. I cannot thank you enough for all the advice you've given me! From publishing to just writing. You're a wonderful human and our friendship is incredible – even if you tell me off for reading too quickly... Also, I'm still up for a swap? Jasper for Calder?

To Hannah L. The support you throw my way? Unparalleled. Even when you're busy, you come and hype me up. This book is for you too. This is how I say thank you for our friendship and your kindness, and for all the orange hearts I send you in return for the red ones you send me.

To Danni & Gennie. Though you two don't know each other, you are both my sisters from other misters. I've known you for years, and constantly I've had your backs and you've had mine. Never have you let me down and you've always been there whenever I've needed you, whatever I've needed you there for. The best I could ever ask for. I hope I can always be there for you and I hope I'm always in your lives. You're both boss ass queens, never forget.

To my other writing buddies. You lot are fantastic. You should ALL be proud of yourselves for how much you've written, for how far you've gotten, and for how awesome you are. I will support you, always!

To my buds on bookstagram. Can I just say wow? To all of you? From the moment I released the cover for this book to its final stages, you have been part of the squad. A chaotic yet delightful squad. Starlight squad. Your cheers and shares and comments of love really lifted me up and I don't think I can ever repay that kindness – I hope this book goes a little in the way of that though.

To my "real life" friends. Your support has been incredible. The way you may not know what's fully going on yet see my posts and hype them up no matter what is all I could ask for. You really are people I can count on.

To Gabrielle. You truly made Starlight come alive. You gave it a face, a cover. The artwork is incredible. Even from my really dodgy brief you seemed to capture what I wanted and then somehow *built* on-top of it to create this masterpiece. I am totally biased when I say it's the best thing ever, but I'm allowed to be. And thank you for being such a wonderful human – for answering my emails and dealing with me! You have the patience of a saint.

To Sydney & Lilac Daggers Press Editing. Literally every word in this book belongs to you. You took the trash-fire and made it look like a delightful cloud. Working with you was fantastic and so great! I know I pestered you more than one too many times, but you were always sweet and kind and funny. Oh, and Sydney? I'm going to need your next book pronto, ok? Thank you! I need to fuel my addiction.

To Evenstar Designs Ltd. The designs. The looks. The way this book is, is because of you. Julia, you have gone above and beyond for me, and I appreciate every single drop of care you have given. All the stars in the sky could never shine bright enough to thank you for making the final pieces fall into place for this book. Its beauty is your beauty. It shines because of you. It has life because you gave it. I also want to thank you for your patience in dealing with me and with the way you handled my ideas and worked with them, adjusting them, to make them absolutely gleam.

TO THE END. I did it. Go me! Take a moment and breathe, will you? You wrote a whole ass book. Celebrate that. And then move onto the next one, because you cannot be stopped now.

Lightning Source UK Ltd.
Milton Keynes UK
UKHW010731210721
387515UK00001B/55